THE LAST RUSH NORTH

BOOKS BY BRUCE DOBLER

I MADE IT MYSELF (with M. M. Landress)
ICEPICK
THE LAST RUSH NORTH

THE LAST RUSH NORTH

Bruce Dobler

Little, Brown and Company · Boston · Toronto

SECOND PRINTING

T 10/76

Library of Congress Cataloging in Publication Data

Dobler, Bruce.
The last rush North.

I. Title.
PZ4.D635Las [PS3554.016] 813'.5'4 76-13625
ISBN 0-316-18916-2

Design by D. Christine Benders

Published simultaneously in Canada
by Little, Brown & Company (Canada) Limited

PRINTED IN THE UNITED STATES OF AMERICA

For Patsy
who hates the cold

And I came to know that a frontier is never a place; it is a time and a way of life. I came to know that frontiers pass, but they endure in their people.

—Hal Borland, *High, Wide and Lonesome*

Ballad of a Camp Cook

An army moves on its guts, they say.
And guts? We got 'em, see.
Guts for a brain, guts for a soul,
And guts where guts should be.

You give me men with lucre'd eyes,
The buck their only hope.
And I'll give you men beyond all men,
The men of the Great North Slope.

—Kim Baker, Valdez, Alaska

Author's Note

This is a novel about Alaska and the pipeline. Obviously, there is only one pipeline being built by a consortium of oil companies in Alaska (at least at this writing). Comparisons to the companies, the employees, locations and events of the actual pipeline project may seem inevitable to the reader. Such comparisons will not prove valid, as anyone familiar with the actual events and circumstances of the pipeline construction in Alaska will attest.

After months of traveling in Alaska and a year working on the pipeline while researching this book, I developed a deep affection and respect for the people of Alaska. It was obvious, despite the magnificence of the land and the magnitude of the pipeline project, that my book had to be a story about the *people* first to do justice to my experience. Since, at the same time, I wanted to respect the privacy of individuals while conveying a true sense of Alaska today, only a novel would serve. *The Last Rush North,* then, is a true story in the limited sense that it depicts the *kind* of events, people and locations that a newcomer might well encounter.

But it is a work of fiction, nonetheless, and such similarities as may be noted are there only for verisimilitude. Resemblance to actual characters either living, dead or presumed missing is purely coincidental. Montez and Copper Canyon will not be found on maps of the Terminal area.

Acknowledgments

Very special thanks are due Stan Blumenstein, Jerry Fike and Beverley Cooke, whose encouragement and support meant so much.

The author also wishes to acknowledge the following people and companies for their contributions:

Steve McCutcheon, George Herben, Alaska Pictorial Service; Ken Benway, Farrar Landscaping; Herb Shaindlin, KIMO-TV; Dorothy Clifton; William Powell; Charles Shaw; Robert Gray; Bruce Lynn; George Magnuson, Joy Manufacturing Company; the Du Pont Explosives District Office, Latham, N.Y.; Harry Austin, Brown and Root, Inc.; Hank Rosenthal, Exxon; Charles Towill, B-P Alaska; Tom Brennan, Atlantic-Richfield; General Andrew Rollins, Bureau of Land Management; Chuck Champion, State Pipeline Coordinator; Robert Miller, John Ratterman, N. Roy Goodman, Dean Berg, Dennis Fradley, Sam Akin, Mark Godwin and Larry Carpenter, Alyeska Pipeline Service Company; Elmer Price and Joe Rustin, Fluor Alaska, Inc., and the hundreds of fine men and women he served with on the pipeline.

Gratitude and best wishes should also go to: Cap'n Tom Lewis, Tom McIntire, Buel Lanz and Ron Lowen (fine fishermen); Shorty

Jones, Ernie the Spool, Mulehead Burke, George Bartel, Rusty, and Pete Gravens (storytellers); Shorty Schultz, Bruce Cooper, and Frenchy (the Erector Set); Helmer Olson, Mickey and Fred, Alfred Positive and Alfred Negative Gagnon (good Cats); O. B. Culley, Judy Sexton, Butch G— —, Stevi Bowler and Big Tony (who kept things in place); Jean Pollock, Becky Klein, Margia, Olive, Bev, Anne Nielsen, the Sherries and two sisters (Gentlepersons); G. Christian Chalifour and Gene Parrish (who can keep time); Lou Cancelmi, Wayne Nielsen, Everett Phillips, Dale Hasz, Tom Comeau, Andy Akulaw, Bob Covington, Lloyd Thomas, Gene Easter, Jim Roberts, Pierre, Cary, Manny, Danny and Blue (stouthearted men); the Hair Bear; Rosemary Gaffney, Louie Howland, John Hawkins and Bill Reiss (who kept track).

Apologies to the dozens more who deserve a spot here. Those not mentioned will surely recognize their contribution in these pages.

The poems "Ballad of a Camp Cook" by Kim Baker and "Words That Mean Goodbye" by Rex Lambert originally appeared in *The Campfollower,* a weekly publication of the Alyeska Pipeline Service Company of Anchorage, Alaska, and are included here with permission of the authors.

Part One

Chapter One

THE FLIGHT PATH from Seattle to Anchorage runs along the Alaskan coastline. For those fortunate enough to make the trip on a clear day, range after range of mountains falls away in astonishing splendor to starboard.

Larry Ransom, whose journey had begun a day earlier in Hartford, Connecticut, had been fortunate. He'd picked the right-hand side of the aircraft and managed to get a window seat. The overcast out of Seattle held for several hundred miles, but at Ketchikan, near the end of the narrow Alaskan panhandle, the mountains broke through all at once. Larry's seatmate, a middle-aged woman who had grown up in Anchorage, began immediately to chatter about the beauty of the mountains and how they went on and on.

No more, Larry smiled to himself, than you go on and on. It had been a mistake to tell her he was a reporter. The woman had taken it upon herself to be a primer for his series on Alaska and the pipeline. Still, she was a well-intentioned woman, and Larry paid her some attention as she rambled on about the "real" Alaska. Anyone who doesn't like mountains should stay Outside, because Alaska *is* its mountains.

Larry lived in Walpole, New Hampshire. He had to admit that

the Green Mountains and the White Mountains of New England were mere foothills compared to what he was seeing now. As the plane crossed over Juneau, the sky closed in again. For a half hour there was nothing to see, but when they hit another clear stretch Larry was surprised to discover that the mountains did go on and on.

The woman was talking about the 1964 earthquake. It had not frightened her as much as some and had been, indeed, of benefit, since the pictures in the press and on television showed the people in the Lower 48 that Anchorage was a genuine city with big buildings and real houses. Not igloos. Although, technically, "igloo" was the Eskimo word for house, so you *could* say that people in Alaska lived in igloos. On the other hand . . .

Larry nodded and grunted from time to time to show her he was listening. She was right. When he had seen the photos of the tilting, splintered ranch houses he had been surprised. He'd expected quonset huts, somehow. Log cabins. But the Anchorage Chamber of Commerce booklet he carried with him could have been shot in Springfield, Massachusetts, or in his own birthplace, Dayton, Ohio. Anchorage could have been any thriving American city of about a hundred thousand people.

The other reporters on the *Keene Sentinel* had had the same log-cabin attitude that Larry had when he won the Phineas Garside Grant from the New England Journalist Association for a special research project and announced he was going to Alaska to begin a series of articles on the pipeline. His wife was a local historian, they said; why didn't Larry stay in Walpole, where the money would go farther? Maybe he could dig up something for the Bicentennial? Or, since his articles about the prison troubles in Massachusetts had been so good, why not tackle the nursing homes in New Hampshire? And, besides, he didn't *know* anything about Alaska.

Believe me, Larry's boss had said, I talked to guys who were there in the army. There's nothing up there.

Hope, his wife, had offered only one comment. That he would be away from home again. Just like the last time, with the prison articles.

Larry had tried to limit the scope of the project, a fact he had pointed out to Hope. First he had intended to describe how New Hampshire had looked in 1776, how much wilderness was left, what the quality of daily life would have been like. Then, reading the journals of Lewis and Clarke, he had expanded the project to all of New England from the time of the early explorations. After that, it seemed natural to want to drive to Missouri and follow the trail of Lewis and Clarke, as closely as possible, to the coast and alternate their descriptions with the countryside today.

It was while reading environmental stories about Alaska as the "Last Frontier" that Larry Ransom had had a revelation. There was no need to try and recreate the wilderness, the America that had been. If the reports were honest, there was still a place where a Lewis or a Clarke could find wilderness and game in abundance and water pure enough to drink alongside a canoe. And a place big enough to have parts that were being settled, with men still tackling the wilderness as in the days of the West—those mythic years from 1870 to 1890, when the American legends grew to their full height, tall as the mountains, broad as the valleys.

Larry clenched his hands on the armrests of the plane as the pitch of the jet engines changed. The stewardess walked down the aisle from seat to seat, checking belts. Anchorage: already the stories seemed to be writing themselves. It was Lewis and Clarke and Bret Harte and Mark Twain and Robert Service and Jack London all over again. In a way, Larry wished Anchorage *was* quonset huts and log cabins.

The flap mechanism began grinding deep in the belly of the plane. They were flying through clouds now, and the first glimpse Larry got of the scene below was of ice floes on gray water. To the side he could see dim outlines of mountains rising into the clouds, and a long inlet.

The lady was still talking. She explained how Turnagain Arm got its name, how much damage was done in the quake there, and how dangerous the arm could be for boats: its twenty-seven-foot tides, not to mention the tide bores. Tides of boredom, Larry amended.

And then there were houses below, like the houses near the Hartford airport. The plane touched down, passing a group of snowplows just off the runway, the jet reversers opening and fighting the aircraft down to taxi speed.

Turning off from the main runway, the plane bumped and made a sharp quarter turn to the left and a sharper stop.

The pilot spoke.

"There will be a few minutes' delay, folks. I'm afraid our left gear is stuck in a snowdrift,"

There were mountains somewhere nearby. The plane was stuck in a snowdrift.

It was a satisfying introduction to Alaska.

Malcolm Finch-Smith, top public relations man for Alaska Petroleum Pipeline Enterprises—APPLE—was more than a little miffed. He had foolishly agreed to meet with an East Coast journalist who was due in from the airport, and no doubt the fellow was having the devil's own time getting through traffic. Not that the others weren't having similar problems. Roy Rogers, the senior coordinating engineer for the project, wasn't here yet. Nor was Ed Booth. But that might be no great loss. Booth tended to be a trifle effusive, even if he was the only man in the Montez area who really had the qualifications for the job. As the Americans were so fond of saying, he was a "natural."

Finch-Smith, like so many of APPLE's senior employees, was on loan from one of the eight owner companies, the consortium of oil firms who had formed APPLE for the purpose of building and operating the oil line. Most of the other supervisory people were from American companies such as Pacific-Western, Gulf or Exxon. Finch-Smith came from UKO—United Kingdom Oil—and had been working in the States now for fifteen years. He'd hoped to go back to London when the Alaska opening came and he was strongly urged to take the position.

As a consequence, he now found himself sitting in the lobby of the Anchorage-Westward, his back to the Gold Nugget Gift Shop, studying an enormous stuffed polar bear. He would have preferred to be in London, in the lobby of the Connaught, but Alaska did have a certain ambience that Finch-Smith found attractive. The bear looked to be about nine feet high and its mouth was open, showing teeth bigger around than a man's thumb. As usual, half a dozen brats were clustered around the glass case.

Two black GIs from Fort Richardson appraised the bear judiciously.

"You think a M-16 could stop that thing?"

"Shee-it, that mother come after me, I wouldn't bother with no M-16, I'd run."

Finch-Smith glanced at his watch. The meeting should have started at two o'clock, which was four minutes ago. Of course, with Rondy on, there would be some delays. The meeting should have been held in the Captain Cook. It was quieter and had more class.

"Run?" The other soldier stepped back from the glass. "Run? Man, that bear kin run faster than you."

"Not on what I'd be leaving behind me, he wouldn't. He'd be slipping in shit every step he took."

Finch-Smith heard his name called. It was Bob Pearl from Pacific-Western Oil.

"Malcolm," Pearl said and pointed to his wristwatch. "We're about to start."

Finch-Smith was irritated. Irritated that the man should come to remind him at all and that he should do so across a space of twenty or more feet. Americans had so little sense of propriety. He glanced around to see if anyone was within earshot. "I'm supposed to meet someone. Is Roy Rogers here yet?"

Two of the children turned from the glass case and stared at Finch-Smith. He resisted the impulse to tell them to bugger off. Apparently Roy Rogers was also the name of some cowboy star. He could imagine that wherever the senior coordinating engineer went there would be endless and tedious reference to the cowboy namesake.

"No, pard," Bob Pearl said, "but his horse rode in without him." Then Pearl touched his watch again. "Don't be too long, huh, Malc?"

Finch-Smith turned back to the bear and stared at the impossibly long claws that could tear a man's chest open in one swipe. The owner companies, or at least some of the people connected with them, hadn't grasped yet that APPLE was a separate and autonomous firm. APPLE had to satisfy the owners in its operations, but there was something obnoxious in the attitude of Pearl and some of the upper management toward the consortium. Perhaps when the actual building of the line began that would change.

After the hearing today—on relocating some pipe in Copper Canyon near Montez—there should be no more obstacles to the final permit sometime in late April or early May. Finch-Smith looked forward to that day when the start of construction actually began, when APPLE took over in fact as well as on paper. He, for one, had had enough of standing hat-in-hand in the offices of various officials, environmental, governmental, native and local. Everyone had made their objections, had their say, registered their complaints, doubts and dire predictions for years. Now it was coming to an end. Like Gulliver at last untied, Alaska Pipeline could stand up, flex its muscles, and go on about the business of constructing a pipeline. The biggest private project in modern history would be set in motion and—despite the fact that there would be monitors and snoops and problems—the line would fling itself across the face of Alaska and begin sucking oil out of the ground at Prudhoe and spewing it into tankers in Montez harbor.

And then Malcolm Finch-Smith could go home. Meanwhile, he would be handling publicity for a company that had been reviled from one end of the continent to the other and now, for good or evil, or perhaps good *and* evil, would be a powerful entity. So far it had been like trying to pick up porridge with a fork. Nothing was solid, even the structure of the corporation itself had not been fleshed out. And wouldn't be until May. But then, ah, then, the superlatives would flow. Whatever the company did would be historic, a publicity man's dream.

Or it would be if he could get the owners off his back and handle things properly. There were still dangers. Things could go wrong and they would. Pearl from Pacific-Western was still trying to develop contingency planning and accountability structures to cover minor and major disasters. Who would be permitted to speak, what cover stories might be used.

Finch-Smith knew they were wrong and he would play it his way. The worst they could do was ship him back to London. In the meantime, total honesty made the most sense. Total honesty and a willingness to be "big" about mistakes, to criticize oneself before the papers could find out something had even gone wrong. It wouldn't matter. The job was too big. It paid too many people's salaries.

Finch-Smith liked the Alaskans he'd met so far. Most of them seemed to take a sensible approach to the pipeline. There weren't many people who preferred picturesque poverty to a chance for real money and a sound economy.

And APPLE was not going to damage the environment in any vital way. Not after signing the agreements the state and federal boards had put out on the table after four years of argument and millions of dollars in research. It didn't make good business sense.

Finch-Smith looked at the jaws of the bear. Polar bears, an endangered species, were known to hunt men actively for food. He wondered if this one had ever dined on Eskimo for dinner. He was about to get up and take a closer measure of the beast when a voice addressed him tentatively as "Mr. Smith." The voice came from a tightly drawn down parka, out of which only a nose and one eye were visible.

"Finch-Smith," Malcolm corrected. "It's hyphenated."

"I'm Larry Ransom?" Larry said it as though it were a question.

About half of Alaska's 350,000 people live in the greater Anchorage area. Ed Booth, sitting helpless in traffic within walking distance of the twenty-seven-story Anchorage-Westward Hotel, was sure both halves were in town and that all of them had brought cars. His nineteen-year-old son, Doug, slumped indifferently against the passenger-side door. Doug said it was getting as bad as New York.

Ed Booth regarded the crowds along the sidewalks on E Street. Despite an outside temperature hovering just between nine and ten below zero, the turnout for the annual Fur Rendezvous was impressive. A steady flow of people, families mostly, dozens of kids, all bundled up to the eyelids, moved past the car on the snow-clogged walks. Here and there flags were waving, banners drooped down stiffly from lightpoles, helium balloons bobbed in the breeze. The light on Sixth Avenue changed and released a tide of Rondygoers, threading through the traffic jam.

Even though Fur Rondy had long ago gone commercial, still there was the pride in knowing that Outside, in the Lower 48, few would venture forth in such cold, much less consider spending the day at a carnival or fur auction, or watching the sled dog races over on Third Avenue.

Doug was probably just repeating something he'd overheard at the bar, comparing this traffic, this particular assortment of pedestrians, to New York. Ed was tempted to say so, but there was no use starting things. It just happened that in his present mood, old Anchor Town had never looked better to Ed Booth.

The light changed again and this time Ed was able to cross Sixth. As he had feared, the J. C. Penney parking stack was full. He eased the car up behind a Jeep with a SIERRA GO HOME sticker on the bumper. The sticker was worn and barely legible, a remnant of the early hearings on the pipeline or possibly on Sierra Club opposition to the year-round road from Cordova to the Richardson Highway. At least the pipeline battle had been settled.

There would be a pipeline, and Ed Booth, forty-eight years old, was going to work for it, by God, and with a position of some importance. Ed ran his hands over the steering wheel of the car and leaned forward for a better view of the two towers of the Westward. In that building, once he got through traffic and found a place to leave the car, he was to be APPLE's representative at the final hearing on the pipeline right-of-way for the terminal site in Montez. A six-billion-dollar project. And the terminal alone accounted for a billion and a half of the total. There were to be three public relations offices, one in Anchorage, one in Fairbanks and one in Montez.

Ed Booth's wife, Maggie, whose proudest accomplishment so far had been to take over and run the Montez Club Bar, had told him the position was no big deal. Certainly not worth pulling his efforts out of the bar and upsetting her plans to put in a pizza kitchen, maybe even open a restaurant section.

No big deal! Only director of public relations for a billion-and-a-half-dollar construction job, the biggest tank farm in the world.

Maggie was a proud and single-minded woman, and she hadn't seen it, didn't yet. Unlike his two brothers who had become bush pilots, a calling they thought romantic and challenging, Ed had gone from job to job, never really finding anything that held his interest. Flying people into the bush was, after a time, as dull as being a chauffeur. When it wasn't dull it was terrifying.

Ed had tried to start a contracting company, but he wasn't mean enough to survive in a tight, fiercely competitive economy. The pipeline would change that. Everyone would have more work than they could handle. Contracting had been interesting for a while. He had learned to drive a cat, operate a backhoe, weld, pour concrete, and build with brick or wood.

For a time Ed Booth had thought of becoming a guide and had taken courses on wildlife, on survival, on mountain climbing and boating. Later, he had tried to run a charter service, but the cost of having his own boat proved too much and he sold out. When the pipeline came along he was publishing a weekly newspaper that was seventy percent advertising and he had about given up trying to turn it into a daily. With a daily, he could have traveled, followed the news, attended all the important meetings, and kept his hand in with the local kingpins.

Now he would be with the company that was the biggest news around. It was like the answer to a dream and Ed wasn't the least bit ashamed to admit it. When the Englishman from UKO had come down and proposed the job, Ed had turned from the window overlooking the harbor and told Mr. Malcolm Finch-Smith that he would not only take the job, but that it was the answer to his dreams.

Ed pushed forward, crossing Fifth Avenue (another parking lot full), heading through the dense pack of cars and people toward the huge lot below Third. If he couldn't get in at Third, there was always the railroad parking lot.

The English were funny; the more Ed had talked about how important the job was and what a fine company APPLE was, what a tremendous boon the pipeline would be for Alaska, the more reserved Finch-Smith had become. A dead fish.

As he crossed Fourth, Ed saw the carnival area behind the new Alaska National Bank of the North Building. The banks were the sign of the future. So many new banks in Anchorage. And tiny Montez, which never had a full-service bank, now had three, one built and two abuilding. Three banks in a town of twelve hundred people. And the same was true of Valdez, just down the road. The pipeline was coming all right, maybe by early summer, two or three months off, and it was going to be the answer to a lot of people's dreams.

No doubt there would be a flood of new arrivals from the Outside. But Alaska was big, Alaska had seen booms, Alaska could handle them. Ed Booth was as confident of that as he was confident of life in general now that he had become a part of the APPLE.

A sign over the street ahead welcomed visitors to the MARDI GRAS OF THE NORTH. Town never looked so good.

Ed glanced over at his son, who was idly watching a trio of young girls cross just in front of them.

"Lot of people in town," Ed said. "These dog races really pull 'em in."

Doug turned the radio to a rock station. "I *told* you we should have parked back on Ninth."

Little Nasty and Tiny made quite a pair. Nasty stood five-five in bunny boots. Tiny was a giant, and his bulk was accentuated by the down parka he wore. Little Nasty and Tiny made their way across the street from the Anchorage-Westward Hotel. They had seen a placard announcing the hearing on pipeline construction at Copper Canyon and had debated going in.

"We ain't gonna learn nothing we won't read in the paper," Little Nasty said as they dodged past an Eskimo couple trimmed out in matched parkas of fox, wolf and sealskin. "Hey, Tiny, you see the fur on that squaw? I bet mah old lady'd like one of them coats."

Tiny turned, shook his head. "You don't have the money one of them parkas could cost. That's over a grand on each of them."

"Well, ah will have if they ever get this damn pipeline started up."

The two men came around to the hitching area just north of E Street and the yelping and snarling of the dog teams grew louder. Dozens of trucks with portable kennels were clustered in the bank parking area. The scene behind the starting line was a confusion of sleds, traces, and straining, nervous dogs. An old trapper with his foxtail cap was stepping coolly over the traces of his team, checking hitches, patting each dog, freeing lines.

"Like to see George Attla take it this year," Tiny said.

"Ah wouldn't trade a good blue tickhound for that whole team," Nasty said, watching as the old trapper went back to the sled. They edged along the fence toward the grandstands as the trapper tipped the sled up on its runners and, with great effort, held the team in check and moved up to the starting line.

The back of the grandstands screened the team from view, but not the cheers of the crowd and the deep "huh-huh" of the racer urging his dogs on.

"You know," Tiny said, as they broke out of the narrow file between cars and grandstands, "once we get going with that pipeline, I hear they plan to work year round. We won't be taking no four, five months off like now. That's going to be some real dough in your pocket."

"Ah reckon it's worth the waiting all right." The two men had sat on the bench, passing up short jobs off the ironworker list, in order to keep their good layoff numbers for when the pipeline hiring finally began. In Tiny's case it was no problem. His family lived within driving range of the hall. Little Nasty had family in Louisiana and he found the separation not only difficult, but expensive. Like most construction workers, he made a bundle during the warm months and lived on unemployment through the off-season. Normally that would have carried him through in good shape, but this year he had to stick around and spend money on two households. Tiny had urged him to make the best of it, to see the Alaskan version of Mardi Gras. He only looked around at the crowds, wondering that such festivity could go on at ten below. He'd much rather have been at the real one in New Orleans.

Across Third Avenue, where the dog trail led out east through town, a merry-go-round started up, the riders exhaling frosty clouds of laughter, scarves flying, mittened hands waving at other children eating cotton candy, scuffling through the snow. More snow was falling: tiny particles of white dust sifted from the clouds. Little Nasty (the name had stayed with him on every construction job he'd ever worked) ran his gaze across the entire carnival, the tilt-a-whirl, the octopus, the Ferris wheel and above it, the clean lines of the Anchorage-Westward Hotel. Flipping up the back of his jacket, he bent slightly with an unmistakable look on his face. Little Nasty dropped the coat and punched Tiny in the arm. "Let's go back inside, mah plumbing done froze up on me. Ah cain't even fart."

For some the promise of the pipeline was a dream, for some a grudging, slow wait until the big day. Tiny and Little Nasty waited out the ironworker's call list, as did their counterparts in every craft, in Anchorage as well as in Fairbanks, where the winter was colder and prices higher. For those who lived in Alaska before and had housing, the cost of waiting was not as bad, but the newcomers, would-be boomers of every trade—laborers, carpenters, plumbers, steamfitters, operators, teamsters, sheet-metal men and cooks, pile drivers, oilers, electricians and asbestos workers, the skilled millwrights, the untrained bullcooks who wanted to make beds and do the laundry, insulators, welders, riggers and mechanics, some good, some frauds—began to trickle in from every part of the world. They found bacon and eggs for $3.25, a steak dinner for anywhere from $8 to $12, and cheap hotels with $15 to $20 a night rates. If they went to the movies it cost $3 to $5 admission. If they drove cars, gas might run to 75 cents a gallon or more. For those not on Alaskan salaries, Alaskan costs were brutal.

Jack Price, working as a superintendent on a job in Venezuela, considered the pipeline and, along with two friends, decided to put in for Alaska just to see what it was all about. Pipeliners, members of the Tulsa, Oklahoma, Local No. 798—some working in the desert, some in jungles, or working the oilfields of Louisiana, East Texas, even adding pipeline in New Jersey, in Joliet, Illinois, in Los Angeles—began to write notes, call old friends, to see who would go when the time came, whether the Alaska job would be worth it.

And there were others for whom the pipeline would be an easy move, with no waiting on benches, no deals with union business agents or scheming for position. Engineers, auditors, cost and scheduling experts, payroll men, designers, structural geologists, safety men, analysts, explainers, understanders, doers, builders and bossmen—all felt the tug, the ripple on the waters, a breath of air from the Far North.

With each article in *Time, Newsweek,* and *Popular Science,* each Sunday feature in the papers, men and women began to speculate and consider and write letters to Alaska Petroleum Pipeline Enterprises. Each received discouraging replies, but daily the border station on the Alaska Highway recorded more cars, more trailers, more personal goods passing into the state than in any year previous for the date. They came with a variety of hopes and expectations, and many would turn back. But still they came.

Larry Ransom let Mr. Finch-Smith lead him through the crowded lobby of the Anchorage-Westward. The red-carpeted, dark-paneled elegance of the lobby was not at all what Larry had expected, nor was the hyphenated Mr. Finch-Smith. It was like being received by William F. Buckley at the Americana Hotel in New York. Finch-Smith had a patrician charm. He casually tossed off comments, gesturing here and there as they passed a globe of the world, a shopping mall, a bar, snug in his double-vented gray suit of a subtle and expensive texture, undoubtedly off Savile Row.

Larry was sweating in his parka, trying not to bump passersby with his overstuffed duffel bag, doing his best to keep up. They were ascending a broad staircase beneath a gold-on-red sign: The Klondike Ballroom.

As a reporter, Larry wished he could slow events down. The confusion of getting through the airport, realizing he might be late for the meeting, had given him scant time to look over the passengers or order his impressions at Anchorage International.

There had been many native people, he realized, some in furry parkas, some (older women) in brightly colored print parkas that looked as if they had been fashioned of calico. He'd seen sourdoughs who probably prospected in the summer and ran traplines in the winter. They looked out of place in civilization and acted it, walking through the airport lounge uneasily, touching chairs tentatively before sitting. Larry would have loved to get into conversation, but there had been no time.

The bus, when it came, was an odd, boxy affair, dark green—a bread truck with windows. Larry had managed to make some talk with the driver, but the traffic was so bad the driver had finally broken off, hurling the bus into the thick of autos and people like a kamikaze pilot. Fur Rendezvous.

At one point they had crossed Northern Lights Boulevard; a futuristic neon sign at the corner advertised the Northern Lights Shopping Center. An old woman on the bus had asked Larry where he was from and then asked if he didn't find it difficult living with so many people.

There seem to be a lot more people here than in Walpole, New Hampshire, Larry had told the woman.

Anchorage isn't Alaska, she had said firmly. She lived out in the bush, a place named Aniak or Uniak, where she taught school. Never ate store-bought meat. Shopped twice a year. Could understand some Eskimo and two or three Indian dialects. Other than schoolbooks, her only reading was the Bible, and there was no need to read any other book than that. The woman got off at the Roosevelt Hotel.

"They get bushy," the driver had said, twirling a finger at the side of his head, launching the bus into traffic once more.

Downtown, to Larry's surprise, looked like a downtown. There was a Woolworth's, a J. C. Penney's, a big movie theater. There were department stores, tall buildings, a huge post office and courthouse.

And now the Klondike Ballroom, with its red, textured wallpaper and crystal chandeliers, heavy draperies and thick carpeting. Larry dumped his duffel bag in the last row of steel folding chairs and stood with Finch-Smith at the back of the room.

A long table had been set up on a dais and a half-dozen men were seated there now. Finch-Smith quickly filled Larry in on the names and positions of those present. The two men on the left were Bob Pearl and Tom Cunningham, from Pacific-Western and UKO respectively. Larry jotted the names on a pad and, for his own purposes, added *Kissinger and Ehrlichman—Oil(y) men.*

The man next to them was the senior coordinating engineer, Roy Rogers. Larry wrote it down without comment and identified the man with three initials: *LBJ.*

The man in the center of the table was, Finch-Smith thought, the most valuable for interviewing (not that he was trying to tell Larry how to do his job). The man, still unnamed, was joint monitor, which was to say, the man who coordinated state and federal pipeline activities—a watchdog. He would make Alaska Pipeline live up to the environmental stipulations, could even shut down the entire project.

Finch-Smith seemed to have a particular fascination for this man, this watchdog. He pointed out that the joint monitor also had a certain responsibility to the State of Alaska to see that the pipeline did get built, which was a devil of a job. Finch-Smith wouldn't touch it with a ten-foot pole.

"What's his name?" Larry asked.

"Sorry. Dan Curry. Marvelous chap, really." Finch-Smith waited for Larry to finish writing.

Larry put in the man's name, took another look at Curry, the square shoulders, powerful build, large nose, thick hair, narrow but friendly eyes. He wrote: *Poor man's Paul Newman.*

The man who came in last was from public relations. Larry wrote the name, Ed Booth, and added: *Big Windbag.*

"Did you say the town where the terminal's going is Mon-tez or Mon-teez?"

"Mon-teez," Finch-Smith said. He drew the final syllable out as if he found it pleasurable. "There are two towns there, so close you really can't tell them apart. The smaller one is Val-deez and the larger one is Mon-teeeezzz."

Finch-Smith then excused himself and went up front to pass out informational material. Larry glanced again at his notes and at the lineup sitting at the table. Booth and the monitor—Don, no Dan, Curry—were deep in conversation. He'd have given ten bucks to hear what the watchdog was saying.

Dan Curry patiently listened as Ed complained about the traffic, the absurdity of arranging a meeting during Rondy, and the ungratefulness of teenagers who no longer seemed to respect their parents or their elders. Ed Booth was a real sufferer, no doubt about it, but once he got through complaining he seemed happy enough. There were worse brothers-in-law to have than Ed Booth.

Dan asked after his sister, Maggie, and Ed said Maggie sent hugs and kisses which he felt he'd better not deliver under the circumstances.

"Are you glad about the job?"

"I feel like a little kid on his birthday," Ed whispered, and then glanced away. "I can't even talk about it. How's your job? How's Paula and the kids?"

The job was eating away all his free time, Dan said, and Paula and the kids sometimes didn't see him for days at a time. On the way to the job from bed, or on the way to bed from the job, as Paula put it.

If it was like this now, what would it be like in May when actual construction started?

There was another reporter in the group, and, as Finch-Smith had promised Larry, there was no mistaking him: Gil Wolfe of the *Fairbanks News-Miner.* He had a curly mop of hair and a green ecology flag stitched to the sleeve of his jacket. Larry sat down beside him.

A book lay in Wolfe's lap: *Oil on Ice*—A Sierra Club Battle Book. From under the cover a sheet of legal paper stuck out about five inches, and there were questions neatly block-printed on every other line. One had to do with nesting birds in Copper Canyon.

Larry waited until Wolfe had finished inserting a fresh tape in his recorder and had checked the battery level. He introduced himself directly, explaining what he was doing in Alaska.

Wolfe reached up absently and plucked a pencil out of his hair. Such hair. A perfect hemisphere of shaped blond foliage. Larry wondered if there were other things besides pencils hidden in it. Extra batteries? Tapes? That kind of thing got in the way if you wanted to be a good reporter.

Gil Wolfe made pencil marks next to the questions at the top of his list and told Larry he had been in Alaska two years and for the last few months had been free-lancing articles—with little success. He was also determined to, as he put it, "screw up the pipeline people as much as possible." But he admitted he wasn't getting very far. Gil especially didn't like Finch-Smith, because Finch-Smith reminded him of William F. Buckley.

The meeting began. Roy Rogers fidgeted through his introduction and then began to read a long, boring statement full of map coordinates and various technical and legal terms dealing with a pipelaying over Copper Canyon in the township and borough of Montez. He spoke slowly, with a trace of a drawl. If he'd come from Texas he'd been away a long while. Larry supposed he took a lot of kidding on the name.

Larry liked Roy Roger's use of "we." All *we* want to do is pick the pipe up from where *we*'d planned and move about a mile and a half of it closer to the edge of the canyon. *We* were going to elevate it over Angel Falls. Now *we*'re going to bury it in solid rock. *We*'ll tunnel under the channel. Roy Rogers continued to advance arguments, moving into engineering specifications.

Ransom's attention wandered and he found himself looking at the audience. It seemed about evenly divided between people in denim or work pants and those in suits. Larry supposed there were various civic and government people whose attendance was mandatory.

One man in particular seemed to be taking in every word spoken. He had a large head and flowing hair that would not have looked out of place in a Dore Bible. A prophet. Roy Rogers spoke and the prophet nodded his head in neither agreement nor contention.

Copper Canyon sounded terrific, wherever it was. Roy Rogers said that it was the most difficult pipelaying on the line, both because the "rugged beauty" of the area had to be preserved and the high, narrow shelf on the east rim was barely accessible in places.

Rogers scratched at the back of his head and seemed to be considering whether he had said enough. "Well, the best part, I guess, is that we make it easier on the eyes and easier on the mountainside. After all, we do want to minimize the wear and tear on the environment . . . despite what some of our detractors say."

Now it was Finch-Smith's turn. "What say we look at the slides?" A secretary in the back row wheeled a projection table into the aisle. Finch-Smith quickly set up a screen that had been resting across some chairs in the front row. The projectionist turned off the room light. A map of Alaska snapped onto the screen.

"I don't have a pointer," Finch-Smith said, shading his eyes with one hand as he stepped into the screen area. "Please excuse my pen." A dark line, set with dots and triangles, jogged first left, then right, down the eastern third of the state from the north to the south coast. He tapped his pen at the north end of the line. "For those of you unfamiliar with our project, the oil wells are here. I know it says 'Arctic Ocean,' but actually this part of it is properly termed the Beaufort Sea."

Finch-Smith tapped his pen all along the dark line, indicating pump stations and pipeline camps. The oil would flow 800 miles south; would rise to 4,800 feet in the Brooks Range, veer slightly southeast at Prospect Creek, and pass north and to the east of the City of Fairbanks. From Fairbanks the pipeline would remain in close proximity to the existing state highways for the last 350 miles. It would climb to 3,600 feet in Isabel Pass and to 2,800 feet in Thompson Pass.

The next slide was a close-up map, showing the southern half of the pipeline only. Finch-Smith circled the Copper Canyon area, lying halfway between Thompson Pass and the town of Montez. This, he said, was the section in question, the canyon stretching from Mile 17 to Mile 20 on the highway. The steep canyon walls might vary from 100 feet to 700 feet at the highway edge. Above the shelf on the east rim, the mountainside peaked at 5,000 feet.

Gil Wolfe's tape ran out. He flipped the cassette over.

Finch-Smith called for a new slide. There was a contour map of the canyon. Finch-Smith showed the original plan for the pipe and the proposed relocation. For the most part the line would be a quarter mile from the rim except in two spots where it ran within five hundred feet of the edge.

The next slide. A map that showed a rocky wall with a crude tunnel entering it near the highway. "At this location," Finch-Smith said, snapping his fingers for the next slide (a view of a lovely, braided waterfall), "and at Angel Falls, the line approaches the canyon."

Other views of the canyon. A second waterfall. A river. Automobiles at the side of the road, with families taking pictures. An aerial shot of the canyon, showing the highway. Another shot of the tunnel, which, Finch-Smith explained, was an old railroad tunnel that had been abandoned seventy years earlier. "A bit of a problem, this, but a fine example of poor engineering."

The last slide was of a fox peering out of a stack of 48-inch pipe. There was snow on the pipe and the red fox was foxy, indeed.

"We will," Finch-Smith assured the audience, "use the heavier of our two grades of pipe in this area."

Finch-Smith asked for the room lights to be turned on. Lowering the screen, he introduced Ed Booth, "a long-time resident of Montez and a most welcome addition to our public affairs staff."

Ed stood and looked solemnly at the audience.

"I'm not going to b.s. anybody. I'm Alaskan, I love Montez, and I think Copper Canyon is one of the finest pieces of work that the Good Lord made when he created this great state."

Finch-Smith smiled faintly and pressed his fingertips to his temples. Ransom felt sorry for him immediately.

"But I tell you true—this company has been over every inch of ground up here and everyone in Montez is plenty impressed with the job they're doing. Our highway engineers looked over the surveys and I can say that APPLE has done *beaucoup* paperwork." He held his hands a foot apart. "They presented us a copy yea thick—and this was before I joined the team, just for the record. Well—what I meant to say, what I was supposed to say, was that the highway department and zoning commission held a meeting. The state engineers were there and the safety men, too.

"From our point of view this relocation is not only A-OK, it's the better plan, safety-wise and environment-wise. But I guess Dan Curry here can fill in the picture on that."

Curry rose. His shirtsleeves were rolled up. He looked like a man about to start muscling the line into place on his own.

Curry reviewed what Ed Booth had said about the meetings. All sides were satisfied and Dan Curry was satisfied. He, too, had grown up in Montez and, like Ed Booth, he thought the company had done a good research job. He explained his position as joint monitor and the purpose of the public hearing. As required by law.

Gil Wolfe's tape ran out again. This time he merely set the machine on the floor.

"Any questions or comments will be added to the permanent record. If any of you can provide information that we have overlooked, it will be up to me to decide if a further hearing is necessary. And believe me, if we've overlooked something, a further hearing will definitely be necessary. Questions?"

Gil Wolfe was first to his feet. "You say there will be no damage to the environment. Suppose you destroy Angel Falls? Are you and all the king's men going to put that all back together again? And what about a quake?" Wolfe dropped back into his seat and waited to block in more questions.

Dan answered calmly, with no hint of impatience.

Not everything was known about quakes, Dan Curry said, but there was next to zero possibility of starting one with dynamite. He compared the relative displacement of a quake to that of a large dynamite shot. Even a detonated nuclear warhead barely jiggled a seismograph fifty miles away. And the small amounts used in blasting could be likened more to sculpting a channel in the rock.

"As to the last," Dan said, "we couldn't get APPLE to rebuild Angel Falls, but from an engineering standpoint, the falls are not in danger. And if I thought they were, I would be the first person in the world to put a stop to this pipeline."

Roy Rogers thumped a hand on the table. "And the one person in the world who could, too."

A pair of natives stood, and one spoke up loudly.

"Me and him come down from Cordova," the man said. For a minute, Ransom thought he might be Irish from the lilt in his voice. "We're natives and we understand there's goin to be natives hired to work on the pipeline. We hear it's goin to pay a thousand a week. Is that true? We want to sign up, but we don't want to waste all day at this meetin, cause we have a friend in the dog races, you understand?"

Malcolm Finch-Smith explained the local and native hire agreement. He handed each of the men business cards. Others in the crowd demanded cards as well.

"That's all Alaskans really care about," Gil Wolfe whispered. The gold rush all over again.

The prophet raised his hand. Dan acknowledged him.

"Mr. Curry, you say you have the interests of the state at heart and I am sure that you mean what you say. You strike me as an honest man.

"You watch over the environment and you also ensure that the state gets its pipeline.

"It seems, Mr. Curry, you serve two masters, the economic and the environmental. Yet you are, as has been said by the senior coordinating engineer himself, the one man who can raise his hand and stop this mighty march of progress at the slightest transgression, no matter how much money might be invested or how many Alaskans might be on the payroll.

"My question, sir, is—*would you?*"

Chapter Two

AFTER THE HEARING, Larry Ransom asked Gil Wolfe if he knew the prophet. Gil did. The man was Emil Bacich. He was a professor of political science at the University of Alaska and had published many articles on the environment and the pipeline. As a result of his constant efforts to influence local action on the pipeline and his success in mobilizing the academic and scientific communities, Bacich had also received several grants—public and private—to continue the fight.

"If he'd wanted to," Gil said, gathering his gear together, "Emil could have put those people over a barrel today. I want to know why the hell he didn't."

"I'd like to meet him."

"Sure." Gil started up the aisle. "That's Jim Miklov he's talking to. They call Miklov 'Hemingway.' "

"Maybe we should wait," Larry started to say. But Bacich didn't seem to mind the interruption. He took Gil by his right hand and Larry by his left.

"Jim, I got these reporters. If anybody's going to mislead them about what's going on, it'll be me."

Miklov laughed. The resemblance to Hemingway was uncanny. "Okay. Let them go back with half a story. Don't even introduce me."

"I shouldn't but I will." Emil Bacich let the two reporters shake hands with Jim Miklov, a man who was born and raised in Alaska and who, according to Bacich, didn't have the sense to realize that the really smart people were those who came to Alaska by choice.

"He'd have stayed in Texas if he was born there and never have known the difference."

Larry asked Jim what he did for a living.

"When I'm not fighting with Emil I'm usually out in the toolies somewhere taking pictures. Those were my shots you saw today."

"Where are the toolies?"

"The bush. The boonies. I think it comes from the tule bush, but I'm not sure on the spelling."

Gil Wolfe wasn't much on small talk. Apparently he was no friend of Miklov, either. "I'd like to know something, Emil," he said. "I'd like to know why you didn't push harder today. You could have made those bastards sweat and all you did was ask one question. One question. Are you giving up, or what?"

Emil Bacich turned around to look at the table up front, where people had gathered in small groups. The hearing was a foregone conclusion, he said. If there were no new facts, no new statistics to add, then there really was no reason to quarrel. Alaska Pipeline and the oil companies had already won the right to bring 150,000-ton oil tankers into Montez harbor, the right to pour oil through a 48-inch pipe that crossed the worst earthquake zone in the state, and the right to go up on the tundra and drill oil wells until they ran out of room to stand. "The very most we could hope to do today would be to keep them from relocating a few feet of pipe."

After all, Bacich added, the right-of-way was sure to be granted, and in two months or so the pipeline construction would begin. You had to fight where the battles were and he was now switching tactics. Bacich pointed to the head table. "That joint monitor, Dan Curry, that's the man to watch. If he does his job the damage will at least be minimized. All I was trying to do was convert *him,* not his plans."

Emil touched Larry on the chest. "You're a reporter. You come and interview me and I'll do my best to convert you, too, if I can. Now let's get the hell out of here and have a drink."

Stepping out of the elevator on the twenty-seventh floor of the Anchorage-Westward Hotel, Bob Pearl led the way to the Petroleum Club's private entrance. Tom Cunningham of UKO and Finch-Smith followed, chatting about North Sea oil and England's future. "I'm glad it has one," Malcolm Finch-Smith said softly.

At the entry desk, Bob Pearl signed the book for all three and the steward offered them menus. Finch-Smith would have preferred a snack; he wanted to watch the Rondy from the top floor of the hotel. But the other two were trying to cut the calories. Drinks would be bad enough, Pearl told Finch-Smith, patting his belly tenderly.

"The Fossil Bar is open," the steward suggested, extending an arm toward the heavy swinging doors.

Rather than stools, the bar had deep, leather-bucket seats on swivels. Fossils were embedded in clear plastic on a background of sandstone. Animal heads and pelts adorned the walls over the long row of booths. Finch-Smith slipped into a seat at the bar and gazed at the nine-foot relief map behind the bar. Alaska hung on the wall of the Petroleum Club like a trophy.

"You guys sound different," Bob said, after drinks had been served. "You from different parts of England?"

Finch-Smith let them talk. Eventually they decided that to Americans Finch-Smith sounded British, and to the British, American, whereas Cunningham sounded British to everyone.

"I believe," Finch-Smith said, "that my accent is referred to as being *mid*-Atlantic."

"Quite right," Tom Cunningham agreed. "That calls for another round."

More drinks. Bob Pearl reviewed the hearing as he saw it. Naturally he had only the highest compliments for Finch-Smith's presentation.

Finch-Smith said nothing. All during the hearing he had been uncomfortably aware of the presence of the two owner-company men at the end of the table. It was his show, of course, but there was still that damned reluctance to turn APPLE loose. As if the major oil companies were in any position to give lessons in image building. APPLE was real enough, by God. Today's hearings proved that.

Bob Pearl was rumbling on about Gil Wolfe and Emil Bacich. He asked about Larry Ransom and Finch-Smith told Bob as much as he knew. Seemed a decent sort of chap. Probably do an honest job.

Finch-Smith gazed at the map. With people like Bacich and Wolfe around, not to mention Dan Curry and his people, it made sense to be honest.

"I suppose it doesn't matter," Cunningham said. "We have nothing to hide, do we?"

The map showed mountains ringing Anchorage. Chugach Range. Seven thousand feet average. Then, almost immediately above them, the Alaska Range ran in a long semicircle a third of the way up the state, filling much of the space between Anchorage and Fairbanks.

Mount McKinley, North America's highest mountain, with its double peaks (the taller over 20,000 feet high), stood somewhere off to the left of the highway leading to Fairbanks. It was surrounded by glaciers. On clear days you could see the mountain from both cities, which were 350 miles apart. England could be picked up and dropped in there and not be found for months.

". . . the best thing we could do," Bob said loudly, over his third drink, "is buy up all the prints of that Bambi film. You know, it's these Bambi people . . ."

Then above Fairbanks was the great, broad valley of the Yukon, and above that, reaching down into Canada, the Brooks Range—and beyond the Brooks, the North Slope.

Tom Cunningham and Bob Pearl were especially fond of the slides and thought the one with the fox was very positive. Cunningham had doubts about Ed Booth, but then Malcolm had been over here longer and no doubt knew the local situation well enough.

Finch-Smith pressed his palm to the cool plastic bartop. Beneath his hand trilobites, echinoderms, coiled cephalopods lay frozen.

Millions upon millions of the creatures had fallen in ancient seas and been buried and moved with the slow drift of a continent to a climate of bitter cold and short summers. Each organism had died and given up an infinitesimal droplet of oil to the sand that held it. And the oil gradually seeped into pools and migrated upward, floating on deep layers of water. Some escaped, bubbling through to the surface, and some collected under slabs of impermeable rock. Much was dissipated and lost, but in places, where fault lines or domes of rock contained the droplets, vast pools of oil formed and waited underground.

Across a land bridge between Siberia and Alaska the first men came, perhaps fifty thousand years ago, most of them turning south, migrating like oil until something stopped them, a mountain range, or good hunting, or just the weariness of a thousand years of nomadic wandering. A few of them turned north and settled along the coast of the Arctic Sea. In spots traces of oil percolated through to the surface and floated on small ponds. But the aborigines had no use for it, preferring the more obtainable and useful oil from seals and whales. The land bridge sank, and for close to fifteen thousand years men roamed over the north coast of Alaska, often camping two miles above the largest caches of oil on the continent. They did not suspect it was there, nor would it have mattered to them.

The Russians came and took whales and furs. The Russians were followed by the Americans—whalers, trappers and prospectors. But the oil had stayed in the ground, unsought, unsuspected. Only in the 1950s did geologists begin to probe. They knew there was oil somewhere, even if it was too much trouble to get out.

By 1968, it *was* worth the trouble to get out. Within a year Alaska had been given $900 million so that the eight oil companies might make holes in the ground and remove this long-sleeping memorial to a trillion dead life forms.

And, after all this time, Malcolm Finch-Smith knew it couldn't happen fast enough.

Chapter Three

THE WHOLE FLIGHT from Anchorage to the Brooks Range had been overcast. It was Larry Ransom's first time in the air over the pipeline route and he couldn't see a thing. At long last, after two hours, the clouds were breaking up and he was catching glimpses of mountain peaks, ravines and valleys frozen under layers of snow. Gil Wolfe, facing him, watched with absorption as did the other passengers. Finch-Smith seemed, of all of them, the one least impressed by what he saw. He might have been looking out a train window at a familiar Cotswold village.

Larry's association with Gil Wolfe had worked out better than he'd expected. Gil had a big apartment and he had put up Larry for four days. They had seen some of Anchorage, met a lot of people, and Larry hoped he had done Gil some good. He looked at the bare patch on Gil's jacket where the ecology flag had been and could not help but smile. Now if he could only tighten up Gil's writing and interview style.

Mountain after mountain drifted slowly past. There seemed to be no foothills, no easy ascents to the peaks. You could draw pictures of them with three or four perfectly straight lines. Like pyramids.

A photographer behind Larry asked Finch-Smith how he'd like to make a forced landing in that. Finch-Smith smiled.

It had cost nearly three hundred dollars to get outfitted. But Larry, in his Sorel pack boots, his down parka and pants, the fur-backed Everest mittens, face mask and survival scarf, was glad he'd stopped off in Seattle. It was worth the money. Jim Miklov, the old sourdough photographer he'd gone drinking with the first day, had told Larry you couldn't overprepare for Alaska. When Larry told Miklov what he'd bought, it was as though he'd passed an initiation test. Jim Miklov congratulated him for using his head. He didn't care for "savages and puppy dogs"—natives and wolves—but he respected anyone who respected the wilderness.

Larry watched the engine, the blur of the propeller, and, below, the wild landscape. If they did go down and he survived the crash, Larry, with his Eddie Bauer gear, had some hope of staying alive. The pilot's only announcement at takeoff had been that food, first aid and other survival equipment was in the right engine locker and that the key to the compartment was in his right-hand pants pocket. "Just in case," he added as the plane taxied out onto the field.

Larry peered out the window. The mountains were thinning out. There were places where a landing might be attempted.

They were passing over Galbraith Camp and there was a Hercules cargo plane unloading at the airstrip. The Herc could carry a 60-ton load. Larry could see a row of tiny buildings beyond the landing field. Galbraith was the first camp on the Slope side of the mountains. An ice road was used to haul freight from Galbraith to the other camps north of the Brooks. A haze close to the ground erased the surface features. It was like flying over water.

Finch-Smith apologized to the man from *Fortune* that visibility was not better. There was ice fog close to the ground. The reporter reassured Finch-Smith. Everything was fine. He was getting a great story. The photographer already had some great shots.

Everyone was looking down, trying to make out the ground. The plane came lower. The sun grew fainter. A squat building appeared off to the right. Then a strange balloon-tired vehicle. The photographer began snapping away again.

"That's our refinery," Finch-Smith said. "We make our own fuel here. Better than hauling it, you see. We call it superknock."

A series of trailers and steel-shell buildings fell away under the right wing and the plane banked on in, dropped, bounced gently, and rolled to a stop beside a two-story corrugated iron hangar. There was not much else to see.

The pilot stuck his head into the cabin. "You guys better put your booties on. It's forty-two below, with a wind-chill of forty-eight and ice fog. Let me know when you want out."

Finally the pilot came around the outside and opened the door. As he did, the photographer in the rear of the cabin began to swear loudly. Larry drew himself down into his coat. The air that rushed into the plane struck like a body blow.

The photographer cursed again, shoved a camera back into its case and put on a pair of mittens. "How the hell am I going to take pictures in this?"

Larry stepped down from the ramp. The snow squeaked underfoot. The inside of his nose webbed over with cold. He rubbed it with the furry back of the mitten. You were supposed to do that every minute or two to prevent frostbite. Out of curiosity, Larry took his hand out of the mitten and tested the air. A half minute later he had the mitten back on and was banging the hand against his chest.

Finch-Smith cautioned him not to touch bare metal and then explained to the group that it was the ice fog as much as the cold that made breathing difficult. Larry looked back toward the pale sun as Finch-Smith directed and he could see the tiny glints of light falling in soft swirls through the air. Ice particles. Frozen fog.

A van with the Pacific-Western logo on its side came around the corner of the hangar. The driver told them that they could try his scraper on the inside windows if they wanted, but that only the front window could be kept completely free of frost. It was a quarter mile to the PW headquarters, but in such cold even that was too far to walk.

The dormitory-office building they drove toward was surprisingly large and modern. It was obviously made of modules, which Finch-Smith said had been barged in last summer. The building stood on stilts—telephone poles—that held it three feet above the ground.

The photographer had the driver stop and he jumped out to grab a few shots. Finch-Smith told the passengers that the stilts were so the fragile ecosystem wouldn't tear the building apart with frost boils. All heated structures had to be insulated so they would not melt the ground beneath them.

Finch-Smith conducted the entire tour. They visited the yard where thousands of 60-foot joints of pipe waited for construction to start. The pipe had been there for four years, protected from rust by a special coating. The reporters walked on a thousand-foot drilling pad that held six "Christmas trees," the valve and pipe system used to cap an oil well. By drilling at angles, the six wells on this thousand-foot pad could drain a six-mile-square area. The tour continued: work camps, water and sewage plants, a vegetation test area where tundra reseeding experiments were conducted in the summer.

"These bastards are going to be hard to nail," Wolfe told Larry.

"We'll have to come back in the summer," Larry said. "There may be bodies under the snow."

Bob Pearl was content to tag along and let Finch-Smith do all the talking until the *Fortune* reporter inquired, over a steak-and-trimmings lunch in the PW dining hall, how much oil there really was on the North Slope.

Pearl told him the company was putting out the figure of 9.8 billion barrels.

Was there really that much?

Bob Pearl gave a quick rundown on oil reports in the industry. You always gave a figure that was about two-thirds of what you expected to get. If you computed 15 billion barrels, then you reported 10 billion. That made about 14 billion or so at Prudhoe. The Naval Petroleum Reserve to the west, Pet Four, had 30 or 40 billion barrels. The whole North Slope, according to the United States Geological Survey people, had 100 billion barrels; all Alaska could have 300 billion. Prudhoe alone also had 26 trillion cubic feet of natural gas. More than 25 percent of the U.S. oil reserves and 10 percent of the gas reserves. The Canadians probably had another 100 billion barrels in their Arctic.

Bob Pearl picked up an ear of corn and rubbed it on the stick of butter in the dish. "This building'll be here a lot longer than just this one pipeline. I expect this job is just the beginning."

The man from *Fortune* asked Pearl if he was sure on the figures. Pearl nodded. What about the Arabs? Wasn't this more than most of those countries had?

"Sure thing."

Didn't this affect the whole energy crisis? What about the shortages? The Arab stranglehold. Why the hell then didn't people in the oil industry tell anyone about all this oil in Alaska?

Pearl put down his ear of corn and wiped his mouth with a napkin.

"But I did. I told you."

"Nationally. In Washington. In your ads, for God's sake!"

Pearl looked at the man sympathetically and explained that oil still underground didn't count. It has to be proven and accessible to matter. You have to find it, punch the wells, transport it to market. All the talk about shortages had to do with proven, accessible oil.

The reporter accused Pearl and the oil companies of deliberately holding back on vital information. Finch-Smith buttered his bread and chatted amiably with the photographer, who was not interested in the conversation.

"Are *you* going to print what I told you?" Pearl asked. "I've given this information out before and nobody seems to use it. Are you going to?"

Pearl pushed his tray aside.

"Well, there it is. Everything up here is so incredible you just don't know what to believe in. Here we are, three hundred miles north of the Arctic Circle, fifty below outside, not a living soul around this camp for miles, and I'm going to get up and fix myself some apple pie à la mode. And that," he pointed a finger at each reporter in turn, "is the kind of thing your readers will believe."

After Prudhoe, Fairbanks, with the temperature at five below, seemed pleasant, almost mild. Larry waved goodbye to everyone in the plane and stepped off the apron to watch it taxi back onto the field behind an Alaska Airlines 727 with a giant Eskimo face painted on its tail.

Larry was immensely pleased. From Finch-Smith he had an introduction to the Fairbanks office of APPLE and permission to ride north with a convoy of trucks on the winter road over the

Yukon River ice bridge. And, before he headed back east, Ed Booth had promised to show him around Montez. Larry picked up his duffel bag and went inside the modern terminal building to see about getting a ride into downtown Fairbanks.

Along the left side of the terminal, toward the parking lot, were three car rental agencies, and on the right, a few small air taxi services and then Alaska Airlines. Beyond he could see another airline facility. Wien Consolidated Airlines. The terminal seemed to be much larger than it needed to be. There weren't more than fifty people in the whole waiting room.

A small group of soldiers sat dejectedly in a corner near a sign for Fort Wainwright. A cowboy was asleep on a chair, his feet up on his luggage. Businessmen and natives (probably Indian rather than Eskimo) mingled at ticket counters. A polar bear in a glass case menaced an old woman vacuuming the carpet near the main entrance. It didn't look to be as big as the bear in the Westward. But it was big enough. Larry went out and found a cab. It cost a buck forty just to get in and slam the door.

"Where you going, pal?"

"Polaris Hotel. It's on Second Avenue."

"No shit," the driver muttered and picked up his mike. "Coming home," he reported. "The cab office is in the Polaris. And if you're wondering about the fare, it's six bucks. You watch and see."

So far they had been traveling a divided highway, passing warehouses, a place for kids called Alaskaland, barrackslike apartment complexes. The driver headed into a residential section, houses and occasional large log cabins, otherwise a street in any town out west.

Downtown was both larger and seedier than Larry had expected. There were more bars than there should have been and fewer restaurants. Most of the buildings were old. The town had a raw look. The Polaris was one of the biggest buildings around, seven or eight stories high and almost a block square. It, too, had seen better days.

"Well, what'cha think of it?" The cabbie pointed to the meter. It said five-ninety.

Larry dug out some singles and kept a quarter from the change. "I like it."

"Yeah? It looks like a goddamn dump to me."

In their apartment above the Montez Club Bar, Ed and Maggie Booth were sitting at opposite ends of the living room.

Ed looked out over the harbor and absentmindedly fondled a soapstone carving of a seal.

"You're wrong, Ed." Maggie's voice was dull, cold. The lamp tinged her hair a bronze gold. She was wearing a white bodyshirt with white tailored overalls. At least they looked like overalls. The bib barely covered her breasts. Maggie was big, almost six feet, with big bones. Ed had maybe an inch in height. In his prime he only outweighed her by ten pounds. "I can see Doug going to work the pipeline. He's young and he could get enough together to make some kind of start in a few years. But this thing is only going to last three years, and then what? We've got this bar. I want to put in a pizza kitchen, add a small café. This is the time for us to build up what we have."

"There could be other work after the pipeline. I've always wanted to do something professional. You know, public relations. They might keep me on."

"Ed . . ." It was an old, old argument. "I know what's troubling you and all I can say is, forget it. There is nothing wrong with owning a bar. Especially one that's going to go like this one will. Don't be like my mother."

"There's nothing wrong with your mother."

Maggie smoothed her long hair with one hand and went to the door.

"There's no reason to be ashamed over running a bar. What are you, some kind of *gentleman* like that phony Englishman you work for?"

Maggie went out.

Sunlight touched the peaks of a mountain at the east end of the harbor. Small boats bobbed in the darkening water.

Lavinia Curry, Maggie's mother, would probably be sitting in the chartroom, watching the sunset or perhaps peering through her telescope at sea otters or whales out in the bay. Lavinia Curry had never said anything one way or another about what she thought of Maggie owning a bar. She had stopped coming down off her hill shortly after the town of Montez had been rebuilt on her old land. The family had lived in the old town when the quake hit. Afterward, when she gave Montez the new townsite out of family land, saving the upland half for herself, she had less and less to do with the place. Now Ed was one of her few visitors.

Possibly Maggie was right. Maybe the old woman had gotten so respectable that she no longer had any peers. But he was welcome there, along with Dan Curry. Dan's brother, David, even though he was now chief of police, got a cooler reception.

Well, the women were strong-willed and Maggie had yielded to her mother in only one area. She had married Ed Booth.

Ed wondered if that was what she really had against her mother.

"Are the kids in bed already?" Dan Curry closed the door behind him and slipped his coat off.

Paula was curled up on the end of the sofa reading *Travel and Leisure*. "Hours ago."

"Too bad. I have some good news."

"Oh." She lowered her magazine. "You were fired?"

He shook his head.

"You quit and we're going back to San Francisco."

"Honey . . ." Dan dropped wearily into the recliner. "No . . . I just thought you might be glad to know that I rearranged my schedule and I'm going to be free for two days to take the kids to the Arctic Games. All day, both times."

She went back to the magazine. "That's wonderful. I'm dazzled."

Dan Curry went to the kitchen to make a drink. "It's not like this job is unimportant," he called back to her. "Right now is a critical time." There was no reply. "I'm doing it for the future of the state." He returned with his drink. "So that your children and mine will have an environmentally pure and economically sound future." He lifted his glass to her. "North to the future."

"I think I'm going to take the kids back home for a few weeks."

"A few weeks?"

She put down the magazine and he could see tears brimming in her eyes.

"Yes, just a few weeks. I'm so sick of snow and cold and . . . everything." She wiped at her eyes. "I'm sorry, Dan, I guess it's just a bad case of cabin fever. A few weeks in the sun, maybe some concerts and plays, I'll be fine."

Dan sat beside her, taking her hand.

"You'll be all right for two weeks, won't you?" she asked, and the tears started again. "It's not like you're home that much as it is."

As he stroked her hair and watched the flames in the fireplace, Dan also tried to soothe the old misgivings that were growing in him.

Alaska is very hard on marriages.

The next morning when Larry Ransom went into the Alaska Pipeline office for his temporary ID card he was surprised to find two people he recognized. The senior project engineer, who didn't recognize him, and Jim Miklov, the photographer.

"Well, lad, I see you're still at it. Thought you'd have the whole story by now."

"Just barely scratching the surface."

"Atta boy." Miklov punched him in the shoulder. "One thing I hate is an expert."

"You know, it kind of amazes me that I should run into you up here. And that other fellow. Roy Rogers."

"Hell, Alaska is nothing but a small town. Just happens to be spread out over a couple of million acres. You stay here a while and you'll know people wherever you go. And that isn't a bad question, by the way. Where the hell *are* you going?"

"I'm trying to catch a ride with a trucker up the haul road. I hear there's an ice bridge over the Yukon River and I'd like to see it before it melts."

"That won't be until May, but you're welcome to ride with me if you don't mind stopping every hundred feet or so to take pictures. I've got a Chevy Suburban and there's room."

Outside the air was even harsher than at Prudhoe. It didn't make sense to Larry.

"Up there you had ice fog. Here you have ice smog. Look at the cars you see parked around here."

Larry looked. Nearly every car at the sidewalk and in the parking lot across the street had its engine idling.

Jim told him that when people came in to shop or on business they kept their engines going. Up on the Slope engines ran twenty-four hours a day, but there it didn't matter. Fairbanks sat in a low place, however, and often had inversions; the pollution could get real bad. APPLE, not wanting to be accused of contributing to the already unpleasant situation, had installed plug-ins throughout the company parking lot. Restarting a car was no problem with plug-ins.

Miklov's Suburban was, nonetheless, idling. "Of course, with the camera equipment, I'd rather get into a warm car."

All the cars Larry had seen in Anchorage and Fairbanks had extension cords coming out of the front grilles. Here they were being used. Many cars had twenty or more feet of cord wrapped around the sideview mirror. Rear and side windows often had oblong transparent panels stuck on to lessen the frostup. Tires, Miklov told Larry, often froze so hard in the morning that you would drive a mile on the flat spots caused by the weight of the car. It could be very bumpy, especially with nylon tires.

Jim arranged his equipment in the back. Two cameras, a Hasselblad and a Nikon, went on the front floor, under the heater vent.

On the highway, north of town, Larry finished a doughnut and told Jim that he thought he looked like Ernest Hemingway when he first saw him.

"And now?"

"What?" Larry looked over at Miklov.

"Now who do I look like?"

"You still look like Ernest Hemingway."

"I thought so, even years ago, when I met him."

"You met Hemingway?" Larry sat up.

"I was on a boat to France. A couple of people had stopped to stare at me on deck one day and the next day I found the stewards tipping their hats to me. Couldn't figure it out. So I went in the bar to think things over and then I saw this guy sitting at a table, all alone, and he looked a lot like me. I smiled and he smiled and we just naturally had a drink and started talking."

"You knew he was Hemingway?"

"Well, I wasn't sure. Somehow we never introduced ourselves. But he talked about fishing off the Keys and about Spain and hunting, so I figured. He was very interested in my stories about hunting bears in Alaska." Jim flashed a smile. "I've got some good bear stories, by the way."

"But it *was* Hemingway?"

"Oh, yeah. And, you know, he was getting pissed off that I didn't recognize him. But somehow I got so interested in topping his stories that I just wouldn't give him the satisfaction. I could tell it was kind of eating at him. Finally the last day out he leans over the table to shake hands and he says, 'By the by, I never introduced myself. The name's Hemingway.' Then he arches his eyebrows kind of and adds, *'Ernest.'* So I nod, and I say, 'My name's Miklov. *Jim.'* He just got up and left the bar." Miklov reached into the backseat for an apple.

Larry laughed and settled back to watch the scrub roll by.

"Are those some kind of pine?"

"Swamp spruce, a lot of people call them. Some are black spruce, some white. They're not much to look at, are they?"

The road diverged from the main highway and the hills grew steep.

"Permafrost here," Miklov said, pointing to the foot-high scrub. "Some of these trees are fifteen or twenty years old. The ground is frozen almost to the surface. You dig down in these spots in the middle of August with the temperature in the eighties and you'll find frozen ground six inches from the top."

All the way to the Yukon, Miklov pointed out features of the landscape and Larry Ransom made notes.

Those white birds are snow buntings . . .

The town is Live-n-good, not Livin' good. It's named after a prospector, Jay Livengood . . .

This part is Alaska Pipeline winter road. It was built at the start of winter and it'll melt in summer. It's four hundred miles long. By next fall APPLE is going to have to make a year-round road out of gravel . . .

You didn't see it? It was a lynx. I can still see him. Gone . . .

And at last they rounded a curve on a hilltop and down below was the sinuous white band of the Yukon River.

"Did you see the bald eagle?"

Larry shook his head in resignation.

When they came down the curve and stopped at the river checkpoint, Larry was puzzled. "The road just crosses the river. Right over on the ice. Is that all an ice bridge is?"

Miklov explained. Normally the river froze to a depth of two feet. Water had been pumped over the ice and allowed to freeze in layers until, in a section about 150 feet wide, it was six to eight feet deep. Ice that thick could hold a D-9 Cat, even a big scraper. Larry wondered why the ice bridge didn't look thicker.

"Hey, even back in New England ice floats low in the water. The more they piled on, the deeper the section went. It's only about a foot higher in the middle than at the edge."

Jim rolled the car slowly out onto the river and held the speed down to ten miles an hour.

"Next summer you can come back up here and piss in the Yukon and you'll have one of the three qualifications for being a sourdough. The other two are to hump a klootch and kill a polar bear."

"Hump a klootch?"

"Screw a savage girl. A squaw. Native woman."

"A savage?"

Miklov shrugged. "I don't mean anything bad when I say it. Just stating a fact. They brag about their heritage all the time and I consider what it is. They ate raw meat, left old people to die, screw right in the same room like a dog or cat would, no concern for the rest of the family, rub grease in their hair, give their wives to each other. Savages. Finch-Smith wanted some pictures of them doing work on one of the camps so I gave it to him in an envelope with 'Photos of Savages' on the front."

"Was he mad?"

"Yeah," Miklov admitted. "So I scratched it out and wrote in 'Aboriginals' instead."

They reached the far edge of the bridge. Soon they came to Five Mile Camp, a collection of trailer units put together with an enclosed center corridor that was heated. Enclosed ramps led everywhere—to the mess hall, to additional quarters, to a small recreation unit and to some of the offices.

A truck-trailer with a generator inside was parked at the edge of the road, supplying power. Its diesel was a constant background noise in the camp.

A cleared area behind the camp held silent rows of construction equipment. Road graders, bulldozers, a few backhoes. Some of the equipment had tape and shipping labels still stuck over windshields.

"They already bringing in equipment for the job?"

Miklov looked over at the storage yard. "Hell, that stuff has been around—four years. They thought they were going to build this pipeline back in 1969, and they made a haul road and built camps and dragged millions of dollars worth of this equipment up here."

"Did they just reopen the camps, then?"

Miklov pulled the car around to the end of the first set of barracks and nosed it up against a plug-in. "They just kept five or six guys in each camp as caretakers. I used to come by and visit once in a while. Half the guys up here were nuts from the boredom. I'm surprised they didn't kill each other." He shut the car off and began getting his gear together. "There's about forty people in this camp now, getting it ready. I expect when the go-ahead comes they'll tear most of this out and put up a new, bigger camp. They've been shipping housing units over the river the last couple of months."

Larry took some gear and went in. Reinforcements were on the way.

"Take the first one that's empty," Jim said.

Larry knocked on the first door. He opened it. Empty. Two beds with a table between them. Two closets. Spartan. He tried to imagine it for four years with nothing to do but keep an eye on things. Larry put his duffel bag in the tiny closet and sat on the narrow bed.

What strange passages of time some men took for their lives.

Dinner was pork chops and potatoes au gratin. Larry and Jim Miklov sat with a chopper pilot and two surveyors. The chopper pilot was interested in writing. "I've been thinking of doing a story on this place," he told Larry. "But nothing ever happens. The whole thing would be 'I got up and ate breakfast and then I worked all day, ate dinner and went to sleep. The next day was the same.' "

The surveyors laughed.

"But then," the pilot continued, "one day I ate breakfast and went to work and I saw a bear and then I worked all day, but nervously, ate dinner and went to sleep. And I almost had a bad dream."

"A wet dream," one of the surveyors corrected. "If it was a girl bear."

"You know," said the senior surveyor at the end of the table, "that's interesting you should mention that. I had three wet dreams just last night. I would have had four, but I fell asleep."

"There are no girls in camp?" Larry asked.

"No booze, no broads and no guns. That's the rules."

"Don't girls work in the camps?"

The three shook their heads in unison.

"I guess they will when things get going. I heard some women's group in Anchorage is going to sue the unions if they don't take 'em in."

"Then, there's really not much to do here, is there?"

"We get movies once in a while."

"We take showers with five-fingered Mary."

"Ah, Mary," the chopper pilot said softly. "You know, I play with myself so much in the shower that now whenever it rains I get a hard-on."

"You going to put this in your article?"

Larry nodded. "I better. I was wondering if I was going to get up here in time to do any stories about the pipeline and I found out I'm about two months early."

"So you'll see Alaska as it was," Jim cut in. "Although even now it's too late. Maybe Montez, when you go there. It'll be the most impacted by the pipeline of any town. It's got twelve hundred people now and it'll have six thousand or more when things are in full swing. But I guess you would have had to be here ten years ago. It's the people, mostly." Miklov put down his fork and wiped his hands on a napkin. "Used to be you couldn't walk anywhere without getting a ride. Now people hardly stop for a hitchhiker. I don't, except in winter out somewhere on the road.

"Used to be you could leave your cabin and come back six months later, you might find a note on the table from somebody who had used the place for a month, thanking you and telling you he'd replaced the food he ate. Maybe there'd be some money on the table and it would more than cover what was gone. Now you're lucky to come back and find the cabin. I even know a guy who found some hippies in his cabin and they told him it was their right, that land and empty cabins belong to the people. He had to take them out of there at gunpoint."

"Why do you suppose that is?" the chopper pilot asked. "I noticed a big change like that everywhere after I came back from Nam."

"Ah," Miklov got up. "These kids today! If they can't eat it, smoke it or fuck it, then they piss on it like a goddamn wolverine."

On the way to Old Man Camp, Larry did see a wolverine, but he didn't recognize it.

"What in the hell was that?" He craned his neck at the low, dangerous creature, half cat, half bear, that darted across the road and turned sharply as if to confront the car. They bounced around a corner and he lost sight of it.

"Wolverine." Miklov said. "Meanest animal, pound for pound, you'll ever see. I ran over one the last time out."

"I wish I had seen the lynx."

"I understand last night the guard saw a pack of wolves, running along the bank of the Yukon."

After lunch at Old Man, a group of four trailers on a bald knob of rock lashed down with cables against the wind, Larry saw two moose.

The country grew strange. Hills reached up to the left, and outcrops of rock that looked like ruins of forts, ancient castles. To the right, the land dropped into a valley that swept for miles to the horizon, ending in another series of hills.

The sun, even at two in the afternoon, hung low in the sky. They had not passed another vehicle for an hour. The road, a path of flattened snow, wound crazily off onto distant hills, appearing suddenly on a rise, then losing itself, showing again as a scratch on a hill.

"Well, lad," Jim said softly. "We're in God's country here."

"It's beautiful, all right."

"That's not what I meant," Jim said. "This is God's country. One mistake and we're in His hip pocket."

The sign at Prospect Creek Camp bragged that the coldest temperature in North America had been recorded there. Just a fraction short of eighty below zero.

Dinner was good, the men lonely; Larry wished he could call Hope.

At forty below Larry went out and looked at the night sky. The aurora was out, and it looked just the way Larry had seen it described in books. A curtain. Glowing. A phantasmagorical curtain behind which those strange lights played. Twice the curtain disappeared and came back. The folds deepened. A laser of light began halfway up the sky and slowly rotated, beginning and ending nowhere. Larry rubbed at his nose and cheeks and stomped his feet. The curtain was gone and a funnel of light, dim in the center, its sides flickering, poured down the sky. On impulse, Larry ran to the radio shack and told the operator. The operator, a tall black man, shrugged and pulled on a parka to take a look.

Away from the building he cupped his hands to block out the light from the nearby windows. Then he looked at Larry.

"No colors." He started back toward the door.

"Colors?"

"Yeah, man, when the lights are working good there's green and purple and pink. Lemme know if it gets good."

Larry stayed until he had the uncomfortable sensation that the surface of his eyes had grown cold. Had anyone ever frozen their eyes? Did eyes make body heat? Larry hurried back to the warmth of his tiny room.

Miklov laughed at him. "Well, eyes won't freeze, but for a Cheechako you at least had the sense to come in out of the cold."

"Cheechako?"

"Native lingo. A greenhorn. Until you've spent a winter or two, seen the seasons go around and know how to stay *alive* in Alaska, that's what you are. A Chee-chaker."

Larry said nothing. Miklov's words were meant as an explanation, but he had taken them to heart. Lying in the darkness of the room he turned Miklov's words into a challenge. That was the difference about being in Alaska, all right.

Anyone could live in Walpole, New Hampshire.

Honey, he said over the telephone in the Montez Club Bar. You can't believe how beautiful this town is. All the way from Fairbanks it got nicer and nicer. We flew over rolling country and then the mountains just got bigger. I'm in a bar across from a harbor, a big harbor, the whole town is surrounded by mountains. I guess the harbor winds in from Prince William Sound, but you can't really see it from here. It's like a movie set.

Ed Booth, sitting on a nearby barstool, couldn't help but overhear. Larry didn't care.

And it's the same size as Walpole, practically . . .

Of course I'm coming home soon. In fact, I'll be home in a few days. I'm here too early. Nothing's really happening yet. I'll have to come back in May. I wish you could see this. Ed Booth says it's a natural fiord and people call it the Switzerland of Alaska.

He made a kiss over the phone and hung up.

"She's going to love it," he told Ed. "I just know she will."

"You sure made the right pitch. Fiord, Switzerland, the whole nine yards." Ed motioned to Maggie for another drink. "He just told his wife he was going to move her up here."

"Well, I didn't actually tell her yet. I thought I'd better do that in person."

"Good idea," Maggie said. "But you might want to start looking for a place to live. Once they get this project going, there won't be much for rent. I might be able to put you onto a used trailer with a space."

Larry stared down into his drink. "I'd appreciate that, but I think I better take it slow. Hope and I like to do things by agreement. She doesn't like it if I go off and do something without the two of us discussing it and . . . well, agreeing."

Maggie jerked a thumb at Ed. "Tell *him* that, would you?" She leaned over the bar. "If you weren't so good in bed," Maggie whispered to Ed, "I'd throw you out in the street and let you starve."

"You want to do impact," Ed said, "you ought to talk to Maggie's brother. He's chief of police here."

Ed was driving through the town, which was laid out in a long rectangle with three cross streets at the harbor end and a connecting street against the mountain. There were eight blocks in between, but they started in from both long sides of the rectangle and dead-ended at a park strip that ran down the center. From the air, coming in, it looked to Larry like a football field on which most of the yard lines had been erased down the middle.

"We'll go there now," Ed said, turning into Curry Drive.

Larry looked at the street sign. "That's no relation to the Curry who was at the hearing, is it?"

Ed slowed the car. "Maggie's mother is Lavinia Curry. She owned all this land. This piece over here," he motioned to the wooded hills on the right, "still belongs to her." He stopped the car at the corner of Curry and Aurora.

Lavinia's driveway was a short distance from the water at the end of the street. For the first few years, while the town was being rebuilt, Lavinia had bustled about, encouraging people, pitching in to feed kids while the parents cleared the lots, attending town meetings. Then, with no explanation or warning, she just stopped coming down from the hill. If she went anywhere now, it was to the airport and a yearly vacation to Scotland and England, where she had family.

She wasn't crazy, Ed insisted. In fact, she seemed brighter and more quick-witted than ever. She had always been quirky, but at the same time very strong. He admired her. Unfortunately, Maggie couldn't get along with Lavinia.

Larry thought it strange that the woman who owned all that land was Maggie's mother and that Maggie worked in a bar.

Ed laughed. Maggie owned the bar, even if she did work in it. It was no fault of Lavinia's. Maggie simply refused her mother's help after Lavinia stopped coming in to town. And the quake *had* considerably reduced the family's income. At the time Lavinia had given the land, it wasn't worth much. Of course, now it looked like house lots would be going for ten thousand each. Maggie had taken, in the last few years, to calling Lavinia "Queen of the Hill."

If Larry wanted to do any articles on Montez, though, it would be nice if he could interview Lavinia.

"Would she talk to me?" Larry asked.

Ed pondered the question. "Give me a month or so to soften her up. She might. If she did, though, it would be a first. But I might be able to work it."

"I saw your brother David," Ransom told Dan Curry back in Anchorage.

"What did he have to say?" Dan was tempted to ask if he'd smelled booze on his breath. David was one person that pipeline impact was not going to help.

"He's funny. It was like talking to a bear. He told me they might get organized crime, prostitution, gambling, drugs, con men, all the rackets following the pipeline money." Larry shook his head. "And he's got, you know, this little three-man department."

Dan nodded. He was glad his brother had finally achieved some distinction, even if only as a character.

"Well, I asked David what he's going to do when all this hits. And he sighs once and he says, 'I guess I'm just going to have to put on three more men.' It's like nothing fazes your brother."

Good, Dan thought, good for David. "Now, Larry, what about you?"

"Well, sir. I thought I could spend a month and get some articles, but this thing is just too big. I'm going back and bring my family, maybe stay the summer."

Dan pushed a copy of his job description and the summary of the environmental guidelines across the desk.

"I hope they like it here. It's a terrific place for kids. At least I think so."

Part Two

Chapter One

"THIS PIPELINE . . ." Captain Ackerman paused until he had the attention of the forty or more men sitting at the movable writing desks. "This pipeline is the biggest private construction job since the pyramids and the Great Wall of China." Two men in the rear of the improvised classroom were talking. Ackerman stared at them coldly. They stopped.

"The Great Wall of China cost two hundred thousand lives. We don't want that. We don't want anything like that. Now this pipeline is going to be eight hundred miles long, and I've heard it said that we'll lose one man for every mile before it's finished. You pay attention today, especially this afternoon after your physicals, you remember what you learn in orientation and we might keep that number down." Ackerman handed the first man in each seat a packet of cards and indicated they were to be passed back to the others.

"You take this seriously today and you might keep yourself off the casualty list. I've been with the army in Alaska fourteen years and we've learned one thing well. The Arctic can kill you before you know you're in trouble." Ackerman dipped into a box and began handing out pencils. He was wearing maroon slacks, a white belt, pink shirt, red tie. His manner and movements were crisp, military. After passing out the pencils he returned to the center of the room and stood, legs wide, hands on hips.

"I realize most of you are not actually going north of the Arctic Circle, so let me amend what I said. *Alaska* can kill you fast. This is unforgiving country. You'll find temperatures in Glennallen and Tonsina down to sixty below and worse. In Montez you get wind out of Thompson Pass up to eighty miles an hour. Even a forty-mile-an-hour wind at twenty below can freeze exposed flesh in thirty seconds."

Ackerman pointed to a chart. "We'll post wind-chill charts like that in the camps and we'll talk more about it later. I know it's the first week in May and you guys are thinking about summer already, but the weather can change fast here and winter will be on us again. As I said, Alaska has a very unforgiving climate. Not to mention that working construction is in itself a dangerous occupation." He smiled at the men.

"That's for sure." A middle-aged bantam of a man in the front row held up his left hand and displayed the loss of his little finger. Heads came back to the front and several men laughed.

"Hey, Little Nasty, I told you not to put your hands where they didn't belong."

Nasty turned around and pointed at the hulking ironworker who had addressed him. "Ain't you ashamed, Tiny?" He looked at Ackerman. "That's the dummy that gave the operator the signal to dump a twelve-ton beam on me. You let him on the job and we'll lose more men than the China Wall, the Panama Canal and the Golden Gate Bridge put together."

Ackerman glanced at his wristwatch. "Okay, men, we have just enough time to fill out these record cards and then get to the clinic for your physicals."

"You sure this ain't the military?" Little Nasty demanded. "I wouldn't want no more soljerin."

"Perish the thought," a kid said.

Little Nasty looked at the boy, at his shoulder-length hair, the embroidered shirt.

"Perish the thought," someone a few rows back whispered, and there were chuckles around the room.

"When you men get to the part about ethnic groups, I want

you to use the terms I've written on the blackboard to your left."

The men looked up and Ackerman began to read the list.

"We have Caucasian, Negro, Alaska Native—" he broke off, pointing to the bracketed words at the extreme right of the board. "Alaska Natives should specify if they are Eskimo, Aleut or Indian."

A hand went up.

"I'm Athabascan," the man said.

"Indian," Ackerman shot back, and went on down the list. "Oriental, Filipino, American Indian and Latin. Latin is anyone with a Spanish surname in case you're not sure. Questions?"

Little Nasty waved Ackerman over. Ackerman nodded. "Caucasian, I should have explained, is white."

"Texan, too?" someone shouted. Little Nasty laughed loudly.

"What you laughing for, dipshit?" Tiny rocked forward in his seat. "You're from Tex-ass, aren't you?"

Nasty held his card out at arm's length to read it. "Cain't see good without my cheaters, but it looks like I wrote Gretna, Loozeyanna, for place of birth." He smiled. "You great big sack of hog's nuts."

"For craft," Ackerman was saying, "include your union local. Teamsters, nine-fifty-nine, operating engineers, three-o-two, whatever."

"Carpenters, twelve-eighty-eight," a voice supplied.

"Seven-ninety-eight, welders," another called, louder.

"Ironworkers . . ." Tiny began. "Laborers," someone shouted.

Ackerman cleared his throat and the room fell silent.

"When you gentlemen have filled out your cards you may board the bus in the parking lot. The bus will bring you back here and you can take lunch at the Big Boy or Grizzly Burger. They're both on Northern Lights Boulevard, about a block over. We resume at one-thirty."

The boy with long dark hair got up, handed Ackerman his card, and walked gracefully to the door. After he left, Tiny made a face and delicately traced one eyebrow with the tip of his little finger.

Little Nasty beat Tiny to the head of the line.

"Your robe don't fit so good." He tilted his head back for a better look. The men had been given disposable paper gowns and Tiny's had torn under both arms. He was now trying to keep the rear vent pinched together, using first one hand behind his back, then the other. The nurse came in with a clipboard and motioned to Little Nasty.

"Name?"

"John Hill." He stepped up on the scale. "Hundred and thirty-eight pounds. It don't never change."

She slid the weights around and nodded.

"Always weigh the same," Little Nasty told her and started to step down.

"I need your height."

"Five-six," he told her. "And that don't never change even more than the weight."

She looked him over and raised the measuring rod, extending the headpiece.

Nasty stretched upward, rising slightly on the balls of his feet.

"Stand flat," the nurse snapped and bent to look at the rod. "Five-four-and-a-half."

"Take this with you to X ray." The nurse handed Nasty a sheet of paper. "You know, Mr. Hill, a lot of famous men have been short." She sounded like a nursery school teacher.

Little Nasty raised a leg and let out a fart. Snatching the paper, he strode off down the hall.

Nurse O'Brien shook her head. "Nasty little man," she said.

"That's his nickname," Tiny told her, getting on the scale. "Better start with the big one on three hundred," he added, moving the weight himself. She asked his name.

"Well, they call me Tiny on the job, but my real name's Vance Moss." He spelled it. Nurse O'Brien slid the smaller weight a few inches.

"Well, Tiny, you're a pound under three-twenty."

He patted his belly. "I'm usually heavy after a winter. I'll be down to three-o-five in the summer."

He had to help her adjust the height scale.

"Six-foot-five." She wrote it down, handed him the paper. "X ray."

Tiny started to walk away. "What do they need X rays for?" He halted in midstride.

"Spinal injuries."

He shook his head in disgust. "You mean so they got evidence in case someone claims he hurt his back."

Nurse O'Brien shrugged. "Or so you can prove that your back was okay when you took the job. Cuts both ways. Next . . ."

The physicals had been going on since the last week in April, when the pipeline right-of-way had been granted, both in Anchorage and up in Fairbanks.

So far the only person rejected in a physical was a man who went directly from the clinic at Fort Wainwright in Fairbanks to the hospital. He had actually suffered a mild stroke during the examination period.

The old were passed, the half blind, the semicrippled, those with histories of asthma and heart trouble, the diabetics, the partially deaf, obvious alcoholics, coughers, the burnt-out and the pathetic along with the vigorous young and old, the physically overfit and the general run of middle-aged, overweight, stolid men who patiently shuffled through this final obstacle to the big paycheck, the solid gold job. Some of them were new, but most, in these early weeks, due to union lists, would be the men who had worked Alaska before, who knew each other from building the DEW line, the navy job at Adak, Amchitka, the Aleutians, oil rigs in Cook Inlet, truck runs, sheet-metal shops in Anchorage, power lines in the Matanuska Valley.

Many hired in these first weeks were those who had played the "lists" right, managing to stay at the top of the union A list by borrowing money so they could pass up jobs that would pay two or three months and then leave them at the bottom when the pipeline calls came in. Some had gone broke and taken the short jobs, or just given up.

After the A lists were called, there were hundreds more on the B lists, and then, for those who were outsiders and had no hours in on Alaskan construction, there would be weeks and months of sitting on the benches. Few would come off the C and D lists this soon.

The smart hunters, coming in from the Outside, hearing that Alaskans were hired first, got Alaska driver's licenses, Alaska plates, Alaska mailing addresses, and claimed to have lived in Anchorage a year or more. This early, no one would check.

If you had to lie or to borrow six or eight thousand bucks to afford the twice-daily showup in the union halls, then it was worth it finally to land a thousand-a-week job.

For those waiting in camps up and down the line it was as though war had finally broken out. Reinforcements came. Communications were beefed up. Supplies and logistics were tripled, quadrupled almost every day. Planes and trucks poured in. The camps north of the Yukon, isolated from each other as the winter road began to melt, built airstrips and helicopter pads. Where there had been camp managers and engineers, there were now superintendents, project directors, senior field engineers and APPLE reps.

Fifteen hundred men were to be assigned to building a year-round haul road. Hundreds more would build new barracks, and when those were ready, they would be filled with men who would build twice as many.

They came from all over Alaska. Men from Kenai and Homer, from Anchorage and Fairbanks. Workers from Cordova, Whittier, from Healy and Wasilla. Natives from Copper Center, Point Hope, Nome and Barrow.

Electricians turned up from Colorado and Los Angeles, pipeline welders from Oklahoma, Texas, Libya and Venezuela.

Construction companies with home offices in Houston sent Texans, those with offices in Riverside sent Californians.

Special skills brought in men from Puerto Rico, Singapore, the Mideast, and even, in one case, an expert fresh from a safari in Kenya.

And, to satisfy the right-of-way permit, every single one of these men was required to take a physical and go through orientation in Anchorage or Fairbanks and to carry the small yellow certificate of orientation on the job.

So it happened that Captain Eugene B. Ackerman, born in San Antonio, Texas, raised in army bases in Georgia, Germany and Spain, came to be teaching, among forty other men, one Isaac Ahgutuk, born in Barrow, Alaska, a full-blooded Eskimo, about the history and ways of the land that had been Isaac's for centuries past counting.

Everyone blinked as the lights came back on in the orientation room. Captain Ackerman sat on the edge of a worktable to the side of the room.

"I know that wasn't much of a movie, but you do get some idea from it of the history of this project, such as it is." He held up a small booklet. "You've all got these books . . ."

Several men picked copies up from the desks where they sat. The cover featured a crude pen-and-ink drawing of a child and adult Eskimo wearing what appeared to be sealskin parkas. They were standing on a hummock of snow-covered ice, perhaps on the shore of the Arctic Ocean, with icebergs drifting nearby.

An Eskimo seated near the back of the room pointed to various details in the picture and the Indian sitting next to him stuck out his lower lip and shook his head slightly.

Ackerman opened his book and waited until most of the men in the room followed his lead.

"Staying Alive in the Arctic." He began by reading the title of the book.

This is the law of the Yukon, and ever she makes it plain:
Send not your foolish and feeble; send me your strong and your sane.

He looked around at the men. "That's Robert Service, as you can see, and if you passed your physicals you may be strong, or at least not terminally ill. Whether any of you are sane remains to be seen." He paused for laughs. "This book, if you read on, has two purposes: to help you stay alive in a survival situation and to prevent you from getting frostbitten, or lost and maybe injured on the job. What does the book mean by a survival situation?"

No hands went up.

"A survival situation is one in which every action you take is directed toward saving your life. The best way to defend against a survival situation is never to get into it in the first place. This book can help you. It has ten rules on survival: I want to give you four simple rules that may help." He held up a finger.

"The first is the buddy system. Never go anywhere alone in Alaska in the winter."

He extended his middle finger.

"Advisement of intent. Give your ETD and your ETA. Let people know where you're going, when you plan to leave, when to expect arrival."

Ring finger.

"Remain in position if lost. Stay with vehicles. Don't wander off."

He touched his little finger with the index finger of his left hand, tapping it several times before speaking.

"Carry enough clothing and equipment to get you through twelve, even twenty-four hours without help. And, I should add, that if you do remain with a vehicle and sit there running the engine with the windows closed, you might kill yourself with carbon monoxide. By the time you realize it's getting you, there's nothing you can do. We took a man out of a deuce-and-a-half a few years back, and when he came out of the hospital he told me that he was aware he was dying but he couldn't move to open the window. He just had to sit there, engine idling, waiting to die. The man couldn't even respond when we came to get him out of the truck. I thought he was dead already."

Ackerman moved off the edge of the desk and smiled. The men were silent and watching him. "Did you all have good lunches?" There were murmurs, a belch from Little Nasty. Ackerman rubbed his palms together. "Fine. I hope you enjoy our next presentation." He strode to the back of the room, flipped on a slide projector, and knocked off the room lights.

The first slide had a date and name.

January 21, 1972 Temp −41°
S/Sgt Billy Joe Henderson

"Cracker," Tiny called out, and two or three men around him laughed.

Ackerman hit the changeover switch and a full-screen picture of a man's right hand, the fingers and palms red, blistered and displaying patches of missing tissue, replaced the name.

"Oh, shit," a voice said from the back of the room.

"This man was working on a Jeep one fine day in January. The sun was out, he was working hard, and he dropped his wrench down into the engine. Sergeant Henderson felt warm all over and he forgot the outside temperature. He couldn't get hold of the wrench with his Arctic mittens on, so he took one off just long enough to reach in, grab the tool, and lay it on the fender." Ackerman paused for a long time. "The only problem was that he couldn't let go of the wrench. It was frozen in his hands and it burned . . . cold burns like hell. So he grabbed the wrench with his left mitten and gave a tremendous yank and the wrench came free, along with about an ounce of meat."

The slide went off and the next one showed the same hand with larger blisters and black areas.

"This is about two weeks later, and some of the tissue is already turning black and beginning to slough off."

He hit the changer.

"Here the fingers are almost totally black, and it will be necessary to amputate. This is five weeks."

The next picture showed a hand with only a thumb. The palm was black.

"Guy looks worse than Nasty," Tiny said loudly, but no one responded.

"It was too bad that Sergeant Henderson was on a road ten miles from camp when this happened. If he had gotten in and warmed his hand carefully in water about a hundred and five degrees he might have had enough left to stay in the service and make his twenty years." Ackerman cut to the next slide. There was a stub of hand left, reddened at the seam, where his palm had been.

"This is after his last operation, fourteen weeks later." He changed slides.

December 8, 1969 Temp −28°
Cpl Michael Spernak

The first photo of Spernak showed both hands a dull, angry red. Spernak had been driving a diesel Cat and didn't realize how cold it was. He had light driving gloves and for a while the cold hurt, but he thought he had gotten used to it. "Normally on a Cat, the engine fan blowing back would keep a man warm, but Spernak had gloves that let his heat drain out. Also, he was on rough ground and he kept grabbing onto the metal around him to steady himself. Then, when he went to unzip his parka, because his *body* was warm, he realized his hands were frozen. He couldn't even move them."

Ackerman changed slides. There were gasps and the baby face in the front row put his head down, not looking.

"Both hands are black after only six weeks and much tissue has begun to slough off. Spernak knew about warming your hands carefully and not moving the fingers so the blood vessels wouldn't break and tissue wouldn't shatter. So he crawled up on the cab and warmed his hands over the exhaust pipe. Right over the exhaust pipe."

Next slide.

"What Spernak didn't know was that the exhaust on a tractor varies from nine hundred to fifteen hundred degrees. He fried the meat real good."

Ackerman ran through three more slides and then there was a new name, Pvt Kevin Waters, who walked six miles on his heels, had his boots cut off, and warmed his feet in warm water until the pain forced the medics to put him under. All but two toes were saved.

And a trapper who cooked one hand off, realizing the trouble he had made only when he looked down to see the water in the pot boil over while his hand was still in it.

There were airmen with blebs on their cheeks that went away and left scars: the men could never live in cold climates again. And there were soldiers who had no ears but who now looked better with earflaps down than up, and a carpenter who out of sheer habit had stuck a handful of nails between his lips at thirty-eight below and would no longer need to worry about chapping.

The frostbite show lasted an hour and was followed by a slide show of the animal, plant and fish life of Alaska. Ackerman described the dangers of removing the insulating blanket of vegetation that made up the tundra. Not the least of these dangers was immediate dismissal from the job. Or termination, as they called it on the pipeline.

There would be no operating equipment off roads or specified work areas without permission, no operating in streambeds, no disposal of waste on the ground or in the water, no littering and no feeding animals.

The men in the room were restless. Ackerman hurried on, already bored, but facing the prospect of giving the same lecture six days a week for the rest of the project.

The listing of camp rules drew the loudest disapproval. "At least . . ." Ackerman tried to smile ". . . at least we may be losing the restriction on women. It looks like the unions are going to be dispatching women next month. And for those of you in camps south of the Yukon, booze is accessible in roadhouses or, at terminal camp, in nearby Montez."

He sighed heavily and flipped through his notes.

"I shouldn't forget the last part of your orientation. Human relations." He looked over the group of men. "There are going to be men here from . . ."

"And broads," Tiny shouted enthusiastically.

"Aw, shet your mouth lard ass, ain't no women going to look twice at some overgrown toad like you."

Tiny leaned back in his chair, but Ackerman cut him off before he could return the insult.

". . . As I was saying, there will be men here from every race, every culture, every part of the nation. Take the time to listen to the boy who comes from a different part of the United States and see if he means what you think he means before you fly off the handle. Rather than squabbling about racial differences, try to gain some insight into other ways of life. You can learn from those whose backgrounds are different from yours." Ackerman pulled at his collar and tried to think of something else to say, then began gathering up his materials. "Dismissed," he said.

A circle of men immediately gathered around him, asking questions about plane schedules, bringing cars, what to take, whether or not they could have single rooms.

"It's all on the information sheets in the packets I gave you." He nodded at one of the men he knew and then called Isaac Ahgutuk over. "Isaac, could you have added anything to my cold weather talk?"

Isaac tried not to laugh at Ackerman. But laughter comes as easily as breathing to most Eskimos.

"Only what my dad say in Barrow." Isaac touched the side of his head. "He always say all white men are nuts."

"How's that?" Ackerman said.

"Fifty below, some white men came and built a radio shack." Isaac shook his head. "Nobody works when it's that cold. That's why he says all white men are nuts."

"That's good," Ackerman said. "Huh, men, isn't that good? I mean, how's that for a cultural difference?"

Isaac smiled at all the men who were smiling at him. "That old man was never wrong," he said, and left the room, still smiling.

Chapter Two

WALPOLE, NEW HAMPSHIRE, is the archetypal New England village. No tourist could ask for more. Yet this town of less than two thousand inhabitants stays much to itself, the tourists either passing it on Route 12 to the south or flying by on Interstate 91 through Vermont, just across the Connecticut River.

At night the local teenagers sometimes "scoop the loop" and race four or five times around Washington Square until the lights begin to go on in the narrow clapboard colonials, the saltboxes, the slate-roofed cottages. On the square are a town hall and two churches, each with proper, prim New England steeples. Life in Walpole is determinedly rural.

As in many northern New England communities, the town divides sharply on most issues between the natives and the people the natives like to call the country club set. Some of the country-clubbers are rich, some well educated; most live in places like Walpole because they value a simpler way of life, or would like to.

Until he got to Alaska, Larry Ransom had been one of the country-clubbers. His wife, Hope, born and raised in Walpole, was a rich, educated native, which, if it did not endear her to both factions, gave her enough assurance for it not to matter.

She would not send her children to the New Hampshire public schools and she let it be known that she would not. At the same time, unlike her parents, she and Larry could not afford private schools. Hope was proud. She decided to teach at the experimental Walpole Grammar School so that her daughters, Caitlin and Netty, could attend free.

The travel trailer, standing on Elm Street in Washington Square, had drawn natives and country-clubbers alike. School was out and it was a perfect June first, a glorious, brilliant Saturday, with the promise of a great summer to come. The trailer was thirty-two feet long, a fifth-wheel model, hitched on a heavy steel plate in the bed of a pickup truck. The pickup, a three-quarter-ton Crew Cab Dodge, had four doors. The total length of truck and trailer was fifty feet. The truck was a sky blue, and under its model name, "Adventurer 200," the kids had taped a sign that read "Alaska or Bust."

The window cover on the front of the trailer, far above the heads of the neighbors and friends who had come to say goodbye to Larry and Hope Ransom, had a green shamrock decal. In the center of the shamrock were the words "Northern Indiana Trailers." Here, too, the children, Netty and Caitlin, had taped a sign: "Alaska Highway or Die Trying!!!"

Larry, outside, was showing the hitching mechanism to Mr. Bundy, the college librarian, and Mr. Bundy's father, both of whom lived in the rambling house across the street; to the Habersons, a devout pair of fundamentalists who lived next door; and to Mike Dunham, the mail carrier.

Inside the trailer, Hope was explaining to Mr. Bundy's girlfriend, Selma, and the two Weston sisters how the kitchen worked, where the shower was, what had to be done to change the kitchen table into a bed. A slender, tall woman with blond hair and fine features, Hope seemed too genteel to show off a trailer, much less to live in one. If she was not comfortable, she seemed at least determined.

Neighbors wandered in and out, peering underneath, standing on tiptoe, seeing much and saying little.

"It's just like a truck and a trailer." Larry pointed to the greasy hitch plate, the release bar, the electrical hookup. "When I want to use the truck, I put down the jacks and pull out. When I want the trailer I back in, retract the jacks and I'm in business."

Larry couldn't tell what the Habersons were thinking, but then, no one knew what the Habersons thought.

"What's in the compartment?" old man Bundy said. (Only he didn't say "comp*ar*tment"; he said "comp*ah*tment," as any proper Yankee would.)

"Generator on the right, propane tanks on the left." Larry opened the panel and pressed the button. The generator purred into life.

"Onan," Mrs. Haberson said, shocked.

Larry looked at her. Mr. Haberson leaned in close, read the label on the generator, and clucked his tongue. "What a name to put on something." There was no mistaking his disapproval this time.

"A-yuh," old man Bundy said. "At's a good name fer a self-stahtin' gen-a-rate-uh."

Larry put the cover back on.

"What's an Onan?" Dunham demanded.

"Onan," Bob Bundy's father said softly, "spilled his seed on the ground and the Lord slew him."

Dunham leaned against the truck. "I still don't get it."

The interior had been done in green and there were Irish touches throughout. Clay pipes and high hats decorated the mirror in the bathroom. The linoleum floor had shamrocks nine inches wide. The curtain at the top of the short staircase leading to the front bedroom was peopled with leprechauns.

"I'm not crazy about it," Hope told Nancy, who had come in to have a look. Nancy taught fifth grade at the grammar school. "But it was the only one we could afford and it had the best interior arrangement. We saw a Yellowstone we liked but we couldn't take delivery until July, and Larry is already a month behind and has to get back."

Nancy brushed back her hair and sat on the barstool just opposite the entry door.

"You will be here for the fall semester, won't you?"

Hope shuddered. "Don't even suggest the possibility that I won't. Larry seems to think Alaska is the promised land, but the more he tells me about it, the less I want to go."

"Oh, but it should be interesting. You've never been west."

Hope frowned. "I think Alaska's beyond that. You know, I was looking forward to helping out with the historical dig this summer. I thought I could spend a few months poking around in old cellar holes, maybe write some poetry, get away from the kids. Now I'm going to be cooped up with them all summer." She patted Netty, the eleven-year-old, on the hand. "Sorry, lovey, but Mommy has her limits."

Nancy lit up a cigarette. "I don't know. It might be fun. At least you'll see something new when you look out the window every day. And it beats sitting home alone while Larry is out re-searching."

"Maybe," Hope said. It was true she hadn't much liked it when Larry was running all over Massachusetts during the prison troubles. And after all, Larry had told her (and told her) the project would take two or even three months. He couldn't expect her to put up with that long a separation. The notion of dropping the project had, of course, never occurred to him. He owed it to her to find a way to bring the family. Hope owed it to him to come. What else was there to do?

Outside, they could hear the men talking.

"I'd hate to pull this thing five thousand miles and up over that Alaska Highway." The mailman.

"You know, you're doing just like that preacher and his family in Michener's book. You know, *Hawaii.* They left from Walpole when they went out to Hawaii." Bundy, the librarian.

"Course the film was taken down at Sturbridge Village." Old man Bundy.

Librarian again. "I hope you have a better voyage than they did."

"Can't miss." Larry. "We have the luck of the Irish with us. This is the Leprechaun model."

Chapter Three

THE DE HAVILLAND TWIN OTTER is one of the real workhorses among bush planes. It has high wings, seats nineteen (seats can be removed for cargo), and can take off from and land on a very short field. It is slow, boxy, inelegant, but for bush flying, with rough fields and worse weather, it is a safe, reliable means of getting around.

Dan Curry wasn't crazy about the Otter. It was too cramped—single seats on the left, two abreast on the right—and the smell of exhaust always managed to creep into the cabin. Flying in an Otter reminded him of bus rides he'd taken in Mexico years ago. Still, it was good to get away from the office and see a part of Alaska that even few Alaskans had seen, the stretch of country the gold rushers had once trod between Livengood and the Brooks Range.

Each camp along the route north of the Yukon River was now isolated, each building a section of gravel road in both directions to link with other camps. Two observers, one from the Federal Bureau of Lands, the other from the State Department of Land Use, were posted in each camp to supervise operations and road building as they affected the environment. Roving teams of state fish and game specialists, geologists and anthropologists also visited camps and work sites. Special environmental observers, hired by the state for expertise in waste control, soil erosion, permafrost effects and watershed mechanics, were brought in to the camps as needed. Soon, several teams of university archeologists would be working along the route of the pipeline, digging in likely spots and watching for signs of artifacts in the company's excavation.

All of these people had their salaries and expenses paid by Alaska Petroleum Pipeline Enterprises; all of them, either directly or indirectly, were responsible to Dan Curry.

Today he was accompanying the combined state-federal teams on one of the weekly flights. The shift for the men was a week on and a week off, with adjustments made for unavoidable weather problems that might prevent a team from leaving or coming on duty for two or three days. This had already happened. One of the men with Dan had flown up to Galbraith for three days straight, only to turn back at the mountains. Finally he was put down at Happy Valley and taken in by chopper from there during a break in the weather.

Not all the camps had airstrips yet, so this procedure was necessary even in good weather. Today they had dropped a team at Five Mile and were skipping Old Man, which had only a helipad. Four men would get off at Prospect and at Wiseman.

It really was the gold rush run. From Five Mile, just north of the Yukon, there was Old Man, Prospect Creek, Coldfoot, Wiseman and Dietrich, all busy towns at the turn of the century and now, except for a dozen people living near Wiseman, abandoned. Coldfoot Camp had a miner's cemetery right at the entrance, and the men in camp had been careful to fence it off. Someone was making a permanent marker for the graveyard and a cabin nearby. Surveyors, laying out the haul road, had neatly bypassed an old cabin north of Wiseman that had been built on a small stream called Nugget Creek. An observer went to check out the cabin. In 1930 somebody had carved his name on the table, so it was abandoned by then. Another name had been added in 1963.

Now there would be a road beside this once isolated cabin. In four more months, by the end of September, a new road would be built where there had never been a road, a gravel road 360 miles long into an area the size of California.

A section of that road, pushing south from Prospect Creek, was visible now ahead of the plane. Curry, sitting at the front of the cabin, leaned into the cockpit and asked the pilot to drop down and circle the road so Jim Miklov, sitting on the right, could get some pictures.

"Haul road shots," Dan shouted to Jim. "And get some of the camp, too. I want some aerials of the creek near the camp."

Like the official observers, Jim Miklov was assigned to Curry's teams when needed, all at APPLE's expense. The company, in order to secure the work permit, had agreed to pay all the costs of policing itself. And that included office space in Anchorage and Fairbanks for both teams as well as every piece of office equipment, phone bills, secretarial help—right down to the last stamp. To get the oil, they would have signed anything.

The plane banked in a long right turn, descending over the haul road. A pale strip of ground showed where the trees had been cleared. The clearing was now being filled with gravel in a pad two to four feet thick. From the air, circling, the progress was imperceptible. But the reports showed miles of progress every day.

The country below was hilly and forested. At Coldfoot the hills became foothills and at Wiseman, mountains. Observers got on, got off. Dan Curry exchanged pleasantries, but he was just along for the ride and to have Jim Miklov take pictures. Jim was one of the few Alaskans Dan knew who had really spent time in this part of the country.

When the haul road was finished, and the project over, the road would be turned over to Alaska to become part of the state highway system. If the state chose to open the road to tourists, others would see a part of the country that was once so wild that gold rushers heading north from Prospect Creek had turned tail for safer country.

Dan looked down now on Coldfoot Camp as Miklov took more pictures of the road. Perhaps Emil Bacich and his followers had the wrong target. The pipeline itself wasn't nearly the disaster they suspected it to be. But a little gravel road into a country as big as California might change the state more than any of the forecasters and analysts could imagine. For it would be open not only to campers and visitors but to businessmen, to mining companies and more seismologists, fortune hunters, speculators and prospectors. And would that be good or bad for Alaska? Dan, and people like him, were going to have to decide things like that soon. And that was the only certainty.

"I'm so tired," Tiny said, stretching his arms over his head. "I don't know if I'll be able to get on that bus and go back to camp or not."

Tiny was sitting on a flopped-over wire spool at the edge of Montez harbor. He was surrounded, on the edge of the dock, by the other three members of his rigging crew, Little Nasty, Sonny, and Dale. Dale was an old man who had smoker's cough and difficulty breathing. But he was having no difficulty breathing today because there had been no work. And Sonny, the native trainee, had had nothing to learn. Somewhere in the Gulf of Alaska, or possibly in Prince William Sound, a tugboat with two barges of housing modules was headed for Montez. It was already a day and a half late.

"Easiest two hundred and fifty dollars I ever made," Little Nasty said, leaning over the edge of the dock to spit into the water. Sunday, their first day on the job, was double time. At seven in the morning, after picking up their work tags at the brass shack, Jack Price, dock superintendent, had told Tiny to take his crew to the dock and unload the barge when it came. It was now ten after five.

"You know . . ." Tiny looked at his watch. "I don't believe those mods are coming after all. You guys see anything?"

All four men peered out across the water. The water was calm and the long low mountains three miles across the bay were doubled. A deep valley split the range directly across from the terminal, where Gold Creek ran along the western edge of Montez. The town, like the terminal, sat on a shelf of land that rose swiftly from the water's edge. The high school at the far end of town was a few dozen yards from the abrupt upthrust of the mountain. In Montez a man might walk over, lean one hand against a nearly vertical wall of rock, and tell a stranger that his property ran right to the mountain, which was a nice mountain, about six thousand feet.

On the opposite side, where the terminal was being built, the shelf was steeper, and much of the rough site preparation for roads and housing consisted of terracing and leveling. The dock area, which was considered temporary (although it had been built at a cost of four million dollars), was basically a dirt and gravel fill with pilings and a concrete sea wall to hold it all back.

"I don't see nothin out there," Nasty said, shading his eyes with one hand. "I believe you're right. He ain't coming."

Sonny and Dale agreed. There was definitely no barge in the harbor.

"I suppose we ought to wait until a quarter after to git on the bus." Tiny stretched again and rested both hands atop his hard hat. Like most ironworkers, he wore the hat backward on his head. The contractor's name, Bartel, had been altered by an afternoon of thoughtful scratching with a penknife to read "Fart."

Nasty turned around to see if the other crafts were knocking off yet. There were two contractors on the terminal, Hyatt and Rueter for the permanent storage tank facility and Bartel, who was putting up the temporary work camp. (Temporary for three years unless another pipeline was begun, or so the unofficial word had it.)

H&R's men were already coming down off the mountain and heading for the boat, which was odd. They usually quit later. Probably they had some blasting to do, Nasty thought, putting the question to Tiny.

"Yeah, I thought I heard a whistle. Too bad we can't go up and watch." Tiny scaled a rock at a gull standing on one of the pilings. He missed, and the gull, extending its wings momentarily, settled back down and preened itself. "Like to see if those boys got any class, Nasty?"

Nasty and Tiny had done some demolition work with explosives, hitting the Lower 48 during the off-season in previous years. For a while business got so good they had thought of forming a company, but there wasn't enough work in Alaska to keep them busy at it and neither one would have considered going back Outside on a year-round basis.

"You couldn't blow a stump outen a swamp with a blockbuster," Little Nasty said. "Come on, dead ass, the carpenters and fitters is going in. No use us staying."

The men gathered their jackets, gloves, and lunchboxes, and walked up the hill toward the shore road and the waiting buses.

A 28-ton forklift with the operating engineer foreman and an operator rolled by. The driver beeped and flipped a finger at Tiny. The forklift operator, the operator of the 225-ton crane and an oiler had also sat idle all day, waiting for the barge. Another crew of riggers with a forklift and crane were presumably idle, since they had been sent up to the dormitory laydown area to unload modules from trucks. Three flatbed trucks, with drivers, were to transport modules from the dock to the laydown area. The drivers slouched in the cabs of the trucks, reading, dozing.

Two teamster warehousemen, whose job it was to check the manifests of incoming cargo, had taken their shirts off to see if they could get a tan. It was, they told Tiny, very unusual to have a sunny day, or even a day in which rain did not fall, in Montez. Good, warm, seventy-degree weather was to be taken advantage of.

After lunch, when it became obvious that a wasted day was ahead, Tiny asked the warehouseman if goof-ups like this were common. He'd never been on a construction job before where the bosses didn't get excited when the men sat around with nothing to do.

Well, that's the difference, said one teamster. You were on jobs. This isn't a job, it's an honorary position.

Talking with the other crafts on the way to the bus, Tiny was beginning to believe what he heard. Out of the fifty or sixty men gathering at the brass shack and the buses, maybe a dozen had done any work at all.

Tiny removed the small plastic tag with his five-digit number and handed it to the timekeeper in the shack window. "Hey," he said after the old man hung the tag on a nail under a painted number. "What the hell is this brass shack business anyway? How come we got to pick these tags up and bring them back?"

The man scooped up a handful of tags that were thrown on the narrow counter by a crew of laborers and sorted them by number. He looked at Tiny, looked *up* at Tiny looming in the doorway.

"It's nothing personal." He shuffled the cards in his hands. "It's to make sure that a man's actually here on the job and not laying in his rack. You know, some foremen might put a guy down when he isn't actually on the site. You understand, I'm only saying that *some* foremen might do that."

Tiny laid a huge fist on the counter. The man glanced down.

"This . . ." Tiny motioned to the shack, the rows of nails and tags, "is here to make sure foremen don't cheat the company?"

The old man nodded.

Tiny leaned into the shack so far that the man was brought up short against the wall. His shoulders twitched as the nails pricked into his back.

"That's the most chickenshit thing I ever heard of on a construction job in my whole goddamn life." Tiny once more banged his fist on the counter and sent some of the tags skittering off onto the floor. "Well, my crew was here today, every damn one of them, and we *worked.*" He shuffled off the wooden walkway, talking out loud to the flow of men coming by the shack. "Harass a man after he's worked himself half to death . . . Can't trust a foreman you oughta can him . . . Call me a liar."

Little Nasty was leaning against the bus, and he shook his head. "You big old peckerwood, if you ain't something. Pick on an old man like that."

"You should have seen him, Nasty. He looked like one of them fakers in India, lying on a bed of nails."

"Hey buddy. You best not to be messing with me like that. I'll tear your face right off."

"You boys going to town tonight?" A forklift driver stepped between Tiny and Nasty. "I hear they got good bars, good music and bad women."

"I was just thinking I might do that," Tiny said. His next sentence was cut off by a sound, a sharp wumping report that you could feel in the chest and stomach. "Blasting," Tiny said, as small, dark chunks of rock fell through a cloud of rising smoke, high on the mountainside. Then the echo came, a mushy rattle, from the mountains over on the Montez side of the bay.

In camps north of the Yukon there were no towns, no bars to go to, no women to dance with or wish to dance with. Liquor was not allowed, but it came in with the luggage by air or occasionally in the mail, packed safely in sweaters and long underwear.

At Wiseman, in the foothills of the Brooks Range, the local Medevac pilot spent Friday evening shuttling liquor from Bettles, a native village, to his own camp and Prospect Creek. The flight log at Wiseman listed a four-hour navigation test run. Men who drank in their rooms and caused no trouble were tolerated.

North of the Brooks, at Sag River Camp, the wind-chill had sent the June temperature down to ten degrees. The men stayed inside. They watched the Clint Eastwood movie and discussed .44 Magnums afterward. There was nowhere to go, even if it had been warm. Sag River, in the middle of the North Slope, sat on one of the flattest pieces of real estate in the world. With the wind blowing dust and fine snow, even the horizon was missing. The snow, it was said, blew in from the polar ice cap, traveling hundreds of miles to sift under doorways and around windows and coat the sides of vehicles with powder. It was snow that might have fallen months or years ago and blown from place to place since then. Perhaps, one man told another, standing at the window of the rec hall, looking out at the hazy 11 P.M. sun, the snow had fallen on Siberia a hundred years ago and blown to Canada and then back to the Pole and lain for a while in the lee of an iceberg and then come down to Sag River to melt at last. Something to ponder.

It was Friday night and everyone had paychecks of six, seven, eight hundred dollars "take home pay." Some banked by mail, some paid to the order of their wives and scribbled short notes to enclose with the checks. A few men just stuck the checks in the drawer with the other checks.

A story was going around about one woman who did get into Deadhorse Camp. According to the newspapers, she had told Alaska Pipeline's public relations man that she wanted to write an article on life at the North Slope. She spent the first week in March at Deadhorse hooking, first for $500 and then for $100. After six days she flew to Fairbanks, having earned $5,300. Then she checked into the hospital for a week to be treated for nervous exhaustion.

At Sag River Camp, the version was that she had told the company she wanted to sell magazine subscriptions, that she sold four and came back with $8,000 and had to go into the hospital.

A news reporter, in an article syndicated for the wire services, wrote of a woman who, posing as a salesman, went to Deadhorse and earned $5,800 in a week, collapsed, and was rushed to the hospital in Anchorage. "I said I was selling," she was quoted as saying. "As a matter of fact, I sold two hundred dollars' worth of subscriptions to various magazines."

The APPLE rep at Franklin Bluffs, who personally knew of the incident, told a group of visiting journalists that the story was true about her getting into Deadhorse, but that the men wouldn't pay those ridiculous prices. The most she got was a hundred, and the last three days she'd go for fifty. She was furious, and had a fit when the camp manager charged her ninety dollars a day for room and board, but that was what it cost to keep the construction men in the camp. Ninety a man. She'd come out with maybe fifteen hundred dollars.

This version was backed up by some of the men at Deadhorse, who had heard of the woman, but somehow not actually run into her during the week. Which was reasonable since she was in bed, working.

The story at Deadhorse was that a bullcook smuggled her in and charged her room and board, but she had still cleared almost three thousand in only four nights. The story she'd given the papers was to get publicity for herself so she could work the camps south of the line in a Winnebago.

This version was accepted by many at Fort Wainwright in Fairbanks, where APPLE had most of the field engineering and managerial staff. The newspaper interview was done for pay, though, since her trip had been a bust.

Malcolm Finch-Smith, asked if he had indeed given the woman permission, said that for the life of him he couldn't imagine where the story had gotten started since no such woman had ever appeared in his office. In fact, from the way he had been quoted by her, it was quite obvious to him that she had never spoken with him. He would never, for example, have told her to "watch her cherries, those are some horny guys." Nor could he imagine saying that "she should keep her mouth shut about it, otherwise every broad working her way through college will be in here."

Gil Wolfe, working in the library as Larry Ransom had suggested, read the story and made notes. It might come in useful for an article on prostitution. Or impact. Emil Bacich had told him to watch the human damage from the pipeline. "See what it spawns."

So far it had spawned a phonograph record about Texans, hippies and Okies invading Alaska and not finding things to their liking. Like the record, a locally produced game called Taps appeared, billed as the genuine pipeliner's game. Among the movable pieces in the game were an oil baron, a Texan and a little old lady in tennis shoes. The June 2 sermon at the Glennallen Community Church was entitled: Angels: God's Pipeline of Mercy.

A man in Manistee, Michigan, for a reasonable cost of only two hundred dollars, had offered to be a "wagonmaster" and lead a three-hundred-trailer caravan of job-seekers to Alaska.

A bulletin was issued within the Alaska pipeline company asking that management employees responding to job inquiries enclose a copy of the brochure "Hard Facts About Alaskan Employment." All press releases were to include a closing paragraph pointing out the high rate of unemployment and the preference for hiring Alaskan residents as well as the high cost of living.

Still, the job-seekers came and, despite disclaimers, they found jobs and wrote home to friends and relatives. And they came, too. Or planned to come.

By driving hard, Larry and Hope had made Ottawa the first day on the road, arriving there just at twilight on Saturday. Setting up for a late dinner, Larry opened the control panel on the refrigerator and found that the 12-volt system, used for travel, was not working. He went up front where the fuse box was supposed to be and discovered that it had been improperly located under the mattress board in the built-in bed. He lifted the mattress and removed a cut-out panel. The fuse was blown. He put in another and it blew.

Hope shined the flashlight into the narrow fuse compartment. She asked if it was serious.

It wasn't, Larry assured her, since the refrigerator could operate on 12-volt, 110-volt, or gas. Things would stay cold enough while they were traveling, or he could take a chance and run on gas until he figured it out. Naturally it would have to be fixed before they sold the trailer.

He went back to the refrigerator, flipped the switch to 110-volt, since the trailer park had electrical hookups, and checked the inside of the unit. The glass shelf over the vegetable crisper had shattered and the broken pieces of glass lay among the lettuce, tomatoes and carrots. Hope cleaned out the tray while Larry went outside to start the water heater so they could shower before bed. A sheet of plastic, he told Hope, would be just the thing for the crisper.

Later, when Hope went to bathe, she discovered that the bracket for the flexible shower head had broken off. These, Larry said, were the kind of problems you always got with a unit that hadn't been thoroughly shaken down. It was good that it had happened in Ottawa and not somewhere out on the Alaska Highway. He'd look after it the next day, find a trailer dealer. He meant to do that anyway since there were a few things he had forgotten to buy, such as a tool for removing the valve on the propane tanks, deodorant for the toilet, grease for the fifth wheel plate and some kind of curtain to cover the window on the short stairway leading to the bedroom. They'd installed clear glass instead of frosted. Maybe he could spray it with something.

Neither of them remembered that the next day was Sunday until breakfast. Larry was disappointed; he'd originally intended to be back in Alaska by mid-May and hoped they could make the run in ten days.

Netty and Caitlin were slumped on the tiny sofa that faced the bar in the space between the kitchen and the bedroom. They were reading comic books and kept jostling each other for room.

"Caitlin," Netty snapped for the sixth time. Larry sent them outside.

"They're bored," Hope said, looking out the window to where the kids had staked out opposite sides of the picnic table. Another fifth-wheeler was parked next door and a clothesline was strung along it from front to back. "Laundry." She rubbed at her temples. "How are we going to do laundry?"

Larry didn't look up from the refrigerator instructions. "There's places, even on the Alcan. I read about them in *Milepost* when I was in Anchorage."

"We don't *have Milepost.*"

"They must sell them when we get farther west. They'll have them in Dawson." He put the instructions down. "I don't understand the setup here with the wiring. I think it's worth hanging around until Monday to see a dealer about it. There's a number I can call, too, in Indiana."

"You *will* be able to fix it?"

"No problem. And we'll sell the thing in Montez and pay for the plane trip home. Everybody up there told me it was the right move. People will be desperate for housing by the end of August. And a crew-cab truck can't miss. They love them."

Larry and Hope spent part of the morning trying to trace the wiring in the trailer, opening cabinets, peering up under decorative edgings, unscrewing light fixtures. A handle on one of the cabinets fell off in Hope's hand when she tried to open it. Larry fixed it by filling the holes with matchsticks and replacing the screws.

"One thing," he told her, as he spread a tarp and inched his way under the trailer to look for the main power cable, "I'll be some kind of handyman by the time this is over."

That evening the old couple next door, who had sold a grocery in

Des Moines and hit the road a week later, came to visit. Larry told the man about the refrigerator, and the man said Larry should run on gas, that 12-volt cooling was too much for the battery. It'd kill you if you stopped an hour somewhere.

The bracket in the shower looked like a standard item, and most people ended up replacing the crisper tray cover with plastic instead of glass.

"Have you had much trouble with your trailer?" Hope wanted to know.

The old man covered his nose with his hand and picked at it slyly with his thumb. "The usual things. Furnace went on the bum, doors don't fit right. Air conditioner drips inside on really hot days. Course you won't need air-conditioning where you're going, will you?" They had seen the signs the girls had made.

The woman, a frantic chain-smoker, had always wanted to go up there, but they'd heard such bad things about the gravel stretch on the Alcan. She wanted to go because the water was pure and the air was breathable.

Larry told them about his first trip, how flying at night from Fairbanks to Anchorage he had seen only one tiny cluster of lights in three hundred and fifty miles.

He described his pipeline travels, and the old man asked if unemployment was as bad as the papers said it was.

Larry didn't know for sure. The pipeline would provide many jobs and leave others open when people left town for the camps. But the feeling of Alaska was what he liked, the optimism. You felt you could go there and just decide what it was you wanted to be and then be that. The phrase "land of opportunity" had real meaning there, as did the Alaska license plate slogan, North to the Future. If anything, the phrases were modest, applied to Alaska.

"Here, in the Lower 48, it's like everything is nailed down." Larry sat back and put his arm around Hope. "Up there, once you tough out that first year, you can go as far as you want to go. At least, that's how it hit me. I found it exciting."

Hope sipped at a glass of white wine and said nothing. She'd heard all this before.

The old man shook his head wistfully.

"So I guess you folks must be moving up there permanent. Maybe get jobs on the pipeline?"

"No, just a visit. We have a home in New Hampshire."

"In Walpole," Hope said.

"Way you talk," the old man said to Larry, "you about sold *me*."

INTEROFFICE MEMO—Alaska Petroleum PipeLine Enterprises—
FORM IM-101

TO:	B. R. Young, President	DATE:	June 11
FROM:	M. Finch-Smith, Public Relations	LOCATION:	Anchorage
REF:	Your phone call, this A.M.	SUBJECT:	My dept. input for monthly progress report

Sir:

There can be no doubt that employees need to be informed as to the monthly progress of the pipeline. However, a company newsletter would be superfluous as we will soon pick an editor for our newspaper, a weekly with projectwide distribution. (We haven't settled on a name yet, but *Tundra Times* and *The Piper* have been suggested.)

However, I quite agree that those of us in the Anchorage office are "out of touch with the men in the field." The remedy for this, it seems to me, would be to prepare, in this office, a monthly progress report in the form of a slide show with script. I have an experienced photographer, Mr. James Miklov, whose transparencies we presently feature in the community-involvement programme.

As I understand from the architect, the new building will have a conference room with rear-screen projection which should provide us with splendid viewing facilities. For the time being, we can use the empty suite on the second floor, since both doctors have moved out. By the way, the dentist in the office across the hall from me will be leaving next week and I have reserved the space for our new editor. As soon as the gynecologist goes, the entire first floor will belong to us! Last week a woman accosted me in the hall, told me she was "spotting" and wanted to know if I could have a look at her.

I have only one additional comment. I read in the paper last week that you said something to the effect that "our compliance with Mr. Curry's construction delay at No Name Creek should satisfy even the most rabid environmentalists that Alaska Pipeline is complying with state and federal permits." The intention of this statement is admirable, sir, but I question the use of the term "rabid." I know they feel they are at war with us, but I think we do not want to give our "opponents" the feeling that *we* are at war with *them*.

FROM THE DESK OF B. R. YOUNG . . .

Ten-four on that, Malc.
By the way, why don't we call the paper *Pipe 'n' Hot News?*

bry

Chapter Four

JOE AKIN, the operating engineer foreman, and Al Godwin, currently running the big forklift, had been buddies for years. They had met at Fort Hood, Texas, in the late fifties, driven heavy equipment for Uncle Sam, and then boomed around the country, following the big jobs—dams, power plants, highways. Joe was quick-moving, an extrovert, short, muscular, fair-haired, a man with small features and piercing, deep blue eyes. He always took the lead with the jobs, the women, the escapades. Al Godwin, hiding behind dark hair that swept down over his forehead, a thick, old-fashioned moustache shading his mouth, moodily followed Joe's whims.

Once, coming into a bar in Montana, he found Joe Akin in conversation with two men. As Al Godwin edged in along the bar, Joe turned and said, "You're in, aren't you?" He had a tenspot on the bar.

Without question, Al opened his wallet and laid a ten next to Joe's. The bartender scooped both up, jotted down a number on a card for each man, and tossed one to each of them.

Scarcely glancing at the card on the way out, Al Godwin finally asked, "What am I in?"

"We're riding broncs in the rodeo Saturday. Free-style competition."

It was no use saying he hadn't ridden before. Neither had Joe Akin. He'd called Joe about every name he could think of, but Al went in the chute Saturday morning and fell off in the pen when the horse bolted free. He'd only torn a ligament. Joe broke his arm.

Akin's lead usually worked out well on jobs, since Joe generally ended up foreman and then Al Godwin got the good jobs, unless it happened to strike Joe as worth a few laughs to stick him down in a sewer running a compressor or operating a little BobCat in the dead of winter. "You got to keep cool," Joe would tell him, in either case. Nice, cool sewer, the rest of us up here sweating. Nice fresh air on a BobCat. None of that smelly, hot air blowing back off the engine like on a dozer.

And if Al got second choice on the women, with Joe in there working on them, both choices usually looked pretty good. Joe Akin had even found him a wife when they decided to settle down in Alaska. She wasn't the best wife. In fact, she wasn't even a good wife lately, Al suspected. But at the time, Al Godwin had been grateful. And, considering what happened with Joe's first wife, he could have come off worse. Joe had quit a good job to look for her and the man she ran off with. In Tulsa, he'd found the man in a bar and shot him three times. Joe Akin had done five in McAllister for that one, and would have got more, except that two of the men on the jury had also been looking for the man Joe shot.

Joe had been on Al now to do as he was planning: buy a trailer lot and move the wife and kids down to Montez. It made sense, Joe figured, since the terminal job would go on the longest of all, five more years while they finished off the west tank farm. Five years was more than a quarter of a million dollars' wages each. With the wives working in town, it could be more. Otherwise you'd get sick of the nine weeks on, two weeks home, and eventually you'd drag up and come back to town for three or four months. What did it matter if a trailer lot alone cost $5,000. Twenty, maybe twenty-five thousand would put your wife and kids right there. And, Joe Akin had told him, if you're really worried about your old lady chippying on you, it's the only thing that makes sense.

Coming back to the room with the mail at the end of the workday, Al found Joe at him again about moving.

"This does it." He waved a bunch of printed sheets at Al. "I don't believe this shit. We have got to move out of this phony, fucking camp."

Al put two letters for Joe on the table and took the cup Joe held out to him, sniffing it.

"Whiskey and Coke," Joe said. "It should be good. It's your whiskey."

"My friggin Coke, too." Al sat on his bunk and threw his hard hat into the corner of the room. "Screw the pipeline."

"What pipeline?" Joe said automatically. It had become a standard response. "You working hard?" That was another standard.

Al was unlacing his boots. "Hardly working."

The two men sat on opposite bunks. Al slipped his boots off and sipped at the whiskey-cola. "What's got you so torqued?"

"This shit." Joe read the heading on the sheets of paper. "Rules and regulations for the construction camp. Welcome to the friggin camp."

"Is that what it says?"

"Welcome to the camp. What is this, Fort Hood all over again? Can you believe this garbage? Five pages."

He began to read it to Al, skipping around. Personal radios off after 10 P.M. Accountable for missing blanket, pillow and linen. No smoking in bed. Occupants responsible for the tidiness of the rooms. Regular inspections. *Inspections.* No firearms, gambling, drugs, alcohol or intoxication. No fighting. Some chance. No camping, hunting, shooting, fishing or trapping in camp or within five miles of the pipeline route. What pipeline?

Joe flipped through the pages. "Here's a beaut. He says violation of the rules can result in immediate termination, and then he says he wants to make living conditions as pleasant as possible. Sounds like McAllister all over again."

There were twenty-three rules of conduct, all of which could lead to termination.

"Horseplay." Joe held his hands out to Al. "No horseplay. And at the end it says additional rules will be established as necessary. What do they think this is, a goddamn Boy Scout camp?"

"You won't last here five more days, Joe." Al reached out to take the sheaf of paper. "You better hold off on the trailer. Where did you find this?"

"Nailed up on the goddamn door. We find the guy who did that, he'll get terminated for damaging company property. Unauthorized use of tacks. We have to get out of this joint. Did you see the sign they put up at the entrance to the jobsite over there? Pollution leads to termination."

"Job's oversupervised. This has to come from people who have nothing to do."

Joe nodded thoughtfully. "You must be right. We don't have anything to do, so I guess management must not have anything to do, either. How much actual work did you do today?"

"Twenty, thirty minutes. But I put in about three hours yesterday morning cleaning up from the last barge."

"I don't see hardly a man out there working like you would on a hard-bid job. This cost-plus is usually cozy, but I never seen anything like this. Can you imagine how long we'd last on a real construction job working like we do here?"

"Some crafts work hard. Those drillers and powder-monkeys drag in here kind of sorry-looking, but I hear it's worse in Fairbanks and on up the line." Al finished his drink and tossed the cup in the wastecan. "Guy up there told the teamster foreman that everybody's standing around waiting for this, waiting for that, not a damn thing to do. I got a feeling that a lot of people are looking to stretch this job out more than three years."

Joe took the paper, crumpled it, and threw the wad in the can with his cup. "Let's go to chow."

There were two dorm arrangements in Copper Camp. Most of the dorms were square buildings with a central shower, toilet, laundry core and five rooms in each half of the unit. Joe and Al lived in one of the four long dorms, two-level buildings with twenty-five rooms on a floor. They were identical to the units that were being set on steel pilings across the bay. Eventually, most of the crafts would live on the other side, which would cut an hour's travel time off every day. As well as an hour's overtime.

The mess hall, like everything else in camp, was modular, a wide, low-ceilinged building with an entry hall to the right, a serving line, drink and snack tables and then a large dining room with tables and folding chairs. Each table had a dividing row of bottles running down the center. Ketchup, syrup, mustard, steak sauce, Tabasco, soy sauce, Worcestershire, pickles, relish, sugar, salt, pepper, gherkins, hot peppers, toothpicks, honey, jam and peanut butter. During mealtimes, the bullcooks, who made up the men's rooms daily and helped out the cooks, continually circulated through the dining hall, checking the bottles, replacing or refilling empties, wiping tabletops, taking away trays.

Twice a week, steak was served, as much as a man could eat. The rules had been posted on a steak night and it had probably been intentional, since the men were generally in a better mood on Wednesdays and Saturdays.

A guard sat at the entrance to the serving line and it was his job to ask each man to show an ID before admitting him. Joe, as he did every night, started to walk through without showing his.

"I forgot," Joe said, flipping the card out of his pocket, where it had been clipped, and letting it dangle from his shirtfront. It was the way most of the men wore their badges.

"I know," the man said. "You always do." He spoke as if to himself.

Joe looked back at Al, who hated this sort of thing, and then at the man.

"I always do," he repeated. "If you can remember that, then how's come you can't remember me so I don't need to show it?"

"Hey, you bums." A shout went up behind Al. "You holdin up the works."

"Hey yourself, Nasty." Al moved forward behind Joe and picked up a tray. "You working hard?"

"Ain't hardly workin." Nasty grabbed a tray and held it up to the light to see if it was clean. He then checked his knife, spoon and fork. "Cain't be too careful," he told Al. "Some of em still have food on, and some don't. I like to get the ones with the food, so's I get a head start on the groceries." He nudged Al with the tray.

"Two, well done," Joe said.

The cook repeated it to the grillman.

Al held up two fingers. "Well done."

"Burn me a big one." Nasty leaned in. "And this time I don't want no blood dripping on my taters."

"Next," the cook shouted. The grill behind him was covered with steaks in various stages of being overcooked.

"You don't like bloody meat?" Al asked.

"Hell, you should have seen what he put on me last Satu'day. I seen animals hurt worse than that get better."

They went down the line, adding fries, corn on the cob, green beans, rolls, coleslaw, macaroni salad. Nasty asked for a serving of spare ribs along with the steak and skipped the vegetables, filling the rest of his plate with fries.

The three found a table.

"You see them rules and reggy-lations?" Nasty asked, his mouth full of steak.

"Don't start him," Al cautioned.

"It's ridiculous. Who the hell do they think they got working in these camps, a bunch of Girl Scouts?"

"Ah wouldn't mind a couple of Girl Scouts in mah room, stead of that damn Tiny. But you right, mister." Nasty poked the air with his fork. "Ah used to be a seven ninety-eight welder fore I came up here. Now those boys are men and they are the best damn welders there is. That ain't braggin, neither. That's why them boys are the only ones that can weld this pipeline together."

"What pipeline?" an old man next to Nasty said. Everyone ignored him.

"Those boys come in, *they* ain't going to put up with this bunch of Sunday school bullshit. No way! You wait till the seven ninety-eighters get in here, you'll see some changes." Nasty dug into his meat again.

"He's right," Joe told Al. "They aren't going to get men to stay in these camps under those conditions."

"Thousand dollars a week, they'll find men," the old fellow said. "They'll find plenty."

"I wish I made a thousand a week," said the kid at the end of the table. Joe and Al looked at him coldly. He was the one who'd sat up front at the orientation. Leslie Collins. He'd turned out to be the assistant safety man. "I guess I'd put up with a lot for a thousand a week."

"Foremens make more," the old man told him. "I bet Joe Akin there pulls down fifteen hundred, right?"

"I do okay," Joe snapped. "Nasty is right. It's chickenshit to put rules like that on the men in these camps. No *man* is going to put up with it."

"How bout candy ass down there?" Nasty said.

"They'll tear up these friggin camps, APPLE keeps this up," Joe said. "We don't have boys working here. We got men."

Al held up a piece of meat to Joe. "Does this look well done to you?"

"They both like that?"

Al cut into the other steak and nodded. Joe reached over, stabbed both steaks with his fork, lifted them off the plate, and dropped them in the garbage can on the cleanup wagon.

"Go get yourself some more steak. Let em start treating us like *men* around here."

After presenting the yellow card certifying the completion of orientation, new pipeline employees were issued photo badges, to be worn at all times. The badges permitted movement in and out of camps, access to company transportation and entry to the dining halls. In Anchorage, the photo room was under the same roof with the orientation center. At Fort Wainwright, in Fairbanks, it was across a neat, grassy quadrangle that Alaska Pipeline shared with the base quartermaster's office and the Army Personnel Movement Center. Pipeline workers trudging across the quad were likely to pass officers, civilian secretaries or the occasional GI picking up paper and butts.

There was, from time to time, some cause for friction in these passages, as might be expected when a man on his way to earning a thousand a week, after months of waiting, encountered brass, a woman or a poor slob who made less in a week than a pipeliner made in a day.

Today not even a bird colonel could walk by without getting ragged salutes, shouted calls to attention and random, obscene suggestions, both visible and audible. Two women had somehow gotten dispatched from the Teamsters and were being sent up the line. They walked together, one outfitted in a thin blouse and tight slacks, the other, slightly older, wearing a short-sleeved work shirt and pair of faded denims.

"Hey, Pam, if you promise not to snore and you keep yourself clean I'll let you room with me." It was the bearded guy again, turning around to look down the front of Pam's blouse. She'd left the top button open.

One of the men stood aside at the entry to the badging center.

"Ladies first?" he asked as the men began to pile in.

"Screw em," one said, shoving on by. "They want to be treated like men, now's their chance."

Jill Jones started in the door and a tall kid with silvery sunglasses edged in ahead of her.

"Dog eat dog world, baby."

"Asshole," someone behind Pam said. "You ladies go raight on in, don't pay that hippie no mind."

Pam Allen laughed and skipped through the door, Jill resolutely following.

Inside, a short corridor led to a bare room with a table, a camera and a chair at the far end. A stand with colored curtains stood behind the chair to provide proper backdrops according to job classification.

Pam was joking with the bearded man, who was asking again if she was going to bunk with him. Pam slapped him playfully on the arm.

"What do you think, Jill? Should I make him wait his turn like all the others?"

Jill shook her head. "For one thing, he's married. And for another, I'd never sleep with a man that asked me in front of his buddies."

"Balls," the kid in sunglasses said. "What they got you doing out here, sweetheart? Driving a truck?"

"That's right, junior, and I've done it before. Drove for Matanuska Farms, drove cabs, drove buses and even ran a semi with my ex."

"I'm working in the warehouse," Pam Allen said.

"How do you spell that?" Sunglasses asked.

"My name is Vern Blue," said the beard. "Didn't mean to be piggy. Just trying to make friends."

"You going to Sag River?" Pam asked.

Vern Blue nodded.

"Well, we'll just have to see then, won't we? I've always had a soft spot for men with beards."

"Yeah," he laughed, "and I know just where that spot is."

Finally Pam got to the badging desk. A girl and an elderly man were working the operation. The girl filled out forms; the man took pictures. He moved slowly, arranging the backdrop cloth carefully, fiddling endlessly with the camera settings.

"Name," the girl at the desk said.

"Pamela Sue Allen."

"Camp?"

"Sag River."

Vern Blue was waiting for Pam. "Room number?" he whispered.

Jill laughed. Pam laughed, too.

"Craft?"

"Teamsters. Nine-fifty-nine."

"Dispatched as . . ."

"Warehouseman." Pam looked at Jill. "Excuse me," she said to the girl at the desk. "My friend said maybe it should be put down as warehouse*person.*"

Pam sat down at the photo machine.

"Should I smile?"

The man looked up from his knobs and plastic envelopes.

"Yes, look natural. Just look in the mirror."

Pam's eyes went up and she automatically smoothed her hair. She smiled and the flash went off. Pam joined the new line of people waiting for badges.

Jill gave her name.

"Camp?"

"Wiseman."

"Wise*person,*" a man in back shouted. Laughter.

"Heavy-duty truck driver," Jill said to the last of the questions and sat down on the bench.

"Look at the mirror."

Jill looked, saw black hair in a pageboy framing a face that had seen better days. Her jaw was very slightly canted to one side, the result of a solid roundhouse thrown by her former husband. She had been wired together on that one. Her full lips, now set in a frown, showed wrinkles at the corners and a tiny, almost invisible scar that caught one side of her mouth. That was from childhood; a neighbor kid had hit her in the face with a coffeepot. She had a nose that her mother called Roman and her father said was roamin all over her face. It hadn't been broken, but since the car accident it had a small bump. Nevertheless, men found her pretty and said so. Her eyes were her best feature, deep brown, wide, honest, with nice crinkles at the corner. Long lashes, full eyebrows. The eyes were the best. The thirty-five years showed everywhere, but Jill liked what time had done to the eyes.

"Smile."

Jill met her own eyes and relaxed her mouth to make the frown go away. The flash left a purple spot in the center of everything.

INTEROFFICE MEMO—Alaska Petroleum PipeLine Enterprises—
FORM IM-101

TO:	Messrs. Finch-Smith, Booth, Curry	DATE:	June 14
FROM:	B. R. Young, President	LOCATION:	Anchorage
REF:	Curry report, this date.	SUBJECT:	Bears in camp

Do something about the bears, will you guys?

bry

Nasty came back to the men gathered beside the bus.

He jerked a thumb toward the state game wardens and the photographer. "Guy says they's repeating shells. Shoots a couple hunderd yards and then the popper shell goes off. Same's they use at airports to run birds off."

"I'd sure as shit hate to rile a bear up with that popgun," Al Godwin said.

"They done thought of that, too. That other feller's got himself five loads of double-ought buck in his twelve-gauge."

"Well," Joe Akin said, moving toward the bus, "they can wait until I'm gone."

"That's what they're doing, dum-dum," Little Nasty told him. "I'd laik to stay and watch. Bet that old bear just humps hisself when that shell goes off under his ass."

"Man, I'll tell you something," Joe Akin said. "I'm not afraid of nothing in the world. Nothing scares me. I mean that, *nothing*. But bears scare the shit out of me."

That night at the Montez Club, Isaac Ahgutuk broke a promise he had made to his brother. He went out drinking. At ten o'clock he was still there, perched on a barstool with Clyde Baranov, an Aleut who claimed to be related to Baranov the Russian, the one that started the settlement that had become Sitka. Isaac told Clyde that the Indians down there were Tlingit, not Aleut, but Clyde argued that Baranov had brought Aleuts along to help the Russians build and that Baranov had kids by the Aleut women.

Clyde Baranov was now telling this story to Nate Jourdan, the black man who was, like them, a laborer. Isaac leaned over the bar to get a better look.

He was laughing again. Isaac was always laughing.

"You shut yourself up, you dumb ass," Clyde Baranov said.

Isaac just laughed all the more, and Clyde Baranov went on talking to the big man with skin as dark as a seal and teeth as white as polished ivory. He wasn't laughing at Clyde. It was the black man. Isaac laughed whenever he saw Nate. He was so big and had tiny bristles of hair, black hair, black skin all over, except his palms were pink like a white man's.

"How come you got hands like a white man?" Isaac asked Nate, but Nate didn't hear him, just went on listening to that fool talk about the real Baranov. Maybe he figures he'll get a land claim in Russia, too, Isaac thought. More laughter.

"Hey," Nate Jourdan was calling to him.

"What do you want, sealman?" Clyde Baranov was looking at him, too, but Isaac could barely focus. He wanted to say something, but instead he took another pull at his beer.

"Hey, man." Nate prodded him. "Borrow me ten dollars till payday."

"You buying?" Isaac asked hopefully. The man had said something about money.

"Lemme hold a tenspot till the eagle shits, man."

Eagle? "You buying?"

"Clyde," Nate said. "Just lemme ten until tomorrow."

"Nate," a new voice said, and Isaac looked up. It was a hippie from the labor crew. "You want ten?"

Isaac watched with interest. These white men, and really Nate was a white man, too, they had strange ways. Always grabbing each other on the television when they play sports. Always slap-assy. And make noises all the time when you talk to them. You say something, they shake the head and make a noise at you. Nate and the hippie slapped hands.

"I mean, if you need ten bucks, man, I'm good for it."

"Shit, you give me ten, *you'll* remember it tomorrow."

The hippie laughed, slapped hands. Isaac held his hand out. Nate slapped.

"You got hands like a white man," Isaac said, but the sealman didn't hear him.

"Hey," Nate said. "Clyde, did you see those dudes with the popguns today? Pow! Pow! Hey, you got ten dollars, Clyde?"

"Who's buyin?" Isaac asked. "You guys. You ever shoot bear?

Me, I shoot all kinds of bears, all kinds. Shoot polar bear, silver tip, brownie, blackie. My brother and me. We go shoot polar bears next spring, maybe. Good mating time, next spring. Bears come in."

Clyde Baranov banged his hand down. "Those guys today, they don't hunt good. Don't know how to get bear. I get biggest brownie you ever saw."

"You dudes is big hunters, huh?" Nate shoved his drink at the good-looking redhead behind the bar, asking for a refill. "You shoot a polar bear, Isaac? For real, now?"

Isaac stuck his lower lip out and looked at Nate for a long time. "You wanna know something about bears?" he said slowly. "Bears can read your mind."

Clyde Baranov nodded. "Bears . . ." he trailed off.

"They can read your mind," Isaac repeated. "Clyde knows. He's native, he knows."

Clyde Baranov banged a hand down again. "Those guys today, they don't know nothing. Bear read your mind, if you look at him."

Isaac reached for his glass, but it was empty. He pushed it to the edge of the counter, but the big woman with the big titties walked on by like she didn't notice. Isaac watched her walk down to the other end of the bar and then looked back at Nate.

"When I hunt bear," he said, " when I get out there and hunt for bear, I *never* look at him. Maybe catch him once, twice, from the corner of my eye."

"And don't think . . . *bear,*" Clyde Baranov said.

"That's right. Don't think *bear.* Think about seals or fixin the sled, think about titties, little babies, but don't think about the bear. I just creep up and think about my sled, or a bird I saw in the morning and try not to look at that old bear until I'm close. Then I look and then I shoot." Isaac stared off into space. "And always the bear turns and looks just then, just when I think 'bear' he turns his head to look. But it's too late."

"Those guys today, talking about bear, thinking about bear, they don't know," Clyde said. "They don't have good heritage. I got heritage. Native heritage. Russian heritage."

"Kin you lemme hold ten dollars, man?"

Clyde straightened on his barstool. "Hiii-eeeee!" he shouted and stretched out his right arm, moving it sideways. "Hiiiii-eeee—yoowwwwaayyy." Clyde chanted, waving first one arm, then the other. "Hii—hiii," he grunted. "Hiii-yiiii-how-aaaaaaa . . ."

Isaac was trying to clap his hands, but he couldn't find the right rhythm.

"Howww-iii-ya," Clyde said, and the redhead woman came over smiling.

"Okay, chief, you going on the warpath or what?"

"That's my heritage."

The woman put her hand on his wrist. Clyde stopped. "Chief, we got entertainment already. And rain dances in Montez, we don't need."

"Can I have another whiskey?"

Nate touched Clyde on the shoulder. "Ten dollars, man. You get it back tomorrow."

Dawson Creek, in northeastern British Columbia, is the start of the Alaska Highway—or what used to be called the Alcan. It is a town of 12,000 with a newspaper, a radio station and three channels available for TV watchers. In downtown Dawson, a milepost, claiming to be Mile Zero of the Alaska Highway, shows 918 miles to Whitehorse, 1,521 miles to Fairbanks. A stone cairn in a traffic rotary two blocks away also marks the official "Mile O, Alaska Highway."

Larry and Hope sat in the apron of a service station just off this rotary, waiting for the welder to strengthen the support for the hydraulic jack on the trailer. Like so many other parts on the 32-foot, $9,000 rig, it had proven defective, and Larry wanted to catch it before they got out on the highway. He had already installed the plastic bubbles over the headlights and the bug screen and radiator protector, but he wanted to be sure. So far, something had broken or gone bad on the truck and trailer every day of the trip. Often it was nothing serious. The light globe over the kitchen table fell and shattered. A cabinet door came away from its hinges when Hope pulled it open. The fuse continued to blow on the refrigerator.

But Larry had managed to fix things, or to at least stay even. He'd rewired the 12-volt refrigerator, running a separate power line, with fuse, from the battery. They'd found a new light globe, after some searching, in Regina, Saskatchewan. The cold water stopped working, but that was only a clogged filter. Larry had taken the faucet apart and put it back together in a morning. The worst was in Edmonton, when Larry, angry about the refrigerator not working, had unhitched the trailer and jumped into the truck to go into town for a part. In his haste he had forgotten to lower the tailgate on the truck and the hitch pin caught it dead center. It looked as though a powerful man with a sledgehammer had stood in the bed of the truck and directed one mighty swing at the gate. Since they had to get their money out of the truck, they'd stayed the extra two days to replace the gate at a cost of just over a hundred dollars.

Now, with the jack being rewelded, they would at least begin the trip up the Alaska Highway with everything working.

Hope, sitting beside him, read *Milepost* in tight-lipped silence. So far it hadn't been much of a summer for any of them. And it looked as if they were going to miss the longest day of the year, the start of summer in Fairbanks, with a baseball game that began at eleven in the evening, sundown. The sun would rise before the game ended. The twenty-first was less than a week off, but Larry didn't want to rush things, not pulling the trailer. Still, even here, it never got completely dark. Even at midnight, once they got past Edmonton, there was some light in the sky.

Larry looked over at Hope. On the road, out her window, cars with trailers were slowing at the rotary and heading up the street that also happened to be the Alcan.

Netty leaned forward. "We're never going to get to Alaska, are we?"

"I wonder what Candy is doing," Caitlin said in a low voice. She had been warned by Hope not to complain. "I bet she's swimming. I think Red Cross lessons would be starting by now."

Larry put a hand on Hope's shoulder. "It could be worse. Things could be going wrong with *our* parts. Someone could be sick."

"That's next," Hope said, and laid the book across her lap. "I wish you wouldn't joke about it. I haven't the slightest doubt that things are going to get worse. I can feel it." She looked over at Larry and smiled, but her lip was trembling. "And the worst part about it is that we can't go back. We have to get to Alaska to get the money out of this . . . fucking . . . trailer and we don't even have any choice. We have to go on doing this thing, dragging this trailer around."

"Honey," he said, "we're almost there. And I can always fix the things that go wrong."

"It's not going to get better," Hope told him and picked up the book.

Netty put her hand on the back of the seat near her mother's shoulder, hesitant to actually touch her.

"Even the truck is called an Adventurer," she said, and when no one replied she took her hand away. Netty retreated, like her mother, into a book.

The summer solstice came, bringing almost nineteen hours of sunlight to Anchorage, nearly twenty-two to Fairbanks, marking the halfway point in the twelve weeks of daytime at Prudhoe Bay. In late November, the North Slope would enter ten to twelve weeks of darkness, but now it seemed as if night could never come.

Others on the Alaska Highway, once north of the 60th Parallel, noticed the gradual lengthening of days. Larry and Hope spent the solstice in Whitehorse. They did not enjoy it. They had broken an axle on the trailer and were waiting for a replacement, if obtainable, from Edmonton.

Others were bound for Alaska, as tourists and job-seekers, and they, too, had their troubles. It was not unusual for cars to slide off to the edge of the road after a water crew had dampened the highway to hold down dust and remove ripples. In sections where the surface was mixed with clay or coal dust, even trucks turned over from time to time. A camper rolled at Mile 342, north of Fort Nelson, and the weight of the truck demolished the shell. The family drove back in the truck, their possessions heaped in the now empty bed, covered by a tarp. A local scrap dealer had given them twenty dollars for the gas bottles, stove and refrigerator, about the only things worth salvaging.

One family, with three children, got as far as Mungo Lake when the road flooded. They spent their vacation, along with over a hundred others, sitting in cars, waiting for the road to open.

A man and his wife in a brand-new car, so the story went, broke down near Whitehorse and waited five months for new parts, in fact were still waiting. In exchange for room and board they were helping a family clear land, and the husband had become a skilled hand with both ax and chainsaw. When the new parts came, they would continue their trip to Fairbanks, where he hoped to find work on the pipeline. And where they could sue the car manufacturer.

One young couple, newly married, also started on the Alcan in a brand-new car, and their experience was told and retold up the line as far as Tok. Afraid of damaging his Chrysler, the husband was seen to get out of the vehicle every few hundred feet to roll the larger stones off the road. Whenever another car or truck approached, inevitably spraying gravel and even rocks, he stopped as close to the edge of the road as he dared.

A gas station attendant at Mile 101—the start of the true wilderness country—saw the couple when they pulled in after only eight miles of gravel. The wife seemed to be impatient to get on, but the husband was hysterical, demanding to know how much more bad road there was. A thousand miles, he was told. Fifteen minutes later he was back, the wife driving, the husband sitting beside her, crying like a baby. They started back home that day.

There were those making their annual trips and those who would never do it again until the road was paved the whole way. There were truckers hauling loads from Georgia; a caravan of Airstreams, this year Alaska, next year, Mexico.

There was even a specially designed, sleeping, eating, sightseeing bus tour of German ladies who had begun their trip in New York and who would end with a ferry ride to Seattle and a long run to Los Angeles International Airport.

For some it went better than others. Those who had driven back country roads found the Alcan to their liking. Those who had spent their lives zipping along midwestern superhighways tortured themselves and their cars and trailers to death by jouncing along at fifty and sixty miles an hour, heedless of ruts, mud, oncoming trucks and bad weather.

They drove up mountain passes, through tiny outposts and towns, along the shore of Muncho Lake, set among mountains, its water turned a brilliant blue-green by copper oxides. They passed streams and canyons and forest, caught glimpses of game, went 600 miles through British Columbia and then entered the Yukon Territory with its rugged mountains and deep valleys. Bigger in area than all New England, the Yukon had 20,000 inhabitants. All but 5,000 of them lived in the city of Whitehorse.

Past Teslin Lake they came, in greater numbers than they had ever come before and bringing more belongings. According to customs reports they were a mixture of tourists and immigrants, some going to jobs on the line, some to assignments with the military and many going to see what might be had.

On the way through the Yukon they passed Watson Lake, where so many stopped to leave a sign with the name of their home town on the cluster of signposts next to the road. A few put up homemade signs. Others, who had made the run before, brought legitimate signs. Tampa—City Limits. Welcome to Davenport. Stay More. Monroe. La Mesa. Village of Dummerston. Leaving Blue Ball.

Seventy-two miles of Teslin Lake was followed by Quiet Lake, just up the Canol Road where a pipeline had been built in the forties, by Squanga Lake, Marsh Lake and finally Whitehorse at Mile 919.

From Whitehorse north the land grew wilder and the travelers passed the largest lake in the Yukon, the Kluane. White River (which was too dangerous for boating), mountains and endless forest; and at last they reached (most of them, anyway) the boundary at Mile 1221 and entered Alaska and found themselves once more on paved highway. At Tok they sought out the high-pressure coin washers and removed layer upon layer of mud and dirt from cars and trailers. Most of the vehicles would need new windshields, and almost everyone spent the first night in Alaska washing, showering, trying to feel clean for the first time in a week or more. A few drove the Alcan in two days and kept on going.

Another day would put them in Fairbanks or Anchorage or Montez. Alaska, or what little of it was accessible by road, less total road miles than the State of Rhode Island actually, lay open at last.

If the going on the highways occasionally brought accident and loss, the same was true on the pipeline. The first month had been good, but by the end of June there had been deaths. A man at Wiseman had been killed when a seven-foot tire from a loader hit him. The tire, used on the big, ten-yard loader, got away from the tireman while he was changing it and rolled down a hill. The tireman shouted, but the laborer, standing next to a dump truck, did not move quickly enough. The tire bounced once and hit him in the chest, crushing him against the fuel tank of the truck.

A carpenter who was part of a joint-rigging crew had his head crushed while setting a 12-ton dormitory module on the steel foundation at Sag River. He had never rigged loads before and had stuck his head between two mods while one unit was in the air. No one saw it; he had been alone, on the back side. The crane operator at Sag River quit the next day.

Cables snapped, brakes either released or did not set, hands missed their hold on scaffolding, feet stumbled, men wearing two-foot-long spearlike tools called spud wrenches hanging from their belts misjudged steps, and the wrenches entered muscles, fatty parts of the leg, ankles, heels. Physician's assistants, medical techs and aides patched, bandaged, splinted and, in the worst cases, called for Medevacs.

Men got drunk and broke up their rooms or went crazy—or both—and had to be taken out, sometimes turned over to troopers, sometimes to doctors.

The press reported all this with great concern, which was as it should have been. Reporters descended on the pipeline like ants and carried away whatever tidbits of edible news they could find. Gil Wolfe began, in free-lance articles, to point out the human damage, some of which Emil Bacich showed him, some of which he saw for himself on visits to the camps. He was certain, he wrote, that the lack of concern by those who wanted only to finish the pipeline at any cost would not change until a grave disaster occurred. And such a disaster, he claimed, was only a matter of time.

Malcolm Finch-Smith sent copies of the article around the office building. Wolfe, he said, is at the door and will not go away. We must demonstrate the extent of our concern and make it public. After all, the chap might be right. The one thing APPLE did not need, before the actual pipelaying got underway, was a major disaster that the press could build up. Or that Dan Curry might levy a severe fine—and severer restrictions—against.

At Montez Camp, Leslie Collins, assistant safety man, reported to his superior that some of the men were *simply* not cooperating with him, not cooperating at all. It was most trying.

That night Little Nasty, with a pound of bacon he had stolen from the kitchen, stayed on the job after the buses went back. He could catch the launch across the bay, he told Tiny, go home with the dynamite crew. He'd been around bears down south, back where he could still find bears. He got a blackie that he'd been baiting every day at quitting time, and he led the bear, tossing bits of bacon, to the blue storage van used by the operating engineers for a dry shack and tool shed. The bear came around the corner. Nasty, hiding behind the steel door that was open, tossed the bacon inside and stepped back. A moment later he heard the scuffling inside and he banged the half-door shut, latching it. Joe

Akin, the foreman, would be there early in the morning, ahead of the others. Nasty laughed all the way back to the launch. He never did care for operating engineers much. The ride across the bay was peaceful and beautiful. Serene mountains and still waters.

Paula was already in bed when Dan Curry got home, and he undressed quietly in the dark and slipped under the covers.

"Kiss," Paula said, and he jumped. Her voice was clear, alert. He'd thought she was asleep and told her so.

"No, I was waiting for you. Of course, I did expect you some time ago. But I'm not sleepy."

"I'm beat," Dan said, and briefly filled her in on what had happened in the Brooks Pass. The company had been told not to divert a stream into a narrow channel, and then, when the observers went out and the weather closed down, they diverted the stream for two days and had it back where it belonged by the time the new team showed up. One of the workers had reported the ruse to the team over chow, but it was too late to do anything much. He'd debated fining them and hoped the press wouldn't pick it up. Anyhow, no great harm, probably. He kissed her and spoke in a drowsy voice.

"It was nice of you to stay up."

"I'm not the least bit sleepy," Paula said, touching him on the shoulder. "In fact, I'm wide awake." She snuggled in next to Dan and was about to say something else when she realized he was snoring very softly. She didn't have the heart to wake him.

Joe Akin walked up to the timekeeper's shack and stepped under the roof, out of the drizzle. The old man had just opened up, as the two of them had come across the bay ahead of the buses: Joe to supervise the generator startup, the timekeeper to be ready with the brass tags when the men arrived.

The old guy already had Joe's tag out on the counter. He knew the number without being told: it was an ability he seemed unnecessarily proud of.

"There 'tis," he said.

Joe Akin looked at him for several seconds and then, as in a dream, reached out to take the tag. He hung it carefully on the snap that held his ID badge.

"Say," Joe said, moving his head ever so slightly. The old man came close to the window. "Tell me something. Is my hair gray?"

The timekeeper looked Joe over.

"No," he said. "No, it doesn't look gray to me." He sounded uncertain. Many of the men didn't like the brassing system and he was continually wary of sarcastic and bitter remarks.

"It should be," Joe said.

"Oh?"

"But it's not gray?"

"Nope." The old man rubbed nervously at the back of his neck. Joe often deadpanned, but usually there was a trace of a smile at the corners of his mouth and his eyes squinted some. There was no smile. "Why should it be gray?"

Joe blinked.

"I just went in the operator's shack to put my lunch on the shelf and I looked down at my feet because I kicked something that wasn't there last night." The wrinkles in Joe's forehead deepened. "There was a bear in the shack. A goddamn bear is lying on the floor of the shack and I kicked it, just a little bit, with my toe because I didn't see it in the dark."

"You're kidding me." The timekeeper looked over at the blue storage van next to the temporary warehouse section. The doors were closed. "A bear? Just now? In there?"

"He is still in there," Joe said, and fainted.

The June progress report was well received at the Anchorage office, particularly Miklov's photographs of work along the line, some taken in cool weather with traces of snow, some showing men sweating in T-shirts as they cleared brush away for the haul road.

"The big picture," Finch-Smith told his audience, "shows work activity quickening everywhere as the number of employees on the line increases." Women, too, were beginning to show up in the camps as bullcooks, secretaries and in a few of the crafts.

The July progress report, delivered a month later on August 6, also closed on an optimistic note.

39. Aerial: Haul road with belly dumps	*The month of July showed us ten days ahead on construction of the haul road and final linkup should be completed by October 1, well within the target date.*

Although only 110 miles of the needed 360 miles are complete now . . .

40. Baggage check-in, Fbks. *. . . projected manpower increases through August should speed up the construction pace considerably. Daily, at the airports in both Fairbanks and Anchorage, upwards of 100 men and women fly to the camps, adding to our growing work force.*

In the discussion period following, B. R. Young complimented Finch-Smith on the presentation, especially the close-ups of the bears.

"I wonder, though, if we don't want some pictures of women working in the camps?" he mused aloud. "With some black and white prints for the papers."

Malcolm Finch-Smith thought it an excellent idea and so did the others.

On the same day the progress report was given, Bartel Construction took positive action to solve the bear problem at the terminal (the popguns hadn't worked out). A bulletin was issued regarding employees feeding or disturbing bears. The warning was clear.

HENCEFORTH, ANY EMPLOYEE OR EMPLOYEES SEEN CONGREGATING AROUND A BEAR, OR BEARS, WILL BE SUBJECT TO IMMEDIATE TERMINATION!

In addition, Isaac Ahgutuk, due to the intercession of the native counselor at the camp, was appointed "bear guard" at the terminal and issued two 2½-foot lengths of two-by-four.

He was to patrol the perimeter of the work area during the day and, on spotting a bear, clap the two-by-fours together loudly to frighten it away.

Ed Booth wrote up a brief article on Isaac, who because of his native background was presumed to know something about bears, and he sent it to the editor of the *Pipe 'n' Hot News,* but it was never used. Instead, two weeks later, a poem written by a disgruntled employee was printed. The poem did not sit well with Bartel management, but Finch-Smith excused his editor on the grounds that the paper belonged to the men in the camps. The poem was signed only "L.C.," but it was obvious that it came from someone at the terminal.

Termination Blues

Now old Montez was my destination
After I got done with orientation
And I flew down with trepidation
With my buddies from around the nation.

We had it good, we had it made
A thousand bucks was compensation
For rain and cold and condensation—
Oh, it did look good when we got paid!

Then they hung some rules up on our doors
And I can see not spitting on floors
But one thing there was abomination
"Drink and girls lead to termination."

Well that was just the germination
Of finding things to get us fired.
To look at bears we were not hired
And a little fun leads to termination.

Now termination camp's my home,
But I'm about to start to roam,
Since according to this occupation
EVERYTHING leads to termination,
And that includes intoxication,
Fornication and congregation.
So watch it, boys, with desperation
ORIENTATION LEADS TO TERMINATION.

Chapter Five

THE TRIP HAD BECOME a nightmare, but now, a half hour from Montez, it finally seemed to be drawing to a close. Larry drove in silence: Lot and his wife and his two daughters.

Their stay in Whitehorse had dragged on to the end of June. They had reached Fairbanks on the Fourth of July and spent two nights camped at a truck turnoff when they couldn't find space in town.

Larry's tooth, which had given him trouble the last few days coming up the road, got worse, and a dentist removed the cap. Apparently an earlier root canal operation hadn't been successful. The dentist in Fairbanks cleaned out the tooth and told Larry to keep it free of food so pressure wouldn't build up.

He could have it fixed in Anchorage, the dentist said, or, if the visiting dentist happened to be in town, in Montez. The dentist gave Larry enough pain pills to last two weeks and, despite a muddy, difficult drive over a thirty-mile stretch of road construction, they made it to Mount McKinley Park with little trouble. It was the first time they had gone two nights in a row with nothing breaking on the trailer. Then, after a stayover in the park, with Larry drifting along on the bus tour, high on medication, the rear axle hanger spring broke loose and almost sent the rig over an embankment. Larry couldn't believe his good fortune that repairs would only involve a simple welding job. He thought the axle had broken again.

As they were being towed back to Healy for repairs, Netty said that the trailer had been misnamed when they called it a Leprechaun. "They should have called it a leper since something falls off it every day." Caitlin began singing the leprosy song—"Leprosy, it's crawling all over me!"—and Hope suddenly started to laugh, laugh so hard that Larry became concerned.

Anchorage, though, was the worst. They stayed at a trailer park on the edge of town and Larry attempted to arrange both dental appointments and pipeline interviews. He saw Dan Curry and Finch-Smith and spent an evening with Gil Wolfe, who was now selling pieces and working as a stringer for a weekly digest. Gil managed to find some stronger pain pills for Larry, just in case he needed them.

Larry went to a dentist who X-rayed, prodded, dug with a metal probe and told him finally that two more root canals were needed in addition to a new job on the hurting tooth. The infection was bad. He could lose at least three teeth if he put it off. The bad tooth would be done first.

Larry had flown to Prudhoe for another visit the day after the root canal and it was like a dream. Time flexed in and out like an accordian. He came back with disconnected images of brown-green stretches of flat country pocked with lakes and puddles, of tiny flowers, of ground that sank when he walked on it, a helicopter ride through hills that were tundra covered, nubby, cozy, flocked, beckoning . . .

When drinks came around on the flight back he was not offered one, but that was okay since the trip took only ten minutes although the landing lasted close to an hour.

The next two weeks—even now, driving through the Tonsina Valley and starting the long, gradual rise toward Thompson Pass—were difficult to sort out. The pain had grown worse even though the teeth were done. Hope had driven him back and forth to the dentist, and in between trips he lay in bed in the trailer under the translucent bubble dome, never even knowing the time of day.

It seemed that whenever he went for treatment it was raining. Hope had rented a television set. Sometimes when he woke it was playing. Other times it was off and Hope was asleep beside him. On occasion there was no one in the trailer when he woke, and he would look at his watch and at the sky and not know if it were ten in the morning or ten at night.

Then he was back in the dentist's chair and the tooth was pulled out. Of all the pain in the grayness of days and nights, this one was the greatest. He cried in the chair, cried on the way to the car, and he remembered waking, next to Hope, with the sensation of a metal band cutting into his head and tightening with every breath.

He cried, Hope woke up, the children woke and tiptoed in. They had never seen him cry before.

The motor lugged and Larry shifted into low as the road steepened through the pass. It was cloudy well below the top and they entered fog.

The pain had been a fog and Larry remembered only vaguely a conversation about a gun, then stumbling through the trailer with a towel wrapped around his head, hollering something, perhaps just hollering, and then, in the hospital, the murmur of voices and a needle. At last he could tell the passage of time. If the shades were down it was night. He counted three nights and when he woke the pain was gone.

Larry glanced at Hope. Two full weeks, she told him. No one knew exactly what was wrong, although an infection and dehydration played a part in it. He guessed it must have been harder on her and the kids than it was on him.

Despite the fact that he'd gotten no research done and it was mid-August, he was grateful to have the pain over. Today was the first day he felt good and he was already trying to figure ways to make up for the incredible expenses of the last month. The grant money was about used up. The essential thing was to get a good price for the trailer and truck so they could afford to fly home. Breaking even might be good enough.

They were descending now, and as they broke out of the clouds, Larry saw a long view of a valley ahead and hills, and beyond the hills, snow-capped mountains.

"Beautiful, isn't it?"

Hope looked out at the mountains and nodded. The kids were awake, but they seemed to take no interest in what they were seeing.

"The waterfalls are nice," Hope agreed as they drove through Copper Canyon.

Montez was disappointing. The rain fell and the mountains were cut off by low clouds. It was difficult to make anything out across the bay. When they got to the trailer park, there were no water or electrical hookups left. They would have to run the generator for power, haul water and sewage two hundred feet every day.

Larry held the five-gallon can as Hope unscrewed the pressure cap to the water tank. She removed the cap and stood back, huddling in her raincoat, shivering slightly.

"Cold?" Larry asked.

"Miserable."

He nodded. "I guess this hasn't been much of a vacation for you, has it?"

Ed Booth was pleased to see Larry back in town and offered to take Larry and Hope out to dinner on a Friday evening, two days after their arrival. Larry agreed on the condition that Ed say nothing to Hope about his past plan to move the family to Montez permanently. This was not the opportune time and, anyhow, he was having his own doubts about Alaska.

Ed took them to the Pipeliner, a bar-restaurant with a model oil well set inside a foot-thick slice of the actual pipeline. The pipeline company, then called Taps, had presented the piece to the owner of the bar back in 1969 when he had been mayor of Montez. He was no longer mayor, but he'd kept the souvenir and welded it firmly to the building alongside the entrance. It was a good gimmick, though oddly enough, the one bar in town that had attempted to capitalize on the pipeline turned out to be the one least patronized by the workers. Perhaps it was just as well; it left a place for the locals to go and feel comfortable.

Hope had stopped on the way in to touch the piece of pipeline. "So that's it," she said. Inside, she was surprised at the elaborately decorated lounge—the plush booths, the flowered trellises arching everywhere, the deep carpeting and the uniformed waitresses dressed as French maids.

"It's the same at the White House," Ed said. "Very classy."

"The White House?" Hope looked around the room.

"No, not that White House. *Our* White House. The big motel and restaurant on the harbor. It's owned by someone named White and that's what he called it. It's not even white. It's gray. Stained pine. I did come contracting work on it a few years back and we extended a wing. We matched it perfect, I think." The waitress came and they ordered drinks. "At any rate, it's about the fanciest spot in town and the bar overlooks the water. We'll go hoist a few down there after dinner."

"This place certainly has a lot of bars," Hope said. "Larry told me there are six. I guess the weather drives people to drink."

Ed looked at the tight lines set in her face. He wondered if the girl had what it took to tough it out in Alaska. She was pretty enough—those long legs, the model's figure and face—but there was a certain "eastern" quality about her. Protected. Coddled, even. Come to think of it, Dan's wife had the same look, but Paula Curry wasn't from the East at all. Paula was from San Francisco.

There was no point in telling her that she would harden after a winter or two and get used to the weather, that Alaskans were comfortable at fifty and sixty, that seventy was balmy and eighty downright uncomfortable. Ed had gone fishing in the rain and camping in the snow. You took what the country gave.

"So what do you think of the town itself?" He caught the warning look from Larry and gave the lad a quick wink. No harm bouncing a few ideas off her.

"I suppose you'll think I'm terribly provincial, but I'm very much attached to the way New England looks. This is . . . interesting, I suppose."

Ed had seen pictures of New England in the yachting magazine he'd subscribed to. Stuffy little white churches and everything looking the same. A little of it would be okay, he guessed, but it would be hard to imagine, say, Lavinia's house in the middle of all that, Lavinia's house with its redwood timbers, the panoramic windows, the observation deck, the arklike immensity of it.

"I guess I'm just a traditionalist," Hope said. "It bothers me to walk down a street and see a trailer and next to it a Swiss chalet and then a French country house with a mansard roof."

"The owner here has the mansard," Ed said. "Built it when he got elected mayor. I like it."

"By itself," Hope said firmly. Ed knew it was time to change the subject. He told a few hair-raising stories about people coming up to Alaska to make them feel better and asked if they would like to see Lavinia and her house. He'd been saving that through dinner as a surprise. Lavinia had agreed to talk with Hope and Larry. They could even bring the children. It was unusual, he told them, for Lavinia to see strangers, even more unusual to have children up there, although Lavinia liked Dan's well enough.

His own boy, sullen though he was, seemed to get on well with her when he went up separately. As a matter of fact, Lavinia had asked Ed not to bring Doug with him on visits anymore, as the boy never talked when his father was around.

Without meaning to, Ed found himself talking about Doug, how the boy had never liked him from high school on.

"I've done all kinds of work, but it seems no matter what I do . . ." Ed shook his head slowly. "No matter what job . . . he just flat doesn't respect me. And it can't be that Doug thinks I should be doing something else. I don't think there's anything *he* wants to be. He doesn't act like it, anyhow. He's on the pipeline now, living at home with us, but he'll move across the bay in a few weeks when the big camp starts to open up. I don't know. Seems like gap-wise there shouldn't be any problem. For years we were both trying to find ourselves and now we've both found *something*—the pipeline."

"That's nice that he found a job on the pipeline," Larry said for lack of anything else to say. "I wouldn't mind a shot at that myself."

"Well, I sure as hell wouldn't," Hope said.

Ed laughed. "You're genuine sourdoughs, then. She's gone sour on Alaska and you've run out of dough." It was the oldest joke of them all.

It happened so fast Maggie almost didn't see it.

The two guys at the end of the bar had been having the usual sort of drunk argument, not enough for Maggie to do much but give them a warning now and again. Then the big fella leaned in close to the fat guy and whispered something. He sat back with a shitty ass grin and the fat guy whipped up a bottle, busted it against the counter, and shoved it in right under the grin.

The music stopped; for a moment it was like everything stopped—the guy with the bottle in his hand, the guy with the bright, impossibly liquid mouth opening under his chin, Maggie's voice that wanted to shout but couldn't. And in that pool of stillness in the room, when the only light was the glistening light gathering at the throat toward which the big man was fluttering two clumsy, leaden hands, the fat man moved like lightning. He struck a second time, a third, a fourth and the hands of the big guy were like damaged birds in flight. And then David, Maggie's brother, no longer slumped over his drink, no longer the teary-eyed Friday night cop on a bender, moved as a dancer, spun, cut in on the pair and took the fat man for his partner. The fat man dipped against the bar and let the bottle fall in splinters on the floor.

David brought his mouth to the man's ear and whispered. Maggie heard it. He said: "Freeze, asshole, I'm a police officer." The words were fogged by drink, but it was an order. Fatman moved, David moved, and a bone gave way. David let the fat man slide to the floor, screaming about his broken arm. He unsteadily made his way to the man whose throat had been slashed, the big man who now lay on the floor (when had he fallen?). Maggie leaned over the bar to see, but the crowd had come alive and was pressing in.

This had all happened, she was later to relate, in the space of time it took to fill two beer glasses, side by side.

Maggie reached beside the register and called for the ambulance, then buzzed upstairs for Doug. He could help settle things down, help David. Maggie went to the end of the bar and the men gave way to let her pass. David was kneeling with the man and he looked up at her vaguely.

"Son'vabitch might actually make it." David. "It's not spurtin too bad. I broke that other bast'ds arm, din' I? Din' I?"

Maggie nodded.

"Hey," David shouted. "You're goin to jail, smart ass."

The sirens wailed, red lights outside the window, the bustle of police and attendants. Maggie went behind the bar, the music went on. A few people got up to dance. You had to expect some bad incidents. As long as they kept it under control. She smiled at Doug, who carefully mopped the corner around the bar.

The band played "Yellow Ribbon."

As soon as word of the incident reached the White House, Ed Booth tossed a twenty at the waitress and excused himself.

Larry said they'd be right over to the club when Hope came back from the ladies' room.

He explained what he'd heard on the way over, described the place from the last time he'd been in.

"Guess it's changed a lot. If you think it's too rough or you don't feel comfortable, we can leave."

Hope, walking through the chill night air along the harbor, everything gleaming with the mist, laughed softly, kicking at a pebble.

"Comfortable? I haven't been comfortable since we left Walpole."

Ed was behind the bar with Maggie, and she was telling him what had happened. There didn't seem to be anyplace to sit. Conscious of the number of eyes on Hope, Larry rested a hand on her shoulder and scanned the room. It was too bad he didn't know anyone. The place had sure changed. There was no room at the bar, the tables were full, a line of guys two deep ran down along the long wall toward the toilets, the poolroom was jumping. Even the dance floor was jammed.

Hope nudged him. Two men, one small, middle-aged, the other a real bruiser, waved for them to come over.

The little man got up and made a pass with the handkerchief over the chair before Hope sat down. Larry smiled at the big guy, who stuck an enormous hand out. "Name's Tiny," he said.

"Mah name's Jawwn Hill," the other said to Larry, "an ah'm a *pipe*liner. Ain't many men aroun' here can say that." He launched into an explanation of Local seven ninety-eight from Tulsa and how they were the best damn welders in the world.

Tiny insisted on buying and also asked the waitress to bring two more drinks to the fag. He pointed to a dark-haired, slender boy seated by the bandstand. At the table, in front of him, were a dozen unfinished drinks. Daiquiris. Or, as Tiny had put it, da-queeries.

"We're six-packing the little candy ass," Tiny whispered to Larry. "He's one of the safety men, and he turned in some operator for being drunk on the job. I could see it if the guy was doing any lifting, but he was waiting for a dozer to come and build him a work pad, and everyone knew the dozer was stuck on a hill. See what shape he's in tomorrow."

The safety man was, indeed, well on his way to oblivion. It was not, according to Tiny, proper to walk off and leave drinks somebody brought you unless you happened to be a woman, in which case, with the odds in here, it would be impossible to do otherwise.

Within fifteen minutes Larry saw what Tiny meant. Waitresses kept coming to the table with gin-and-tonics for Hope, indicating from which group of men the drinks had come. Hope would look up and a man, or two or three men, would wave at her and smile. Suddenly there were eight drinks in front of Hope and the waitress was coming with another.

"Your seventh-graders won't believe this, will they?" Larry said, but Hope was listening to John Hill, who was telling a story about a hunting dog named Old Blue. He had also offered a toast about breezes and treeses, but Larry couldn't hear it over the music.

The men wouldn't let Larry buy a round. They were making so much money they were looking for new ways to spend it. And Larry had decently driven all the way from New Hampshire just to brighten up the Montez Club with this beautiful woman.

The band played a rock number, "Stagger Lee," and Larry thought of asking Hope to dance, but he figured she was probably too tired. And, he felt, it would be unfair to the men who had offered to share the table and bought them drinks. He listened to John Hill, who seemed to do most of the talking, describe hunting with a ferret in his pocket.

You had to reach in ever so gently, not to scare the ferret, or it would bite you. Slip a hand in the pocket, slowly. Hill slipped his hand over Hope's hand. Tiny nudged Larry, started to say something. Shet up, Hill told him. Reach in real slow like, and just stroke it with one finger. He stroked the back of Hope's hand. Two fingers. Gently. Ever so gently. Hill's voice dropped. Hope looked at him expectantly.

Then you picked him up and stuffed him down a rabbit hole. John Hill picked up Hope's hand and, winking broadly, laid it on his knee.

For a moment she did not take it away. She asked: "What then?"

John Hill banged the table with his other hand and broke into wheezing laughter.

"The ferret's supposed to go in after the rabbit."

Hope returned her hand to her lap.

"She'd make a terrible ferret wouldn't she, Tiny?"

The waitress came.

"Those men, see the one in the cowboy hat? The character in the green satin shirt next to him? Well, honey, they wanted to buy you drinks, but I told them you already had a waiting list. Anyhow, they just said howdy and that I should tell you."

The cowboy took off his Stetson and fanned himself with it when Hope looked.

Larry checked his watch. It was late, considering these guys would be getting up at five, six in the morning to go to work. That safety man had about had it, but Tiny kept the drinks coming to him until the waitress called it quits. There were, she said, twenty on the table. That wasn't six-packing, that was murder.

They talked about the fight, which Tiny had seen up close. He could have stopped it himself, but when you work around construction the usual thing is to step back and give the men plenty of room. Cop did okay, though, considering he was half bombed. John Hill went to the men's room.

"Are you tired?" Larry asked.

Hope shrugged. "Not really."

"Do you mind all the . . . attention? It must make you feel a little conspicuous."

Hope pushed the assembly of glasses together in a tight circle.

"To tell you the truth," she said, as John Hill—Little Nasty—wove back to the table and the band started up again, "it's the first time in the last two months I've felt attractive. I could use a little attention right now."

"Do you mind if I ask your wife to dance?" Hill—Nasty—looked so respectful in asking it that Larry nearly laughed.

"Sure. I mean, if she's not too tired."

He held his watch out. But Hope told him that, tired or not, it was the first time anyone had asked her to do something she enjoyed since she left home.

"Look at that," Tiny said. "She's about a foot taller than Little Nasty."

She wasn't really. It was more like six inches, but it was enough difference for the guy to lean his chin on her breasts when he swept her around. "That your name for him? Little Nasty?"

According to Tiny, John Hill wasn't known by any other name. Larry watched them on the dance floor. Hill didn't look particularly nasty. He was a good dancer and Hope seemed to be enjoying herself, which was probably a good thing. A man at the next table came over and tapped Larry on the shoulder.

"That your wife?"

Larry nodded.

"Can I have her for the next one?"

He nodded again and looked for Hope, but Little Nasty had whisked her off to the other end of the dance floor. Larry helped himself to one of Hope's drinks.

Despite the double-edged sexism of the men around her, Jill Jones found life in Wiseman Camp to her liking. Sure, she had to put up with the catcalls—and the disparaging remarks about the quality of her work. But Wiseman had its compensations. Other women were showing up in camp now and the men had begun to treat her less like a freak. Since they all couldn't have her, they figured no one should. The few attempts made by a drunken pipefitter to kick in her door suddenly stopped. Chivalry had its good side.

The women had first lived in a separate dorm, and since it remained half empty, incidents such as the door-kicking seemed likely to continue. Moving the women to the same dorm with the men worked better, even if it did take some getting used to for all concerned. One clown persisted in walking naked down the corridor to take his showers, a towel tossed over one shoulder. He told Jill he wasn't "ashamed of it."

She congratulated him heartily, reaching out to shake his hand, naked there in the hall. After all, she announced, it's not the size of it that counts, but knowing what to do with it.

At meals, Jill never liked to sit with the women; it was too uncomfortable. The men would always stare from all sides and she found herself dropping spoons, fumbling with her knife and fork like a self-conscious child in a fancy restaurant.

Sitting with the men was simpler. They asked her how she liked driving a Wabco, the thirty-five-ton dump truck with a ladder up to its cab. She preferred the Euclid, she told them, that she'd trained on. But Euc or Wabco, the shifting was simple, the tach said right on it when to shift up, when to shift down. The main thing was learning how much room you took on the right side. It was easier than driving a cab in Fairbanks.

Aside from the job and the people she worked with, there was Wiseman itself, surrounded by mountains, forest, an old mining town nearby where she could wander in the evening (rattling a can of pebbles to warn off grizzlies), poke around, and find a souvenir from the gold rush days, a battered canteen, rocker pans, a broken pick.

And there was Bill Wiggins, the Medevac pilot, younger than Jill, with dark, appealing eyes, a clean, fine look about him. Jill had already qualified for her single-engine license and Bill went flying with her two or three nights a week, often on actual Medevac runs which needed volunteer aid to look after the patient. Although Wiggins was not qualified to instruct, the big, seven-passenger Navaho was roomy enough for them to trade seats after she had flown the plane from the right-hand seat. A few times, pulling down to the end of the runway, they had discreetly switched position and Jill had taken off from Wiseman and Fairbanks. They had reversed the procedure for landings.

Wiggins, because he was not at all averse to making a whiskey flight into Bettles, was something of an underground camp hero. He tried to keep the circle of those who were in on the arrangement small, but, as in a prison, news spread over the grapevine, as some said, "before it happened."

On Friday morning, in the mess hall, Bill Wiggins had told Jill he was making a run into Bettles after work and she could come. He had promised to bring the relief medic and the medic had asked if he could bring JoAnn, the payroll clerk. But those were all that could go.

By dinner, everyone at the table as well as a dozen people who'd dropped by the medical shack during the day wanted to make the flight into Bettles, where they could drink at a real bar, maybe even dance with a local girl. Wiggins agreed to take two couples besides JoAnn and the medic. He took the requisitions secretary and "the Greek," then reluctantly took Jill's foreman, Mack, who had been giving Jill a hard time, and Mack's girlfriend, Marci the bullcook.

By now the camp traffic manager had learned to accept whatever Bill Wiggins wrote on the manifest. He asked no questions and refused to look out the window when Wiggins loaded or unloaded the plane. Even regular evacuations to Fairbanks were getting to be so crowded that Wiggins asked for volunteers *not* to accompany the plane. This had happened after one of Wiggins's would-be passengers told a guy in back that he hadn't been to town yet and since he was bigger, the guy in back could get off. The guy in back turned out to be the evacuee, but he asked Wiggins if he could wait for a less crowded flight.

So Bill Wiggins, Jill, JoAnn, the medic, the Greek, the girl from requisitions who never said much, Mack and Marci piled into the Navaho, and a small crowd of well-wishers and last minute whiskey customers turned out along the strip.

As the plane lifted off in the bright, late evening sunlight and banked against the mountains before turning south, a voice in the crowd came softly.

"Well, there goes the honeymoon flight. I wish the weenie-bird was here so I could go, too."

The weenie-bird was the line-camp reference to Wien Airline's high-wing Fairchild 327-B that flew a regular run up the pipeline every day, bringing in new help, taking out those lucky enough to have reached R&R. *Pipe 'n' Hot News* had already printed a whole series of weenie-bird poems, with no explanation for outsiders who happened to read the paper. "Watch the weenie-bird in southward flight;/ And you will spend a sleepless night./ Come back, oh, weenie-bird, don't go;/ My days are long, my nights are ever slow."

The state surveying team, sitting at a table in the Bettles Lodge, could hardly believe that girls had come in. They bought drinks while Bill Wiggins patiently filled the orders, marking sacks and boxes and storing them in the cargo hold. Then he and Jill went to the bar and tried to catch up with the others.

It was getting on to ten o'clock when the couples straggled out of the bar and into the plane. Jill, who had had the least to drink of any of them, waited at the door to the cabin and then closed it tight, latching it.

Wiggins was having some difficulty climbing into the cockpit and she told him to take the copilot's seat.

Back in the cabin everyone was still laughing, bottles were being passed around. The loud conversation made it hard to distinguish one voice from another.

The sun hung low, very low in the sky. It was setting, but the sky wouldn't get completely dark, and the way back should be easy to find once they located the pipe road and saw the lights of Prospect Creek or Old Man.

The Greek and his girl were across from each other in the first row of seats; Mack and Marci were behind them, with JoAnn and the medic in back.

Jill leaned into the cabin and shouted for everyone to buckle up.

"Whass she doin on that side?" the Greek asked his girl, but she didn't say anything, as usual. He leaned into the cockpit, repeating the question, tugging at Bill's shirtsleeve.

"Oh," Jill said happily, "he can fly it from either side. I wanted to see how it looks over here for a change."

The Greek turned around in his seat and told Mack, who was slumped in his seat, smiling inanely at Marci's big tits. Mack reluctantly shifted his gaze to the front, to Jill snapping switches, making adjustments on the control panel. Mack knew something about planes. The motors revved up, died down, revved up again.

"She's drunk," he told the Greek. "She thinks she can fly the plane, but she can't. Drunks think they can do anything," he said in disgust, and then burst into tears as the plane began to taxi down the runway.

The Greek leaned forward and Bill shoved him back.

"Someone's gotta do it," Bill shouted into the cabin. "She can drive a truck, she can fly a plane."

The plane had turned at the end of the runway. The Greek was explaining the situation to Marci and the girl who never said much and now they were both crying. The medic and JoAnn, in back, didn't know what was wrong and they were trying to sing "Yellow Ribbon," but they couldn't agree on the words.

Jill shoved the throttles forward, held the brake for a few seconds, released, and the plane leapt into movement down the runway.

"Oh, God," the Greek shouted above all the rest, "oh, God." Mack shook his head, looking out helplessly at the ground falling away from the plane, tears streaming down his face. "You're fired," he whispered to the window.

Jill banked sharply and Marci screamed, as did the girl who seldom had anything to say. They were almost to Wiseman before Bill Wiggins finally admitted to the Greek that she knew how to fly. Nonetheless, the Greek muttered prayers all through the descent and later told everyone in camp that he never doubted she could do it.

Mack got off her back and stayed off.

Vern Blue rubbed his beard against Pam Allen's neck and forced himself in deeper. Pam, he groaned, urging his way with her in the narrow barracks bed, Pam, Pam, Pam. Wham. Bam. He chuckled into her ear and stilled himself, trembling. The night crew at Sag River were clumping down the hallway outside and he heard a voice he recognized, but not the words. The light was failing out there on the empty, flat landscape, dark coming down like a collapsing roof.

She spoke under him. It was good, wasn't it? I like it, I always like it best with you, Vern.

There was no room to roll back. Carefully they changed positions so they could lay side by side. Once they had made love in the warehouse when he'd gone to pick up a seat cushion for his dozer. One of the storage vans was filled with slabs of foam rubber and they had burrowed there, almost at the back of the van, and made love during the morning. That afternoon, pushing gravel in a borrow pit alongside the Sag River, he had wondered who else might be burrowing at that very minute, but he'd finally gotten used to her. She did like him best. And Pam never denied him, always put the others off when she knew he was coming to her room.

Vern reached down under the bunk and picked up his cola can, the same one he'd used for a month. He sipped, liking the burn of the whiskey after the softness of lovemaking. Like putting lead back in the old pencil, his pa used to say.

He told her to have one, but Pam declined. She didn't like to drink much, was always down on him for his drinking.

Vern held the can up, and as if reading from the label said: "Malt can do more than Milton can to justify the ways of God to man."

"You know something?" she said after a long time. "You're weird. You really are. You could have stayed on teaching, you could have gone to school and been a college teacher even, but you come out here, live like this, run a bulldozer."

He touched her breasts gently, moving his hand lightly down her back to make her shiver.

"What's wrong with living like this?"

"I don't mean *this.*" She waved a hand at the small, dark room. "I mean all this, the camp, the life here."

"I'd rather be a catskinner than a chalk scraper. Pays better. And they don't mind if I have a snort now and then. Come down with muscatelitis in the morning, no one gives a shit. I can lay in my rack and take a day off once in a while."

"What's the rest of it?" she asked suddenly.

"Of what?"

"The poem about malt can do more than Milton can."

He recited the part about lying down in a ditch and feeling good about it until you woke up. It was the only part he'd ever bothered to learn.

"What does your wife think about you drinking so much?"

Vern dropped the can over the side of the bed onto the floor.

"Women can't stand to see men happy." He patted her on the ass. "At least most women." Vern rumpled Pam's white-blond hair, touched her on the ear, the neck. His R&R would be up for next week but he was going to put it off for a while. If he went home, she might not like him best by the time he came back. And Pam had so far said nothing about planning to take R&R. When she went, he'd go.

"Do you think sometimes about whether or not your wife is chippying on you?" Pam asked, warming up to him again, starting to tighten her limbs where he touched. "Would you hate that?"

"I don't tell her, she don't tell me." He wondered if he could possibly go with Pam again, so soon. He doubted it.

Footsteps came to the door of her room, stopped as if the walker had paused to listen at the door. A faint rapping began and a quiet voice called her name.

Vern relaxed. It was only one of the Kelly brothers, Darwin or Dewey. He got up and went to the door. It was both the brothers. He let them in, and while Darwin unbuttoned his shirt, Vern and Dewey sat on the bunk across the room and mixed drinks.

Pam shut her eyes and lay, arms at her side, like a sleeping princess, waiting for Prince Charming. Vern drank deeply, looking out the window at the deep twilight, the stars lost in the glare of the camp lights.

"Never would have thought working on the pipeline could be like this, huh, Dewey?"

"Gosh, no," Dewey said, unlacing his shoes, never taking his eyes off his brother and Pam. "I'd have thought this would be about the loneliest job in the world."

Vern turned his head from side to side, feeling the false grooves in the wall paneling behind him. The paneling in the bedroom of his house in Fairbanks was exactly the same. "It sure isn't lonely."

Vern took another snort. It was warm going down. Knowing she liked him best was more than enough. He hoped his wife liked him best, too. He smiled benevolently on Pam and Darwin and thought of the phrase, "making the beast with two backs." Shakespeare or the Bible, one. Warm going down, a warm and cozy world. Best ditch he'd found in years.

Chapter Six

PEOPLE HAD COME to look at the trailer. Larry explained the outside equipment to the men; Hope showed wives how the kitchen and the bathroom worked. But no one bought. It looked, with a week left in August, as though Hope and the children were going to be flying back to Walpole while Larry stayed on to sell the trailer.

Then, Monday night, the twenty-sixth, coming back from an evening with Lavinia Curry, they found a desperate note, begging them to hold the trailer until Tuesday after work. A man, his pregnant wife and their toddler showed up. The man agreed to pay the asking price. They could take it over on September 1. He'd see Larry the next evening with the deposit. It was not perfect; Larry would definitely have to stay over until the trailer deal was completed, but he could perhaps spend a few days in Anchorage before coming home. The second half of the Phineas Garside grant money would be due him October 1. They might make it. Hope hardly dared to relax, she was so afraid the deal would fall through, that the man would change his mind.

Wednesday, sun and a luminous blue sky brought an end to the clouds and mere patches of sunlight that had marred the last month. Everyone, Larry felt, deserved a day of real summer pleasure. Slipping out of the trailer before the others were up, he went down to the dock to see about renting a fishing boat. Lavinia Curry had showed him through the telescope two or three coves where the salmon constantly broke the otherwise smooth water. There were seals in the water as well, swimming off Saw Island near the construction site across the bay.

A man stepped from the back of one of the campers parked on the harbor next to the Montez Club and whistled at Larry. Hard hat in one hand, lunch pail in the other, he jogged over. It was the man who had come to look at the trailer. He set the pail down and fished his wallet out and counted five new hundred-dollar bills into Larry's hands as if they were singles. When Larry had carefully transferred the bills to his own wallet, they shook hands firmly.

"Now you have to sell us the trailer, " the man said, and hurried on down the road to where a yellow school bus waited to take the men the long way around to the camp.

Later, bringing Hope and the kids down to the 14-foot skiff loaded with fishing tackle, box lunches, cold drinks in a chest, all rented or bought at the White House, he told her about the deposit.

"Just counted it out like it didn't mean a thing." He laid the five bills in Hope's hand and she laughed. The kids were still giggling over his joke, telling them to go see if the boat full of fishing stuff looked like it belonged to anybody. Hope put the money in her purse and let Larry help her into the skiff.

"I feel like we're stealing someone else's boat," Netty said, sitting alongside Larry in the stern.

Larry was glad he'd thought of it. It was about time they had a good day together.

Hope leaned back against the bow and watched the mountains slowly change shape as Larry took the boat through the channel and headed out into the bay. The water was utterly calm. Lavinia's house, just visible on the knob above the western edge of town, perched, as Ed Booth had said, like a beached ark.

Hope's father had had a boat during the years she was in high school, and they had spent summers at Spofford Lake and sometimes up at Lake Winnepesaukee. As for Larry—he'd taken her on the swan boats in the Boston Public Gardens once or twice.

How odd it had seemed to Hope the other night that Lavinia Curry, sitting on her hill in Montez, would have been so perfectly in context in Boston, a slender, tall, regal woman. She spoke with a fierce intensity that reminded Hope of the descriptions of the suffragettes or perhaps the bluestocking ladies who stumped Massachusetts decrying the execution of Sacco and Vanzetti. What her daughter Maggie had in raw sex appeal, Lavinia had in an indomitable grace and presence.

Larry had been as much awed by her as by her house, which seemed not to have a straight line or expected turn of hallway in it. Somehow he hadn't found a way to ask her the many questions that seemed important to him.

Hope hardly needed this boat ride to cheer her. Talking to the old woman, who was so curious about Boston, the Cape, New England, was like touching on life again. Lavinia had little interest in Larry other than in his intention to discover Alaska for readers back east. She seemed entirely unmoved by his admiration for the town of Montez.

Lavinia had received them in her library. Behind her, shelves of books ran from floor to ceiling. There were paintings of Alaska throughout the house, some by Sydney Laurence, a good number by an artist from Homer. If it was not the kind of art Hope would have chosen, neither was it the cheap, slick scenery painting she had seen so much of in Alaska. Northern lights painted on black velvet were *de rigueur* in most motels and restaurants. Hope could only imagine what the Alaskans had in their own homes.

Out in the middle of the harbor, though, you could easily be on a lake in Switzerland. Hope shaded her eyes against the sun. As they drew away from Montez, the peaks seemed to rise over the town rather than diminish. A Swiss town might be just as bad. Heart-shaped decorations everywhere. Edelweiss, real and painted. Fussy kitsch wherever you looked. It suddenly struck Hope that Switzerland and Alaska were equally far from Walpole—although in opposite directions.

Caitlin, ten, was slender and still very much a child. She touched everything, the fishing poles, the reels, the tackle. She asked Hope's permission to reach over the side and feel the water. Hope told her to go ahead and Caitlin's eyes widened in shock and delight. *Cold.*

She told Larry and put a hand in. Netty, with much shifting of position and careful consideration, tried also. It was the glaciers, Larry said. The harbor was a mixture of glacial runoff and sea water. It was deep, practically from the shoreline. Larry explained it all. Three hundred to seven hundred feet deep at the center. The town and the terminal sat on small mountain plateaus. The harbor was really a valley filled with water.

Caitlin made a face. She had only wanted to know if the water was warm or cold.

They stopped in a cove. There were no salmon, but everyone was already hungry, so they ate lunch sitting on a low, flat rock that would be covered when the tide came up. The children explored some hollows in the rock after Larry made sure there were no bears and that they were not actual caverns. He kept a wary eye out for bears, but with the lack of salmon here, he supposed there was little danger.

Hope thought about walking in the woods in New Hampshire. You didn't need to carry a gun back home. The children could picnic safely. Sometimes deep in the woods on a hillside, thinking you were somewhere no one had ever been, you might come upon a half-fallen stone wall and, if you persisted in searching, the cellar hole of a farm that had existed a hundred or more years ago. The stone walls were even on mountainsides.

Hope had written a series of poems about stone walls. The surprise, the sense of comfort and awe, the way it felt to be hot and tired and to find cool stone upon stone for you to sit on, stone still serving the purposes of man after a century's neglect.

The trip across the bay, running on a diagonal away from Montez, had taken almost an hour. They continued on another ten minutes beyond the Cove of Caves, as Netty called it, and rounded into a tiny, hidden inlet. Larry cut the motor immediately. Everywhere the water was broken. Salmon, bigger than any fish Hope had ever seen, leaped completely free of the surface, throwing diamonds of water into the sunlight. The sharply curved inlet was perhaps two hundred yards across and three times that deep, although it fanned out widely toward the sea. There were rocks down to the water on the left and a thin strip of pebble beach along the forest edge to the right. A creek ran down through a cut in the hills and spilled into the inlet. The water was white and foamed where it met sharp rock. A few gulls drifted back and forth across the water.

They stayed a long time. Hope and the girls had put away their tackle early. But Larry kept on trying. Finally he snagged a salmon and, even though it was the first time in his life, he played it for ten minutes. Caitlin scooped the salmon out of the water with her net. Then she began to cry when Larry proposed knocking it on the side of the boat to kill it. Larry threw the fish back into the water. It seemed the right thing to do.

Hope was content to float in the transparent water. More gulls had come, impossibly white against the fierce blue of the sky. Something good was happening inside her, an uncoiling. She realized suddenly that she was *feeling.* Had she been numb these last two months? She swallowed the momentary terror that caught at her throat. For a second it was as though there were no memories of the summer. The gulls called crazily to one another. Two fish broke the surface at the same moment. Larry and the children watched in silence.

The gulls were gathering at the mouth of the stream. The water boiled. Beneath the boat there were fewer and fewer salmon. Were they going to swim upstream now? Larry whispered to the children that they would start the journey, would spawn and then die. He told Caitlin the deaths did not matter: the fish came here to give birth.

The gulls dove at the water and Hope recollected something she had read of this. They were going after the salmon, trying to pluck out their eyes. The gulls were many now, their mews bringing more predators. Larry watched in fascination. The girls lay, one over each side of the boat, enraptured.

And then it happened. The gulls flew up as one and darted from the creek, filling the air above the boat. Below, the water darkened in thick bands alongside the hull as the salmon retreated to safer depths. In one moment the blue sky was white with birds and the water was black with fish. Hope and her family, of the water and not of the water, of the air yet not of the air, lay suspended between. Then the fish and the gulls were gone.

Caitlin hugged herself suddenly. Netty stared after the departing birds with a look of sweet vulnerability that brought quick tears to Hope. Larry held his hands up, cupped, toward the air. Much later he was to say that he knew what it must have felt like to be Lewis or Clarke on their journey, knew it in that moment. To Hope it was as though Alaska in her great, godlike indifference, Alaska that could make death beautiful, had suddenly decided to bless them. As, thirty minutes later, it suddenly tried to kill them.

The boat didn't even have a name, just the company and a number painted on its ugly bow: *SeaCo 127.* Sailing from the company's home port of Seattle, the ship, modified from a World War II landing transport, had been brought in to Montez to ferry concrete trucks across the bay until the shore road could be relied on for passage around the clock. The dingy green and white vessel carried three, four trucks per crossing and it docked at a gravel berm built between the terminal site and a short, wooded peninsula that ran parallel to the shoreline. The berm stood well above the water and was easily wide enough for two trucks to pass. The lagoon, created by its construction, not quite a quarter of a mile long, would be filled in eventually as rock was removed from the hillsides where the crude oil storage tanks were to be built.

SeaCo 127 would ease up to the sloping gravel spill extending from the berm to the waterline, drop its loading ramp, and disgorge, instead of Jeeps and tanks seeking a beachhead, concrete trucks and equipment. Since the tide put the ramp at a different height every time, a dozer and front-end loader stood by, the loader dropping four or five yards of gravel at the edge of the spill and the dozer pushing the gravel to the boat's ramp, smoothing it for a temporary roadway. If the trucks couldn't make the slight grade coming off the ship, the dozer could hook on and drag them up on the berm while the captain kept the screws running, holding tight to the shoreline. It was a crude operation but it sufficed.

For the loader operator, who had to scoop a load of gravel up about once every hour and drop it by the ramp, the job was a cinch. He got paid for the time in between, and he occasionally left the loader and rode over to the other side in the boat to have a drink.

Al Godwin, the loader operator, was about to make another of his visits and his foreman, Joe Akin, was thinking about going with him. They were watching a small skiff work its way across the bay. No question that the skiff was making heavy weather of it. With the change of tide, the seas were building. Even the old bucket they were standing on rose and fell. The captain was having some difficulty keeping it positioned, but one of the concrete trucks was late coming back and they had to wait. The catskinner would probably have to touch up the ramp by the time he showed.

"I wouldn't want to be out there," Joe said, standing close to Al Godwin.

"They don't either. They're turning in toward us. I don't think they're going across. He's got more guts than I do, going out in that open water with a little boat like that. You go in the water, you can't last ten, fifteen minutes."

"Maybe a bear came after them," Joe Akin said. "You suppose they were fishing and a bear came? I'd go out in that water for a bear, maybe."

Hope had been in rough water before, and her daddy had always told her not to worry, boats are made for water. She told Larry not to worry, but she could see he was already damned scared. Caitlin, at least, was enjoying it, but Netty had taken a cue from Larry and grimly watched the waves.

Larry called to Hope over the sound of the motor to tell her he was going to head in to the lee side of the big green and white boat. He didn't know anything much about boats and the water, but a wave had partially broken over the stern and he wanted to find shelter. Maybe he could take the skiff out there. At least get the kids ashore.

Hope reassured Caitlin and then, as they neared the shore, she could see the swells roll up and break over the rocks. Alongside the big boat there seemed to be a gentle gravel ramp which might be best after all: most of the shoreline was strewn with boulders.

She wished she had paid more attention to things her daddy told her about using the boat, landing and so forth, but it had never really interested her any more than sailing did.

Larry was waving his arm at two men standing at the rail of the boat and they suddenly disappeared belowdeck. Hope watched and saw them emerge at the ramp, now about a hundred yards off. Another small wave had spilled over the transom. Everyone was wearing life jackets. Hope felt calm. They moved in alongside the ship. It did not seem necessary to say anything to the kids. The men were watching them intently. One seemed about to shout as the skiff touched the gravel just below where he stood.

Water swirled in the skiff and Hope watched it, transfixed. The stern rose once, the boat ground into the shore and a second wave buried the transom. Hope picked Caitlin up and shoved her at the man with the pocket full of ball-point pens. Then everyone was in the water. The boat was wrong side up and Netty, in her bright orange jacket, was adrift. A dark-haired man reached for Netty and missed; a wave went over her. The man ran to the steel landing ramp of the boat and threw himself flat on it, plunging an arm into the water. He snared Netty, almost under the bow. How had she gotten there and why couldn't Hope stand up? Hope kept drifting. She might hit her head on the metal ramp. Caitlin was safe. Larry, a glimpse only, was up to his neck. Probably getting things out of the water, which kept trying to push Hope against the big boat. So confusing. And then the other man was in the water to his waist, getting his clothes wet, the ball-point pens just above water. He held onto a chain that ran toward the upper part of the boat and he grabbed Hope's arm just as the water flowing beneath the ship grabbed at her legs. The propellors! They were what made the water pull her back under the barge.

Hope came out to the kids, hugged them, kissed Netty again and again. Larry and one of the crewmen were hauling the skiff out of the water. There was not much in it, no poles, no gear, just the dip net. Larry went back into the water, ducked down, floundered, as Hope settled the kids. Caitlin wasn't even wet.

Larry gave up. He had found nothing. Nothing. Hope looked in the boat, at the gravel ramp washed by the waves. Larry slogged up to her, head down.

"I couldn't find the purse."

Hope shut her eyes. Three hundred dollars and the checkbook. And the deposit, the five new hundred-dollar bills.

"What'd you lose?" the man with the pocket full of pens asked them.

"Everything," Larry said. "Her purse."

"All our money."

"Much?" he asked.

"About eight hundred." Larry turned to look at the waves,

breaking, falling back, washing gravel down the bank into the sea.
The man reached for his wallet.
"How much do you need?"

"I feel so stupid," Larry said, standing at the counter in the trailer, spreading out the contents of his wallet to dry. There was the sixty dollars he had been carrying and the two hundred Joe Akin had loaned him. "The guy who rented the boat told me to lay in if the weather changed and the water got rough."

"I didn't think it was that rough," Hope said, but her voice said otherwise. If Larry could find a buyer for the truck at a good price, they might make it up. He said he could get rid of the truck quickly in Anchorage.

"At least we're clear of this trailer." Larry blotted the wallet with a paper towel. "Remember how it kept breaking? I was actually thinking we might take a beating on it. But we'll get our money back. Or we would have, except for today." He worked on in silence. Hope sipped at her tea and stared out the window.

"John Hill is coming." She sounded surprised.

Larry went to the door, opened it. "Hello, Nasty."

Nasty stepped into the trailer and unpacked a shopping bag, announcing the contents as he did. "Booze. Milk. Steak sandwiches. Ice cream. Cashews. I come to have dinner with you and hear 'bout your big fishing trip."

"That was nice of you," Hope said. "I haven't even thought about eating."

"We have," Caitlin said, and Nasty stepped over to sit down between the two girls, who had been reading comics.

"So these is the little girls. Your mamma done tole me you was pretty, but you *are* pretty."

Caitlin snuggled up under his arm. Netty smiled, but kept her distance.

"I got some little girls, too. Little older than you, but I got em."

He showed them his wallet. The girls were sixteen and eighteen. Netty asked if they were in high school or college. Neither, he laughed. They were both married. Sixteen-year-old was just turning seventeen and already had a baby boy.

Mechanically Hope put the sandwiches on plates while Larry got the glasses and ice.

Nasty came and sat down. The girls ate on the barstools. Larry told him how Al Godwin had saved Netty's life. Hope began to cry and Nasty patted her on the hand.

Joe Akin had told him all about it; even admitted to giving Larry the money. Nasty asked bluntly if this put the family in a bad way.

"With everything else? Damn straight." Larry told him they had sixty bucks left, a few hundred in checking and close to six hundred in unpaid dental bills from the trip.

Nasty talked about life in the pipeline camp. It was lonely; you missed the kids. In fact, part of the reason he'd come was to have an evening around kids. Hope looked at him sweetly, touched his arm.

Nasty swallowed a hunk of sandwich. "Well, I cain't give you no two hundred dollars, but I think I got enough pull to get Larry on as a timekeeper if he wants the job. Like I say, it's lonely, but the way I figure, a couple of months could set you right. Course it's a non-union job and don't pay much, but there's free room and board."

"You serious? Work on the pipeline?"

Nasty shrugged. "Ah don't know, though. Pay's not too good, like I said. Six hundred a week. But it's easy. You'd be a time-keeper, and I ain't never seen one yet looked like he was working hard."

Hope looked at him desperately. "He could make that much?"

"Gross. I take home more than that myself, being union." He belched loudly and sighed. The kids giggled. Hope leaned across the table and kissed him lightly on the cheek.

It was as easy as Nasty promised. All Larry had to do was tell the payroll supervisor that he'd been in Alaska a year. The man knew he was lying and Larry knew he knew.

"You have lived in Alaska one year," the man said, reading off a form. It was a question on paper, but he read it to Larry as a piece of advice.

"Yes I have." Larry gave the address of the trailer park in Anchorage.

"Your last job?" The man wiggled his fingers over the typewriter.

"Traveling through the state on a research grant."

The man sat back, relieved, and typed it in.

The position would begin September 1. Larry would gross over six hundred a week, probably live in the new camp, the first dorms of which would be ready by then. All he needed to do was go to Anchorage at his own expense for the orientation and physical.

"I'm about thirty pounds overweight. Will it matter?"

"Nobody fails. Welcome to Bartel. The job's nothing. Try to do it right and we'll get along fine."

They met Nasty that night and toured the bars in town with him, finally driving back to his camp at one in the morning, by which time they had been wandering the waterfront, arm in arm, singing a dirty song Nasty had taught them. In the front of the pickup on the way out to Copper Camp, Nasty slipped an arm over Hope's shoulder and made her snuggle down. He mumbled something about hating to see her go back Outside and how he'd keep an eye on Larry for her. The radio was on, the Armed Forces Network, very faint, but knocking out some easy jazz rhythms. Larry knew his life had come to an extraordinary turn. Just when it looked like he would have to leave Alaska, busted, this job had come along. He could stay, do research while making money, and be home the first week in November. Just put in one nine-week hitch and quit instead of taking R&R.

He glanced at Hope and Nasty. The guy had his arm so far around Hope's shoulder that he could almost reach down the front of her blouse. Larry glanced again. It looked like Nasty did have his hand on the upper part of her breast, but the hand was curled, not reaching. If he opened the hand, moved a few inches, he'd touch her nipple.

Larry stared at the road, looking for the turnoff to camp. Should he say anything?

Just then, looking over, he saw Nasty turn to Hope, saw the man's eyes go to the front of her blouse and then meet her eyes.

"Ummm?" Nasty asked her softly, but loud enough for Larry to hear it, even over the radio.

Just as softly, Hope said no. Then they were at camp and Nasty was crossing the gravel parking lot toward his dorm.

As the *Columbia Glacier II* nosed out into the open waters of Montez Bay and picked up speed, Netty and Caitlin stood, shivering, along the starboard rail watching for the place where they had gone in the water. Hope and Larry sat by the picture windows in the passenger cabin facing each other in a booth that seemed more suited to an ice cream shop than a commercial vessel in sub-Arctic waters. Hope didn't look out.

The clouds hid the mountaintops and the water was a bitter gray, churned by a stiff wind coming down through Thompson Pass. The boat rolled heavily, and passengers trying to eat breakfast found it difficult to sip at their coffee without spilling it.

Larry carefully managed his tea, which did less than he hoped for the pain in his throat. He would accompany the family only as far as Whittier and then return to Montez, where he could see a doctor Saturday. He looked at Hope, who was staring down at the water. If only he weren't sick, saying goodbye would have been so much easier. They'd have spent a night in a real bed in a motel. He'd have gone to the airport. They would have promised to write each other and he'd have hugged the kids. There would have been a last chance to make love to Hope, to try to impress their bodies on each other firmly enough for the memories to linger over the next two months.

But last night he'd been too sick. And the whole time in Alaska had been sexually spare between them. Hope's mind was already back in Walpole. Her parting was taking place in an air of distracted indifference. Larry supposed she was depressed by the accident. Hope showed flashes of humor, protested that she was very pleased at Larry's opportunity to earn back the money they had lost. She claimed that if there were any other way, she wouldn't think of forcing Larry to stay and work, and asked if, indeed, it wasn't the other way around. Didn't he prefer staying on for the experience?

The lines of worry and sadness scarcely diminished the loveliness of Hope's face, her hair softly framing her features, those eyes seeming to watch some slow spectacle taking place deep beneath the hard, gray water. Larry's throat ached so much that he didn't dare swallow. He had a fever. Already he felt abandoned.

The children returned and Larry felt like a ghost among the living. The conversation among the three was of Walpole, with occasional references to missing Daddy very much. Larry tried a few times to speak to them, but he couldn't make sounds.

The passage through the narrows was like a journey through a fairy tale by the Brothers Grimm. Dense stands of pine gave way to steep cliffs on the near shore and to rugged mountains opposite, less than a mile away. The fog hung in patches on the water, now stilled to gentle swells; gulls went swooping and plunging in and out of the mist. He expected to see castles atop the cliffs, ancient vessels appearing from the fog, sirens calling from the lonely clusters of rock along the shore.

For a half hour they threaded their way through a series of tiny islands. Then the captain announced they were passing Elf Point and would head into Columbia Bay for a look at the great glacier.

A low, blue-white band of ice lay across one end of the bay, with two sets of mountains rising above it on each side. The vessel continued on toward the glacier for several minutes, and only with the realization that the ice did not seem appreciably closer did Larry begin to understand its scale. He buttoned his coat and, with the children, went to the upper deck to stand outside. The captain explained everything. The bizzare shapes of the smaller icebergs floating by in the water were caused by the ice rotating in the water as it melted, thus presenting different faces to the sea from hour to hour. After a close inspection, some of the glacier ice would be scooped up both for display and for serving in mixed drinks or soda pop for the kiddies. Slowly the peaks, Einstein and Witherspoon, lowered and the front of the ice grew in height and it was possible to make out details, crevasses in the glacier, sections of ice that were distinctly blue and some that were clouded. The icebergs in the water grew more numerous, larger. If you were to fall overboard in these waters you would survive only a few minutes. The children drew back from the rail, hanging tightly to Larry's hands. It was no good to wait for the roaring thump of a giant chunk of ice to fall in the water; by the time you heard the sound the action would be over. Larry, like the others, scanned the face of the glacier. He was lucky enough to see a piece fall. It was called calving.

"The glacier," said the captain, "is over three miles across at the face, up to four hundred feet high. That last chunk that fell was probably the size of an eight-story building. We'll be heading on to Whittier now, as most of you will be making a train connection from there to Anchorage, and we do want some time to look for whales once we get clear of Glacier Island."

On the way back from Whittier, before stopping at the glacier again, Larry saw a whale spout, but his fever was up again and he didn't go out on deck to look at it.

Hope and the kids were probably pulling into Anchorage. He'd told Hope about Whittier and the Kenai Peninsula, a little of which she would see. Alaskans, he said, went down to Seward and Homer the way people in Massachusetts went to the Cape. She told him not to talk, to take care of his throat, get plenty of rest, write. It hadn't been much of a goodbye.

Dozing, he missed the glacier altogether.

There wasn't much the doctor could do. The infection was not serious. No doubt the exposure to the cold water had reduced Larry's resistance. He gave Larry pills.

The family that bought the trailer met Larry at the bank and it was an effort for him to follow the transaction. He refinanced the pickup truck and would sell it later, while he was living in camp. The trailer was all paid off. Larry no longer owned it. Tuesday he flew to Anchorage and Wednesday went through the orientation and physical. The doctor complained that he should have been home in bed, but passed him. It was true, Larry realized as he boarded the plane for the flight to Montez and life in a pipeline camp, no one failed. It wasn't that kind of physical.

A bus met them in Montez and took them on the shore road to the camp across the bay, where they were photographed, registered, given meal cards and issued keys. They were lucky, the camp manager said, as each one left the office, to be the first group of men housed in Terminal Camp. Larry was especially lucky. He got a second-floor room with a view of the harbor, within sound of the waves breaking along the shoreline a few hundred feet away. He shut the window, pulled the curtain, and fell back in the narrow bed.

He hadn't the strength to unpack and fit his belongings in the tiny closet. He stared at the ceiling, waiting for the inevitable constriction of his throat. God, he thought. Terminal Camp. I've come to the right place.

Malcolm Finch-Smith pressed the slide changer. B. R. Young sat with both hands on the desk, supporting his chin, a pose mimicked by several of the low-echelon executives. The slide was of a woman in a hard hat, about to climb up the ladder of a 35-ton dump truck.

Finch-Smith read from the script.

"Meanwhile, one of the many women hired through the unions during the last month prepares to climb aboard her 'rock buggy' at

Wiseman Camp. A heavy-duty driver, Jill Jones works for Hyatt and Rueter and reports that she gets along fine with the men. Departing from the text, I might add that we have a front-page picture story on Jill Jones in next week's *Pipe 'n' Hot News.*"

The next slide showed Dorm One at the terminal, with carpenters putting final touches on the snow tunnels above the entryways.

"Terminal Camp was made ready for its first hundred tenants and should be up to its full capacity of twenty-eight hundred in a little less than a year. Occupancy was planned for the first week of September and eventually we hope to phase out Copper Camp. Two operating engineers at the terminal, it is reported, saved the lives of a family of three who sank a hundred yards offshore in a gale. The husband's name was Barry Fanshow, or Grandshaw, but we don't know who the operators were."

B. R. Young swiveled his head a few degrees toward Finch-Smith and nodded almost imperceptibly. A little drama. Just the sort of thing the old bastard liked.

Part Three

Chapter One

JILL JONES WAS FEATURED on the front page of *Pipe 'n' Hot News* with a series of pictures down the left-hand column and a full five-column, 36-point head. The kicker, in 18-point italics, said "Jill Jones Gets Her Fill," and the head beneath it was: "WOMAN WORKER WOWS WISEMAN WISEGUYS."

Pert, pretty Jill Jones stands 5′5″ tall and doesn't weigh much more than a single set of tire chains for her Wabco Dump Truck. But every day for eleven and sometimes twelve dusty hours she hauls fill for the gravel road that is nearing completion between the Yukon River and Pump Station One. Although some of the men at Wiseman made the expected jibes about women drivers (and liberation) Jill takes it all in stride.

"Most of the fellows have been real sweet once they got over feeling strange about having me around. I guess there's a few who think we belong in the kitchen and not behind the wheel of a truck, but the first time I got out and did men's work and found it was no harder than women's work—and paid more—I was hooked."

Asked if she was bothered by "male chauvinist attitudes" on the job, Jill tucked a curl under her hard hat and allowed that it got to her from time to time. "But mostly I don't have time to think about that. We're in competition with other camps to build the most haul road and, all day, mister, I'm in that truck and just flat boogieing."

According to Jill, a lot of the men who complained the most at first now say that camp life is more pleasant with women on

(See p. 4, Woman)

Jill circled slowly above Sukakpak Mountain, with its oddly canted side peak sticking out in the direction of the haul road. All day she had been working a material pit near Sukakpak, taking on gravel from the pair of loaders and hauling ass down to the south end of the road near a crossing of the Koyuk River Middle Fork. The article had caused her some embarrassment: phrases taken out of context, her observations condensed to an approximation of what she'd said. The photographer had taken some nice pictures, but the tape recordings he'd sent back of the interview must have been considerably revised.

"You're getting a little close," Wiggins shouted over the noise of the engines.

Jill corrected and swung north toward Dietrich Camp, which she soon saw glowing in the odd bulge of the river. Dietrich and Wiseman had already linked up, and you could drive all the way from Five Mile to Coldfoot, a distance of 112 miles. Soon the camps would all be connected; trucks could come from Montez and drive all the way to Prudhoe. The weenie-bird was on the ground at Dietrich. Jill banked sharply and made for Wiseman again.

It had been good to get up in the air, get away from the sudden surge of publicity. Those who were on her side, of course, were full of good words for the article, but a lot of nasty comments had come down the line in the mess hall. A sheet-metal worker had practically knocked her over trying to get ahead at the salad bar. After lunch, climbing up in the cab, she had found a copy of the paper stuck in the steering wheel with a circle around "woman in the kitchen." "I like it in the kitchen," a note in the margin said, "but it's better in bed."

Wiggins hadn't pressed her to discuss any of this and she was grateful to him. It was true that most of the men had been nice, but the ones who were mean could be mean in ways that ruined a whole day. If one of *them* had to stop and take a leak, nothing was said. But if Jill pulled her truck off the line to jump into one of the little green portables, there was always somebody waiting outside to comment on the event.

She reached over and put a hand on Wiggins's arm. He took the hand momentarily and turned his dark eyes on her. Jill began her descent. On the ground, there was the usual scramble to be in the proper seats when they rolled up to the flight office.

A half hour later, instead of engines roaring in their ears there was the rush of water from the shower and the soft, booming sound of the metal partition flexing in and out as Wiggins rhythmically pressed Jill's buttocks against it for support. She had both legs wrapped around his waist and clung to his neck, eyes closed, water streaming sometimes off his back, sometimes on her upturned face. She wished he didn't boom so on the wall, but he was getting close now and his hands tightened spasmodically on her ass.

The shower curtain slid aside, and Jill, eyes closed, fumbled for it, trying to pull it shut. The fabric resisted. She saw a close-set pair of eyes under bushy, dark eyebrows. The camp manager. Jill knew she mustn't scream. Instead she backhanded the man across the bridge of his nose, yanked the curtain away, and called him a bastard. Wiggins pulled out. Until Jill swore, he hadn't realized that anything was wrong.

"It was that damn creep who runs this joint," she said. "I think I gave him a bloody nose. Teach him to stick it where it doesn't belong."

"Jesus," Wiggins said. "He'll fire me sure as hell."

Jill peeked out.

"He's gone now. Maybe he didn't see who you were. Get your clothes together and get upstairs to your room." She pushed trousers at him. "Don't dry off, just move ass."

Wiggins ran, clutching underwear, shirt and shoes in his arms. As he rounded the corner out of sight, the resident camp manager and the teamster steward appeared at the other end. Jill stepped back in the shower. She was on good terms with the steward, a tall Italian fellow. His name was pronounced "Guloochi" but it was spelled funny. She never could get it right.

"She's in dat one dere."

Good, he did have a bloody nose and was still holding it.

"She might have been in there," the steward said, "but I don't know that she's in there now. I know I'm certainly not about to pull a shower open on a woman." His voice was mellow, reasonable and, as usual, dripping with implied threats. "Suppose she thought I was attempting to rape or molest her? I could get worse than a bloody nose and no jury would lift a finger against her."

Jill soaped herself under the shower. Guloochi, or whatever his name was, had come from New York where he managed some big nightclub. He never said he had connections with the underworld, but he did little to discourage such assumptions. A timekeeper had come up to him during the lunch break and asked how to pronounce his name. The steward had gotten up, stared at the kid until his clipboard began to tremble, and without a trace of a smile said, "With great respect."

The RCM was running water in a sink now and tearing paper towels off the wall. "Ah," he went a few times, and his voice came back to normal. "Jones," the resident camp manager shouted. "Is that you in there?"

Jill turned up the water and ignored him. If there were wet footprints leading to Wiggins's room, they'd be dry by the time he found out Bill was gone.

"Perhaps the young lady, if indeed it is a young lady in there, can't hear you over the shower. I suggest we wait. Of course, this is a callout, you realize. I get four hours' pay for a callout at the end of my shift."

"They hear us all right," the RCM muttered. "I knew it wasn't going to work, having women in these camps. They never should have let them in."

"You should have told the reporter that. It would have been an interesting aside in the story about Jill."

There was silence out there. Jill washed herself thoroughly, rinsed, and then shut the water off. She heard the floor creak outside and pulled the curtain, making no attempt to cover herself. As she'd expected, the RCM made a big show of averting his eyes.

"Hi, Gulooch."

The Italian turned his great dark eyes on Jill and she found herself reaching for a towel. Dark eyes in a man! If a man had good eyes, she could forgive the rest.

"Hi yourself," he said. "Is there someone in there with you that I don't see from here?"

"He's gone, obviously," the RCM said. "But I saw the two of them in there, heard them down the hall. I got a witness, one of the guys who was taking a shower and heard them in there going at it."

The Italian stared at the ceiling, lost in thought. "You could hear two people making love under a shower? All the way down the hall?"

The RCM stomped up onto the adjoining shower and put his knee against the wall, popping the partition in and out for demonstration.

The steward nodded. "I always thought those shower stalls were too damn sleazy."

"Anyhow, this ain't a court of law. This is my camp and I'm the manager. I saw the two of them in there, never mind her assaulting me, and I want her and the guy on the next plane out." He stopped talking and looked at Jill, who had slipped into a robe. "In fact, it could have been that pilot, Wiggins, who was in there. Was it Wiggins?"

"I never ask the names," Jill said. "Besides, I had my eyes closed. They all look alike in the dark."

"You don't actually *know* that it was Wiggins?"

The RCM waved his arms. "Oh, the hell with Wiggins. Who gives a damn? It's her that's causing the trouble. I caught her having intercourse in the shower and I'm going to see that she's terminated. You're the steward and I just wanted you here as a witness. The girl admits it."

"The woman admits it."

"Girl, woman, what's the difference? You did it, didn't you?"

Jill took her cue from the Italian and shook her head enthusiastically. "Sure did."

"You can pack bags, sister," the RCM said. "You're going down the road."

"I'm still waiting to hear what you're going to type in on the termination where it asks for a reason," Guloochi said.

"That's right," Jill said, stepping down off the shower platform and backing the RCM up against the sink. "You show me in any contract and union agreement where the teamsters say they won't fuck in the showers."

Two days later, when the business agent backed Jill a hundred percent, the RCM told the steward bitterly that he should have kept the dorms separate. "If the boys and girls want to visit they can visit in the mess hall and the rec hall, but not in each other's rooms, not in the showers."

"I don't think they want to visit," the steward told him after much thought. "In fact I'm sure of it. What they want to do is fuck, and I don't think you want them doing that in the mess hall and the rec hall."

The RCM was Irish, a Catholic. At times like this it showed in his manner and voice. He folded his hands and looked up. "Sure, and it was a sad day for the camps when the women came into them."

Vern Blue stopped the dozer, but left the engine idling. The other catskinner and a loader operator were heading for the dry shack and he waited until they got through the door before reaching into the toolbox under the seat and pulling out a pint of Jim Beam. He took a nip and slipped the bottle down into the large side pocket of his denim jacket and jumped from the mud-clotted tread to the ground. Early in the morning the ground would be hard from the September frost, but by noon the gravel pit had pockets of mud where he swiveled the dozer. It wouldn't be long before the cold came and stayed.

Inside, Fat John, who ran the other D-8, was leaning back in a corner with one foot up on the bench. Three sandwiches, four cans of apple juice and an assortment of cookies and sweet rolls were spread on the table beside him. He was reading the company paper to Bagge, the new kid who ran the loader. Bagge was young, but he had the feel of the loader. Even the teamsters who hauled the gravel away had good words for him. Bagge let his load in easy and never banged the truck with his bucket.

Vern took a spot opposite Fat John. Fat John scooped up a sweet roll absentmindedly. He set out a sandwich and hard-boiled egg. "John," Vern said, "what are you going to do the day you can't fit in a D-8 seat anymore?"

The kid at the end of the table smiled shyly. He was too new to join in ragging anyone yet. Another week, and he'd be comfortable calling Fat John names, but not yet.

"No shit, John, you keep up all that sugar, it'll kill you. I been on a high protein diet." He lifted the bread off the table and tossed it in the garbage. Vern had packed about a half pound of roast beef for the sandwich and he waved the slices at Fat John. "I knocked off fifteen pounds in the last month."

"Yeah. And about two pints of booze at each meal. Don't tell me about killing myself."

Vern stuffed a few slices of beef in his mouth and chewed slowly.

"You see where this teamster girl says she's getting on good with the men? I bet she's getting on. Probably stands up to take a piss. Looks like a dyke in the pictures."

"I thought she was cute. Of course I prefer our own teamster."

Bagge, the kid, pretended indifference. Vern watched him. He knew Bagge had heard stories about Pam and wanted to ask if it was true. Probably wanted to be invited in for a quick bang. He'd wait forever if he was depending on Vern.

John laid the paper on the bench. "Ain't you afraid to get the clap, fooling around with that stuff?" John shook his head. "See you two together, think you was married to her. Don't that make you feel funny sometimes?"

Vern thought about it a minute and decided he wasn't being mocked. John really wanted to know.

"She's a bum. I know that. All you have to do is pat her on the head and her drawers drop down. But what can I do?" Vern Blue smiled blissfully at the two men. "I love her."

It was Larry's third day in the brass shack and this morning he was working alone. The old man had moved up to chief timekeeper and was breaking in a girl to handle time cards, a boy just out of high school to check equipment.

The sun was shining, something Hope had never seen in Montez. It was a pity. The new snow on the mountaintops was dazzling. Termination dust, they called the first whitening of the peaks. It signified the end of summer. Back in Walpole the leaves wouldn't even be changing yet, not for another month.

Still, the early sun had already pushed the temperature up noticeably since he left the barracks and crossed over to the mess hall an hour ago. He looked at the number tags hanging in neat rows. Soon the parade would begin and the men, some of them, would begin bitching that it took him too long to find their tags, that the old man knew the numbers. A few obviously hated the brassing system and everyone connected with it. "New stoolie?" one of them had asked, seeing him the first morning.

Life at the camp, even after three days, had taken on a dull routine. Larry got up at a quarter to six, washed, had breakfast.

After the daily struggle to make a lunch at the two chow-up tables, he opened the brass shack. At eight o'clock he began his rounds, seeing foremen, checking on work crews around the job site and, at five, going back for another hour in the shack. After dinner there were movies—a new one every night—pool, Ping-Pong, shooting the breeze or hitting the bars in town. At nine, the men in the camp began to straggle back to their rooms, and by ten or ten-thirty most of them were asleep. Some came in from town night after night at midnight, or later, and went to work with a few hours' sleep or none.

Already Larry had lost track of the day of the week. The men said that with the long daylight or the long dark you would soon forget what time of the day it was as well.

One of the men Larry had eaten breakfast with this morning was the son of Ed Booth. He remembered meeting the kid back in February. Doug Booth told Larry he was glad to get away from the old man; he called Ed a bag of clichés and said he was a phony. Bad scene at home. Couldn't really rap. A drag. There was no end. Bad vibes. Tell you what he's into, he's heavy into the whole plastic trip, that's what.

Larry leaned over the counter. Joe Akin had come by to pick up his tag. Akin said that it was a nice day to go fishing and walked away without even cracking a smile. Never a mention of the two hundred dollars he had loaned Larry.

Larry's roommate was a teamster rigger who hated Joe Akin and said so even when Larry described the fall in the water. Fortunately, the guy, who snored all night long, was leaving on R&R in a few days.

The first of the men, a crew of pipefitters, ambled down the ramp at the far end of the old metal schoolhouse, left over from an army post that had stood on the terminal site. Larry glanced at the number code on the wall so he'd know where to start looking.

The first man stepped to the window and snapped his fingers. Fifty-two-o-seventeen. Larry found it just as the man leaned in and began pointing. Fifty-two-o-o-eight. On the left, fer Chrissakes. Fifty-two-o-sixteen, thata boy! Getting sharp.

Larry handed out the next tag and the man handed it back. Twenty-two, not fifty-two; I'm a nail bender not a pipe mender.

The men began to pile up in the aisle of the shack and Larry handed tags out as fast as he could. As the ranks thinned out, Larry heard laughter, whistles, catcalls, hoots.

It was Tiny, all six-foot-five, three hundred and some pounds of him. Tiny had a babushka over his hard hat, lipstick and two melons or softballs tucked in under his sweatshirt. His pant legs were rolled up and he had some calico material bunched up around his waist like a skirt. Little Nasty was wearing a faded woman's dress and carrying a handbag. Larry looked closer. Over the dress and the skirt both men had their working belts, complete with spud wrenches.

"All right," Tiny bellowed, "watch your mouths now, let's show some class around here."

"We got to educate you peckerwoods so's you'll know how to treat wimmen."

Sonny, the native trainee in Tiny's crew, sidled up to his foreman and tentatively squeezed his melons. Tiny slapped him away ineffectually.

"Heavens, what an awful thing to do. Can't you see I'm liberated?"

Dale, the old man in the crew, had to sit down and hold his head in both hands.

"You guys read the paper," Tiny shouted to the circle of men. "We're gonna have to learn to act decent on the job now. No more swearing, no spitting, no scratching your nuts in public, and most of all—watch your dirty talk. We got snatch coming to work on these jobs and Nasty and I thought maybe we could help you get used to it."

"It's not working," Al Godwin hollered. "I can't drive a loader when I'm sexually aroused."

Little Nasty put a hand behind his head. "Eat your heart out. I ain't giving it away no more."

A truck went by and slowed suddenly. Tiny pulled at his skirt and exhibited a thick, muscular leg. The driver stopped and put his head down on his arm.

"Too much for him. Well, you guys'll have to get used to it. It's a good thing you got Nasty and me around here, so's when the cunts come on this job, you'll know how to treat em."

A melon dropped and he caught it quickly, pushing it back to his chest. He looked at Larry in the brass shack. "I guess I'm going to have to walk all the way over there to get my tag."

"I'll get it," Sonny shouted and paused a moment to look at the melons. "Darling."

"Naw, I'll get it for the both of them." Another ironworker.

"I'm getting Nasty's," a welder said, and there were other shouts, boasts. The aisle at the brass shack immediately jammed with workers, shouting out numbers for the two brass tags. Sonny got one and the big labor foreman got the other.

The surveyors, who usually trained their scopes on girls in fishing boats just offshore, set up later to catch Tiny and Nasty, who were cavorting between loads on the dock. During some of the more complicated picks, Tiny would forget the fooling around completely and then revert to his act, thrusting his ass out, lifting a leg, caressing himself, as Nasty did a bump and grind.

Finally at ten the dock superintendent came over and put an end to it. Leslie Collins, the safety assistant, had asked that it be stopped—for "reasons of detriment to the safety of the unloading area."

Tiny threw his melons, one after the other, against the side of the dry shack.

"Why didn't the candy ass come and tell me to my face?"

Nasty tore the dress off and dumped it in a trash barrel.

"We'll git him, one of these days. They's more ways to kill a dog 'sides choke him to death on okra."

Finch-Smith had gotten permission for Gil Wolfe to attend the progress report the previous week and now Wolfe was back in his office with more questions. Why hadn't anyone mentioned the number of deaths during August? Three surveyors and a chopper pilot had gone down at Prudhoe. A driller had fallen into the Yukon from the edge of a caisson and been swept away. Yet a newspaper article failed to include these deaths in a report on pipeline safety. Shouldn't the progress report have made some mention?

Finch-Smith explained the difference between pipeline deaths and deaths occurring among nonproject contractors. The surveyors were with an oil company over which APPLE had no control. The driller was a subcontractor to a state outfit building the Yukon River Bridge, for which APPLE guaranteed to cover half the cost. The company would hang the pipe under the bridge, the state would build a road over the top. They were, in a sense, pipeline deaths. But not deaths directly related to APPLE as a company. Gil settled for that.

As Finch-Smith talked to the reporter, he realized that Wolfe had changed from early spring. He dressed better, he'd cut his hair shorter, but the main thing seemed to be a change in attitude. His questions were as direct as always, but they seemed less loaded, delivered without the edge of belligerence he had once displayed in meetings.

He told Gil Wolfe of other accidents, just to make sure it didn't look like a whitewash. There had been a multiple stabbing incident near Old Man. A laborer had gone berserk, inflicting minor knife wounds on three co-workers, very nearly killing a job coordinator who stumbled into him during the struggle. At the pipe storage yard near Tonsina, an oiler had been paralyzed from the waist down when a forty-foot joint of pipe had slipped from the jaws of a loader and crushed his lower back. Finch-Smith denied that any of these accidents were a result of pushing to complete the job at any cost. There had never been a job, perhaps with the exception of atomic plants, with so much supervision and safety control.

The phone buzzed and Finch-Smith spoke briefly with Sherry. He looked at Wolfe.

"Speak of supervision and who shows up?" The door opened. Dan Curry stepped inside, saw Gil, hesitated.

"No, come on in; Mr. Wolfe just stopped by to chat about safety."

Gil shook hands with Curry and began to gather his materials, thanking Finch-Smith for his time. "Good to get the facts straight, at least. See you later, Dan."

Curry shut the door and took a seat near Finch-Smith's desk. "I must say, that Wolfe is a persistent sort. Has he been on to you much, lately?"

"A little." Dan shrugged. "Sounding me out, you know. Just waiting for me to give him an excuse to dig in. I suppose he'll get a good chance tonight. I'm having him over for dinner with Emil Bacich and your photographer."

"I never could understand why Bacich and Jim Miklov were so friendly. Jim usually doesn't have much patience with conservationists, preservationists. Whatever."

"Well, they'll be in a good mood tonight. I've got some news that may cheer Emil up. You won't like it much, though."

Finch-Smith raised his eyebrows.

"I've had to reroute about ten miles of your haul road between Sag River and Happy Valley. Nesting area for peregrine falcons. In fact, that's why I'm here this morning. I just gave B. R. Young the bad news. He got some engineers, patched us in on a conference call to Rogers in Fairbanks, and we came up with about a three-hundred-thousand-dollar expense for the road and more than twice that to relocate the pipeline to the west. It'll have to go aboveground, not through the river channel."

"A million dollars to save some falcons."

Dan looked at him.

"That's what the state hired me to do. I don't know, maybe the falcons would just move, but they're stubborn rascals. The people on the top floor aren't very happy with me."

"Million-dollar move saves falcons." Finch-Smith said. "Something like that. Has your staff alerted the newspapers about this yet?"

Curry shook his head. "We can barely answer our mail. I guess I'll put something out in a day or so, when I get all the facts together. Guess this makes a tough job for you."

"For me?" Finch-Smith looked off in the distance. "It has its positive aspects. You'd be surprised."

Emil Bacich showed up at the Currys' just as dinner was about to be put on the table. He brought a copy of the evening paper, the *Anchorage Daily News.* The lead story told it all. "APPLE's Million-Dollar Move Saves Birds." What a crock. You told me you were going to order the move, now they take credit for it.

Paula put a hand on Dan's shoulder. Everyone happy with wine? I'll have water, Gil Wolfe said.

Here's a good one. "When APPLE engineers learned that the route passed through a peregrine falcon nesting area, they immediately held a companywide conference to take action to change the blueprints. A company spokesman, Malcolm Finch-Smith, observed that the cost was high, but APPLE is concerned about the environment. If the last peregrine falcon disappeared from the face of the earth you couldn't make another one for a million, or any amount of money."

If it was the *last* one, Wolfe said, as Paula brought the water, you still couldn't make more. That's right, Emil said.

Dan helped Paula serve the steaks. Gil Wolfe looked as though he hadn't eaten a good meal in months.

Emil read on, commenting on almost every other line. At last he came to the end. "APPLE, the firm responsible for the design, construction and operation of the trans Alaska pipeline, announced that their decision to move the line and road was being made in conjunction with the office of the Joint Monitor, Dan Curry." In conjunction? They were given an order by you, Dan, and they make it look like they thought it up. Can never make another one, my ass. Dan laughed. Finch-Smith knew what he was doing. The story was accurate. Accurate? Gil Wolfe swallowed quickly. That Finch-Smith is some miserable son-of-a-bitch. What are you going to do about it? Would anyone like steak sauce? I have some steak sauce and some Béarnaise. Comes in a jar . . .

Cleaning up afterward, Paula was silent, moving through the living room, emptying ashtrays, picking up glasses. Dan followed, gathering napkins and coffee cups. Cornering her in the kitchen he asked what was wrong. The way she was banging things, not speaking, something had to be wrong.

She denied banging things, but, yes, something was wrong. When you can't even relax at dinner without arguing over the future of Alaska, something is definitely wrong. All she ever heard was the pipeline. She began to cry. They held each other in the kitchen and later in bed, but it didn't seem to help. Dan asked her if she'd like to go away. She wouldn't, not alone again. The pipeline was planning a two-week slowdown, practically a shutdown, around Christmas. Some of the contractors were closing down for three weeks. They could take the triangle. Fly down to San Francisco and stop off in Hawaii for a week on the way.

It might help.

Without Hope, Larry found the Montez Club a different scene: without hope. It was Saturday and there weren't more than six girls in the place. The odds were thirty to one. Since four of the girls had dates, the chance of finding someone to dance with was just about nil.

Al drank moodily, watching the blond, Gloria, stoop at a table taking an order. Gloria had great legs. Larry watched, too.

"You can have her for a hundred bucks," Al said. "*If* she likes you."

"*If* she likes me?" The glass slopped some beer on his arm. Larry wiped it off. He was getting a little drunk.

"That's what she told me Thursday night. She said she liked me and I could have her for a hundred, so I asked what she'd charge if she didn't like me. She told me that she didn't make a date if she didn't like the guy."

Make a date! On Fourth Avenue in Anchorage a hooker asked Larry: "Wanna date?" Larry, walking around town with a sore throat and fever had brushed on past. Funny. Last spring he had spent evenings in Fairbanks and Anchorage and the girls asked if he wanted a party. Now it was a date.

Larry watched the girl. A few weeks away from Hope and he was already horny. He supposed it was the atmosphere of the camp. You could feel sexual tension in the air. Larry shook his head sadly as Gloria came up to the bar with her tray and began moving empty glasses to Maggie.

"I'd as soon have the redhead," Al Godwin said, smoothing his moustache down. Traces of beer foam showed in it above his lip. "That's a hell of a woman, and her old man's a jerkoff."

"Ed? He's okay." Larry turned around so he couldn't see any of the women. The band had just come in and was scattered around at tables, talking before going to the stand. "*If she likes you.* That's really depressing."

Ahgutuk, the little Eskimo laborer, walked up the center of the dance floor. He'd been hanging around the pool tables in back.

"Lot of money for a lay," Al said.

"It's not the money that's depressing. Look at what we've got in this town. You come in for a night and you don't score with the local girls, so what? Look at the odds. You try to dance and there's nobody. Maybe you don't get a single dance all night long. That's sad, but I could handle it. But imagine, you come in here with a hundred bucks, you find one of the few hookers, and she doesn't like you. There's rejection and there's rejection. I don't think I could stand coming down with a hundred bucks and not even scoring with the local whore."

Gloria went by and Larry seemed to panic.

Al nudged him. "I don't think she heard you."

"Some town. Can't even make it with the hookers."

"It'll get better," Al said. "Few months, there'll be more whores than you can shake your dick at. Price might even come down. Free competition. Isn't that right, Isaac?"

Isaac Ahgutuk focused on Al with great difficulty. His whole body wavered as he stood there beside the two.

"You buyin?" he asked.

Al ordered Isaac a beer.

To Larry it seemed that natives drank past the point of intoxication. He'd seen people passing out drunk in Keene and even at some of the parties in Walpole. But the natives often looked as though they were in another world altogether. They might weave slowly across the floor in a bar and stop in the middle of the room, oblivious to the noise and hilarity from tables around them. Their eyes seemed to be fixed on a point just off the floor. Isaac was like that now. The drink had come and he didn't notice. He might have been wondering where he mislaid his keys. Gradually he came out of it. He looked at Larry. "You buyin?"

Larry nodded. "Al bought you a beer. By your elbow.'

Isaac turned, his eyes passing over the glass of beer several times before he saw it. Still, when he reached, the move was sure, steady.

Al and Larry talked in low voices, turning away from Isaac for the moment. Eskimos, Al said, were the best mechanics in the world. The Canadian Air Force used them as jet mechanics. Trained Eskimos in a tenth of the time they could train a white Canadian.

Why was that? Larry wanted to know. Why should that be? Al thought it was because when they went hunting they watched every sign, every shape of the landscape, even turning back to see how it would look on the return trip. After five days they could retrace their way across a flat landscape of ice and snow, remembering every step. Maybe when they took engines apart they did the same thing.

Larry looked over at Isaac, slumped on the bar. Eskimo villages were sad places to visit, Al told him. Drunk natives everywhere, mothers offering to let you sleep with their daughter if you'd bring home some beer, filth in the streets and outside the windows of the shacks. If you visit Barrow, go in the winter, when it's frozen. The smell can get to you in hot weather. Or go in spring. When it stays near freezing.

The band started with an instrumental number, "Tequila."

Nobody got up to dance.

Isaac was asleep; Maggie shook her head when she brought refills to Al and Larry. Al had his arm over Isaac's shoulder. He told Maggie that the little man had had a busy day. She didn't say anything. Schultz, the Dutchman, stood in the near corner. Schultz had come last night; he was hired as a bouncer for weekends.

Larry looked at the dance floor. They were playing "Peggy Sue." All six of the girls were dancing now, two with guys Larry recognized from the sheet-metal crew. Lucky bastards.

"How come Eskimos can't drink?" Al said thickly. "I can drink. You can drink. Why can't Isaac drink?"

Isaac opened one eye. "You buyin?"

During "Yellow Ribbon" Isaac woke up and began patting his knee in time to the music, singing. A native woman had done that beside Larry in a Fourth Avenue bar last February. The song kept coming up on the jukebox and the woman would sing it even when something else was on. She'd asked Larry if he was in Alaska because of the pipeline. "Get back on the bus," she would sing and look at Larry, lips twisted in amusement, "go back to . . . *California?*" She'd swear then and struggle to light a cigarette or take another swallow out of the glass. Five minutes later she would be singing happily and then lean close to Larry. "Get on the bus." She stopped. "Go back to . . . Texas? Louisiana?" After she had named about ten states she stopped singing and poked Larry in the arm. "Where you from, anyhow?"

She'd never heard of New Hampshire. Kept asking for the state. Not the city, the state. Don't you know nothing? The state.

He told her that he was a writer and hadn't come to take a job from an Alaskan (and now that wasn't true; he had).

"I'm Aleut," she said. "Pribilof. Pribilof Islands." She began to swear. From what Larry could make out, something terrible had been done to the Aleuts of the Pribilofs, but when, and by whom, he could not determine. The woman looked around the room. A tall, rough white man with a potbelly and half his teeth missing was dancing dreamily in the center of the room with an even fatter native woman not more than half his height. When he turned, eyes closed, his face a mask of rapture, Larry got a look at his partner. She was one of the ugliest women he had ever seen. Her face was round and puffy and, in profile, went in across the nose as though someone had bent her face in with a baseball bat. They were both drunk, both smiling. Their friends, white men, native women, shouted encouragement from nearby tables. A man fell off his chair in the far corner of the room and no one moved him.

A native man about fifty went to the serving rail at the bar and waited.

"See him," the woman told Larry. "He's Eskimo. I'm Aleut. Hate goddamn Eskimo."

Larry studied the man's features. "How can you tell he's Eskimo?"

The woman found the question hugely funny. "Got his hand out and his mouth open. Eskimo." She swiveled her head back to Larry. "Paleface," she said, and began banging her glass on the bartop. The man behind the bar snatched the glass away from her, bringing it back a few minutes later, holding it away until she paid. On the other side of Larry, on one of the barstools shadowed by the wall where you had to squeeze through to get to the toilet, a woman pushed her glass over the bar edge and it shattered on the floor.

The man swore, striding quickly to where she sat. "Get out of here, you scum."

The woman sat up straight. To Larry's right, the Aleut was singing "Yellow Ribbon." The other woman mindlessly began to mouth obscenities. Some of them didn't make any sense at all.

The bartender threatened to put her out on the street. Finally he'd had enough. Lifting a section of the counter, he stepped around and dragged her off the stool, slamming her into the wall. Larry stared. He was, due to the angle of the wall, the only one in the place who could see what was happening.

"Goddamn slut." The bartender banged her against the wall and Larry heard her head hit the plaster. "Foul-mouthed little bitch."

He punched her in the stomach, banged her into the wall, punched her again. "Cunt." He backhanded her across the mouth and then slapped her. Turning, he kicked her, unlatched the door, and heaved her into the alley, slamming the door behind her. Going back behind the bar he smiled at Larry and wiped his hands on a towel. "You get em all in this business, you know what I mean?"

Everyone applauded the band and Isaac howled. "Yellow Ribbon" was a popular number at the Montez Club. Ed Booth had come in to see Maggie and he spoke for a few moments with Larry, asked about Hope and the kids. Larry had a letter. They were glad to be home and the kids missed him very much. The usual. Larry told him that Al Godwin was one of the two men who pulled them out of the water. Saved Netty's life. Al shrugged.

"He buyin?" Isaac asked.

Later, Larry and Al Godwin were discussing Eskimo sports. They do a kick, Al said, that you wouldn't believe. Both feet together. Up and down.

Larry had never seen it.

"Do you know the kick, Isaac?" Al shook him by the arm. "Isaac, you know the two-foot kick?"

Isaac nodded. Put something, a ball, he said, from a string. Six, seven feet up. Run, jump with both feet together, kick ball with feet together, and land feet together.

"I know a man in Barrow, can kick a stone right off the top of your head. But I can't do it."

Al leaned back to watch the dancers. It was a polka and only one couple really knew what to do. A young girl and a middle-aged man were at the far end, jitterbugging.

"They do sports with one hand, one leg, things you wouldn't think somebody could do. You ought to go sometime, you get a chance."

Isaac sat lost in thought.

"I can do the seal race," he announced. "I can do a good seal."

"What's that?" A slow number had begun. All the girls were up and dancing.

Al made tight fists and held them up to his chest, facing out. "They lie down and go on knuckles and toes by wriggling their bodies. Some of them make a seal noise."

"That must be tough on your knuckles. What do they do it on? Snow?"

"Last time I saw it they went across the hardwood floor of the City Gym on G Street. It's brutal."

"I can do it," Isaac said. "Got good knuckles." He held his hand out for Al. It trembled slightly.

Al patted Isaac's hand and turned away to watch the dancers.

"I think I may catch the next bus to camp," Larry told him, and Al looked at his watch. "I may go, too," he said over the sudden laughter from the tables between them and the dance floor. A woman shrieked and both Larry and Al looked out at the floor, startled, unable to make out what the trouble was. People at tables next to the dance floor were standing up and the dancers had begun to separate.

"Awk, awk" Larry heard. And then there was Isaac pitching off across the dance floor, barking to the left and right as he scattered dancers out of his path.

"Sheiss" Larry heard, and the Dutchman was making for Isaac. He scooped the Eskimo up easily and carried him to the side door, disappearing outside as if nothing had happened. The band went on.

Remembering the woman in the Anchorage bar, Larry dove through the doorway, followed by Al. Outside, the Dutchman was lecturing Isaac sternly.

"That does not go in zis bar. Such monkeyshines is not allowed. You vant Frau Booth should gif you eighty-six?"

Isaac shook his head and stumbled down the road toward the bus stop for the camp.

The Dutchman brushed off his hands. "Zese natives." He touched his forehead. "It's good ting I vork here. Like Herr Booth says, ven poosh comes to shoff, shoff hard. So now I work as shoffer. Take gut care, your buddy." He tapped his forehead again.

Sunday, Maggie, Ed and David Curry had a big midday dinner. The weather was good, sunny off and on through the day. The nights were cooler now, late in September; the camper trucks had thinned out along the waterfront. The town council had ordered David Curry to issue tickets to those who parked more than a night or two, but he had done little more than suggest that some of the families move their trucks every other day.

Town meetings were getting as raucous lately as they had been in the few years following the great parceling out of lots when the new town had been settled. Everyone who owned property in the old town was entitled to the same footage in new Montez, but they had to sign an agreement to develop the property within a certain period of time. There were squabbles over location, over excess undeveloped property from the old town. HUD had been called in at the beginning, but the price of their planning was a four-hundred-dollar charge for each lot. Lavinia had given the land away, intending that former homeowners have the land for nothing. A tax writeoff for the gift had been agreed to by the town fathers and denied by HUD. Owners of property in the old town refused to abide by the condemnation orders and said they would move the old houses five miles down the road to new sites. Houses in the old town mysteriously burned, and the blame was placed variously on HUD, jealous townspeople and angry contractors. No arsonists were ever convicted. Some of the property had been sold off to a group of San Francisco businessmen who promised to develop but didn't, and, it turned out, twenty percent of central Montez actually belonged to Japanese investors.

Still, as residents built new homes and got businesses going, the town had quieted. In 1969, with rumors of pipeline money and people coming in, the squabbling flared up briefly and then, until this year, settled down again.

Now the town was hopelessly split. The council claimed that they wanted to discourage growth that would leave Montez overdeveloped after the pipeline left. They voted down appropriations for new housing sites, would not approve new trailer parks or the expansion of old ones. APPLE had come in and offered the town nearly four million dollars to build a new sewage treatment plant, but the town, considering its taxes on the property across the bay and possible royalties, held off. APPLE contributed a million for impact studies and promised more if the studies showed that the pipeline was causing economic hardship to the town. In addition, the company offered to take over all maintenance costs on the public schools and to pay the entire cost of any new building resulting from impact. A tract of fifty modular homes was to be built for the company managers at the northwest edge of town, and at the end of the terminal project, sometime in early 1980, all but twenty of the houses and lots would be turned back to the town.

The council held back, fought expansion. One faction in town accused them of holding back because they already had money or wanted to create a tight market to inflate further the value of the holdings they were selling near Copper Canyon. Maggie and Ed Booth felt that the town should ride the crest of the wave. David Curry held with those who wanted to keep it small simply for the sake of preserving the amenities of small-town life. If town meetings went on as they had been going the last few months, David and his department would have to attend merely to keep order. Prices, property, costs were going up. Old-time residents who had never owned a home were now being forced out, forced to leave as landlords increased rents—up to $1,200 for a two-bedroom apartment.

Fear, conservatism, speculation and a nervous, intense greed pervaded Montez and all the towns along the pipeline route.

If Delta was crowded, Fairbanks was becoming inundated. Traffic crept through the streets. Making a phone call, always a problem in Fairbanks, now became a nightmare. You might wait a minute or two to get a dial tone. When you got the dial tone, the circuits would usually be busy. If they weren't busy and you made a connection, the connection was often a bad one.

The police department deserted regularly and headed north, once the men found that pipeline jobs paid guards a thousand a week and better. It was not possible to bring in new men, for there was no place to live, not on an ordinary salary. The Salvation Army hall was filled to capacity, men living hand to mouth for weeks until the number came up at the hall and they went from Sally handouts to the big dollar at Five Mile, Wiseman, Chandalar, Sag River, Prudhoe. It was rags to riches. For those stuck in the middle, it was bitter, burdensome.

APPLE had rented whole floors of local hotels, filled the streets of Fairbanks with green pickup trucks (green APPLES). Roy Rogers and his management operations team (the MOT Squad) met with the city fathers. Texan jokes were told. Why do Texans wear those hats bent up on the sides? So you can get four in the front seat of a green APPLE. Texan and green APPLE jokes and then the meetings. The situation would be studied and then APPLE would pay. Roy Rogers stood up, grim. We have to get our sights on these problems. We've done our cost and scheduling. Fairbanks needs a chance to plan, too. Outside, horns blared in the streets. Afterward, two girls asked Roy if he wanted a double date.

When supper was over, Maggie, Ed and David moved to the balcony overlooking the harbor. Maggie and Ed had coffee. Since he was off duty, David said he'd stick with bourbon.

Next week, Ed said, the company would bring in a Sikorsky Skycrane. It had six-bladed rotors seventy-two feet in diameter, and could lift a D-4 Cat assembled, a D-7 in two trips. There were only seven commercially used Skycranes in the world, and APPLE had managed to charter one for the weekend to put the drills and equipment on Copper Canyon. The crane would come back the first week in November to take everything off the ledge for the winter. By then the pioneer road would be roughed in and blasting nearly completed for the pipeline. In the spring the road would be finished and the pipe brought in.

David was almost embarrassing in his admiration for Ed.

"You really know the facts and figures don'cha? Hear that, Maggie, old Ed's got it down, don't he?"

Maggie looked out to the harbor.

"I think," she said, "Ed must have memorized every blueprint they have over there. I heard him talking to that writer from *Tomcat,* and it was all this many million barrels, so many gallons per minute and miles per hour."

"*Tomcat.* I talked to that guy, too. Sure I did. In the club, I talked to him. Told him all about it," he said, as if to himself. "Told that *Tomcat* man we're getting three thousand new people this year. Might go to seven thousand next year. Six cops. Told him all about it. I wonder if I'll be in it. I didn't see anything about us next month in the back of the magazine."

Below, a car pulled up in front of the laundromat next door. Two women and a half dozen kids got out. A native man, shirt open to the waist, stumbled out of the shadows between two campers, pulling at his fly. He walked toward the White House and greeted two construction workers sitting on the stone wall along the small boat landing.

Maggie took it all in. "Used to be," she said softly, "I could sit up here after the season was over and not see a single person I didn't know. Now if I do happen to recognize someone on the street, half the time we're not speaking."

It happened in prison, it happened in the army, and it happened in pipeline camps. Somebody who had gone along quietly would suddenly and thoroughly go to pieces and, as if to make the outer world conform to the inner, begin breaking up his room. Sometimes it would happen in the mess hall, the laundry room or even on the job, but usually it happened in the man's own room.

Wiseman's first incident occurred during the middle of the afternoon when the camp was almost deserted. An oiler, Petter Larsen, a stolid, melancholy Norwegian, told his roommate he wasn't going to show. He didn't feel like going. Felt sick. The roommate went to work without giving him a second thought.

When the bullcook opened the door to Petter's room at two to make the beds and bring in fresh towels, he froze in the doorway, unable to make sense out of what he was seeing. The wall paneling had holes in it, some the size of a fist, others two or three feet across. The window was broken; the drapes were stuffed in one of the larger holes along with the shredded remains of a pillow. The mattresses were sprawled in one corner and the bed frames had been wrenched apart, and one of the side rails dangled from the ceiling where it had made a deep gash. The light fixture was gone, two wires dangling in its place. The table had been ripped from the wall and the closets had no doors. All of the drawers had been removed, their contents scattered, and the drawers themselves smashed to kindling.

There was a loud, shattering crash in the toilet. The bullcook tiptoed to the center of the corridor and peeked around the corner in time to see Petter, his face twisted in anger, smash the porcelain sink, torn from the wall, into a toilet bowl. Water ran out across the floor. Petter came out of the dorm a moment later, howled at the bullcook, and suddenly veered off down a line of barracks. The RCM, the bullcook and two security men followed a few minutes later, but Petter had headed across the river toward a large dome of rock. While the security man in charge called for more help, the other three followed Petter at some distance. A moment later they saw him emerge on the knob, throw back his head, and scream piercingly at the distant mountaintops. Then he dropped to his hands and knees, still shouting and howling.

"Jesus, Mary and Joseph," the RCM breathed. "Do you suppose he's in pain? Or is he just off his noggin?"

Petter stopped scrambling, looked around, and slunk off to one side of the knob, out of sight. Then he appeared halfway down, running, waving his arms, tearing at branches and low bushes growing among the cracks and shelves of the dome.

Petter was a big man, six-three, a solid 190 pounds. The guards, numbering eight, were equally divided among ex-cops and those who considered their jobs that of watchmen. The watchmen won out. The men would form a large circle and observe Petter, attempting to keep him in range so he wouldn't be lost. Later, when the workers came back into camp, they might find someone he'd listen to, maybe talk him down off the knob. In the meantime, he might tire himself out. The medic came, conferred with the camp manager, and said he wanted no part of sticking a needle in the man to quiet him down. He wasn't hurting himself or anyone else out there on the rocks. The RCM approached the knob and called Petter's name. Petter began biting the bushes and screaming through his teeth.

"Poor fellow's gone daft," the RCM said, and went in the shade to sit down.

When the men came back it turned out that Petter had no friends, not even the crane operator who usually worked with him. Some of the biggest men volunteered, and under those circumstances, even the medic was willing to give it a try. A party of twenty approached the knob; Petter watched them warily. Another hundred or more workers stood along the banks of the river, watching, among them Jill Jones and Bill Wiggins. If they got Petter down, there would certainly be a Medevac. Wiggins was already turning requests down even though several people literally begged him for a chance to get into Fairbanks. He would take Jill and five strong men. Maybe the medic. Half of the men in the group approaching Petter were doing so out of hope for a ride with him into town.

"Petter, come on down," one of them called.

"Hey, old buddy," another shouted, "how's about a nice plane ride? See the pretty country?"

The medic told them to all shut up. Petter was bouncing up and down as the men fanned out and surrounded the knob. He looked in all directions and, as the medic was preparing his hypo, Petter screamed and threw himself off the knob, tripping on an upended slab of rock, sprawling in the gravel at the feet of the men. Four piled on immediately and Petter lay so still that one by one they let go, fearing that he was unconscious or worse. Petter lay contentedly at their feet, staring at the fingers of one hand.

The medic knelt beside him and put the needle back in his bag.

"Petter," he said. "I would like you to get up and come back to the camp. Okay?"

Petter raised his eyes to the medic.

The medic extended his hand and Petter took it, allowing himself to be helped up and led back across the shallow river. An hour later, the medic called to the flight shack and said Petter was ready to travel. He had taken a mild sedative and should give no trouble. Of course he would be strapped in at the rear of the plane.

An ambulance would meet him at the airport by the cab stand.

Wiggins shut his eyes, turning away from the crowd. "Please," a man pleaded, pulling at Wiggins's sleeve. "My girlfriend's in town for the week, I could see her for an hour or two. I haven't seen her for three months. I'll pay, Bill, anything. You name it."

Jill stood to one side, tearing up a sheet of paper into small pieces. She put them in a hard hat and whistled through two fingers.

"We'll do it by lottery. There's five pieces with an *X;* they go to Fairbanks."

The men surrounded her, grabbing for numbers. There were two extra and Jill unfolded them. "Zeros," she told the men. "Okay, see what you got." The fellow who wanted to see his girlfriend whooped loudly. There were curses, a few cheers. Five smiling men followed Jill to the medic's shack where Petter waited. They escorted him back to the plane, and the conversation was about what bars they might go to, whether or not there would be time to get laid, who they'd call. Petter and Jill walked together. He was docile. She stood aside to let the others on the plane and Petter obediently waited at her side. She told him to get in and he sat down, letting her strap him to the reclining stretcher seat. The mood in the cabin was festive.

As they took off, the men in front cheered. "Tommy's Elbow Room Express," one called out. Three men began to sing "Hurray, hurray, I'm going away with the men in the little white coats." Petter Larsen stared quietly up at the ceiling, lost in thought.

The plane pulled up along the side entry at the Fairbanks airport. When Jill opened the door, the man who wanted to call his girl ran right on into the terminal without waiting to unstrap Petter. Wiggins had promised to stay on the ground for three hours, but threatened that he'd leave anyone who wasn't back in time.

He taxied the plane alongside a small hangar and asked Jill to meet him by the cab stand.

"I'll call a cab for us to make sure," she shouted, but Wiggins couldn't hear her.

"I got a friend home on R&R," one of the escorts said in a loud voice. "I bet he'd come out and get us. Maybe line us up with a chick."

"Shit," another said. "I only brought thirty bucks!" He stomped his feet in anger. "I could have got laid and I forgot to bring money."

The man next to him flashed a roll of bills, peeling off two hundreds. "Take this. Give it to me payday."

"Let's get Petter inside," Jill urged. "Sooner we get him in the ambulance, sooner we can go."

The terminal lounge was crowded. The evening Wien flight from the camps was due in soon, bringing back the men coming home on R&R. Girlfriends, wives, parents clustered eagerly around the reception gate for the pipeline flight, craning their necks at any activity out on the ramp. The army had brought in a large contingent of GIs from Richardson in Anchorage and they filled up the center hall, waiting for transportation to Wainwright.

Jill, Petter, and the four remaining escorts moved to the cab ramp and Jill went outside, looking all around the parking area. There was no ambulance.

She came back and one of the escorts was gone, making a phone call to his buddy. She looked at Petter, who stood patiently next to the car rental desk, and said she had better call the hospital as well as a cab. She went to the phone. After several tries she got a dial tone, but the hospital line was busy. The phone wouldn't work at all after that.

She went back to where Petter and the escorts had been and couldn't find them. Apparently the ambulance had come after all. Wiggins surprised her, catching at her elbow.

"Well, sweetheart," he said, smiling happily, "let's go check out the action."

"I'm not sure if the ambulance came," she said, still looking for the escorts. They went outside. There was no ambulance. The escorts weren't around.

"Maybe they put him aboard and left."

Just then two of the men came outside and waved from the next entrance. "He get off all right?" one shouted, and Jill shook her head, hurrying after them.

"I left him with you," she said. "Didn't you put him on the ambulance?"

The two men exchanged glances. "I thought you said we should call for a cab."

"No, I went to call a cab."

It took fifteen minutes, but they eventually located all five escorts. None of them knew what had happened to Petter.

"He's lost." Jill stared across the mob in the waiting room. "We lost him. I don't believe it."

"My girl's coming down to pick me up. Can I just go?"

Wiggins doubled his fists. "You bastards lost him, you can find him. You leave now, you're not riding back on my plane."

They spread out and made two passes through the lounge, Bill explaining to the airport cop who followed them on the second pass what they were looking for. The ambulance came, sitting outside the cab stand, lights flashing. Then men went outside and began looking while Bill explained they were having some difficulty with the patient.

On a hunch, Jill went to the row of army buses and, braving the comments, boarded each bus to look over the men. On the third bus, still half empty, she found Petter sitting behind the driver, who had turned in his seat to talk. Petter looked at the man with an intent, yet blank, expression as the driver told him loudly what he would do if he were mayor of Fairbanks.

Jill tapped the driver on the shoulder. Leaning forward, she explained what was wrong, who Petter was, where they were taking him.

"I'll be damned," the driver said, as she led Petter off the bus. "I'd have never figured him for a nut. I thought he was one of us."

Larry waited in the telephone line outside the mess hall, rereading the letter from Hope. His grant was already long spent. The insurance had lapsed because he hadn't made a payment when they left Walpole; all the medical bills from Anchorage would be out of pocket. The air fare was another $600. Hope had outlined the expenses and asked if he could hold out until Christmas, perhaps come home on R&R and then go back for a second hitch.

There were two ahead in line. One telephone for four hundred men. The phone was on the wall next to the coat racks where people came out of the dining room. No privacy.

Larry read the letter again. It sounded cold, dispirited. She'd signed it "With love," but there was no sense of love anywhere in the letter.

He folded it. The man at the phone was turned to the wall, speaking in a low voice. "Honey," Larry heard. "Aw, honey."

The two men ahead of Larry were talking about the weather. More dust on the mountains. Cold nights. Already had snow in Thompson Pass. Snowed hard at Galbraith this morning. The first man talked in quick, jerky phrases. He hated the weather in Montez. Dry cold was okay, but Montez could freeze you at forty degrees above.

Finally the man on the phone hung up and looked sheepishly at the line of men, now ten or more deep. The next man called, snapping at the operator for making him repeat his name.

He didn't turn away to speak. "Listen you bitch," he shouted, "I don't want you bugging my brother about when I'm coming home. You'll see me when I'm goddamn good and ready to come home. What? Listen, you dumb twat, you fly out here to Montez, you can goddamn well get right back on the plane . . . I'll shit meet you at the Montez Club."

Mart, the warehouseman, turned to Larry. "Shame we don't have more phones. Or at least some privacy."

Larry nodded.

"You hear some awful things standing here."

Larry nodded.

The man at the phone was shouting obscenities.

"I heard a guy last week asking his wife if she still loved him, telling her he was sorry he'd beat her up. Broke her arm, it turned out." Mart clucked his tongue. "These are some working conditions, huh? I did time in a federal pen. The guys would have rioted, they had to live like this. No privacy on the phone. Two guys to a room. No hot lunch. Stale sandwiches. Movie theater where you can't even see if you don't sit in the first two rows. That's right. We would have rioted."

The man at the phone demanded to speak to Melissa. "Melissa," he crooned. "Hi, sweetheart, it's Daddy. Are you being a good girl? You doing what your mommy tells you to do? What's that? Hey, Daddy loves you. Let's hear a big kiss. Big kiss." He lit up. "Okay, honey, you hang up now. No, I already talked to Mommy. Bye, sweetie."

He hung up the phone and stood for a moment with his hand on the receiver, smiling.

Mart dialed, hung up, tried again. After five minutes he got the operator, but the line was busy at home. "We'd have had a riot," he told Larry, handing him the phone and trudging back to the end of the line to wait another turn.

Larry stretched the phone cord so he could face the corner. He tried to keep his voice low, but the connection was bad. Hope said she had tried to explain to the grant director that Larry was still doing research. The children would be disappointed if he missed Thanksgiving, but as long as he got home at Christmas, it would be fine. Larry asked: should he come home on R&R or stick it out?

Hope thought *he* should decide. After all, he was the one away from home.

"Are you happy to be home?"

"I can't hear you."

"Are you happy to be home?"

"God, yes, the leaf season is great. I've gone for some drives. Alaska may be magnificent, but New England is lovely. I've got a poem started. And I'm going to a reading next week. That German, Kurt Schall, who used to teach at Keene State. He's doing the elf king and playing the theremin."

Larry frowned. Schall was the curly-haired smart ass that got kicked out of Keene State College after the Kent State shootings. He remembered that Kurt had made much of the play on Kent and Keene in some of his "poetic-revolutionary" speeches. How distant that all seemed now. And irritating.

"Do you miss me?"

"What? I can hardly hear you, Larry."

"Do you miss me? Are you lonely?"

"Going where? There's a bad echo on the line now."

Larry glanced over his shoulder. The line had pressed closer.

He cupped his hand over the mouthpiece, enunciating carefully. "Do . . . you . . . miss . . . me?"

"I still can't hear. This is a shame. And I bet it costs a fortune. You'd better write. Take care of yourself, Larry, and don't worry, we're all fine. Can you hear me?"

Larry stared at the wall, the scribbled phone numbers, the obscene suggestions.

"I hear you."

Vern Blue lay on his back, a cola can resting on his bare chest. Pam Allen, against the wall, snuggled into his side. She was going home on R&R and this would be their last night together for a few weeks. Twice, when someone knocked at the door, they had lain still and waited for the visitor to leave. Pam found this difficult and it showed in her eyes, darting from Vern to the door, but his tiny whispered plea was enough. Now he reached down beside the bed, fumbled through his pants pockets with one hand, and brought out a scrap of newspaper.

"I saw this in *Pipe 'n' Hot News* and I thought . . ." he scrunched the paper flat on his belly and Pam steadied the cola can. "I thought I could read it." He sighed heavily. "It's not by me, but it's how I feel and if I could read it . . ."

"Sure." Pam rubbed the palm of her hand gently along his side, making Vern shiver momentarily. "I like to hear you say poems to me."

He squinted sideways. "How'd you know it was a poem?"

"I saw it when you held it up."

He looked from the poem to her like it was a hand of cards.

"You seen this poem already, the one about saying goodbye?"

"No, did you write it?"

He checked. "Rex Lambert wrote it. I didn't write it. It's Rex Lambert and I don't know who he is, but he's a goddamn fine poem writer. You sure you didn't read this?"

"Nope."

"It's called 'Words That Mean Goodbye.' "

"I didn't read it, Vern."

"Okay, then." He sniffled loudly and took a sip from the can, setting it back on his chest. "Words that mean goodbye," he said.

Lying beside you, loving you more than myself,
I cannot find the words that mean "goodbye."

My tongue is like a frozen river, my heart is heavy
And dark at the thought of leaving you here.

Outside, winter dawns like pale fire over Fairbanks.
The cold, bitter air cracks white like a dying ember.

Tomorrow night, when the southern camps settle
Into dull and dreamless sleep, weary with the laughter

Of lonely men, I will ask myself again to trust
That this is not forever, that we will be together soon.

Lying beside you, loving you more than myself,
I cannot find the words that mean "goodbye."

Vern sniffed. "Rex Lambert," he added huskily, and turned to look at Pam. She was blinking her eyes, crying silently.

"That's so beautiful. It has all our loneliness, yours, mine, all the men, their women."

Vern swallowed hard and his mouth trembled. "It makes you wonder if all this is worth it," he managed to say at last.

Pam sobbed, "I know. I know. That's why, when I see these men out here and I think what they're going through, I just have to do something to make it better. They come to bed with me, and for just that little time, they don't seem so lonely."

"My tongue is like a frozen river. A frozen river."

Pam, her eyes moist, a line of tears on each cheek, allowed a faint smile. "Funny, it's such an easy thing for me to do, and yet it means so much to them. Don't you think so, Vern?"

His eyes shone in the half light as he looked at her, brushing a damp curl away, gently, with one finger.

"I love that about you, Pam. You are so generous." He began suddenly to blubber, turning into her, upsetting the can of whiskey. "So generous."

She held him.

"Generous."

Outside, down the long hallway, she heard the laughter of lonely men with hearts that were heavy and dark.

Crews from Coldfoot had pushed north down into a long flat valley with a ridge at the far end. Over this ridge, Wiseman road builders were bringing their section of haul road toward Coldfoot in a sweeping curve. Where the curve bottomed out, stakes had been driven, two pairs a few feet apart, marking the "no man's land" where the final linkup would take place. Both camps put up arguments as to whose crew should dump in the final load of dirt that would finish the 360-mile road from the Yukon River to Prudhoe Bay. A compromise was reached. The final load of gravel would be dumped by Wiseman and smoothed out by Coldfoot. A truck driver and operator were chosen to represent each camp.

Finch-Smith was delighted that Wiseman's choice had been Jill Jones, and he made certain that Miklov took extra close-ups of her as the vehicles were brought into position. A hand-painted billboard had been erected alongside the spot by the carpenters, and one of the camp artists, with help from some friends, had created a landscape with the road, the camp names at each end, the date. He stood by now, brush in hand, to put in the exact time.

B. R. Young, beaming under his white APPLE hard hat, allowed Miklov to move him around for shots with the equipment, with various officials. Dan Curry and Roy Rogers stood on the sidelines, chatting, relaxed for a change. A contingent of workers from each camp gathered at both ends of the narrow gap, which had been partially filled in by hand so that Jill's load would, in fact, complete the job. Reporters drifted in and out and Miklov was continually shooing them away from his photos.

A portable PA system had been set up, and Miklov finally got it moved to a spot where he could catch the dump truck backed up to the gap and the dozer sitting alongside, pointed in the opposite direction, ready to spread the gravel into place. Young, his vice-presidents, and Roy Rogers would group at the back end of the dozer, just under Jill Jones's cab window. Once Young was set, the movie cameras moved into place with Jim. Other film crews had set up across the gap to get head-on shots of the dozer.

At the last minute, Curry was pushed into the picture to fill a spot alongside the truck's bumper (which was a beam of steel about even with his shoulder). Dan rested a hand on the deeply ribbed tire that stood a few inches above his head, but the safety man came over and warned him off, moving the line a few feet from the truck.

Jill's steward, the Italian, climbed up in the truck and sat down on the opposite side of the cab. As high above ground as they were, no one would see him in the pictures.

"Hi, G'looch," Jill said in a low voice.

"Hey, why the frown? Don't you know you're about to become a part of history? The woman selected to finish one of the most expensive dirt roads ever built."

She shrugged and looked out at the cameras, reporters, workers.

"I'm getting laid off tomorrow. They said the road was done and they don't need so many drivers. I got selected for that, too."

"I heard. But it's not just you, you know. We're losing eight drivers. Laborers are dropping ten men, operators another six. You go back to town, you'll be out again in a week, I guarantee it." He pulled a card out of his pocket, scribbled a name and phone number on it, and pressed it into her hand. "I guarantee it."

She tucked the card into her jeans. "Thanks, I will."

"Tell him hello from me. That make it any better?"

Jill shook her head. "Bill Wiggins took off at two this morning to Medevac the super who had the heart attack. He hasn't got back yet."

"Maybe the guy wasn't that sick and Bill's waiting to fly him back up from Fairbanks."

"I had flight call for me. The super's in intensive care. Bill took off about five. He never showed up. At least he hadn't by lunchtime . . ."

Jill was being called by B. R. Young. She stuck her head out the window.

"When I give you the word, you drop the load. What's going to happen is, we give our talks, me last, and then everyone gets a picture for the record. Then dump when I say. Got it?"

Jill put her arm on the door and leaned out as Miklov had told her to do.

"Maybe—" the steward said, "—maybe Bill picked up an emergency call on the way, either from another camp or on the emergency channel. Never know. Could be a hunter in trouble, somebody else down in a plane. It would have been practically daylight by the time he got up here. I can't see why he would have trouble."

Outside, Roy Rogers extolled the cooperation of state and federal agencies that made the permit possible, the wonderful cooperation among various crafts, the spirit of the men—and women—that had built a 360-mile highway over treacherous terrain in only five months.

The vice-presidents were brief. B. R. Young considered the road a tribute to the tough, frontier Americans who had taken a first great step in taming, without destroying, the great Alaskan wilderness.

Miklov framed the scene in the viewfinder of his Hasselblad: Wabco truck, D-9 dozer, business suits and hard hats, frozen smiles. Necktie tossed askew by the breeze. Catskinner wearing a plastic orchid in the lapel of his striped denim jacket.

High above the others, Jill looked off into the sky. A Canada Jay, or Camp Robber, lit on the side mirror, just over Jill's head and, like her, cocked its eye at the sky.

Miklov pressed the release; the scene disappeared into the camera. History.

He rolled off two more and stepped back. The fill lights went on. Cameras began to whir.

Jill looked down just as B. R. Young spoke.

"Drop it, baby," he said.

It was bad, sitting on the runway, waiting for Wien to take everyone out. Most of the passengers were going on R&R. The terminations had been staggered over three days and Jill was in the last bunch. Even the men laid off were happy to see the plane circle in. Jill had prayed it would be the Navaho. But she knew in her heart that Wiggins was gone. Of course there had been a search—and it would continue another few days. At the same time, the RCM had suggested they put out a possible stolen aircraft alert to Canadian and northwest airports. Jill had overheard him in the mess hall.

"I'm not saying the poor fellow didn't, God forbid, go down in the mountains somewhere. I'm only saying that it was clear weather, just a wee bit of breeze blowing, and not a peep out of his radio after he left Fairbanks. Crazier things have happened. Hell's bells, if a man wanted to, he could be in Mexico by now, someplace no one would ask any questions, know what I mean?"

Turning around, Jill had thrown a full cup of coffee at him. A dozen men swore it was an accident, and one even pointed out a smear of jelly on the floor where she slipped.

The plane pulled up in front of the crowd and one by one they filed aboard, cracking jokes about town and old ladies and going for a little I&I—intercourse and intoxication.

After too long a time, the plane picked up and climbed out of the ring of hills and mountains surrounding Wiseman. The river gleamed below. Snow was creeping down the mountainsides. The next storm would leave traces in the lowlands.

Jill pressed her face to the window and peered intently at the scene below, into ravines, up cliffs, over ragged mountaintops and down again. She penetrated crevasses and dark, shadowed valleys, searching the corners, the hidden places: Alaska and its secrets.

Chapter Two

NASTY HAD BEEN laying for Leslie Collins ever since the "dress incident" (as it came to be known among the officials who were called in to negotiate with the unions involved) and his chance finally came. Collins had reported that few of the ironworkers who were going up on the barges to rig loads were wearing life jackets. This was a violation of OSHA policy and Collins, as assistant safety man, went to the dock and told Tiny, the foreman, what had to be done.

Nasty complained that he hadn't never fell in the water while rigging and he didn't intend to start now. Tiny told him life jackets were ridiculous, considering the height a man could fall, say on a double-stacked bargeload of housing modules.

Collins persisted and the next day Tiny's crew went to work in life jackets. Nasty worked very slowly, constantly watching over the edge, creeping along the modules as if terrified of falling.

The dock superintendent, Jack Price, asked what the snafu was, and Nasty told him Collins insisted the work be done that way. It was a one-man "slow wobble" all morning. Then, at lunch, Nasty called a safety meeting. What if a man was unconscious in the water? Life jacket wouldn't help. An ironworker in a motor launch should circle around all day to pick men up. And how about the ladders they used to climb on the barges? The tide moved them up and down so they couldn't be secured properly. What was needed, then, were ship's gangplanks with railings on both sides, a swivel foot at the base to account for tides, cross-treads down the ramp for traction. The ironworker's fab shop could put it together. And, considering safety, why should composite crews set the modules in place? Let the whole crew be ironworkers, with a few carpenters to make the final placement measurements. They already had a carpenter hurt bad, trying to play rigger.

The wobble spread. Whenever management, at any level, asked what was going on, the men said it had been Leslie Collins's idea. Collins spent much of the day denying it, but he was in the doghouse. Meanwhile the wobble hit other crafts; the stewards for the laborers, pipefitters and carpenters called in business agents, complaining that jurisdiction had been violated.

An ironworker got into a fistfight with a sheet-metal worker installing a ventilator grid in a prefab steel building. Another business agent was summoned.

An operating engineer moved a loading platform that had been used for ironworkers erecting the steel prefabs, and to help a man out, he transported a load of pipe. The teamster warehouseman reported it to his steward, claiming that the work should have been performed by a teamster forklift driver, not an operating engineer.

According to the general project labor agreement, unions involved in construction of the trans Alaska pipeline had agreed not to strike or to cause a work stoppage. The company warned those engaged in the wobble that they could be terminated. Each union promptly went into a safety meeting lasting from seven in the morning to five-thirty at night. The ironworkers were granted the man in the motorboat and the two gangplanks. The composite rigging crew remained the same but would be bossed by an ironworker foreman. The ventilator grids would be installed by ironworkers, but the fans belonged to sheet metal.

The teamsters, claiming that Leslie Collins had put them up to it, demanded and obtained four ambulance drivers, day and night shift on both sides of the bay, as well as a standby Medevac plane. The warehouseman who complained about the operating engineer on the forklift received an extra day's pay. The laborers and pipefitters remained in safety meetings, some said because they hadn't thought up any demands yet. The operators worked at intervals, calling safety meetings every few hours during the day. Their men spent much of the day in transit.

Larry Ransom walked down to the dock, hoping to catch the operating engineer foreman for his signature on a time card. Missing him again, he decided to wait in the ironworkers' dry shack. Nasty was leaning back in the corner, looking at the latest *Pipe 'n' Hot News.* He told Larry he liked the story he'd done, it was in the best Alaskan spirit.

Larry's story was about the new Sikorsky Skycrane, which had turned out to be much more powerful than anticipated. Riggers at Copper Canyon were surprised to see it carry not only D-4 Cats, but a few D-9s and several tons of Pourvex dynamite. It was only when a worker noticed the unusual interest the Skycrane had in bare arms that they realized this was a lone mosquito refusing to call it quits for the season. When it tried to mate with the Sikorsky, a general alarm had been sounded, but the Skycrane seemed to take it well enough. Further difficulties had arisen when a crew of black bears had refused to hibernate, demanding union cards and work rigging on the mosquito loads.

"I suppose I should do another one about the big wobble. Begin with bears demanding chastity belts to protect themselves from Texans trying to become sourdoughs."

Old man Dale laughed himself into a coughing fit. "You piss in the Yukon yet?" he asked Larry.

"Pissed in it at fifty below."

"On it," Tiny said. "At that temperature."

"No, in it. They were making holes with a steam pipe to check the thickness of the ice bridge, so I got there before it froze over."

"Now ya got to lay a native gal and wrestle a bear," Dale told him, coughing again. It was bad today. "Or, better, try it the other way around."

"I done it the other way."

Everyone looked at Nasty.

"I humped a bear."

"I believe it, too," Tiny said.

"I'll tell you about it sometime. It ain't a pretty story."

Larry hung his hard hat on a peg and sat at the table. "I hear they got a junior sourdough test for Texans."

Nasty peeked at him over the top of the paper.

"Instead of urinating in the Yukon, having intercourse with an aboriginal and engaging a bear in a wrestling match, Texans can tinkle in a creek, masturbate in the woods and badly frighten a bunny rabbit."

The men traded dirty stories, most of which Larry had heard already. His new roommate was an avid collector of them and wrote the best down in an appropriately filthy and dog-eared notebook. At least he didn't snore.

Eventually the talk got around to R&R and what you could do. Nasty planned to hold off until Christmas and go back to Gretna, maybe bring his wife back and keep her in Anchorage. Tiny was thinking of Hawaii, but he'd been there too often. Sonny, the native trainee, was going to Las Vagas on a free trip. All he needed to do was buy some chips. Air fare, meals, room were free. The guys thought he was crazy. Sonny laughed. He'd come back fifteen hundred bucks ahead last year.

"This guy 'L.C. from Montez' has a song in here," Nasty said. "It's like that 'Sixteen Tons.' "

"I seen it," Tiny told him. "You ain't going to sing it."

"Jist the chorus and the last verse. It's the truest thing they ever did put in this paper."

Dale nodded, coughed, and lit up another smoke.

Nasty's voice was gravelly, but pleasant.

You work seventy hours and what the heck?
Uncle Sam takes half out of your paycheck.
St. Peter don't you call me 'cause I can't quit,
Those deducts just don't leave me shit.

"I noticed it didn't say 'shit' in the paper," Tiny told him. "How'd you ever figure out what the blank was for, numbnuts?"

"It rahmed, you humongous, sorrowful sack of horseturds."

"Sing," Dale gasped.

For nine long weeks I toiled away,
And I sent home what was left of my pay,
R and R came and I had me a fit,
'Cause my wife run off and left me with shit.

"I wonder who the dude is, wrote that," Tiny said. "Prob'ly works for Hyatt and Rueter. Poor bastard, bet it happened to him, too."

"Wouldn't be the first time," Nasty said. "I knowed a guy in Iraq, sent home 'bout twelve, thirteen thousand, gone without drink or a woman for four months. Got back and his old lady run off with the kid next door."

"That's nothing." Tiny pointed a finger at Dale. "You remember that redheaded Swede, the big honcho on the Adak job? Well, he stayed out eleven months, sent home thirty thousand bucks, and not only had she run off with his dough, she'd stripped the goddamn house down to the bare floor, cashed in his insurance and sold both his cars. I mean, you want to see one sorry son-of-a-bitch, you should have seen him when he come back out to work."

"I been married three times so far," Dale said. "This last one I finally got smart. You work like this, you don't want no woman you care that much about, just one you can get along with good." He spit a hocker in the corner. "That way she goes chippying around, what do you care, huh? Long as she's there when you get back home a few weeks."

"Nobody comes 'round my old lady," Nasty laughed. "She's so mean, I'm the only man can stand her. An' ugly? She'd scare the buzzards off a gut wagon."

"I bet she's not," Sonny said.

Nasty pulled out his wallet and flashed her picture at Sonny, who shook his head.

"Well, she's got nice eyes."

"Crossed. An cain't hardly see out of the left one. But God help me, men, I love that woman. I bring her up here some time, she can arm rassle. Put that college boy down on the table, I bet."

"I can see where this kind of life would be rough on marriage," Larry said, since everyone was looking at him. "Doesn't give you much of a home life."

"You got the worst deal," Nasty told him. "You up and married one of them beauts. Where you say she's living?"

"Walpole." Larry frowned at Little Nasty. "New Hampshire." He resented him for what he'd tried that night after the celebration, although he found it hard to stay angry considering what Nasty had done in finding him the job.

"Well, if you don't think they's some guys trying to chippy around with her back in Walpole, you must have got born this morning."

"Hee, hee," went Tiny. "They'll back her up to the wall and give her the pole."

Old Dale nearly had himself another coughing fit, and he went outside where he wouldn't have to listen to any more jokes. Larry went with him.

That night Larry got a letter from Hope, filled with news about the kids. Then he went to see a movie about a man who had been asleep from birth and awakened after thirty years. The man was a child, but Larry found himself fascinated not so much by the problems of educating and caring for this man-child, but by simple scenes of men and women walking together in the sunlight, sitting in a living room by a fire and listening to music. They were scenes of another world, a life he had already forgotten. It seemed the slightest hint of emotion, the commonest touch of domesticity and love brought tears to his eyes. He wrote to Hope and in the process found himself crying. What, he wrote, can this mean? Is something wrong with me?

It was late, but Larry went to see Joe Akin and Al Godwin. Joe still hadn't gotten his family moved down to Montez. They were sitting in a darkened room, drinking. Joe was on the edge of his bed, Al on the edge of his, hunched forward, talking quietly.

Larry sat on the folding chair and didn't speak, letting his eyes get used to the light. He opened the can of Coke he'd brought and sipped at it.

"Same thing with the camp manager here," Joe said, his voice tired, sad. "He sends forty bucks a week to some orphanage in Korea. Forty a week."

"I never knew that." Al's voice was heavy, too—heavy with drink and sentiment. "He never told me that."

"Never told me. I found out from the rec director, Josie. There's lots of guys do things like that. And you know, here we are, living for free, eating steak, good food, know what I mean? Never want for a thing. And what do you take home a week?"

"Seven-twenty, sometimes seven-eighty."

"And I'm knocking down eight-twenty-five a week. Eight hundred and twenty-five goddamn bucks a week. Am I worth that much? Is there a man here that's worth it? Or that really needs it?"

"I don' need it."

"Guy sweeps the floors, takes out the garbage here, brings home six hundred a week. What do they call it? Menial. Menial labor. Some guy in Asia, South America works his ass off... works his ass right off for twenty, thirty bucks a month. Kids starving. You see them in the magazines? Big eyes, big bellies."

Al Godwin sniffled and Larry could see him in the dark, wiping at his eyes.

"I got kids. Do my kids need eight hundred bucks a week? Shit, no." He rattled the desk drawer. "I ain't even cashed my last three paychecks yet. There's guys here got nine or ten checks in their pockets when they go home on R&R. Their kids need all that?"

"My kids," Al cleared his throat. "My three boys are in football camp. Costs me three, four thousand a year, put those kids in a football camp. You and me learned football in a sandlot somewheres, didn't cost nothing. Maybe a new football once every couple of years."

"Guy told me you can keep a kid alive for thirty bucks a month. I could do that just like those guys do."

"My wife says they need football camp. They like the coach, he likes them. Bastard's probably in my living room right now, drinking my liquor."

The three sat in a long silence. Footsteps came and went down the long hallway. A washing machine, out of balance, chugged madly and clicked off.

"We're greedy, Al, you know that? We are really greedy. There's gen'rous people in the world, but we ain't among em."

"You loaned me two hundred," Larry said, and Al jumped.

"Jesus, I forgot you were here."

"That was nothing," Joe said. "Two hundred."

"You didn't even know me. That was pretty generous."

"Shit it was. Any American would do a thing like that. You'd lost your dough, had an accident. I just did what any American would do, isn't that right, Al?"

"I don't know," Larry said. "I've been in parts of the country where that wouldn't happen."

"Any *real* American."

"He's from out East."

"Oh. Yeah. Alaska's got real Americans. Anyhow, that was a loan. That wasn't generous. But forty a week—now, that's generous. Never think he'd be the kind of guy who'd do it."

The door opened. The three men shielded their eyes from the sudden intrusion of the light.

It was Dago John, the concrete foreman.

"Hey, you dudes wanna buy a ticket on a couple of whores?"

"Whores?"

"Yeah, we got a thing set up in town with these two foxy hookers from L.A. Five bucks a chance, get's you an hour. We're selling a hundred chances."

No one spoke.

"You can take both girls for a half hour, both of 'em together. One's a redhead, the other's kind of a blond. Big tits. Real pretty. Two on one for a half hour."

Joe put his head down. Poured whiskey into a cup.

Dago John clapped his hands loudly. "Or how's this, a half hour with one, followed by a half hour with the other?"

He waited in the doorway. "Or you can look the two girls over and take a whole hour with the broad of your choice. Drawing's going to be first payday in December and the winner don't need to be present. Five bucks a shot, huh, how can you beat that, hey?"

He waved a chain of tickets in front of Al.

"Well, check you later. Think about it, huh? I'm buying four tickets myself. I mean, what's twenty bucks, way I look at it?"

Over the next few weeks, Hope's letters began to change. She became cheery and often joked about walking fast, cold showers, general horniness and keeping busy. In one she enclosed a German poem about loneliness. Even if you didn't know the words, she said, the sound of the poem was lonely. Hope explained, as an afterthought, that she had heard the poem at one of Kurt Schall's readings. He was staying with a local artist, living in a refurbished henhouse, where he "hatched poems." The theremin, which was played by waving a hand over some kind of electric rod (Hope supposed), made the eerie music often heard in horror films. Kurt had gained some recognition, even in New York, by combining the theremin with German and English poems. Sometimes the lines were part English and part German, and you almost felt, listening, that you were understanding the foreign language and even, on occasion, that you no longer knew English. Everybody in Walpole was crazy about him.

Larry wrote back that Kurt was an ass, standing over that bunch of gadgetry, eyes closed, waving his hands like a hippie Lawrence Welk. There was no way he could get into the letter the disgust he had felt the one time he'd seen Schall perform, the skinny, sensitive rich kid, with his mop of blond curly hair. Gil Wolfe had hair like that when he'd first met him.

Hope answered and said that Larry sounded jealous. Jealous? You could say that. Living in camp was tough enough. A guy down the hall had been standing in the shower with a letter from his wife and a leather belt in his hands, no clothes on. He looked wild-eyed.

Larry asked what was wrong. His wife had addressed him as "George," not "Dear George" or "Dearest George." And instead of signing it "Love" she had written her name, nothing else. No x's and o's like usual.

Larry read the man's letter. She had, she said, written in haste to tell him her grandfather died and they were rushing to catch a plane. She didn't want him to worry if he called home and got no answer. He went back to the room, compared the sloppy handwriting of the letter to that on her other letters.

The man said he probably wouldn't have killed himself. He'd already calmed down when Larry came by and was just going to file for divorce as soon as the lawyers went to work in the morning.

Hope's next communication was a telegram. It said, three times, "I love you," and ended with a word: "Phone."

After an hour-and-a-half wait, Larry got through.

"I'm quitting my job. We're coming up to Alaska. Can you find us a place in Montez?"

"What?" was all he could say. "What?"

"It'll just be until spring. Can you find a place?"

"Not here."

"Anchorage then? I want to at least be in the same time zone."

"I can take my R&R, maybe find a place. You quit your job?"

"You said I could find work in Alaska. That's true, isn't it?"

"Oh, sure, plenty of work. But . . . I can't believe it. You're actually coming up here." Larry ran on for five minutes, describing the things they could do, places he could rent. And he'd be able to afford a phone call every day if he wanted. "I just can't believe it," he said over and over. "What made you decide?"

Her voice came back, dead, flat. "We'll both go crazy this way. There didn't seem to be any other choice."

They discussed what she should bring, how to rent the house in Walpole. She could fly up and use the truck around town, as he hadn't sold it yet. Or he could trade it in on a smaller car. Hope said she would come as soon as he sent for her. Anytime after November first would be fine.

November brought shorter days to the North Slope. After the second week, the sun would drop below the horizon and remain hidden until late January. The darkness would not be complete. For a few hours at midday the sky would grow lighter, a pale twilight that, as it threatened to break into a tinge of sunrise, began once more to dim into Arctic night. While temperatures in Montez hovered around the freezing mark, camps in the interior stood at zero and below. Those beyond the Arctic Circle, an imaginary line running about fifteen miles south of Prospect Creek, found the complete lack of sun as chilling as the subzero cold.

Vern Blue, riding a dozer down the gravel pad on which the pipeline would be built, watched the sun set at 12:58 P.M. It spread like a red line, clinging to the edge of the horizon, then ebbing away. The red stayed in the sky for a long while, and the flat, snow-covered earth was colored with it. The temperature was eighteen below, the air still. Vern and the other skinner, Fat John, had put up the canvas sides on their dozers. The heat from the diesel engine washing over them would make it possible to work in temperatures down to fifty below.

The dozer bumped and rocked over the frozen tundra, and Vern abruptly swung his Cat back onto the workpad. He'd polished off a full pint of Beam at lunch, and the warmth from the engine was making him drowsy. He hoped no one would notice his tracks off the pad. In summer it would be enough to get a man run off the job. Vern watched ahead. In the half light, in a landscape on which a man might see fifteen miles in all directions and not find a prominence anywhere, it was sometimes difficult to stay on a road or follow a course. Just last week a team of surveyors had run their snow machine off a six-foot embankment, confused by the diffusion of light from a cloudy sky on a white, level landscape. Days when the wind came, bringing total whiteouts, and the chill factor dropped to seventy, eighty, even a hundred and ten below, work efficiency fell to nothing. It was almost impossible to see, and no cold weather gear could keep a person warm.

Vern was comfortable now. He was moving toward camp. Any moment, the light on the camp's microwave dish antenna would appear over the horizon, like the mast of a ship sighted at sea. The Slope was one of the few places on land where a nonsailor could routinely see and apprehend the curvature of the earth. Vern smiled to himself as the light appeared a few degrees to port.

He idled down, approaching the end of the workpad where a team of surveyors were staking out the next dogleg of the pad. Vern looked back at the area they had already cleared. The flags, set two feet on either side of the pad, made a zigzag pattern off into the distance north. He could barely make out the flags in the twilight, although they were bright orange and yellow. The zigzag had something to do with expansion and contraction of the pipe. It would be elevated, but allowed to move on its supports. The project director told Vern it would also prevent an earthquake from ripping the pipe in two if the ground cracked and moved apart. The pipe could simply straighten out.

Vern put the dozer in neutral. Fat John was coming along now and the gravel trucks were due any time. A flatbed truck, loaded with hard foam blocks in two-by-four panels, stood at the end of the present pad. Two laborers were unloading panels. As Fat John drove up behind Vern and got off, a school bus came up the haul road, turned down the access alley, and zigzagged along the workpad. It stopped at the end of the road alongside the flatbed.

Vern got down and went over, followed by Fat John. The driver, a native girl named Tina, opened the door. She was wearing an insulated vest jecket, sleeveless, and against the absurd thickness of the down her arms seemed tiny, fragile. The heaters on the bus were roaring at full blast and a crew of a dozen laborers was sprawled around, legs over seat tops, some dozing, a few lying down with feet across the aisle.

"Jesus Christ," Vern shouted, "what a bunch of deadbeats. Don't you know we got a pipeline to build!"

He was pelted with orange peels and crushed paper bags.

Tina snapped her fingers, turning in her seat. "I knew I was supposed to tell you something. The environment people said we can't take so much gravel from the pit here, so we have to use more styrofoam."

Vern swore. The double-thick layer of foam meant they could get by with less than half the gravel they needed on bare tundra, but the work went by fits and starts. The laborers would get down a section and then he and John would put gravel on it to keep it from blowing away, rushing like crazy, and then wait an hour for the workers to get ahead.

Fat John knocked at the bus door and Tina swung it open.

"You're beautiful, honey," John said, panting as he climbed over a pair of legs and found a seat in the third row back.

Tina had come to work a week ago, arriving on the same plane that had brought Vern Blue in from R&R. She was a cheerful kid, just eighteen, she said, and she looked even younger. She'd dropped out of the University of Alaska in Fairbanks to take the bus driver job. Now she was making more than the president of the school, a fact that she brought to the attention of Vern and anyone else who chided her for quitting.

"So how come you guys ain't working?" John asked loudly.

"Waiting on our push," a voice in back answered. "He's riding up with another truck of insulation."

"What's a *push*?" Tina leaned across the aisle so she could talk to Vern. She seemed to like him, had sympathized with him at the airport when Pam failed to show up as expected. Pam still hadn't come back. Tina had never worked construction.

"A push is a foreman," Vern told her in a low voice. "The honcho. He runs the job."

She looked back at the men. "I heard one guy say he liked this work better than operating an idiot stick." She lifted her eyebrows. "I was afraid to ask."

"Shovel." Vern smiled, glanced at the time on her wristwatch, barely discernible in the half light. A cloud of smoke and swirling snow moved in the distance. The other truck. Three trucks. Probably bringing floodlights up. About time. They'd been getting by with two portable stands, but with so many men working, they'd need more light. The Wien flight would be coming in at dinnertime. Perhaps Pam would be on that one.

"You miss her, don't you?"

Vern shook his head, startled. "Miss who?"

"You have an easy face to read. You aren't so tough as you like to act."

"I don't like the dark and the cold." He looked out. The two laborers with the flatbed had turned on the small floodlights. "Yeah. Sure. I miss her."

"Maybe I shouldn't say anything." Tina edged closer to Vern. "I heard the union steward talking about some woman coming in on the plane today. All I know is, he said something to the housing manager about making room for a warehouse*person.* It wasn't my business, so I didn't ask. You know, Vern. Being new and all."

He nodded, didn't speak. The girl turned back in her seat, resting her arms on the steering wheel, leaning her chin on the spoke and peering out into the dark. Over the noise of the heater, Vern could hear her humming; the melody was happy and unfamiliar.

After dinner, Vern went over to the radio shack next to the

airstrip and traded stories with the operator, an old drinking buddy from Fairbanks. When the plane came he ambled out to see if anybody he knew was aboard. A fellow skinner he'd palled around with at Adak was the first off the plane, and he grabbed Vern and tried to get him in a headlock. Vern easily threw him off and they shook hands, promising to get together later in the rec hall, if the man could find it. Vern told him the camp was all under one roof. Just follow the tunnels.

A woman got off, short, dark-haired, nice-looking. Vern told her which way the check-in office was and then realized, as the ramp was folded up, that she was the one Tina had been talking about.

Vern caught up with her.

"You working in the warehouse?"

The woman nodded, impatient. Vern offered to help her with the large duffel bag. She surrendered it with a halfhearted thank-you.

"I was looking for a woman who used to have the same job," Vern said. "Pam Allen." Both stared in sudden recognition.

"Orientation?" Vern said.

Jill nodded. "I thought you looked familiar. Whatever happened to the sexy blond?"

"That was Pam Allen. Don't know. She went home same time I did and never came back. Just disappeared I guess . . . I keep looking for her."

Jill quickened her stride. "Tell me about it." Her voice had a mean edge to it.

On Larry's first trip to Montez he hadn't really noticed much. Now, going back to Anchorage, early in November, with the first heavy snow on the ground, he saw the country. It was magnificent. After all that had happened last summer, it seemed to Larry that following the family back home to Walpole was not only inevitable, but desirable. Working the long hours, bored as much as tired, walking through mud and rain, hardly daring to think about the loneliness, the near tragedy with Netty and Hope in the water, Larry had little enthusiasm for a permanent stay.

But today there had been Thompson Pass and valleys with mountains towering beyond the hills. Then, with the sun low, the peak of Mount Drum, tinged pale pink, floated in the evening sky. Last night, looking across Montez harbor, he'd seen the same illusion, ghostly peaks in the moonlight. And below, a razor of lights stretched from the town of Montez to the airport and reflected in the black water. He'd stood outside the barracks, having packed his bags, and gazed at the scene, the double line of lights cutting through the blackness and then, far, far above, the mountain peaks, hanging.

Perhaps he would not stay in Alaska, but at least his family was coming back to him. They could see some of it, get it out of their system. At worst, they might hope to survive it again.

Larry carefully followed the sharp, steep curves of the road, slowing down to catch a longer view of some new canyon, the occasional stand of pines. Stopping to relieve himself, Larry shut off the car lights and listened. The trees creaked in the wind. If he'd known the road better, he could have driven with the headlights off. The moon cast crisp shadows on the snow. He was parked on a high curve and he walked across the road to look out over a deep valley. Within the valley were lesser hills and valleys. There were mountains at his back, mountains across the valley, mountains that shone in the moonlight, their peaks softened only slightly by the snow. In all of those mountains no person walked, no lights were visible. Larry was looking at wilderness just as surely as Lewis and Clarke had seen the wilderness. Alone, staring into the shadows and depths of all that wild land, he felt terrified; he fled to his car.

Larry stopped several times on the way toward the city, standing alongside a wild river that had not yet frozen, walking away from the road. Always he felt a deep unease and afterward a profound exultation. Whether they stayed in Alaska or not, Larry would carry a few good memories, a few times when he had perceived the world as it had been made, not as it had been reshaped. The mountain, the valley, the stream, even the day when the air and water above and beneath the boat had come alive with the salmon and the gulls.

He thought of Jim Miklov and the trip up the ice road, the game they had seen, the visible pleasure Jim showed with every mile put between him and Fairbanks. Out in the toolies.

In New Hampshire, if you didn't watch where you were going in the woods, you were likely to stumble into a cellar hole. Still, he had wanted to chuck it all, drag up at work, catch the next plane out to be back in Walpole, back with Hope. And would now, if she weren't planning to join him in Anchorage as soon as he found a place to live.

Larry saw a faint glow ahead in the sky. It might have been Palmer, one of the small towns on the outskirts, or Anchorage itself. To Larry it was eating in a kitchen, sitting with his family, lying in bed with a woman again. Things had been strained between Larry and Hope, even before the trip. But in bed it was always good, except for the months in the trailer. They had a lot of catching up to do. Thinking of that, Larry hoped he would find a place right away.

He spent two days looking for a decent apartment, making all the mistakes a person in a strange town can make. He wasted time driving to blind addresses and finding himself in some rundown section in front of a building with a "now renting" sign that was as old and faded as the building itself. Many of the ads with good apartments and no price listed turned out to be luxury high-rise buildings that started at $300 a month for a utility.

Larry was talking to a waitress at the lunch counter in Woolworth's on the third day when a man sitting across the bend of the counter asked loudly what price range he was looking for. Several people at the counter watched with mild interest.

"Depend on the place," Larry said.

"Obviously, but are you looking for a flop until you get work or do you want a nice house you could put a family in?"

"He's a family man, I bet," said a heavy-set woman nursing a tulip sundae. Larry smiled. "I got a wife and two kids. Big kids, girls," he got in quickly, just in case.

"Ought to try the Inlet Towers," the waitress put in. "Get a nice two-bedroom for around three hundred, three-fifty."

"More like three-fifty," the sundae eater said, wiping her mouth with a tissue. "And that's high as far as I'm concerned."

"So you want a place for your family? Right? Well, I got a nice duplex just about three blocks from the towers on K Street, just off Fifteenth. Two bedrooms, fully furnished, and I mean immaculate."

"If it doesn't run over three-fifty, take it," the waitress said.

"Does it?" Larry asked.

"I'm not through. It has a heated garage, you have the front part of the house, wall-to-wall carpeting, kids go to Inlet View School, everything modern. Utilities included, naturally, and what's more, you can move in today."

"How much?" asked the lady, tapping her spoon on the tulip glass.

"Four-fifty." The waitress shuddered expressively, a man sitting at the bend of the counter between Larry and the landlord waggled a hand in the air, not so good, not so bad.

"I'll take it."

At four-fifty? The woman dug into her sundae sorrowfully. He must work for the pipeline.

Larry smiled around. Yeah.

"Do you like it?" Larry whispered, one arm under Hope's neck, the other resting across her middle.

Even in the faint light of the room, he could see her eyes move toward him and then back to the ceiling. A snowplow was grinding on bare pavement somewhere down the block. The noise ceased abruptly.

"The house or Anchorage?"

"Either."

"I'm not crazy about being in Alaska, you know that." Her eyes wandered over the dark ceiling. Larry supposed that Hope thought he couldn't see her. He wondered what she saw of the room. She had poor night vision. Perhaps she could make out the twin bulbs of the hanging lamp, the looped gold chain running from the center of the room to the wall and down alongside the heavy vanity mirror. There was a large painting of a ballerina on the wall beside the closet door. The pink skirt made a pale patch of gray.

"What about the house?"

"It's very fancy, isn't it?"

"You don't like it."

Her eyes moved toward him, lingered a moment. He could see the whites clearly in the violet glow from the streetlamps outside.

"I'm sure it'll be very comfortable. The heated garage is terrific."

"Something, all right. Two months ago you went home broke and now you're in a four-hundred-and-fifty-dollar -a-month apartment, there's a six-hundred-dollar color TV out in the living room and tomorrow we're picking out a new car."

"How will we ever get the TV back home?"

"Ship it. I figure you'll be alone here eight, nine weeks at a time, cold out, you'll want comfort and entertainment. And it's for the kids, too. You'll see. It's not the end of the world up here."

Her eyes disappeared; Hope had closed them.

Larry lay beside her, wanting to ask if she was glad to be with him again. She had seemed strange at the airport, had looked at him curiously when they undressed. He had asked her about that look. Hope hadn't seen him for a long time. He'd put on some weight, ten pounds. Life in the camp. Good eats. Hope breathed softly and after a time Larry realized she was asleep.

In the morning, jokingly over coffee, the kids out for a walk to explore the neighborhood, Larry asked if anybody had tried to flirt with her while he was gone. He suggested a novelist who taught at Frost College over in Vermont. Hope said he was right. The novelist had hung around, mooning about, asking for Larry, expressing his willingness to come over anytime if she needed him. Larry was amused. The novelist was about a hundred pounds overweight and his hints and innuendos were so badly put, so trite, that he was never taken seriously. As far as Larry knew the man had never, despite a life dedicated to the ideal of total hedonism, actually been unfaithful to his wife.

Hope touched her upper lip with the tip of her tongue and looked sharply at Larry. A thing *had* happened though, quite unexpectedly. She and some friends had gone to hear Kurt Schall read and then visited Schall's studio in the henhouse. Hope had been invited to read her poetry and she had spent some time with Kurt in the next few weeks talking about poems, putting her poetry through a complicated analysis of his that involved algebraic formulas.

Larry grew impatient, pushed her cup aside. What had happened then?

Nothing to be concerned about, she assured him. She told Larry it was nice to see he cared and moved closer to him. She continued in a low voice, although they were alone. She giggled once or twice. The whole thing was silly. Kurt and several of her friends had come to discuss a pulp mill that was trying to relocate in Walpole. Kurt had written a poem against it which called for such violence, including the murder of collaborators, that three people left during the reading. The discussion ran on, but one by one the guests, except for Kurt, went home. She and Kurt were seated on the big sofa, talking about revolution and poetry, when Kurt reached out and caught her face in his hands.

Larry listened, his face showing no emotion. The living room was visible from the kitchen. Luggage still lay on the carpeted floor. Some of it was his.

"I thought he was going to say something about poetry. He'd shouted for me to listen, took my face in both hands, you know how pretentious and dramatic he can be, and instead of speaking, he kissed me."

Larry relaxed. "You must have been surprised," he said. "What did you do?"

"You're going to think this is stupid, but I didn't know what to do. I guess after the summer I was glad that somebody found me attractive. Maybe I was lonely. But until he did that, I was moping around and feeling like a dishrag. Even the kids at school noticed it and asked me if I was sick."

"You let him kiss you?" Larry made a small smile.

"I wanted him to kiss me. I kissed him back. Oh, it was dumb. I felt like an idiot, just like being back in high school. That's just what it was like. Two high school kids, suddenly making out on the sofa."

"He's a creep."

Hope didn't reply.

"What else did he do? Were you there a long time?"

"Not long. Fifteen minutes, maybe more. Nothing else. It was ridiculous, like I said. We could have been sixteen."

Larry nodded, When he was sixteen, he'd been to bed with a girl. "He get in your pants?"

"No, it was nothing, really. I only told you because it was so silly. I sent him home."

They went back and forth, and Larry suddenly felt like *they* were high school kids, having a high school argument. He rubbed at his chin. Hope leaned over to kiss him on the cheek and he let her do it.

"I don't believe you," he said. "It doesn't make sense. Not two people in their thirties. Did he touch your breasts?"

Hope admitted that he had, but only outside of her shirt, not on bare skin.

Larry remembered the phrase from high school.

So he got covered titty. Did he get bare twat? Covered twat and covered titty. What did you get? Nothing. No covered Kurt?

It went on. How long had he done each? When Larry had all the answers he sat, thinking.

"I've made you upset." Hope put an arm on his shoulder. "I didn't want to make you upset. I never should have said anything."

Larry listened to her going from remorseful to cheerful. It meant nothing. I was flattered. You miss the point. I'm sorry. Ask questions then.

Larry did. How could it be that he wouldn't try to reach down the front of her blouse, not unzip her jeans? The guy had the nerve to make a move like that, he wouldn't stop where he did. She had to be holding back.

For three days, off and on, Larry would suddenly ask Hope a question. Gradually he came to believe her. Not to believe caused too much anger.

After all, Hope said, you should be proud of me. Kurt's fairly attractive and he called me just about every day until I left, trying to make dates, asking me to go out. I refused to have anything to do with him. I could have, she pointed out, and you wouldn't have known a thing about it. Also, and more to the point, I didn't *have* to come up here to be with you.

Larry had only a few more days at home. It wasn't worth fighting about. He tried to ignore the doubts. At least she was with him in Alaska.

Dan Curry listened while Gil Wolfe talked. Dan hadn't made any moves yet that betrayed conflict of interest, according to Wolfe, but he was building a case. He was working on an article about Curry's family ties, particularly the situation in Montez.

Gil had discovered a case of inaction (just the one Dan hoped would go unnoticed—a borderline decision) where the company had not been fined for a temporary river diversion in violation of standing orders. Similarly, despite a threatened state injunction against the seepage from the sewage treatment pond at Wiseman Camp and occasional high bacteria counts at two other camps on the Slope, Curry's office had delayed time and time again to let APPLE tinker with the problems. It wasn't enough, Gil said, to let them solve these problems by hit or miss, to patch up troubles. If the company doesn't know what it is doing, then it ought to get the hell out of the Arctic.

And, Gil demanded, did Dan Curry, in fact, consider the economic potential study of mineral resources along the pipeline to be in the best interest of the state?

Dan looked at the young man across his desk. "I'm not," he said, "going to attempt to answer your innuendos about my family. They are only speculation." Wolfe responded that he knew that; but he was putting Dan "on guard."

"I don't know about the last," Dan admitted. "I know that I have to make some evaluation of the dollar value of the natural resources along the pipe corridor. And, who knows? Maybe if it's low, it'll scare some would-be developer off."

Gil said you couldn't put a dollar value on the environment.

"Well," Dan said. "I have to try. And we're not advocating using up the land, only using it to the best advantage."

"I don't think you care about Alaska or the environment," Wolfe said. To his credit, the tone of his attack was calm, objective. He believed what he was saying and he looked at Dan with some pity. Dan had seen the same look in Emil Bacich, who found the transition from Alaskan wilderness to "wilderness areas" genuinely painful. But how big did a piece of geography have to be to be called a wilderness?

"There are men out there right now raping the wilderness," Gil said. "If you pick up the paper tonight, you can read an article about you and those men. They're performing rape, and you, and this office, you know what you do? You try to pass it off as seduction. You want us to lie back and enjoy it. I wonder if you even realize this. I'd like to think there was a time you did care about this state. Emil says he thinks so, but I wonder, Mr. Curry, I really do. I don't think you even know you're a rapist. Or care."

Dan folded his hands together tightly and spoke in a soft voice.

"I think I'll have to ask you to come back later if you want to continue."

"When you're not so busy?" Gil eyed the stack of folders and letters on his desk.

"No," Curry said. "When you haven't ticked me off to the point where I'm likely to get up and throw you through the door." He smiled. "Forgive me, Mr. Wolfe, but Alaska is something I care about very deeply and its future is something to which I am wholly committed. You can print that as my reply to all of your questions. And before you get excited, I wouldn't really throw you through my door; you might damage my map of Alaska."

Wolfe got up. His interview was obviously over, but he was

unsure whether or not Curry was actually angry at him. He stood at the door, one hand on the knob, looking at Dan for some sign. Seeing none, Wolfe raised his head.

"I suppose if the victim is beautiful enough, there might be a rapist who'd care deeply for her."

At home, Paula told him she'd seen the paper, that he didn't need to read it to her, that of course it was totally unfair, he had given his life to defending the state. She handed him a drink.

Dan wandered around the living room, muttering, sipping from the glass. "Rape of Alaska. Can you believe that?" He walked over to where Paula stood, looking out the window at the lights of the Captain Cook Hotel just down the street. He touched her on the shoulder and Paula whirled around, face tight with bitterness, slapping the glass from his hand.

"Paula!"

Paula moved in like a prizefighter, shoving at his chest, hard, with her fingertips, pushing him back. "Rape of Alaska." She jabbed. "Rape of Alaska." He felt the sudden jab again, simultaneous with the words. It was the way a man, trying to start a fistfight, might shove another man. She hit him again. "How about raping Paula Curry?" Paula swung wildly and caught him across the forehead, openhanded. "You and your damn Alaska. How about raping *me*? That boy was wrong. You don't rape Alaska. You're married to it, you hump it night and day."

She took another swipe at his head and Dan caught her hand, caught both hands and pulled them down to her sides, holding her rigid, close to him.

Paula looked down and then into his eyes.

"That's the first time you've held me tight in weeks." She glared, inches away from his face. "If you had a mistress I could do something, cry, shout, try to be more seductive, see an attorney, something. But *Alaska*?" Tears welled. "What am I supposed to do about that, when I fall asleep night after night alone or with you too tired for anything but a goodnight kiss? I hate it. You know that? I *hate* Alaska!"

Chapter Three

HOPE WAS ECSTATIC. She would start as a secretary for a state-run youth program and in February move up to a teaching position at an experimental learning center for native children. The salary started at $11,000 and would go to $13,500 in February, when she began classes in poetry, literature and creative expression.

"That's twice what I earned in Walpole." Netty and Caitlin looked up from the color television.

"We're rich now, aren't we?" Caitlin said.

"It's true, what you said, Larry. Anybody with some smarts and a few skills can come up here and decide what they want to be. I could have had an advertising job, a dozen secretarial positions, all kinds of jobs in social services, guidance counseling, you name it. A man even asked me if I wanted to go out on the pipeline as an apprentice steamfitter, whatever that was."

"About twelve bucks an hour for a journeyman," Larry said. "You should have taken it. They've got women in everything now, climbing telephone poles, welding, driving trucks. How about you going out there and letting me stay in town?"

Hope laughed. "This is far enough from civilization as it is. But I have to admit that I'm going to feel strange about going home and working for half the money. I'm getting a grown-up's salary and I know it doesn't cost twice as much to live here."

"How long should we stay, then? Until summer?"

"I guess I have to, if I'm teaching. Maybe I should take a plain secretarial job, so we can go back when we've made up our losses."

"Put in a winter, we may as well stick around for the warm weather."

"And the people I met were so interesting."

"Mostly women or what?"

Hope put her hand on Larry's.

"Almost all women. I think the men must be out on the pipeline. But they're just a great bunch. After my interview, the boss, Jackie, actually hugged me. I just got the feeling that these women are really working well together."

"No men at all?"

"I told you what happened with Kurt."

"Sorry."

"You should be. This is the first nice thing that's happened to me in Alaska. Don't spoil it, okay?"

"Did anyone back there know about you and Kurt?"

Hope got up and went to the bedroom. Larry followed.

"All right, you want to cross-examine me again, go ahead. But not in front of the kids."

Larry hesitated. "It's just that if we go back—*when* we go back—I have to make a living there. I wondered if there would be talk."

"Nothing to talk about. I told Nancy. She thought it was funny, but I don't think she'd even tell David. I asked her not to. What else?"

Larry hung his head.

"While you were gone I leafed through your poetry notebooks. You had some lines about a strange hand on your body. What was that?"

"You leafed through my notebooks. Terrific. Exhibit A, Hope Ransom's poetry journal." She sighed. "All right. I thought I should tell you something, but I knew you'd be lonely at camp and you'd probably brood. I can see I shouldn't have said a thing."

"There was more."

"He put his hand under my blouse."

"Under your bra?"

"It was summer. I don't like to wear a bra in summer."

"Did he touch your breast then?"

"Yes. And I told him not to and he took his hand out. I suppose I should have had him arrested."

"You're drunk," Jill Jones told Vern. Outside, the weather was down to twenty below and a gust of wind rattled the windows of the Sag River rec hall. A pool player leaned across the table and angled in for a corner shot. Vern Blue had to tilt his head back not to interfere with the cue handle. From the movie room, the sound track was punctuated by sudden bursts of gunfire. There was an explosion followed by laughter from the audience. Vern nodded at her unsteadily.

"I know I am. But I'd still like to go to bed with you. I can do it with a few drinks in me, don't worry."

Jill nibbled at a brownie, watching him with interest.

"You think you ought to go on drinking after Calkins caught you like that?"

Calkins was the workpad superintendent and he'd caught Vern Blue drinking two days ago. Early in the afternoon he'd driven up to Vern's Cat in a pickup truck, stopped Vern, and searched the dozer. He found the bottle, half full, but Vern hadn't been drinking.

"I'll watch myself. And there's lots of places to hid a bottle, including right in my coat pocket. I don't think he's got the right to search me. Come on, let's go back to my room. You been in this camp a long time, we had dinner together and everything. Don't you think I at least deserve a little courtesy fuck?"

Jill shook her head, trying not to smile.

"I only started talking to you because of Bill Wiggins. I guess I felt sorry for you because Pam didn't come back."

"All right then, how about a mercy fuck?"

"You *will* get run off, if you get caught with a bottle again."

"How about it?"

There were auto crashes on the screen and the sound of people crying out in pain, then more gunshots. The men in the other room were still laughing. Vern wondered what sort of movie could be showing.

"You know something, Vern? You have too good a mind to spend the rest of your life living in these camps and hitting the bottle every night."

"That's what Pam used to say."

"It's true."

Vern put a hand on Jill's knee. She pushed it away firmly.

"But when *she* said it, we were in bed."

Two of the new kids in camp were at the electronic Ping-Pong game.

Peep-peep-peep, it went as the ball hit the sides of the televised field. When someone missed, it honked. Rnnnnk.

"I like you, Vern, but I like you for what you have in your head. Only I wish you wouldn't drink so much."

Peep-peep-rnnnk. Peep. Hroonnnk.

Vern looked up at the game. "I'd rather be treated as a sex object." He met Jill's eyes and blinked sleepily. "Hmmmm?"

"Why do you do it so much?"

"Sex?"

Huurronnnnk.

"No, drink."

"It feels so warm going down. It's true. That's actually why I do it. If lemonade felt that good going down, I'd drink lemonade."

On the movie screen it sounded like a house was caving in and then the reel ended. The laughter trailed off and some of the guys came out for coffee and snacks, smiling, joking with one another, during the reel change.

Vern dragged himself up and headed back to his room, bumping into the two kids at the Ping-Pong machine. They made no complaint.

Vern stripped to his underwear, poured a drink, and turned out the light, lying in bed with the cola can on his chest. "Roonnnnnk." He went and tipped the can back to drink. It was warm going down, warmth spreading everywhere but to his heart. "Rnnnkkk."

Miss.

December seventh was, as noted by several newscasters, the anniversary of Pearl Harbor. It was also the day on which Finch-Smith, in his monthly progress report, announced that the new ice bridge over the Yukon was to be open for traffic. At the terminal, although neither Finch-Smith nor the others knew it yet, December seventh marked the first incident of a fire in the electrical distribution box of a housing module. It was to be the first of six fires over the months of December and January, two of them serious. The fire in the terminal was discovered almost the moment it broke out by Leslie Collins, who was making a safety inspection of the women's dorm. The report helped his standing both with management and with some of the crafts who had long speculated on his sexual preferences.

The temperature at Montez on December seventh was twenty degrees above zero with mild breezes. Just over Thompson Pass, at Tonsina Camp, the temperature was two above zero. At the Yukon River, where the first truck edged across the eight-foot-thick section of ice, the air was still, temperature eighteen below.

At sunless Sag River, seven hundred miles north of Montez, the thermometer had hung at twenty-eight below for two days, with very little hourly fluctuation. Vern Blue had transferred from the workpad to the camp and nearby pump station construction. The new superintendent told Calkins he'd keep a closer eye on the problem child. At lunch, in the operator's dry shack, Vern kidded Bagge about the soft job he'd landed. Bagge was working with the concrete batching plant, which meant that he spent roughly half the day inside the mammoth air structure building that housed a two-story sandpile. The structure, called a beluga (for its resemblance to a whale), was secured by a criss-cross net of steel cables that would hold it together in winds of seventy miles an hour. With winter temperatures, the chill factor at seventy miles an hour would make the building windproof anyhow, it was said, as the heated structure would be jammed with workmen assigned to outside duty.

Bagge claimed the assignment wasn't that good. The change in pressure going in and out of the giant airlock with his front-end loader hurt his ears. And then he would get overheated inside and freeze outside.

Vern and a few of the other men stuck with outside jobs laughed. Overheating was no problem with them.

One man thought it funny that they could spend thousands of dollars to keep a sandpile warm while the carpenters and welders were out in the cold trying to work. This kind of weather, it was said, would separate the men from the boys. Last night a Wien flight had come in, and a mechanic from Texas got off the plane, looked around, threw his tools back in the cargo hatch, and climbed right back on the plane.

"I never mind the cold," Vern said and went back outside. He climbed up on the idling dozer, switched on his headlights, and followed the road to the edge of camp where the rough site work for the pump station was under way. The rubble from last night's blasting still had not been cleared off. Vern pulled out the throttle and cut around the far side of the rubble, out of sight of the camp and prying superintendents.

Feathering the throttle with one foot on the pedal, he reached up over his head, feeling along the canvas snow protector he'd slung under the safety grill. He edged the lump to one side, gave a bump, and a bottle fell into his gloved hands.

Y'er out! he called, and his foot came up off the pedal, lurching the Cat forward. Vern steadied himself and unscrewed the cap, breathing on the mouth of the bottle to warm it. He shook the bottle. The whiskey gurgled.

Carefully, so as not to touch the glass to his lips, Vern leaned back, mouth open, and poured. It was hot going down, too hot, not warm. Vern began a cough, but it would not come. The bottle fell from his hand, shattered on the deck of the cab. No, not hot, *cold,* he realized as the deep, searing agony of alcohol at twenty-eight degrees below zero crystallized the tissues of his mouth and throat, convulsing windpipe and esophagus even as it killed them.

It was not possible to scream. Vern fell to one side of the cab and listened to the roaring in his ears: blood and diesel pistons. The pale Arctic noon fell to night.

A chopper found his dozer seven hours later. As the two crewmen circled in on the floodlit Cat, hung up on an ice hump, its treads chewing away uselessly at the snow, they nudged each other.

"He must have got lost when the wind came up and then got stuck. He didn't get far, did he?"

Vern was exactly eighteen miles north-northwest of camp, on a course that would have taken him to the Beaufort Sea and out onto the pack ice if he'd had enough fuel.

The chopper set down and the copilot plodded through the snow, smiling at the sight of the tracks clawing in the air. The guy on the Cat would probably be furious.

When he got around to the side of the cab where Vern seemed to be looking out to see why the treads were running free, he covered his mouth, swallowing hard.

Vern's face was frosted over with blown snow. Particles of ice rimmed his eyes and mouth. Vern's tongue protruded, frozen: a river of ice.

The operating crew that came to take the dozer back found the bottle, and the autopsy confirmed the circumstances of his death. Everyone had been taken by surprise. A dozer, blowing engine heat back like that, shouldn't let a man freeze to death. And it won't, Fat John pointed out, as long as you're talking about freezing from the outside in.

Chapter Four

ALTHOUGH NORTH SLOPE workers faced subzero temperatures that rendered steel brittle, froze stalled engines solid, and forced men to wear face masks just to breathe, workers at the terminal in Montez suffered in other ways. Montez typically received 300 inches of snow in a winter, beginning in November and running right into April. In town, the accumulation would reach heights of eight to twelve feet along sidewalks. Drivers had to slow at each corner since it was not possible to see approaching traffic on cross streets.

At Copper Canyon, the dozers stranded on the cliff edge by bad weather doggedly continued work, clearing and reclearing snow from the three-mile-long shelf and the steep, partly constructed pioneer road. Tons of snow were pushed over the edge of the canyon, to be carried away by the swift-running Lowe River. Occasionally, dynamite crews planted small charges in strategic locations to keep the river from jamming with ice. Blasting atop the ridge continued at a slow pace. Some sections, in the path of possible avalanches from the higher elevations, were traversed carefully. A guard with signal was posted at all times. An oncoming avalanche, even if it stopped short of the rim, could generate a wind ahead of it strong enough to carry a man out over the edge.

The port of Montez was ice-free, which was one of the chief reasons for its selection as the pipeline terminal. It was the northernmost ice-free port in Alaska, and it sat at the end of one of the two highways in Alaska that reached to the interior from the coast. Temperatures in the area were moderate, the average January temperature just under twenty, or thirty degrees warmer than the average for Fairbanks. Where Anchorage might hit thirty and thirty-five below and Fairbanks sixty below, winter temperatures in Montez seldom fell below zero.

But Montez had extremes of wind and snow; the combination made for a particular unpleasantness. In late fall, winds would sweep down out of Thompson Pass at sixty to a hundred miles an hour. The wind might come with no warning and last for several days. Wind-chill factors of twenty and thirty below were not uncommon. And the snow, at twenty and twenty-five degrees, fell like wet doilies, fell in great clumps of flakes, hour after hour, fell and melted into the clothing of the workers, plastered hair and beards, eyelashes and cheeks. It was too cold for raincoats, too wet for down parkas. The workers at the terminal wore wool next to the skin, ponchos and slickers against the snow, and spent days avoiding the trickle of ice water down the back of the neck, the inevitable soaking of trousers, collars, sleeves.

Cylindrical heaters, powered by fans, clustered around the project like miniature yellow jet engines, some turned toward open sheds with plastic sheeting, others blasting heat through crude holes cut in the sides of dry shacks. The carpenters built drying racks, and inside each shack, during lunch, during coffee breaks, the men hung coats, jackets, gloves, boots to catch the stream of air.

Those with sinus and respiratory problems suffered the most. Colds were epidemic. The medics jokingly called the various combinations of cold, sinus infection and flu that struck at least a third or more of the workers "the Mon-disease," as doctors in nearby Valdez called theirs "the Val-disease." The newspapers around the world made much of the harsh life at Prudhoe Bay. Terminal workers grumbled that they'd trade anytime if Prudhoe only had a few good bars and some women.

Despite the snow and dampness and the endless complaining, the work got done. Fourteen of the twenty-eight dormitories to be built at Terminal Camp were complete or nearly so. The new sewage plant, a larger mess hall and production kitchen were taking shape. The rec hall grew and the office building, halfway between the dorms and the actual tank farm site, was complete, although without water. The secretaries complained bitterly about using the portable toilets scattered along the perimeter of the building, and hourly a van service shuttled the women back and forth to the toilets in their dorm.

The blasting and general site work at the ballast treatment area was complete, and the rubble had been cleared and dumped in a landfill between the old ferry landing and Jackson Point. Three tanks would be built here, on the shoreline, each holding 410,000 barrels of ballast water from the tankers that would be docking here. The oil would be separated from the ship's ballast and the water treated before being released into the harbor.

Above the ballast tank area, a broad shelf had been blasted out of bedrock as foundation for a crude oil storage facility, the tank farm. By Thanksgiving, the east tank farm, which would have fourteen tanks, each capable of holding 510,000 barrels of oil, was a level area, ready for the concrete rings, 250 feet across, that would serve as bases for the individual tanks. A trail had been broken to the west tank farm, and surveyors, the advance scouts and commandos of the pipeline, slogged in on snowshoes and skis to lay out the second storage area.

Larry Ransom, covering all this in a pickup truck, day in, day out, was no longer impressed. He wrote letters to Hope in which he described activities at work, and she wrote back about the women, the stories she was hearing about Alaska. The kids wished he could be home for Thanksgiving. Larry sent them a copy of *Pipe 'n' Hot News* in which holiday menus were listed. He sat in his room, listening to someone's tape player down the hall blaring out country music, and tried to think of things to tell her. Even the menus failed to cheer him, although they were discussed widely on the job, mostly with an attitude of disbelief.

Sag River Camp was promised:

SOUP
Chicken Noodle

SALADS
Shrimp Salad, Relish Tray, Fruit Compote, Tossed Green Salad, Coleslaw, Crab Salad, Cottage Cheese

ENTREES
Roast Tom Turkey with Sage Dressing
Giblet Gravy
Cranberry Sauce
Baked Virginia Ham with Cherry & Wine Sauce
Roast Beef with Brown Gravy au jus

VEGETABLES
Cauliflower, Creamed Peas, Asparagus with Hollandaise Sauce, Creamed Whipped Potatoes, Baked Potatoes, Candied Sweet Potatoes with Orange Slices

PIES
Pumpkin, Mincemeat,
Dutch Apple with Cheese

DESSERTS
Fruit Cake, Fresh Fruit,
Orange Sherbet

CONDIMENTS
Assorted Nuts & Candies

Some of the other camps had selections based on the chef's nationality. One camp offered Authentic Italian Ravioli, Caesar Salad, & Genuine Italian Ices. Along with the standard turkey, another had Cornbread, Baked Southern-style Sugar-cured Ham, Southern Fried Chicken, Candied Yams & Black-eyed Peas. Larry thought those at Livengood most fortunate. A third of the items were in French, including Roast Long Island Duckling à L'Orange & Roast Prime Ribs of Beef Au Jus Vert Pré.

What with Cornish Game Hens Stuffed with Wild Rice, Roast Baron of Beef & Virginia Baked Ham, Terminal Camp put on a good feed, Larry felt, but many of the men were disgusted at not having turkey. The kitchen manager locked himself in the back office for the entire meal.

The season dragged on and Larry settled back into the routine, marking off the days until the Christmas break. Because he was one of the first timekeepers hired, Larry was guaranteed two weeks off out of the three-week slowdown. Little Nasty got tired of waiting and "drug up" so he could go home before the holiday rush. It didn't matter if he quit; Nasty was owed several favors by the business agents. He'd be back in late January. Isaac Ahgutuk got sent home early to dry out, and the native counselor assured him he'd be back in sixty days. Clyde Baranov teased him, saying he, Clyde, could hold his liquor because he had good Russian blood in his heritage.

December seventh, the mail clerk wished Larry a "Happy Pearl Harbor Day" as he came to pick up the mail. There was one letter in the box with no return address. It was postmarked with the Walpole zip code.

Larry sat down at one of the circular tables in the pool room and opened his mail. Several of the workers had taken up chairs around the lounge, too impatient to wait until they got back to their rooms to see what had come.

"Look to your wife," the letter began. "We have never spoken against you in town. Your wife did not come from godless people. I was relieved to hear she had joined you but now I learn that even in that distant country you do not live together as man and wife. Think of the children, Ransom. Mark 9:42.

"Think of your wife. Proverbs 7:7–13, 18–21."

The letter was signed by Mr. Haberson, their neighbor. A fundamentalist puritan in the old New England tradition, always trying to legislate other people's morals, a self-righteous busybody, as was his wife, always dropping notes and gossip to the people in town. This was the first Larry had received. He crumpled it up and threw it in the wastebasket. A moment later he was back inside the rec hall, smoothing the letter out. It might have been that Haberson was on his old tack about the breakdown of the family, which to him was a natural result of leaving the state of New Hampshire. Or it might not.

But where could he find a Bible? The chaplain had hours posted on the bulletin board in the mess hall. Larry went there. The man was due tomorrow. He tried the camp manager's office, but he was out. He went to Al Godwin's room and Al just laughed. "That'll be a scarce item in these parts."

He knocked on the door across from his. It was Dale, the ironworker. His room was a blue haze of cigarette smoke.

"You got a Bible?"

"A Bible?"

"Yeah. You know. Bible." Larry squared the air with his hands. "Book."

"What you need a Bible for?"

"I need it." Larry glanced around. "I'm in a hurry."

"You suddenly get converted or something?" Dale laughed and caught himself before the coughing started. "Naw, I don't have no Bible. You want a Bible, go see Banjo."

"The pipefitter?"

"Right, big guy with the handlebar moustache. Banjo-eye Kelly. He's with that A.A. bunch. He's got dozens of Bibles."

Larry asked around, received a few sympathetic handshakes

from some of Kelly's anonymous members. Finally he found the room, knocked at the door.

"Whattaya want? I'm in bed," came a voice.

"Uh . . . a Bible," Larry said. "I can come back."

The door opened and a large man in underwear, a man with big eyes and a handlebar moustache, reached out to shake Larry's hand, dragging him into the room and switching on the light.

"Hiya, pard, my name is Banjo-eye Kelly and I'm an alcoholic." Now that Larry was inside the room, Kelly used both hands to grip Larry. "So you finally saw the light."

"Not exactly," Larry said.

"Hey," Banjo-eye patted him on the back, "you came to see me, that's good enough. And you're a believer, huh?"

"Believer?"

Kelly went to his closet. It was indeed full of Bibles as well as stacks of printed folders and booklets. Kelly was pawing through them, selecting one of everything. "Yeah, a believer in God." Kelly turned, his hands full of booklets as well as a Bible. "You do believe in God?"

Larry thought of trying to explain, but simply nodded.

"Sure. Sometimes."

Kelly handed Larry the books. Poking him in the chest to emphasize his words, Kelly said, "I'm glad to hear it, because that's going to make things a lot easier. You show me a guy that doesn't believe in God and I'll show you a real asshole." Kelly poked again. "You know what I mean?"

"All I really wanted was to borrow a Bible."

"Borrow, like hell. That Bible's yours. And the senenity prayer on the plastic card inside. Tuck that in your wallet." He punched Larry on the arm lightly. "Gets me through the day. I'll be six years old next month."

"Six years . . ."

"Off the booze six years. You can do it, too. You believe in God. That's a step. You have a sincere desire to stop drinking alcohol, that'll be your next step. I could see this coming."

Larry looked up, puzzled.

"I watch the men and I could see a change in you this time out. I knew something was going on. Shit hit the fan, huh?"

"Kind of," Larry mumbled. Kelly was patting him on the back, squeezing his elbow, moving him toward the door.

"Right. I got to get some shut-eye, kid, you come back anytime after chow and we'll talk more. And, Larry—"

Larry, in the hall, turned back. "Yeah?"

"You got friends in this camp, now. Don't forget that. You got some of the best friends you're ever going to have."

Larry went back to the dorm feeling good. He drank seldom and rarely got drunk. He hoped Banjo-eye wouldn't be too disappointed.

The first reference Larry found was about not offending the little ones and the millstone around your neck.

Larry turned to Proverbs and began to read.

> 7 And beheld among the simple ones, I discerned among the youths, a young man void of understanding,
> 8 Passing through the street near her corner; and he went the way to her house,
> 9 In the twilight, in the evening, in the black and dark night:
> 10 And, behold, there met him a woman with the attire of an harlot, and subtil of heart.
> 11 (She *is* loud and stubborn: her feet abide not in her house:
> 12 Now *is she* without, now in the streets and lieth in wait at every corner.)
> 13 So she caught him, and kissed him, and with an impudent face said unto him,

Larry angrily skimmed the next few verses and started in at eighteen, checking Haberson's letter.

> 18 Come, let us take our fill of love until the morning: let us solace ourselves with loves.
> 19 For the goodman *is* not at home, he is gone a long journey:
> 20 He hath taken a bag of money with him, and will come home at the day appointed.
> 21 With her much fair speech she caused him to yield, with the flattering of her lips she forced him.

Their living room faced the bedroom of the Habersons' house.

If the Habersons knew, everyone knew.

Larry went to the phone. It was late, there was only one ahead in the line. He called Bundy, and only when he heard the sleepy voice did he remember the five-hour time difference. Eleven P.M. in Alaska was 4 A.M. in Walpole. He apologized, but Bundy was glad to hear from him, asked if he and Hope were back together.

Back together, Larry thought. No, he told Bundy, they were living three hundred and fifty miles apart, by highway, about half that by air. He took a chance.

"I suppose you know about our troubles."

A pause. "Yes. Frankly I was surprised when she left Walpole to go back up there. But you aren't together."

Bundy was too circumspect to come right out. Larry sighed.

"I found out from the Habersons about the situation back there. And from Hope."

"Well," the relaxation in Bundy's voice was noticeable, "I didn't want to say anything. I wasn't sure if we were talking about the same thing. You know, if Hope and that Schall fellow hadn't spent so much time together, her over there, or the two of them staying after poetry readings, we might not have thought much about the car. But that really had me convinced you two had split up last summer on your trip."

"The car?"

"Yeah, you know, Schall leaving his car parked right in your driveway all night and then coming out in his undershorts to bring in the morning paper." Bundy laughed. "I'm surprised Mrs. Haberson didn't call the police when she saw that. Oh, well, that's ancient history by now, I suppose. How are things with you otherwise?"

Larry talked a few minutes longer, explained he was just concerned about the kids who'd rented his house and was homesick. He stood, after hanging up the phone, trying to think of what he would say to Hope. A man tapped him on the shoulder.

"You mind?" he asked, slipping by, taking the receiver, dialing.

Larry walked back to his room, ignoring the occasional greetings from other men up late, bent on odd errands here and there through the complex alleyways of snow. In the shower, out of sight and sound, he cried in solitary pain and anger like an army of cuckolds before him.

Mid-December brought layoffs for the holiday, most temporary, a few permanent, in camps on the Slope, where winter had brought work progress to such low efficiency that some outside jobs had to be postponed. The first heavy movement of pipeline workers going out on Christmas R&R began, and gradually the pace of activity in camp for those who remained slowed down. Crews were reshuffled, and those who stayed were transferred into maintenance and operations. Construction ceased.

Maggie and Ed Booth had expected Doug to come home on Saturday, the twenty-first, but since he had no distance to travel he showed up on Friday night. Friday was quiet in the bar except for the bunch of ironworkers in with the big foreman, Tiny, who had won the checkpool. Tiny dropped three hundred of the forty-two hundred he'd won that day, and when he left the bar, Gloria and a stray hooker up from Juneau left with him.

Ed had been glad to see the boy, but Doug as usual was sullen and unpleasant. At breakfast Ed asked about the checkpool, and only Maggie prevented a scene. Doug explained it to her, the use of the last three digits of the check serial number combined with two cards, drawn early on payday and announced around the job by noon. The five numbers were read as a poker hand and the best hand took the pot.

"It must be tough to win. What do guys put in?"

Doug looked at his mother. "Ten bucks a week. This week, because of Christmas, it was twenty. Usually the pot is only fifteen hundred, two thousand."

"One chance out of two hundred," Ed said. "Not for me."

"You don't have to tell me that," Doug replied, getting up and taking his plate to the sink.

"Of course, if Ed was making as much as you laborers," Maggie said, "ten bucks wouldn't mean so much."

Ed laughed. "It isn't the money. Doug just thinks I won't take chances."

Maggie frowned. "Home one day and you two are starting up. I don't want a Christmas like last year."

"I've taken plenty of chances, buster," Ed called at Doug's back. Down the hallway a door slammed. "Kid has no respect," he told Maggie.

"I'll talk to him."

Ed looked at her. "It didn't help having him side with you about my taking this job. He thinks I've sold out."

"Have you been watching the receipts here, Ed?"

He shrugged.

"I'm glad you have a job you're proud to do, Ed, I really am. I guess you need to feel important. Me, I'm like my old man was. I want to take what I've got and make it grow. Your boy is making more than you are. I remember last winter. He didn't want to dig ditches. He had a little of you in him, more than you think."

Ed remembered. Doug had to be talked into it, but not by his father. His uncle, Dan Curry, had convinced him.

"Money's not everything, but neither is a title. Your boy makes good money. He's getting tough doing it. Oh, I know he's not killing himself over there, no more than any of them are, but he's sticking with something. And you want to know what this place is turning into?"

"A sports arena?"

Maggie looked confused.

"We get a fight a night in here at the minimum."

"Between Schultzie and my brother we're not doing too bad. Nobody's tried to break the joint up. But listen to what I'm telling you. This place that I wanted you to stay with is going to take in about one million bucks by the next fiscal year. I figure a million and a half the next year when construction's in full swing. You stand there some night and watch those hundred-dollar bills float across that bar. You don't have to read about the gold rush days in books, Ed, we have it right downstairs. I got Schultz full-time now and we'll get the restaurant open. And in a way, I guess I'm proud of you for sticking to what makes you feel like a man. But don't sell the club short, honey."

"I guess I could help out some in the evenings." Ed rubbed at his nose, head down, looking across the table at Maggie. "You know, a week after the workers started coming in here, I knew you were right and I shouldn't have taken that job. Still, it does mean something to me."

"Hey," Maggie motioned for him to pull back and make room. She sat in his lap and buried her nose in his ear. "It's okay. I'll just have a bigger share of the glory this way."

Ed drew in his breath, shifting his weight under her, letting Maggie know he was interested.

"You think he's too big to send out to the movies?" Maggie asked.

"Who cares? We've got a lock on our door."

Because camps south of the Yukon River were spread over an area with two mountain ranges and some of Alaska's least predictable weather, winter brought a cancellation of all company air charters for employees. Those who wanted to pay their own airfare could make reservations, but anyone seeking the promised free transportation to and from Anchorage now had to ride in buses. The trip from Montez to Anchorage, fifty minutes by air, took nine or more hours by bus. The alteration in policy was poorly received.

Tiny, anxious to get south and spend some of the big winnings, Larry, who burned with the impatience of confronting Hope, and a dozen others had bought tickets on a Polar Airways flight. They milled about in the small trailer that served as office and waiting room. Tiny warned everyone that if they told his old lady he'd won anything over three thousand bucks they were dead. Larry watched out the window. When the buses back to town had left at nine this morning, the weather had been fairly clear. Now it was clouded over, and down the bay, where the plane would turn in from its path over the sound, it looked like snow.

The plane was due at one o'clock, and it was now one-thirty with no word. The flight had left Anchorage. The two men on standby paced back and forth in a narrow space between sofas, counting the men ahead. So far, five hadn't come in, although two had called, and it might be possible to get a few extras on. Weather reports were not good. It was this trip or none.

The ticket woman, who also handled baggage, shipping, local weather reporting and a charter service, shouted for everyone to be quiet so she could hear the radio.

The room fell silent and the men watched Mona's face. When she smiled, they smiled. At every frown and biting of her lip, hearts sank. She spoke into her microphone and removed the headset, smiling prettily around the room.

"He's out there at the entrance of the bay."

Approving murmers were heard. A lineup formed at the desk.

"But he can't find his way in, so he's going back to Anchorage. Sorry fellas. But we might have an extra flight tomorrow if the weather picks up and I can put you all on that one."

There were curses, groans. The men in line began laying tickets on the counter to get refunds. Bad weather in Montez tended to hang around.

Tiny shouldered his way to the desk. "How much to charter a plane?"

"To Anchorage?"

"Where else?"

Men began edging in around Tiny.

"Hey, I'm in, share the cost?"

"Put me on that, Tiny."

Mona went to the doorway and peered out through the window.

"It'd be round trip for the aircraft, you know."

"I don't give a damn where the airplane goes. I want to be in Anchorage so's we can get off to Hawaii tomorrow."

"It would be two hundred and fifty dollars. The plane holds five. If he'll fly."

Tiny laid three hundreds on the desk. "Tell him I'll go three bills."

Mona called and nodded up at Tiny. "You ready to leave right now?"

"Sure as hell am. I was ready a hour ago."

She put the phone down, wrote out a receipt for the three hundred and handed it to Tiny. "Right down to the hanger there. It's the little blue and white Piper Aztec." She put a finger to her lips, appraising Tiny. "I think, considering your size, you can take three with you."

Wads of money began appearing.

"Who's a ironworker here?" Tiny picked out an ironworker. "Any welders?" A hand went up and Tiny motioned the man toward the door. "What the hell?" Tiny said, hitting Larry across the back. "Might as well take a timekeeper, stay on the good side of payroll."

"I knew you'd pay off for fixing up the paycheck number." No one but Tiny laughed.

The men gathered their baggage and straggled down toward the hangar where the pilot was removing the down-filled covers from the engine and air intakes.

"How come a plane can get out?" Larry asked the welder. "That Polar flight can't come in?"

"Something to do with coming up from mountains rather than flying down into them. Anyhow, I hear you can go out through Thompson Pass. That Polar flight might have made it through Thompson if he'd come around that way. It's a little longer. Like coming by car."

"I hope this guy knows what he's doing."

"Sure. These bush pilots know it all. If they go up, it's safe."

Larry nodded, not really willing to pursue it any further. Alaska history, colorful though it was, was crowded with dead bush pilots. And what difference would it make? The way he felt, a ride into the side of some mountain would be as good an alternative as what he had to face at home—both in Anchorage and Walpole. Larry loaded his gear in the rear compartment and stood by the wing, waiting to get on board.

"You don't look very happy about getting out of here," the ironworker said. "Don't you like flying?"

Larry met his eyes. "Got stuff on my mind."

"We were damn lucky. Look of those clouds, this'll be the last flight out of here for quite a while. Might be rough, but it'll beat a nine- or ten-hour bus ride. Hell, they get any kind of slide in the pass, could take twice that before they get to town. By tomorrow, who knows? You can sit in Montez three days easy with no way out of town. Damn lucky," he repeated, patting Tiny on the shoulder.

"That's my middle name," Tiny said, rubbing both hands together. The wind had picked up. Clouds were deepening down toward Copper Canyon. A heavy coldness was in the air. "Oh, baby, Honolulu, here I come!" Tiny clapped his hands as the pilot secured the hatch and climbed up the wing to open the cabin door. Looking over the passengers, the pilot called the welder and ironworker up first, putting them in the rear two seats. Tiny was to sit in the left of the two center seats. Larry got in front with the pilot.

"I can't guarantee nothing," the pilot said, facing the rear of the cabin. "I'm going to try and take us up over Thompson Pass, but I might get to the entrance of Copper Canyon and just turn around if it looks bad. Just wanted you to know."

He started the engines, taxied down to the end of the field. Ran the engines up and down, testing the magnetos, warming up the plane.

"Home, James," Tiny shouted over the engine noise.

The pilot, a middle-aged, husky man, stuck a thumb up in the air and opened the throttles. The plane hesitated, began to roll, gathered speed, grudgingly (it seemed to Larry) took flight, heading toward the side of a mountain and only gradually altering course, banking to the right so as to miss it.

Larry watched, impassive. He had moved through the days since

Haberson's letter as though he were under water. He saw little, spoke seldom, drifted with the tide of activity around him.

The plane banked again, gained altitude. Larry could see the pioneer road, a dark scratch up the long slope of ground rising to form the canyon wall. Snow whipped past the plane. The plane jolted and Larry's head hit the window. The jolt was followed by another. Tiny laughed loudly. "Waa-hooo!" There was a series of jolts and Larry thought of the boat accident, the way the waves had tossed them.

"Rough air," the pilot called. "Keep your belts on, boys, I don't want dents in the ceiling."

"Hot damn," Tiny bellowed as the plane dipped, crabbed to one side, and then straightened out with another harsh jolt. The plane bounced and came down hard three times in a row. Larry watched the wingtips, holding tight to his armrest. The plane was actually slewing from side to side, a very noticeable movement. He had never seen a plane do that before. He glanced from right to left. A steep mountain wall rose out of sight on the pilot's side. On Larry's side it was possible to see up to where the clouds obscured the mountain.

The pilot leaned over. "You ever see weather change like this?" he shouted.

Larry caught glimpses of the mountainside through the mist. The plane crabbed, flew one way, pointed another. Larry held on and shook his head, shouted, "You going back?"

"Can't." The pilot banked sharply to the left and then to the right. He steadied the plane as best he could, keeping his eyes on the mountain. "Too narrow to turn around. Got to go through now."

A sudden death, Larry thought, wouldn't have been so bad. But the terror leading up to it could be done without. The plane bucked. Larry looked all around. Half the time he couldn't see anything off the right wing. He looked down at the canyon, faintly visible. The snow was thicker now and it formed an icy slush in the corners of the windshield. Large clumps of ice gathered along the leading edge of the wing and then were torn away by the airstream. Some of them were hurled against the side of the cabin and they sounded like rocks.

What had been a narrow canyon below was, at high altitude, a gap between mountains, a canyon in the air through which the plane was flying. Up ahead, still higher than the plane, was another gap, high on the left, low on the right—Thompson Pass. Larry saw the pass for a second, then snow and fog, another peek at the gap ahead. The pilot stayed low and Larry wondered if they would manage to climb high enough. Banking from time to time, the plane followed the contour of the mountainside, always staying close enough for the pilot to see something.

A wave of nausea hit Larry and he swallowed. Fear at least might keep him from being sick. He looked for the whoopie bag, but couldn't find it.

"Rough," the pilot shouted and when Larry looked the man was not, as he expected, smiling back to show it was okay. He was tensely watching out the side and front and he looked as scared as Larry felt. Then the pilot turned his head and saw Larry. The smile came, weakly. "They oughta fix these roads, huh? Lotsa potholes."

They cleared the pass by a few hundred feet, never quite losing sight of the ground below or of the mountains. Coming over the pass, the pilot angled the plane steeply to the left and again followed the contour of the mountains. Larry was glad to have the rocky walls off the pilot's side again.

"Damn, Sam," Tiny called out, leaning forward to touch the pilot on the shoulder. "You give a hell of a ride for three hundred bucks."

"Scared?" the pilot hollered back.

"I ain't scared, but that welder in back is leaving permanent dents in the armrests."

"He what?"

A rocky outcrop rose instantly off the wingtip and the pilot reacted with a quick twist of the wheel and jab at the floor pedal.

"Never mind," Tiny told him loudly. "I ain't scared if you ain't."

"You think it's going to be like this all the way?" Larry asked after another five minutes. The sudden reports of the ice striking the fuselage and the occasional, wrenching bumps of rough air were terrifying. Larry doubted he could ever get used to them.

"We should be clear in another thirty minutes or so," the pilot said. "I hope."

Larry considered writing Hope a note of some kind. But what could he say? I forgive you? He didn't forgive her, not by a long shot, not yet anyway. And maybe she didn't want to be forgiven. Something for the kids? I love you both. The way the plane was bouncing, he doubted he could have held the pen on a piece of paper to write anything. And it would be embarrassing, especially if Tiny reached over and grabbed hold of it, just to see what he was doing. Never hear the end of it. Hope would be appalled when he told her. She didn't like flying much. Hope.

The plane hugged the mountains. Here the ceiling was higher and they flew even with many of the peaks. Probably most of them hadn't been climbed. There were dozens, hundreds of mountain peaks between Montez and Anchorage. The mist hid the ground below. They flew in a gray world whose only feature was an unending series of snow-covered peaks. These were the same mountains Larry had seen from the highway driving into Anchorage on the last R&R, the last time, when he had been so eager to see Hope. That trip had been so beautiful. In a way, from moment to moment when the fear subsided, so was this one. It was odd to be elated and frightened all at once. Whatever his emotions, he was indeed *feeling* now. The indifference to his own death had been replaced by a strong desire to keep those peaks away from the fragile, beautiful wingtip, blue with a bright red parallel stripe. The plane, streamlined, sleek, wallowed and skittered its way home.

Five minutes out from Anchorage, after more than an hour of buffeting, the plane broke free of bad weather. Anchorage lay in broken evening sunlight as though floodlit from a bank of stage spots. The air smoothed out and the pilot smiled broadly at Larry. "Sure nice to see town again, isn't it?"

After the landing, Larry stepped onto the concrete and resisted the impulse he felt to lie flat on the ground. Anchorage had little snow; drifts a foot or two high in the corners, the streets bare. Larry stomped on the ground, walking around the plane, enjoying the feel of ground underfoot. His car, a green and yellow Toyota, bought on a trade-in, was parked just off the highway. Hope wasn't there. Probably she was waiting inside. The woman at the airport in Montez had promised to phone everyone's family to let them know a charter was coming in to the Polar Airway terminal. He waited at the luggage hatch.

Planes landed and took off in rapid succession even though, at two-thirty, it was growing dark. Merrill Field was one of the busiest private airports in the world. Everywhere Larry looked he could see movement in the sky, military planes from Elmendorf, commercial flights from Anchorage International, small planes for Merrill.

Larry picked up his bags and walked into the hangar. He'd wondered how it would be to see Hope again, whether he would be glad to see her, angry, despondent or what. As she stepped out of the doorway where the other men had gone to meet their wives, bundled in her parka and heavy mittens, he was more glad than sorry. He was glad to be seeing anybody.

Nonetheless they exchanged only token greetings. They moved to the car. They were less than strangers.

The closer Paula got to the airport, the happier she seemed. Dan Curry was cheerful, talkative. He tipped the cabbie well. The week in Hawaii, followed by a few weeks in San Francisco, would take the pressure off for a while.

There were very few people at the check-in counter and Dan glanced up at the television screen showing departures. As he feared, the Hawaii flight was delayed.

"How long?" he asked as he came to the desk.

"Looks like two hours. If you want, take the boarding passes to the restaurant and we'll cover anything up to six dollars a person."

They reserved two sets of seats on the plane so the kids could be together in the row ahead. Paula also wanted some time away from them. Let the aisle-seat passenger prattle with them for a while, she said, as they walked back down the ramp to the restaurant.

Dan squeezed her hand. In San Francisco the kids could stay with Paula's mother while they got off for a while, maybe even taking a run down the coast to Mexico. With Dan working so much, Paula had been both mom and dad to the children the last several months. Not that he didn't need the break as much as she did.

They found a table near the window, but it wasn't much of a view. A ground crew was crawling over a Japan Airlines 747, putting baggage aboard, loading prepared meals, inspecting. At the next table, several Japanese stewardesses were chatting, watching the plane.

"Have to go to Japan, Hong Kong sometime," Dan said. It was a trip most of his friends had made at least once. Anchorage lay on a great circle route between New York and the Orient as well as being in the path of several transpolar routes. Many transcontinental flights had come to use Anchorage for a refueling stop. The queen of England and heads of state around the world had found themselves in Anchorage on their way to London, Moscow, Toyko, Washington.

"I'd like to see Bangkok," Paula said, glancing up from her menu. "Sometimes you can get a tour. Hong Kong, Tokyo, Singapore and Bangkok."

The waitress came and the children ordered ice cream. Dan and Paula had drinks. Along with the second round of drinks—and ice cream—Dan had a visitor, a tall, windburned fellow who spoke as from the other side of a waterfall. Cap, his name was. Cap something.

"Join you?" Cap drew up to the table.

"We're going to Hawaii," Allison said.

"And Honolulu and California, Sand Francisco," David added.

"San Francisco, California," Paula told the boy. "We need a vacation from the pipeline," she said to Cap, who had something to do with soil testing on the line.

"We all do," he told her, and immediately started in on Dan. The concrete floor for the pump station at Prudhoe might have to be repoured: a storm had torn away the Kelly enclosures and the concrete had frozen before it set. At the terminal, the bedrock for the east tank farm was fractured in one spot and a cavity was going to be blasted and the hole refilled with gravel. He was trying to hammer out some kind of agreement on the minimum and maximum sizes for the fill gravel. Did Dan want to get in on it?

"We can talk about it when I get back," Dan told Cap.

"Good, plenty of time," Cap said, and began describing some of the problems they were having with rock splitting off in the Copper Canyon blasting. The whole area had been subjected to stress, cracks in odd places, unusual failures in samples sent to the lab for strength tests.

Paula moved away from the two men. The Japanese stewardesses had departed hurriedly, and Paula supposed they were on the 747. The loading ramp was in position but there was no movement visible through its portholes.

Dan listened to Cap and watched Paula. She was making the best of it, ignoring the conversation. She looked lovely in the soft light coming through the tinted windows. Lovely, but indefinably strained. Perhaps like the rock on Copper Canyon. Invisible stresses, hairline cracks, unexplained failures. Since the big blow-up, things had been good between them. Basically good.

"Cap," Dan found himself saying. "We're on vacation. I don't mean to put you off, and I know Copper Canyon's bound to cause some problems. But right now, I'm thinking sunshine and sand."

"Read you, Danny-boy." Cap stuck his hand out. "Have a good time. A humongous good time. We'll catch you next year, huh?"

"Next year." Dan shook the hand. "Bye, kiddies," Cap said loud enough for some children two tables over to wave at him. "Bye, beautiful. Don't let those wahines give him a lei until you ask how they spell it. You know what they say in Hawaii." Cap was a laugh a minute. "Kum-on-I-wanna-laya." He made a pistol with his thumb and forefinger, got a quick shot off at David and Allison, and sauntered out of the restaurant.

"One-man crowd," Paula said in a soft voice.

Boarding the plane, it was obvious that some of the passengers were rushing the season that lay some three thousand miles to the south. Flowered sport shirts for the men, colorful shorts for the women, a few of whom were already wearing outsized sunglasses and straw hats. To Dan and Paula both, Hawaii was as much the winter vacation spot as Bermuda or the Caribbean was to East Coast residents. The triangle fare, throwing in a free stop in Hawaii for anyone traveling from Anchorage to Southern California, had made the Islands less exotic to the average Alaskan who flew Outside on family visits and business. Next month there would be a small surcharge, twenty or twenty-five dollars. Worth it.

Dan located the seats and got the kids settled. Allison won the right to sit by the window at takeoff. David, undoubtedly shrewd enough to realize he'd have the window when they landed in Hawaii, put up no fuss at all.

The one thing Paula found strange about making the trip from Alaska was that she didn't go west, didn't need to set her watch. Anchorage and Honolulu shared the same hour: Alaska-Hawaii Time Zone.

"We're actually going," Paula said, buckling her seat belt. "Thank God."

The plane began to fill up. A big, burly man, with a determined, but petite wife, made his way down the aisle, shouting greetings to friends scattered around the aircraft. Perhaps, Dan thought, some group of neighbors or a club. He heard "R&R" and a hoarse "I&I" shouted back a few rows.

"Hey, there's another Coldfooter." There were boos, random

cheers, applause in the forward section. Two men in their mid-twenties sat behind Dan and Paula. Drunks. Dan caught the word "pipeline."

Beside him, Paula extracted the plastic card with the information on ditching at sea and read it, feeling under the seat for the life jacket. She looked to Dan as if she expected to use it.

During the day, while Hope was at work, Larry visited people he knew in Anchorage. Finch-Smith was busily rearranging furniture and materials in the new APPLE building, an impressive eight-story structure on C Street. He took Larry on a quick tour, the high point of which was the "war room," where management meetings were held.

The room resembled a miniature UN. Two U-shaped tables, one inside the curve of the other, filled the center of the room. Chairs had been placed on one side of the tables only, orienting the room toward a blackboard and speaker's rostrum at the open end of the tables.

Finch-Smith pressed a button and the blackboard slid to one side, revealing a backlit projection screen on which a rose lamp was shining. Touching other switches, Finch-Smith dimmed the bank of similarly backlit, translucent graphs on the right wall, the spots illuminating the fifty-foot pipeline schematic covering the rear wall and finally the display of project photographs mounted on the left wall. The overhead lights dimmed automatically, as Finch-Smith demonstrated. Then, touching another button, the rose light faded out and a color slide with the APPLE logo faded in. In a series of lap dissolves, the November progress report presented itself.

"We've missed your stories the last few weeks," Finch-Smith told Larry as they stood near the elevators. "You know you're about the only camp correspondent who gives us copy we can use without rewriting. But then, you're a pro, aren't you?"

Larry thanked Finch-Smith for the compliment. It was true, that last. Even feeling as bad as he did, he was, indeed, a professional journalist. He told Finch-Smith that he had a lot on his mind, couldn't promise anything. Camp life was difficult.

"You ought to get a job here in town," Finch-Smith suggested as the elevator door opened. He held it for a moment longer after Larry was inside. "From what I'm told, that kind of life tends to get rather sticky for a marriage."

Larry visited Gil Wolfe, praised him for the success he was having, suggested a few lines of inquiry into money-wasting, which seemed endemic to the project, at least in Larry's terms. Gil asked if he had any leads on Dan Curry: bribe-taking, conflict of interest, favoritism or out-and-out collusion with APPLE. Larry said he doubted that Dan would be involved in anything underhanded but he'd let Gil know. Emil Bacich could also use whatever Larry ran across in the way of unreported oil spills and sewage plant breakdowns.

"I'll keep my eyes open," Larry said. But he had his own problems and the day with Gil was rambling, distracted. He couldn't get interested. It was just Larry's way of using up dead time.

Nights were bad. Neither of them knew how to act. One minute Hope would be quiet and contrite and the next banging things around and unwilling to speak a word. Larry for his part could be indignant, crushed, forgiving and callous.

"How did it happen?" was gradually replaced by "Why did you do it?" It happened, Hope told him, very gradually over the summer. Kurt had never tried anything at the start, but it was obvious that the love-poem cycle Kurt read one night at the Village Tavern was directed at her. It began with two voices, one in English, the other in German, and the two were intertwined, Kurt using common German words and a surprising variety of cognates to link the two voices. Other poems were more explicit, the last two or three to the point where the woman who ran the Village Tavern pulled the cord on Kurt's theremin before he was through.

Yes, it felt nice to have a good-looking man after me. It's been a long time since I was pursued. He's good-looking. To me and to a lot of other women. Of course, *you're* good-looking. It is not the weight. So you're forty pounds over. You're the one who's changing the subject. He kissed me and . . . all right. All right. I was sitting down. The end of the sofa toward the street.

Larry strode back and forth in the bedroom, drawing it out of her.

Kurt had kissed her and then they had necked, like high school kids, and Hope kept thinking she would stop him. She made him take his hand away when he reached under her blouse, and then, the second time, she hadn't. When he reached down below her waist she had caught his hand and Kurt had begun to speak the poem he recited in the Village Tavern, adding lines, changing it to the moment, to the way she looked.

Like most reporters, Larry regarded poetry as sentences that rhymed. He had never admitted this to Hope. What next?

I think I've been through all this before with my father, about fifteen years ago. Yes, then I did it, I went all the way. I lost control. What can I tell you?

Everything.

Christmas was dismal. No friends over to the house, a tiny tree instead of the usual room-filling Scotch pine. No carolers gathering in Washington Square.

Larry could have replayed the entire seduction with actors, staging, dialogue, movement, lighting. He knew it all. Kurt was not the lover she thought he would be, but he was attractive, interested.

Larry and Hope made love, and although it was desperate, even violent on one occasion, Hope later told him she was glad to at least have his interest.

"I don't feel like a useful piece of equipment anymore. That's all I was," she cried. "A piece of nice, functional furniture, pretty to look at, pleasant to have around, something to show to the guests."

One morning, just after Christmas, as they were making love the bed began to shake. "What is it?"

Hope smiled. "The earth moved."

And it had, they learned over the radio, but only at 4.8 on the Richter scale. The big quake of 1964 had been ten thousand times more powerful and lasted eight times as long.

There were good times, too. Larry watched TV with Hope and the kids, laughing at shows that still had Christmas coming. On one episode, the holiday dinner turned out to be Thanksgiving. Anchorage was weeks behind the Lower 48 in programming. The football game of the week actually took place the week before. Sports fans were torn between reading up on the game and insulating themselves from the final scores so the game would have some suspense.

After the TV went off, Larry sat in the big chair, looking at Hope on the sofa. "Is that really what it was like?" he asked. "Did I really let you feel ugly and superfluous, a *thing?*"

"You were always going away. What could I think? You didn't want to spend any time with me."

Five minutes later, he stormed out of the kitchen with a can of beer.

"You could have told me. You didn't have to keep it to yourself for years. You could have said something instead of doing what you did."

"Until this happened, I didn't completely realize it myself. I kept busy. Did what any good New England girl does when the going gets rough. Put up with it and worked harder."

Some nights they were able to talk about their jobs. Larry told stories about the fights, the practical jokes, the sadness. Hope described the natives, how the Eskimo officials in the program would go into conference and every few minutes there would be wild laughter, then more talk. The work got done, but it was a style that Hope had never encountered, certainly not where she grew up.

The women, for the most part, were divorced and on their second or third marriages. Some had been brought to Alaska unwillingly and had stayed even when the marriage went bad. They told Hope that after a year in Alaska she wouldn't be able to stay in Walpole. She might go home for a while, but she'd be back.

Alaska, Hope had come to realize, was its people as much as its wilderness. If Larry was going to write about the state for readers back east, then he really ought to write about the people. No one had been surprised that Joe Akin had lent Larry the two hundred. Things like that happened all the time. One family had gone broke on the Alcan and a gas station owner at the border had offered them all the gasoline they could carry. They filled milk cartons, jugs, bottles, jars, even baby food jars, everything they could find. True to his word, the man had filled them all. It was two years before they could pay him back.

Eventually Larry had all of the story and the reasons: how Hope had felt then, how she felt now. He surmised correctly that Hope had left Walpole because she was afraid that if she stayed she might have fallen in love with Kurt, even gone off with him. Larry alternated on that one. It pained him that she could really have been that close to leaving him. On the other hand, there was much to be said for Hope's pulling up roots and coming to Alaska, a place she hated, just to preserve a marriage that Larry seemed to care little about.

New Year's Eve, Larry had brought up the difficulty of returning, the gossip, the ridicule. "We'll ignore it," Hope said. They were standing in the bathroom with the door closed. The kids were on the sofa reading.

"Why did you let him leave the car in our driveway? Why didn't you close the curtains? If you were going to do something like that, couldn't you think that the car in our driveway all night would look bad?"

Hope sighed, leaning against the door.

"I'm sorry. I've never done anything like this before. I'm sure if I'd planned to have an affair, I would never have allowed myself to be seen with Kurt. We would have gone to Hampton Beach or over to some Vermont inn." Tears came into her eyes and Larry was sorry he had said it. "It's not like I go around . . ." her voice broke off. Deep within the house, below the cellar even, a rumbling could be heard. It grew louder and Larry felt movement.

Hope threw the door open and screamed for the kids to get under the doorway leading to the living room. The rumble was now intense and the movement of windowpanes, dishes, doors, partitions, added to the noise. A freight train was there, just under the floor, and the house was shaken in all directions. Hope stood, a child on each side, in the living room door. Larry, gripping the frame of the bathroom door, looked at Hope, looked down at the water in the toilet bowl. Its surface was torn by ripples.

Netty had one hand on her chest, mouth open.

All this had taken perhaps five seconds as the earthquake gathered strength. The noise of the train steadied and the house itself began to rock like a passenger coach over a bad roadbed. Larry's eyes darted from corner to corner of the house; he fully expected at any moment to see 90-degree angles begin to shift, become oblique, sharply acute; for the doorway with the children to become a parallelogram or trapezoid. In the kitchen, glasses were falling into the sink. The bedroom mirror began to swing in wider arcs.

"I don't like this," Caitlin said for all of them. With an odd zinging sound, the picture window cracked at the lower right corner. Larry nodded his head and Hope turned in time to see the crack reach up and across the pane.

Larry's watch said five-fifty-five and ten seconds. The quake had only just begun. Behind him, the toilet lid slammed down and Larry jumped out of the doorway just as the quake peaked out and the rumbling quit. Both the children were laughing at Larry, who stood in the small hallway, arms drawn up around his face. "My God," he whispered. Then he, too, began to laugh.

"Daddy was afraid," Netty said. "But I would have been, too, if I'd been standing by the toilet."

"You don't suppose it's going to do it again?" Larry said, turning on the radio. The radio announcer was interested in substantially the same information, and after several calls to geologists, he told his listeners that nobody really knew. But this one was a 5.3, and that's a biggie, folks, as far as we're concerned on this station. That's really ringing the old year out. Somebody must have done something wrong. I suggest we all make better resolutions and stick to them. The old man upstairs, or maybe the one downstairs, might be trying to tell us something.

"Is that true?" Caitlin asked. "The man upstairs?"

The quake did little damage around the city of Anchorage, although a market at 13th and I streets, possibly located on a minor fault line, suffered a few hundred dollars' damage in broken jars and bottles. Other stores reported merchandise on the floor. Homes had cracks. Dishes were broken. One woman was slightly injured when a grand piano suddenly waltzed across the floor, knocking her down.

The epicenter was located in a nearly uninhabited area fifty miles northwest of Anchorage. The quake was felt in Cantwell to the north, in Portage to the south, and in both Glennallen and Montez to the east. No sea waves were predicted or recorded as a result of the quake, which was actually the fourth in the space of a week. One of 3.5 Richter and another extremely brief one of 4.3 went unnoticed by many Alaskans.

Those in Montez seemed to have noticed all four, and conversation along the bar in the Montez Club was centered on nothing else. All New Year's Eve, regulars, the old regulars from before the pipeline, came in and compared notes on the quake.

It was like old times in the bar. Schultz had been let off for the week, as few pipeliners were around and fights had again become unusual. Bill Greenwood had gone down to look at his boat, remembering what he lost in the first quake. Maggie said nothing about losing her father and brother. Others in the bar had lost relatives, friends in that quake.

The band was down to half strength tonight, and the three members sat at a table together. Maggie wouldn't need them until later on, for a buildup to midnight.

Ed Booth was working behind the bar with Maggie, handling the beer tap. The pace was slow, talk relaxed. Maggie had turned the jukebox down. Doug and the Greenwood girl had left just after the quake hit to have dinner and spend New Year's Eve with Lavinia. Ed couldn't figure that one at all.

"I have the feeling we've had this conversation," Greenwood said to Maggie. David Curry smiled agreeably and slowly stirred his drink. He'd been hard at it since four-thirty; the quake had only stepped up the frequency. The way Maggie looked at it, though, New Year's Eve was only once a year. She didn't water the drinks for him this time. "We had this talk," Bill said, "the day that writer was in here from *Tomcat* magazine. What do you suppose ever happened with him? I've looked at the magazine every month but I haven't seen anything."

"If you don't see anything in that magazine," Mr. Greer said, "you must not be opening it to the middle." He and his wife laughed and poked at each other with their elbows.

"He said it would be a while," Maggie told Greenwood. "Everybody's been wondering if he was going to make us look like a bunch of nuts. That was when the blasting first got started and lots of people were feeling jumpy."

"I hope to tell you that little 5.3 we had tonight made me jump," Ed said. "I drove right out to Copper Canyon to see if any of that equipment might have been knocked down. We have a dynamite drill working close to the edge. You know, I didn't even see a single snowslide up in there."

David raised his head. "Be careful, Eddie boy. S'dangerous in these mountains this time o' year. Bad enough without a quake. That whole canyon," he waved a hand in the general direction of Copper Canyon, "whole damn canyon scares me." He banged his hand down. "That's right. Canyon scares me. Whole shitload of snow come right down on you. What could you do, huh? What could you actually do? And blasting in there. How'd you like to be in there, have the whole damn canyon fall on your car? You like that, Eddie boy?"

Ed shook his head. Bill Greenwood toyed with his coaster, smiling.

"Better believe you wouldn't like it. So don't go in there no more, okay? 'Cause I'm the one that's gonna have to come and get you out. And I'm drunk. Christ, I don't have to tell you that, do I? Maggie. Maggie! Police officer here wants another drink. Police *chief*." He watched Maggie mix the drink and then he took the glass from her and one by one toasted Maggie, Ed, Bill Greenwood, the Greers, the three members of the band. "Happy New Year to all of you. You're the finest bunch of people I ever knew in the whole world and I mean that." His mouth trembled and he closed it tight for a moment, fighting for control. "I'm proud to be your police chief, you know that? It's an honor." Tears flowed down his rugged, deeply creased cheeks. "I don't deserve it. A great honor."

"Happy New Year, David," Maggie said.

"Happy New Year."

"Yeah, Dave, Happy New Year."

Chapter Five

IT ALL BOILED DOWN to this: either Larry could forgive Hope and they could stay married or, if the pain just never went away, he could conclude he was unable to forgive and they would separate. Hope didn't want the last, but if he was going to spend the rest of his life dwelling on his hurt, then what kind of marriage would it be for either of them?

The day Hope dropped him off at the orientation and travel center on C Street, Larry wanted to forgive her, forgive her and hunt down, abuse, and finally murder Kurt Schall.

They parted sadly, Hope asking to be forgiven, Larry promising he would try. But always, inside, it ate at him, and Larry could not help exposing some new part of himself to the pain—it was like a complex work of art in which new dimensions constantly revealed themselves. The talk in the waiting room was alternately boisterous and melancholy. Not many wanted to go back.

Leslie Collins sat in a chair across from Larry, scribbling in a notebook, glancing up from time to time so that Larry thought for a moment Collins was doing a portrait. But when Larry got up to pour a hot chocolate, it was words and some scrawls of musical notation.

About a hundred workers, most of them men, were gathered in the dispatching room. A bored man with a head so gaunt it took on character from the shape of the skull underneath walked back and forth, checking travel orders, making notes on a clipboard.

"Sheep Creek," the man beside Larry told the checker. The skull regarded Larry from deep-set, weary eyes. "Camp?"

"Terminal."

"Camp?"

Terminal. Sheep Creek. Tonsina. Terminal. Glennallen. He worked his way down both sides of the room and returned to a narrow counter where a woman hunched down close to a sheet of paper, laboriously filling in lines of information. The two had a conference. Around Larry, men and women spoke of travels, the quake, how tough it was to go back to work this time of the year.

"First time I worked all winter," an operating engineer said. "Usually get in eight months and lay back on unemployment. This year I can afford to take off the summer instead, so I can get some housebuilding done. We been trying to finish off a log cabin for three years now and I just haven't had time."

A laborer on the other side of the long narrow room agreed. But he was going to put in three straight years, take advantage of the situation. "When it's done I figure I can buy a plane, and since I'll really have an extra year in, working the winters, it won't hurt to put down thirty, forty thousand. Then I can bid jobs in Kenai, fly back home once in a while and see Mamma."

"I don't know, I can't see working twelve months a year. You might as well live down in the Lower 48 if you're going to do that. That's what I like about being here. Strong union state. A guy like me, no education, and I can still make enough in eight, nine months to carry me through. Go Outside and try that. It's all screwed up down there."

The men at the Terminal had ragged Larry bad about only bringing home four, four-fifty a week. Tiny had told him it was ridiculous to live in a camp, sleep alone, put up with all the crap for less than seven hundred. Tiny could make four hundred a week working in town and have the weekends to himself, plus be home in his own bed every night.

Several of the men had tried to get Larry to drag up and sit in the union hall. Waiting now for a bus to camp which he would ride at no compensation while everybody else was paid eighty to a hundred dollars for their time, Larry wondered if they were right. Joe Akin took home almost nine hundred a week, and Godwin, when he caught that long-hour generator job, did nearly as well.

There were ways around the long lists. He could fly down to Juneau or Ketchikan where pipeline impact had practically no effect and earn himself an A or B card. When he had the hours in, he could transfer in at Anchorage or Fairbanks and be ahead of all the newcomers.

Nasty told Larry to take a pocketful of money up to Tommy's Elbow Room in Fairbanks and find himself a business agent. Didn't matter much what union. Used to be, Nasty said, you could buy a job in Tommy's for three, four hundred bucks. Course, they were getting greedy now, charging (he heard) a thousand and more. But what the hell? First two weeks of paychecks would clear that up.

Or what Larry should have done, and might have if he hadn't been so upset, was to go to the hall during the Christmas holiday season, when no one wanted to work. He might pick up a two- or three-week job in one of the camps, and when he came back, *if* they didn't keep him on, he'd have his B card and in the spring he'd be right back out.

Joe Akin hinted that, as foreman, he might be able to work out something, slip him in as an oiler. Could Larry wipe a crane down, keep the windows polished, check a dipstick, tighten a nut? Anyhow, did you ever see an oiler look like he was killing himself? It's like the fireman on a passenger train.

Now, listening to the chatter about big money, Larry wished he had done it. They were right. Working away from home, putting up with camp life wasn't worth taking home four hundred a week.

Leslie Collins chewed on his pen and listened to the conversations, too, watching the operating engineer who moved his hands in the air, describing the way his cabin sat on a ledge, overlooking a salmon stream. Only a few hundred feet the other way was a lake, where he could dock his seaplane.

"You've got a plane?" a laborer asked.

"It's not much. Little Cessna floatplane. About ten years old. If you get a plane, like you say, you ought to think about floats. Thousands of lakes in Alaska. Always got a place to set 'er down if you need to. Hell, sometimes I'll be flying along and see a likely lake, I might go in, do some fishing, just to try it out. Of course, you want to look it over pretty good 'fore you put yourself somewhere's you can't get back from."

Larry shut his eyes and rested his head against the wall. Being away from camp these past few weeks, he'd forgotten already the constant discussion of plans, dreams, expectations. Usually he found such talk invigorating. There was a spirit among the workers of almost matter-of-fact optimism. The state was obviously moving into a boom that would long outlast the pipeline construction, a future of fat and unending paychecks. A lot of money was wasted, a lot of men came back from R&R as broke as the day they hired on, but just as many were buying land, building, socking it away. Out east everyone Hope knew was talking about limits to growth, limits to families, limits. At her job, the talk was all of people having babies, buying land, putting up houses, opening new businesses. You could see it in the women, Hope said, the confidence of a mother pregnant with her fourth or fifth child. Larry saw it in the maze of construction activities, one-way temporary streets, clearing of land in Anchorage, a city that still had large areas of untouched land, contoured and forested the way it had been from all time. The skyline of the city in all directions was pierced by the thin latticeworks of cranes, some atop buildings, hauling themselves up by their own bootstraps, others reaching up impossibly into the pale blue sky of Alaskan winter to continue jobs that in any other year would have shut down for the cold season.

Even APPLE officials, although officially pessimistic and noncommittal, privately admitted that a second pipeline would almost certainly be built as well as a trans Alaska gasline. Kenai was booming. Fairbanks, crowded, dirty, untenable, at times practically uninhabitable—Fairbanks was booming. The old state capitol would be moved from Juneau and within the decade a new city built somewhere between Anchorage and Fairbanks. And that all by itself was a boom. If there was a bust coming, no one could see it in the next twenty or thirty years. An area the size of Texas, California and Montana with the most magnificent country and some of the richest resources of any state in the Union was booming and who could say when it would end?

The men and women in the dark, narrow, untidy room rested on plain wooden benches, waiting for the buses that would convey them into the camps, and they spoke of boom times and good times and sad times ahead.

It was tough, though, going back to work: seeing the look on your kids' faces. But where can you make this kind of money, huh? Tell me that. It's worth it on payday. Larry listened and thought of the pregnant women and Hope with Kurt, but Hope could not conceive. Together they had decided on a family of two and the doctor had performed a tubal ligation. So Kurt Schall's sperm had died one by one without causing a new person to be born. Still, for perhaps two days, a part of Kurt Schall had been alive inside of Hope's body. Larry pressed his head into the wall behind him and was relieved when the skull-faced man called for attention.

"We're going to have one bus for luggage. *One* bus. All luggage will be tagged and will go on the *one* bus, except for your survival gear. You will take survival gear with you. We report fifty-eight below from Gunsight Lodge all the way to Tonsina and sixty-to-eighty-mile-an-hour winds in the pass. So you will take your survival gear in the school buses."

"Eighty-mile-an-hour winds," the man next to Larry said softly. "I guess we're a hell of a lot better off in a bus. I wouldn't fly down there from here this time of year. I don't care how long the bus takes."

Larry rubbed at his eyes. He didn't want a ten-hour bus ride, he didn't want another ride in an airplane for a long time, didn't want to be at camp, and couldn't imagine going back to Walpole. Maybe Finch-Smith was right about trying to find work in town. But what would pay enough? He shut his eyes as the man repeated everything he had said, using different words. There was nowhere Larry wanted to be and nowhere else he could be than doing this thing, taking the ride, putting in another sixty-three days. And sixty-three nights.

At last it was time to leave. Outside, at nine A.M. the sky was getting light, the temperature in Anchorage stood at twenty-two below zero. Traffic, as usual, was tied up along C Street at the intersection with Northern Lights. Larry handed the duffel bag to the baggage loader, got on the bus for Terminal, found a window seat halfway back. The bus filled up quickly. Larry stared out the window already frosting up, and when he got around to looking at the person who had taken the aisle seat he was vaguely surprised to see it was a woman.

"Hello," she said. It was a greeting that acknowledged his presence and nothing more.

The woman was not bad-looking and had a deep tan, as did many of the returnees who had flown south for a few weeks in the sun. She wore only a heavy jacket and earmuffs, ordinary woolen mittens. Apparently she had not brought her survival gear onto the bus. Larry turned back to the window and wiped at the gathering frost with his bare hand. The temperature in the bus wasn't much above that of the parking lot outside. Maybe the woman figured if they had an accident the gentlemen around her would lend her gear, keep her warm. The operating engineer with the floatplane and the laborer who wanted to buy some kind of plane continued their discussion in the seat behind Larry. Two men Larry hadn't seen at the Terminal before sat ahead and complained to each other about the cold, unheated school bus, violation of everything in the project agreement, and speculated on the quality of life in Terminal Camp.

"Well," the bristle-cut by the window said, "I'm just glad I finally got on."

"Hell, job's a job. I was looking for a job when I found this one. Pipeline's not the only job in the world, you know. This is any sample, I'm pulling the pin, go back on unemployment."

All the way to lunch, at Gunsight Lodge, not even the halfway point of the trip, Larry had dozed fitfully. The windows were not merely frosted by now, they were covered by a quarter inch of ice. The bus, though, was warmer, so that he could leave his coat open and his gloves off. The window frame looked like the inside of a freezer. In places, tiny whiskers of frost clumped together.

Lunch was simple, provided by the company: hot roast beef sandwiches, gravy and mashed potatoes for everybody. Getting back on the bus, Larry asked the woman if she wanted to sit by the window.

"Are you cold?" she asked.

Larry looked at the icy pane and shook his head quickly. "I don't know what I was thinking of. There's nothing to see, is there?"

"It isn't the most exciting sightseeing tour I've ever taken," she said.

Once more the bus was under way. Larry told the woman who he was, that he had started out to do articles on Alaska and ended up working on the pipeline when he went broke. He left out the accident, Hope, everything else.

The woman had transferred down from the Slope, didn't want to work up there anymore, wouldn't say why.

Up ahead, the conversation had turned to guns. The man by the window who, Larry supposed, had kept the same haircut he'd been given the day he joined the marines, was a hunter. All his conversation was directed toward what kind of gun you'd take if you were after a Kodiak bear, what you'd use on moose in brush country, scopes, charges, grains.

The man on the aisle didn't hunt much, but knew a lot about ammo. He talked for a long time about "stopping power" and only gradually did Larry realize he was talking about people. Apparently a test had been done with gelatin packages that duplicated the consistency of human flesh. Various calibers and loads had been fired into these cells to determine the relative damage of, say, a .38 police special and a .357 Magnum. The article had concluded that the 9 mm load was probably the ideal for law enforcement, as the bullet would have a great enough shock capacity and penetration for the average situation with the added advantage that it wouldn't easily pass through the subject to wound innocent bystanders. The .44 Magnum was regarded as too powerful. The first shot would stun the nerves in the hand of a shooter and render his aim less accurate. After three shots, performances by all but a few shooters had dropped significantly enough to become a danger for bystanders.

Which, to this man, was a load of crappola. For one thing, guy comes in your bedroom at night, you don't have a lot of bystanders. Some clown runs out and tries to pull the car door open on a dark corner, where you see bystanders?

I hit a man I want to know that man's going to stay down. I use a .44. The rest of the family's got .357 Magnums except for my boy. He's only ten and he generally goes with a .38.

Even the bristle-cut hunter didn't respond to that one. The

woman, Jill Jones, looked at Larry and made a small circle in the side of her head. Screwy.

The man persisted. Daughter's seventeen. She don't go out of the house without a gun. Takes the car, she puts it right down on the seat beside her. Course she was raised with guns, like the rest of them. Had pellet guns when they were real little. One day, oh, the girl was ten, the one boy was twelve and the other boy was seven. Three-year-old was in the house. Anyhow, we were out in back of the house plinking away with this one pellet gun. Took repeating cylinders in it, so you could get off several shots. I got mad about something and I remember taking that gun and telling them kids to move it. They started hollering and I pointed it at Chrissie, that's the daughter, and let her have it right in the ass. Made a bruise about the size of a half dollar. She jumped a mile, Jesus! The boy had got down behind the hedge and when he put his head up I zipped one right in on him. Parted his hair and then caught the other one, trying to scootch in behind a tree, right on the toe. Christ, did he jump around. I thought my wife was going to kill me. Well, you know how it is, you hunt. Target shooting's okay, but there's nothing like a live target.

The hunter nodded and bunched his coat up against the window, snuggling down. Eventually the man on the aisle left off.

Several times Larry glanced at the woman, Jill Jones, and thought of saying more to her about what had happened, about Hope and their marriage and how depressed he felt. But he sensed that she was depressed, too, and Larry had seen what happened with the women in camp. Every man with a problem would find his way to a woman and unburden himself.

"You look as down in the mouth as I feel," Larry said after the bus rounded the intersection at Glennallen and started down the Richardson Highway, now halfway to Montez.

Jill, who had dozed lightly the last hour or so, made a faint smile. "I sometimes wonder if all this is worth it. You think this is the way people are supposed to live?"

The operating engineer with the floatplane behind Larry had been discussing the economy in the Lower 48. It wasn't a recession out there and the little ups and downs weren't signs of recovery. The world economy was doomed. That seaplane was his escape ticket. He had a year's supply of staples for every member of his family stashed away in the cabin. The bottom would fall out. You put your money in a plane, fine. But if you don't put the rest of it in food, silver and gold coins and enough ammunition to carry you ten or fifteen years, you're crazy. You get staples, you can eat off this country.

"I'm not even earning enough to make it worthwhile," Larry told her. "Just working as a timekeeper."

"Why not join the Teamsters? You're not regular staff, are you?"

For one thing, when the depression hits, it won't be like the last one. It'll be quick, yeah, it'll happen fast like before, but it'll be worse. Panic, looting, starvation, disease, military takeovers in the cities. First thing, absolutely, is lay in a supply of food. Hey, the Mormons do it all the time, part of their religion. And there's companies that put up food, nonperishables, things packed to stay fresh, bags of wheat, small grain mills, everything including drinking water in cans. They used to just get the Mormon trade, but in the last few years sales to people like me have tripled, quadrupled.

"I wish we could go Teamster. It kills me to hand out those big checks every week. When I first got the job, I thought I'd struck it rich, until I saw what the others were getting."

"The Teamsters have done me some good," Jill said and leaned close to Larry, whispering the story of what had happened to her and Bill Wiggins in the shower. But Wiggins had disappeared. A friend in some other camp had frozen to death. She'd spent R&R in Hawaii and seen a boy killed on a motorscooter. Larry put his arm over the back of the seat so Jill could move closer. They unburdened each other.

There's books about how to get ready for the crash, what to do, where to buy the food. Some places will deliver the food in unmarked packages so nobody will know. That way you won't get people in town talking, maybe the postal clerk and some friends come to your house . . .

The bus swerved violently and threw the left aisle passengers, Jill, the shooter, the food saver, all of them onto the floor. The bus jounced up and down, still swerving, and then slowed, easing back on the highway.

There were curses, complaints, questions.

"Moose," the driver shouted back. "He ran right out on the road, but I missed him. Two of them. One on the road, one by the side."

"Hit him again," a drunk up front shouted, "harder, harder."

"Everybody all right?" the driver called, slowing the bus to a crawl. The people on the floor sorted themselves out. Jill had twisted her wrist slightly, others had aches, but nothing broken or cut.

"Lucky he saw him," Larry said. It was already five o'clock. Red lights blinked ahead on the road and the driver slowed abruptly. Just beyond a dip in the road one of the other buses *had* hit a moose and the mangled body lay on the road to one side of the mangled radiator and front end. The driver, his face bandaged, sat in a state police car while a wrecker crew stood looking at the moose.

"Need any help?" the driver said.

"No, second bus took up the load. Patrol car took a few guys back up to the hospital in Glennallen."

"Damn near hit a couple myself." He swung the door shut and moved on. The blast of cold air that had come in caused further complaints, speculation on the outside temperature. The thermometer at Tonsina Lodge showed sixty below. Larry spit on the fender of the school bus and it froze immediately. After quick coffees and lavatory visits, the workers scooted back aboard the bus, spending as little time outdoors as possible. What heat the bus had built up on the way down was now lost with people getting off and on.

Everyone was cold, tired, uncomfortable and hungry. Jill stuck her hands under her armpits and stomped her feet. The drunks passed bottles around and swore fervently. The wind was picking up now and obscuring the road with snow. Once or twice the driver slowed for suspicious drifts gathering along the roadside.

The front-seat passenger crouched at the driver's side and scraped at the windows, trying to keep up with the ice. The defrosters made two tiny clear spaces on the windshield. In a half hour there was no other traffic on the road.

"Hope the goddamn pass is open," someone shouted.

At Mile 34, the warning signal was dark. The pass was open.

A spray of snow completely obscured the windshield. Even after it had cleared, the air in front of the bus was a swirl of white. Larry tensed, a drunk broke off in midsong, the bus fishtailed. Then the road lay out where it was supposed to be and the bus followed it.

But there was no relaxing. A steady booming began as the bus leveled off at the head of the pass. From what distance it came, there was no way to judge. Larry had dreaded leaving Hope and the kids alone with the possibility of more quakes. Suppose the 5.3 was merely a trembler preceding another giant quake? The booming continued.

"Step on it, you bastard," the man in back shouted, "the frigging snow's coming down on us." The man apparently had an ice scraper when he boarded, and he had persistently kept a six-inch square of window free of ice. "What is it?" someone called back. "What's happening?"

The man got up and shouted that it was a slide. He'd seen it up high, but couldn't tell for sure if it would hit the road. The driver shouted back that he wasn't about to stop and investigate. Just as he did, the bus swerved again and plowed through another low drift.

This time it came to a halt. The driver cursed and tentatively fed gas. The wheels spun. He put it in reverse and tried again. The rear of the bus moved sideways, toward the edge of the road.

The man who stored food reached into his duffel bag and began pulling out cold-weather gear and chocolate bars, which he tucked into his shirt pockets. He looked grimly satisfied.

Larry was glad he'd brought his gear. The best Jill could come up with was a pair of padded ski mittens, and even though the motor was running and the heater still working, she slipped them on. Everyone was suddenly intent on the rise and fall of the wind howling outside the bus. The slide, if there had been one, had died down.

"Well," the driver said, standing up and facing his passengers, "the longer we sit here the more that wind's going to pile the snow up on us. If you men can push me back, I can cut left and maybe bull my way through."

"We could wait for the next bus," someone suggested, but men were already zipping up parkas and moving toward the door.

"My business agent's gonna hear about this," the man behind Larry muttered, getting up and tying a scarf over his mouth and nose.

Larry struggled into his bib-front insulated pants and Jill had to stand so he could get by.

"Hey, sweetheart," the man with the scarf said, "you ain't going out dressed like that are you?"

Jill frowned at him, took her seat.

"Don't forget to save my seat," Larry called back and was pushed along the aisle and out the door.

He found himself in snow above his knees. The wind-driven snow stung his eyes and Larry stumbled along, head down, to take up position at the front of the bus.

The driver leaned out his side window and shouted for the men to begin.

"Now!"

He revved the engine and the wheels spun.

Larry could feel the bus give way for a moment. It moved perhaps a half an inch, but it did not rock back. The men slacked off and tensed.

"Now," the driver shouted, and the men along the front of the bus repeated it so everyone could hear.

Larry strained, heard men around him grunt, heard the wind and the distant whine of tires.

"Dummy can't drive," the man to Larry's right said.

The man was drunk and breathing hard already. He wore a knit cap that was already plastered white with snow.

"Ease up on the pedal, why don't ya?" he called as the driver shouted for another push and the men threw themselves against the weight of the bus. This time it moved a few inches and rocked back, and the men did not need to be told to get in the swing of it.

The bus went backward, stopped, moved forward. The men pushed, farther this time, back, then forward. The bus moved back five feet and stopped. One of the passengers floundered along the edge of the road to the rear and came back to the driver.

"Snow's already drifted behind us. We got to go forward and try to bust through it."

When Larry got to the rear of the bus he found himself alongside Leslie Collins.

"You know," Collins said, laying a shoulder into the bus and bracing himself, "there's a dangerous element about all this that I find vaguely attractive."

"Jesus Christ," the drunk said and moved on down the line to be away from the two.

Jill was not the only one who had failed to bring cold weather gear along. There were five other men still on the bus because they weren't dressed properly and two men still on because they were too drunk to get off. Jill moved to the front, trying to see through the icy windshield, scraping clear spots that froze up almost as soon as she moved from them.

"What are they doing now?" she asked, standing in the door-well, using both hands to move the scraper over the glass.

"In back," the driver told her, sticking his head out the sliding window, ducking back in and putting the bus in gear. "We have to try it again."

One of the men who'd remained aboard moved up front, followed by a kid who had pulled a stocking cap down over his ears. The driver eased down the gas pedal, backed off, tried again. The bus moved a foot and bogged down.

The kid, arms tucked down in the side pockets of his peacoat, nudged the driver.

"Would it help if we got off?"

"You aren't dressed for it."

"Just until they get it moving. We could stand it maybe three or four minutes."

"Sure," the other man said, "we'll just keep out of the wind."

"Suit yourself," the driver said, and opened the door.

On impulse, Jill stepped out into the snow and hunched down inside her jacket. At least her hands were warm. She walked out into the full force of the wind, backing into it all the way to the other side of the road. She could just see the rear of the bus through the darkness and blowing snow. Another twenty feet up the road she could just see the front, could not even hear the bus over the sound of the wind. She cupped her mittens around her eyes and peered down the road ahead and then turned to look back down the pass.

A light glimmered faintly, an orange light. She moved a few steps toward it and then saw the light again. It blinked on and off three times. A dull, low growl sounded during a lull in the wind and Jill recognized it immediately, the sound of a big diesel engine. A road grader or a snowplow. With a blinking light.

Throwing off a sudden shiver from the cold, Jill scuffled through the snow to where the two men huddled out of the wind. The tires were still spinning, but the bus was moving slowly, moved back to where it had been when they first got stuck.

She told the kid about the noise and let him know she was going down the road to meet the plow.

He nodded, arms hugged around his chest. "I'm getting back in the bus."

Jill passed some of the men coming up on the road side to the front of the bus and carefully avoided crossing directly in back of the bus, just in case it should come free and suddenly roll back. In places the snow was blown nearly down to the pavement, and in other spots, drifts of two and three feet suddenly appeared. The tracks of the bus were already covered and she turned to look back, seeing the taillights glowing softly through the wind-whipped snow.

Again she cupped her eyes and peered down the road, listening for the plow. She took a few more steps and hesitated, not sure if she was hearing it. Then she saw the orange light blink again, and it seemed measurably closer than the last time she'd seen it.

Looking back at the bus she could barely make out the taillights and she was hesitant to move completely out of range. She was getting cold and there was no telling how fast the plow was working. In fact, it was possible that it was sitting still, or working on a particular patch of road, maybe a small slide.

Jill smiled at the thought of the driver, moving snow up through this desolate, empty pass and seeing a woman hitchhiking atop a snow bank. She listened, and this time the powerful, throaty roar of the engine seemed to come from just down the road. The snow had let up for the moment, and she could see the orange beacon flicking on and off. Jill took a last look at the bus and began to jog, stumbling in the snow once or twice, but glad to be warmed up. She heard the engine again, but couldn't tell exactly where it was coming from. This time the sound seemed to come from behind her. Perhaps it was the bus. Or another plow.

The wind blew up a sudden gust and Jill ducked, following the road by watching for the metal markers on either side.

The wind eased up again and Jill stopped, puzzled and suddenly apprehensive. The engine sound now came from below, then to the left of the road. Once it quite clearly seemed to come from above.

Jill raised her head to look for the orange bubble light on the plow and felt a wave of sick fear pass over her.

The orange light she was following was one of the overhead markers, a reflector mounted on a metal pole that arched out over the road to show drivers where the edge of the highway was. The marker was loose and it wobbled in the wind, picking up the light of a single, unshaded bulb that illuminated a highway department tool shed, half buried in the snow.

Jill listened for the plow, heard only the wind and the steady creak of the reflector as it bobbled up and down. Then she heard another engine sound for a split second, faint, but unmistakable. The bus.

And then, as if taunting her, the wind snatched sounds of a diesel engine and blew them at her from all directions. A violent shiver went through Jill as she turned and began to trudge back uphill.

"Lose your girlfriend?" the guy behind Larry said as the men settled into their seats. Larry shrugged, nodding toward the back of the bus.

"I guess she found better company."

The kid across the aisle tapped Larry on the shoulder. "If he means the girl you were sitting with, she caught a ride with a snowplow."

"A snowplow?"

Larry looked down. Her bag was still in the bus.

The kid shrugged. "That's what she told me."

"So that's what that was," his seatmate said. "I went over to the other side of the road to take a leak and I thought I heard a piece of heavy equipment moving. I thought it was my imagination."

Larry got up and went to the driver. The bus was well over to the left side of the road and free of the drifts. The driver was scraping ice away from the windshield and two men were helping him.

"The woman that I was sitting with isn't on the bus."

"She got a ride with a snowplow," the driver said, finishing his section of the scraping and putting the bus in gear. He moved out very slowly, testing the road surface.

Jill bit down on her tongue as if to take away the pain she felt now in both feet. It was difficult to run, and for an awful moment she thought the bus had left her. Then she saw the taillights, the bus waiting for her on the road. Jesus, she thought, how embarrassing. They hadn't been waiting for her long, but she'd never hear the end of it. They were probably thinking of sending out search parties.

Live and learn. She stumbled and fell headlong in the snow, dragging herself upright with great effort. This was no fooling though, she was cold and tired and wouldn't be surprised to find a few patches of mild frostbite tomorrow morning.

She moved toward the bus and blinked at a sudden rush of snow. It was odd. She had taken several steps but hadn't come any closer than ten feet to the rear of the bus. She shook her head and lurched forward and dumbly watched the bus recede just the distance she had moved.

Moving. She took two quick steps and understood that the bus itself was moving.

"This is no time for games," she whispered, furious at the driver. The bus slowed, she caught up to it, steadied herself against the rear taillight for a moment and then felt the bus draw inexorably away. Jill began to run in a slow, determined dogtrot.

She caught up again and pounded a fist against the rear panel, pounded in silent, dreamlike gestures with her soft, padded, thickly insulated mitten.

"Stop," Jill screamed, and the words were torn from her lips by a gust of wind. The bus slowed as if in obedience and Jill whipped her mitten off, smacking the steel of the bus with her bare palm. She felt a sudden tug as the bus lurched forward again. Jill stumbled after it on feet that had no more feeling and tried to pull free, but the hand was frozen fast to the metal.

And then she fell, glimpsing in one moment the imprint of her hand—not the imprint, but the seared, frozen layer of flesh with all its intricacies and unique whorls, the love line, the money line, the lifeline, the individual patterns of the fingers—torn loose and mounted like a butterfly that disappeared into the darkness and the snow.

She lay, her ruined hand outstretched in the snow and sobbed, listening to the sound of a powerful diesel engine throbbing into the night, now close, now far away.

As it turned out, Copper Canyon was blocked by a slide and the entire bunch had to lay over at Sheep Creek. It was after the regular meal hour when they got in, only twenty miles from Montez. The cooks agreed to put on a hot meal instead of sandwiches.

Larry sat at a corner table, as depressed as the rest of them, too depressed to join the bunch who were angrily planning to take it up with the union. Leslie Collins the safety man sat at the far end of the table and rubbed the strings on his guitar. Larry didn't know he had it, hadn't seen him bring it in, had never heard Leslie play.

Leslie blew on his fingers and smoothed out the page of his notebook.

"I made up a song on the way down."

Larry laughed. "I hope it's funny. That bus ride was a bad joke."

"You got that right, mate," said a tough-looking kid who was on the edge of the table itself. He was Cockney. "Play," he said, "anyfing at all."

The song was about the good times the pipeline was supposed to bring, the hopes and dreams of the men and women who were drawn to it like moths to a candle flame. It was about sleeping in a bed alone and thinking of someone far away and then being at home, knowing you were going back again. It was called "Black Gold Blues."

Larry moved closer and followed the score. It was signed "L.C. from Montez."

"L.C.," Leslie interpolated, "that's me."

L.C., who everyone knew was single and didn't like girls, sang of families gone sad, the children wonder why and all you can say of the man on the bus is that he's somehow doing this for us.

When he stopped and looked up a dozen men were watching respectfully.

"Do you know any more?" one of them asked.

The next morning word came in over the camp radio about Jill. The plow driver had made a run at 5 A.M. and, glancing to one side of the road to see what he had picked up with the blade, saw Jill's leg protruding from the new bank of snow. He dug her out and brought the body down to Tonsina Camp. Nobody seemed to know who she was, but she had a dispatch from the teamster hall to Terminal Camp.

Larry told the security man, who interviewed the bus passengers, what the driver had said and that the tall kid had told him she'd caught a ride with someone.

"Well, these things happen," the officer said. "You were lucky the rest of you made it, know what I mean?"

Afterward, before they headed on down to Terminal Camp,

Larry looked for the driver, but he had left early for the trip back to Anchorage.

Things happen, the men agreed, and forgave themselves and each other.

Tiny Atigun Camp was nestled into a valley in the middle of the pass that carried the pipeline through the Brooks Range. More than four thousand feet above sea level, the camp was a small maze of interconnecting snow tunnels that allowed workers to pass from their dorms to chow to the construction offices and, at the end of the day, to the recreation hall without ever stepping outside. If the closed system protected workers from weather, it also made the entire camp especially vulnerable to fire. Two days after the new year began an electrical fire had broken out in one of the nearly unoccupied dorms and the skeleton crew of maintenance workers had answered the alarm with extinguishers and little else but determination. The fire was confined to the service room and the adjoining laundry room. Smoke lingered in the corridors for days, faint traces of it seeping throughout the facility.

Dan Curry, on an inspection tour with a state safety engineer, could still smell it. The area around the furnace had the characteristic sour smell of damp, charred wood, but the odor was detectable even in the main hall.

Curry looked at the panel and the adjoining wall and ceiling. In one area, the fire had burned through to the outside and tiny flakes of powdery snow occasionally sifted down. A new, temporary circuit board had been set up to handle the load until a replacement unit could be sent up from Fairbanks. Dan didn't understand much about electricity, but he listened as the engineer talked to the camp's electrical supervisor.

Outside, the wind rattled loose panels of corrugated roofing, whined in the eaves, made electrical wires sing in the sunless afternoon. It was a long way from Hawaii.

The electrical boards had been mass produced and installed in the modular units on an assembly-line basis somewhere in California. The work had not been done by union electricians, the electrical supervisor maintained. He was a member of the IBEW and claimed no union man would do sloppy work like that. Perhaps, he suggested, all of the electrical hookups from Prudhoe to Montez should be redone by union men.

The state inspector asked to be shown the same setup in another dorm. Curry tried to show interest in what the inspector was telling him. The unit checked okay. They went on through four more dorms until they found a discrepancy. The IBEW man was sure the wiring was nonstandard, and the inspector finally agreed that although the load would probably not cause trouble, the unit should be replaced.

This was all explained to Dan in terms he could understand, since Dan might have to write the order for total inspection or total replacement.

Outside it was dark and the wind blew. The haul road stretched from Prudhoe to Livengood, linking the camps into tiny towns spread across the northern half of the state. Where before the camps were like military bases, they were now becoming frontier villages, each with its own identity. Coldfoot had a cabinetmaker who created fancy woodwork for the mess hall. Dietrich was big and bustling. Chandalar was intimate, and had a cook who spread checkered tablecloths and provided fancy coffee mugs. Atigun's sign painter had posted messages and clever sayings everywhere. Galbraith, which sprawled on the edge of the Slope in the shadow of the Brooks Range, housed pipeliners, roadbuilders, truckers, and in warm weather, teams of archeologists who daily helicoptered to a dozen nearby digs. Toolik had spirit, put out its own newspaper, "the farthest north daily in America." They were mountain towns and treated visitors with mountain hospitality.

Caribou wandered through these mountains, foxes, grizzly bears, dall sheep and the small mammals, parka squirrels, mice, weasels. Those who worked in the camps found their days richer for the occasional sighting of game, the silent beauty of a peregrine falcon circling in a mountain updraft, the playful ease of the parka squirrels. This far north, winter brought extremes of cold, but it also brought the wondrous play of aurora borealis. Curry had seen tinges of this morning's lights when he landed at Galbraith for the drive up to Atigun.

It was necessary for Dan Curry to remind himself of these things from time to time, just as it was now necessary for him to follow the inspector's finger as it traced a path through the tangle of colored wires in the circuit box. Dan shook his head and the safety man began again, starting at the distribution line, singling out the one right path in the jungle.

Dan thought of the corridors leading everywhere, the haul road leading south, other places and times. He knew that in the maze of last month's events, Paula had decided to remain in San Francisco.

"Are you following this, Dan?" the safety man asked. "This is the crux of it."

Dan nodded.

Was all this really worth it? And if it wasn't and he gave up the job, took something less demanding in town, would he lose her anyway? Paula was jealous of Alaska. That was the term she used. She didn't know when she was coming back. The wire that seemed to continue on through the circuit actually ran to nowhere.

Fire in the Arctic was as dangerous and deadly as fire at sea. Outside, Alaska moaned and rattled at the skin of the buildings.

For him?

Even in winter the boomers came, crowding into rented rooms, living in hotels, motels, trailers, flophouses and missions. In Fairbanks the cost of a one-room apartment jumped to four, five, and six hundred dollars a month. Landlords rented houses by the night, sleeping men on the living room floor, in the dining room, in hallways, wherever they could find places to stretch out in bedrolls. They charged ten dollars a head and took in as much as four hundred a night, twenty-eight hundred a week. Some lasted a month before the health board closed them down. Rooms were rented for a hundred a week and more, rooms with no plumbing and broken-down beds. But the men paid because they had come so far and there was no way back.

They collected welfare, unemployment, free meals at the Sally or the First Presbyterian. They sold off guns, tools, campers, cars for which they could no longer buy gas. Although the work force had been cut for cold weather and the halls filled up with old-time residents looking to go back out, the newcomers waited on the benches for a union call, waited at the Odd Fellows Hall in Fairbanks to be operating engineers, waited in the modern, red-iron, rose-tinted Teamster Hall in Anchorage, waited for the call that would make them rich.

The wives, who could have found work as nurse's aides, as secretaries, as store clerks, for the most part stayed home in Boise, Shreveport, Ocala and Spokane. The men ignored a hundred jobs that might have kept them afloat in favor of a poverty with some promise. Meanwhile, the cities were run by children. Boys barely out of high school drove taxis with street maps on their laps. Girls who had rarely gone shopping on their own were selling suits, shoes, shirts, records, furniture. Kids delivered the mail, pumped the gas, minded the stores. There were jobs going begging, jobs that would lead—as yet another manager became assistant chef at Pump Station One, as the head clerk went off to drive trucks at the Terminal—to better jobs. The work force simmered and turned over and the opportunities were there, but who would plug into a job for a few hundred bucks a week, when the big call might come any day, for two or three times that money? But there were a few, down on their luck, who reluctantly took a job: maintenance worker for the University of Alaska, electrician for the City of Anchorage, forklift driver with Sea Land, jobs that had been prized in the years before the pipeline and would be again. When the Alaskans came back from the camps, when the war was over, all the good jobs might be held by strangers. It was a chance you had to take.

Larry Ransom's crews got through to Montez after a two-day wait during which Montez was cut off by land and by air from the rest of Alaska.

The lucky ones, those with pipeline jobs, envied by the dispossessed, the haunters of the union halls, settled in with the usual grumbling, roommates who snored or listened to rock or country and western, eggs too greasy, mattress sagging, the weather, the wind, the hours, the choice of movies, the phone service.

Nasty came back, tanned like the others, and in a sunny disposition as well. He looked for Tiny for two days and then ended up with a roommate he found acceptable, Dago John, the concrete foreman.

Tiny got in a week late, just as the labor relations man was considering filling in a termination. "Still hadn't spent that checkpool money," he boasted to everyone.

"Not much left," the room clerk told him, looking over the keyboards. "We're holding a floor for the night shift now."

"Hell, I don't care where you put me. I been in these camps a lot of years and I get along with 'em all." He cracked his knuckles. "I wonder why."

Tiny took the key offered, slung his bag over his shoulder, and trudged up the hill toward the third dorm. Eventually, fifteen dorms would stand on the hillside in parallel rows, each succeeding dorm a little higher than the next. Two other sections of dorms were also being built. Twenty-eight hundred people would live at the Terminal in the height of construction. Tiny expected it would be a madhouse then, both on this side of the bay and the other. He'd never lived in a camp that big. Rat's nest, he thought, as he climbed the short stairway and went inside.

The room was on the first floor, halfway to the center. That was convenient. Too close to the bathroom and laundry was tough for sleeping. Too far from the bathroom could be disastrous after a hard night of drinking.

It was ten-thirty at night. Most of the men were asleep by now. A tall kid wrapped in a towel padded down the hallway and Tiny nodded at him, pausing to check the key number against the door. He heard an electric hum inside the room and thought of knocking first. But what the hell, it was his room, too. He pushed the door open and stared, standing in the doorway, trying to comprehend it all.

On one wall was a color poster picture of a koala bear. It was wrapped appealingly around a eucalyptus tree, nibbling at a shoot. Above the head of the right-hand bed was a red, white and blue sign. FUCK COMMUNISM. That, at least, he could go along with, but on the bed, sitting there cross-legged in his underpants, was that candy-ass safety man, drying his hair with an electric blower.

Collins shut off the blower and smoothed his hair down impatiently.

"You know," he said to Tiny, "I spent sixteen dollars having my hair done in Anchorage and now I wear a hard hat all day long. My hair can't even *breathe* properly."

Jack Price, the dock superintendent, and Little Nasty sat hunched over a small table in the Montez Club, fighting to put each other's arm down. Once Nasty's elbow slipped. One time Price, only a few inches taller than Nasty, was caught gripping the table edge. Sonny, the trainee, was reffing the match. A pile of bills, forty bucks in all, lay in front of him.

It was the middle of the week and the club was fairly empty. A new hooker, a black girl from Texas, was working the club tonight, chatting up the men, laughing, shooting pool in back. Sonny watched her and watched the table.

"Y'know," he said to Nasty, whose neck and forehead revealed veins standing out as if they would burst, "I had a black girl in Fairbanks last spring."

Nasty grunted. Jack Price grunted back. The locked hands trembled, but neither man gave an inch.

"Figured I'd had Orientals when I was in Nam, Spanish chicks when I was in Mexico, white girls here in Alaska and of course my own kind. Aleut. Eskimo. Tlingit. Athabascan. Creoles."

"Can it," Price growled, and leaned into Nasty.

"Funny, everyone figures something different is better. You whites always want a black girl, a native girl. So I was working and had some dough and I saw this black girl walking toward me. Cute little thing. And why not? I had plenty in my pocket. And it's thirty below, so who wants to walk around? She asks me if I want to party and I ask her how much? Fifty bucks. Hell no, twenty I say. Shit, no, forty. So we agree on thirty and go back to her room in this crummy motel. Except her room isn't so bad. Big floor pillows all around, beads hung in the doorways, pretty nice."

"Gahhhrrrrrr," went Price, and Nasty's hand went down a few inches. Nasty squinted horribly from one side of his face. "Huuuuuuu." He brought Price's hand up and started down the other way.

"Well, this whore you see by the jukebox here, you can see she's built. Pretty ass, nice titties. But this girl I was with, out at that temperature, by the time she gets down to skin, there's nothing left. Skinny legs, tiny little ass. And she's wearing this big wig on her head and three sweaters. For thirty bucks she don't take off those sweaters. I reach under the sweaters and tell her it's okay. See, I'm not missing much. Not like this one in here tonight. Good hips on that woman. Just made to rest in."

"Kill you," Price grunted, "son-of-a-bitch." Price had his back to the jukebox and the girl.

"So what do I get for thirty bucks? A skinny lay, sweaters and a face full of Dynel hair. Like screwing a big Barbie doll. Worst piece of tail I ever had. But this one tonight, now I can see has something going. Look at the way she moves on that dance floor. Unreal!"

"God!" Price shouted as Little Nasty suddenly slammed his arm down and, holding him there, reached over with his free hand to scoop up the money.

"Would you look at that little cutie?" Sonny urged.

Price, his arm free, turned around, took in the girl, and then faced Sonny. "That's the ugliest girl I ever seen in my whole damn life."

"Isn't she, though?"

"Well, that's one down," Nasty told Sonny. "I hope Candy Ass gets up there soon. I asked Tiny to meet me down here for a surprise."

Ten minutes later, as Nasty recounted a hunting story about a dog named Old Blue, Leslie Collins entered the bar, guitar case in hand, and went up on the bandstand. In a half hour the rest of the band was in, minus Ken, and Leslie introduced a song he had written about men coming back to work after saying goodbye to their families. Even the town regulars seemed to like the song.

Tiny showed up when Collins was well into "A Boy Named Sue." He had got as far as the table and was about to order a drink when he noticed. Nasty leaned over, watching for the proper moment, and whispered something to Tiny, who jumped out of his chair, knocking it over, and stalked out of the bar without a word.

"There's two," Sonny said, and Nasty laughed, pounding the table.

"Did you see that?" Nasty gasped, laughing harder. "God, was he mad?"

"What you guys do to Tiny?"

It was Al Godwin, picking up the chair and sitting down in Tiny's place.

Nasty jerked a thumb toward the bandstand. "He got the candy ass for a roommate and now he's afraid to snore. Don't know whether he's safer on his belly or his back."

"You must have riled him some."

"Naw, I just asked if he didn't get enough of Leslie at night that he had to come visit him in town, make a public spectacle of hisself."

"I thought so. He sure looked pissed. Like to knock me down on his way out of here."

"Wasn't he mad, though? You should have seen him. He was jumping up and down like a nigger shortstop." Nasty waved over to Leslie. Winked. Took a long sip of his drink.

Leslie Collins looked down at his fingers on the guitar strings. He forced himself not to think of Nasty. Let the words of the song come into his mind and over him. Tonight, before chow, Tiny had confronted him in the room. Want to get one thing straight, he'd said. We'll get along all right if you keep to yourself. But make a move on me and you're a dead man.

His fingers picked out the complicated melody line, his voice filled the room out there with loneliness. Leslie had taken a chance with Tiny, but he had been angry. You've been blunt. I'll be blunt. You have nothing to worry about. You really aren't all that attractive.

The song was over; his fingers picked out a few more notes and without preamble he slipped into "Country Road." The second time through he changed the lines to Alaskan roads, Alaskan places.

> Almost Palmer, Eagle River,
> Chugach Mountains, Matanuska Valley
> Take me home . . . O'Malley Road
> To the place I belong . . . .

The weather turned bad through the last weeks of January. Dark clouds hung over the mountain valley of Montez, hiding the peaks. Some days fog covered the water and the air turned white with steady snow. Larry slogged through it all, filing reports, filling out time cards, checking equipment. He wrote some articles for the *Pipe 'n' Hot News* and his letters to Hope were by turns warm and indignant.

He tried to deal with it in small ways. He grew a beard for the novelty of it. He exercised for his health. He reasoned it out at great length in letters meant to make it acceptable to himself. As he was not in Walpole, her affair was not a choice or preference (he wrote Hope); she had not thereby rejected Larry but only sought solace.

Yet at night, lying in bed, he recognized all these attempts as last dying struggles. Depression gripped him like the snow that engulfed Montez, clotting the streets, altering the shapes of buildings, wearing down roofs, sheds, lean-tos, awnings by sheer accumulation.

Larry began to despise the weather, the clouds that pressed down upon the valley and the snow; the water that swirled with rotten ice picked up off the shoreline, the gray, cold, dead waters lapping at the shore. Alaska had done that to the marriage, separated them, broke Hope, broke him. For the goodman is not at home. He is gone a long journey. He hath taken a bag of money with him and will come home at the day appointed.

Larry walked to the shore. Alaska had almost killed Netty, almost gotten him two or three times. Perhaps he was not wanted here. A truck passed and Larry did not even attempt to dodge the spray of slush. A dribble of mud and ice clung to his beard and Larry left it there.

He'd lost home, no matter what he and Hope came to. It was a different thing choosing to leave Walpole and being forced to stay away. A small town talked. Larry was a reporter, used to dragging other people's dirty linen into public. He knew how the people talked, the snickering, the sly remarks passed at the general store. Like most reporters, Larry had an absolute abhorrence of anyone knowing about his own life and personal failures—aside from those of the printed word. There and only there did he willingly accept the judgment of his townsmen.

The one good thing he could say for Alaska now was that people didn't push too hard to find out what your past was. A frontier had its advantages. You learned not to be too nosy if a man didn't want to talk. The office manager in payroll said that Terminal Camp had nine or ten men on the most wanted list in various states Outside. Alaska was a refuge, the farthest place a man could run. And since that was so, if you couldn't make your way in Alaska, where else was there to go?

Larry exercised, but he drank and ate too much, and he brooded for hours on what he'd do if he met up with Kurt Schall.

Finally he began to consider getting even.

Gil Wolfe began a series that ran in the *Fairbanks News-Miner* with later reprints in the *Anchorage Daily News.* The articles ran under the head: "Dan Curry: Who and What Is He Protecting?"

The lead was essentially a rehash of what Emil Bacich had asked him at the Copper Canyon hearing. Would Dan call a halt if a serious violation occurred? The article described Dan's job in some detail and outlined his powers. Against his power on paper, Gil Wolfe posed the actual pressures that state interest and the construction companies could put on Dan. It would, Gil said, take a man of exceptional integrity to stand against the economic interest, whether real or imagined, of eight oil companies, APPLE, its complex of subcontractors, up to 20,000 pipeline workers, and millions of dollars of eventual tax revenues for the state. He could. *Would he?*

The second article summarized the economic reports and resource potential studies done by Curry's investigative team. Did this, Gil wanted to know, sound like the kind of studies a group concerned about the environment would make? Or was Curry becoming a shopowner, hanging price tags on the wilderness?

The third Gil Wolfe wrote from the perspective of a sports reporter. He described the powerful Dollar team and the impressive Wilderness team. Wilderness had the greatest natural strength, but it was weak in many areas and could be gotten to if the Dollars hit in the right place at the right time. The season had a long way to run, but Gil Wolfe suggested a look at the record so far. One column had decisions won by Dollars and the other decisions won by Wilderness. Since Wilderness had fewer fans and couldn't protest to the umps as loudly as the Dollars they had lost several close ones. The score showed Dollars ahead, 17–11.

The last article was a personal profile. Gil Wolfe quoted Dan Curry extensively, let him respond to the other three stories.

"I have this awful daydream—daymare, I guess—that one day my grandchildren will be saying, 'That's grandpa's picture. He's the one that sold out our wilderness and ruined Alaska.' "

"Do you worry about that?" I asked Curry. "I think a lot of us would sleep better knowing that."

"I worry about that, but I have another daymare that goes right along with it. Suppose they say, 'That's grandpa, the one that wrecked the economy of the entire state. He's why things are so bad up here.' "

This reporter has no doubt as to which of those dreams he'd go for. You can't build a wilderness the way you build a pipeline. People got along up here before Alaska Pipeline began waving petro-dollars around.

Dan Curry says he's deeply concerned, truly committed, and I'll give him that. But the big question still remains: to what?

(Next: a series of articles on wilderness impact. Gil Wolfe

and Emil Bacich ask the old question: "How can you call it a virgin wilderness with 800 miles of pipe stuck up in its middle?")

Malcolm Finch-Smith let the last slide die on the screen, and fade into rosy light. "And that's it for January," he said.

B. R. Young, sitting at the end of the outside semicircle, rapped on the table with his knuckles. Those about to get up relaxed back into their chairs.

"Men," he said, and looked along the curving table. "As most of you know, a fire this morning destroyed three dormitories and the recreation hall at Sag River Camp. We were lucky. Temperature was only five below. No wind. Some light in the sky." He picked up one of the chrome coffeepots and refilled his cup. "Suppose," he spoke slowly as the coffee rose to the rim, "we lost a camp at seventy below in a wind. Everybody tumbling out in pajamas and skivvies. It could happen. Dan Curry let us know loud and clear it could happen two weeks ago and now I think we'll be hearing it again. From Curry, from the press. They'll want to know what we're doing. What will you tell them, Malc?"

"I understand that we are taking every precaution and that electrical supervisors will inspect every inch of wiring in each camp, with authorization to replace or bring up to standard any substandard installations. There will also be fire patrols picked in each camp from various crafts and posted so that no area in the camp housing facilities will have less than half-hour visits, round the clock."

"Check." Young set his cup down hard. "I put Roy Rogers and the MOT squad on it this morning and as you see, they already got back to Malc. Those are good men. They're going to build us one hell of a good pipeline."

Nods, murmurs of approval ran around the room. Young flashed a smile.

"The MOT squad is also setting up the first pipe burial for April 15. We're releasing that story today. If a reporter grabs you on the fire and you can't refer him to Malc, be sure to get in something about the first pipe. That'll be news, right?"

He was looking up at Finch-Smith who had remained at the lectern.

"Assuredly," Finch-Smith said.

Young got up, patted Finch-Smith on the arm, and strode to the back of the room. Chairs swiveled as one, not a squeak among them. Young punched a finger down at the south end of the pipeline display.

"Copper Canyon, April 15. First pipe in the ground. Ceremonies, press, TV, speeches, the whole nine yards. Same setup we had at the haul road link. But that'll be the last party. We talk at Copper Canyon and the next one is when the last weld goes in."

"The golden weld," someone whispered. B. R. Young nodded sagely. Up front, Finch-Smith pressed a button, and unseen, unheard, the two slide projectors behind the rosy screen began to recycle January to "start."

Chapter Six

TWO COPIES of the February issue of *Tomcat* lay open on the bar, one in front of Maggie, the other shared by Bill Greenwood and Tom Farrell.

Coven's article had been titled "Making It at the Montez Club," and there was a sketch of a dilapidated building with an Oly Beer sign in the window and a Winnebago parked around the side. A line of men gathered at the corner of the building, waiting their turn in the Winnebago.

The bar didn't even look like the Montez Club.

Maggie read it aloud.

"You had to know that ten years ago when the old town washed into Montez harbor that Maggie Booth was the sexiest broad in town. And she still is, which may say something for Montez, a seedy, ramshackle collection of houses, huts and trailers that manages to be the ugliest, most worn-out ten-year-old town in the world. Afternoons, before the pipeline workers knock off and come into town to cruise for the few available local girls, the Montezans come into the club to toss back a couple of brews, reminisce about the old days, and boozily brood over Maggie's build. Ah, Maggie! Six feet tall, red hair to the waist and the most gorgeous pair of mammaries west of the Continental Divide (which they immediately bring to mind for a writer seeking an apt comparison)."

Maggie frowned down at herself, and Greenwood, who had been skimming ahead in the story, laughed. "He caught that right, Maggie."

"Bout the only thing he got right," Farrell said.

"Maggie's no dummy, he says about me. I know the value of sex-in-advertising and my bar is the most crowded in town." Maggie found the line. "To men stuck in a construction camp without women for weeks at a time, Maggie Booth must be like a seven-course meal at the end of a five-week fast."

"This crap about your brother ticks me off," Farrell said. "Makes Dave sound like a rummy. Guy can't have a few drinks when he's off duty? And what's all that crap about townies and pipeliners? We got plenty of people in town working over there."

Bill Greenwood thumbed the magazine and read the paragraph about town girls and pipeliners. "Lock up our daughters, small children and favorite household pets. I'd like to see the guy that could get anywhere with my Martha." He shrugged. "Unless of course she wanted him to."

"I resent all that about greed," Maggie said. "So I charge a buck and a half for a beer, two bucks, mixed. This clown came up from the Lower 48 where people don't earn Alaska salaries. What does he know? And how about the landlords, the storekeepers, real estate holders? You don't get a chance to make it big very often in your life. This pipeline is a golden opportunity. The oil companies are going to get rich, the natives are getting rich, the state's getting rich and the workers are getting rich. We're inundated with people, putting up with noise and trucks and traffic and I suppose we should sit back and say we don't want a piece of the action."

"That's right," Farrell applauded her. "We went through some slow years in this town and some hard times putting it back together. I can remember when money was tight, but we had something that made life here worth it. These guys came in and changed the way of life, so we might as well get something for it."

"Still," Greenwood said, "it's too bad that some of the old-timers got forced out when the rents went up. And some of the people on retirement row, when the rents on the trailer sites went sky-high, they had to move into Anchorage. Some families lived in Montez forty, fifty years. Never got enough ahead to buy a house, and then people they'd known all their lives doubled, tripled the rent."

Farrell picked up his beer glass. "Yeah, there is that," he said. "That was a shame."

In camps up and down the line it was the same thing, anger, disgust, disbelief at the article. Although many of the pipeline workers agreed wholeheartedly with the assessment of local residents treating them like sheep waiting to be fleeced, there was little else they conceded. It had been that way with many popular magazine articles. The camps north, isolated from town life, were regarded as curious sociological experiments, disruptions of normal human existence. It was as though there had never been prisons, military camps, lonely outposts. Absent from the articles was any mention of the fact that a great proportion of the men had worked even more isolated jobs: the DEW line, the Adak Naval Station, the nuclear test site at Amchitka, radar installations in the Aleutians. Men had built in the cold, had lived without women for months in conditions far less luxurious than the pipeline camps, and had thought of it as nothing more than a construction job.

Sure the young guys came off the job horny. But so were the hands coming off jobs in Fairbanks and Anchorage. Some of the women in the camps could testify to that, having passed construction jobs in town during the lunch hour.

Rosemary Fay was particularly offended by Mr. Coven's persistent hammering at the big salaries earned by men and women who were not nearly as well educated as he was.

Rosemary had taught second grade in Kenai and, like so many of the male teachers, worked construction in the summer to bring in extra money. This year she had decided not to go back to the classroom in the fall although, appropriately enough, the Teamsters had put her to driving the school buses on the job site. Rosemary was tiny, just under five feet, and had never tipped 100 on the scales. But, as she told the men who teased her, all she needed to do was reach the pedals.

Rosemary sat at the table, angrily flipping through the article while Larry ate his dinner. She shook her head and read a paragraph aloud. Larry tried to appear interested. He wanted to seduce Rosemary, but didn't know how. It was difficult to work up much enthusiasm for it, he felt so unhappy.

"Here's the kind of thing I mean," she said. "John Martin dropped out of grade school in Boise, Idaho, to become a rodeo hand. Now he sweeps floors and carries out the trash in the Fort Wainwright office buildings and makes twice what the average full professor in a university takes home. Mary Lou Lavell barely finished high school and took a job at the cosmetics counter in an Anchorage drugstore. Today she works behind the counter in the Five Mile Camp warehouse and earns about the same income as a doctor in his first year of practice."

"Should have said 'doctor in *her* first year of practice,'" Larry told Rosemary. "Have to have your consciousness raised if you write for publication."

"Well, that's not what torques me. What's he got against the average person making a good living? And which would you rather do, sweep floors or teach college? Sit in a warehouse or be a doctor? How many hours a week does a professor put in? I'm working seven elevens." She shook her head angrily. "You show me a professor, any teacher, puts in seven eleven-hour days, never sleeps at home, lives with damn near no privacy, not to mention sexual deprivation."

Larry watched her carefully. That sounded like a good lead.

"Of course, for you, the last is easily taken care of," he said.

"Pssshhh," Rosemary went and flopped the magazine shut, turning it face down on the table. "Know what that is? That's your average upper-middle-class elitist talking. The kind that can't understand how Eric Hoffer can really work on a dock and actually talk to longshoremen. You ever read Hoffer?"

"No, but I read Erich Fromm. *The Art of Loving* . . ."

"All these people writing about how much we're making are like that. They can't stand to see somebody with no education making a good buck, no matter how hard they work or what conditions they're willing to put up with."

"Like sexual deprivation."

"That, too," she sighed. "You know, it's not as easy for a woman as it looks. And that's another thing these eastern snobs write about. Women making money. Women being able to have harems. Harems! It makes you wonder what kind of world these smart asses would like to set up. A woman in these camps has to give a lot of thought before she sacks out with some guy. There's a lot of talk. And jealousy. It can screw up your work detail. If I want to climb in bed with some dude in camp here, I have to be discreet and so does he."

Larry smiled. "I can be very discreet. Believe me, Rosemary, I won't tell a soul." He leaned across the table. "I like you very much, Rosemary. You know that, don't you?"

She looked at his eyes for a few seconds and then resumed eating. Between bites, she spoke slowly.

"I wasn't trying to seduce you by what I said. I never make it with married men. Almost never. I'm not backing down, just being honest."

Larry sighed heavily. Rosemary patted him on the head and left. Larry stayed at the table, picking at his food, hardly noticing when Joe Akin sat down beside him, pushing with his elbows to make room.

"Sorry there, son," Joe said in a husky voice and then sat back in mock surprise. "Why it's Larry Ransom. I hardly recognized you. You know, buddy, you looked happier the day we fished you out of the harbor. What the hell's eating you?"

Larry thought a moment before answering. He had wanted to discuss the situation back home with another man, but found it embarrassing. Somehow, with Rosemary it had been easier. "Can you keep something to yourself?"

"Yeah, shoot." Akin dug into his mashed potatoes.

"I mean really don't tell anybody. At all. Ever."

"You got it," Akin mumbled, mouth full of food. "Swear to God."

With much hesitation, Larry described what had happened, how he found out about Schall, the whole thing. He finished about the time Akin finished his dinner.

Joe sat a moment, toying with a roll, mopping up traces of gravy. He pushed the plate aside.

"Yeah, I had that happen, too. About the same way. Went off to work a summer construction job, came back, found out what she'd done. So I got a gun and found the bastard in a bar and put three, four slugs in him, jumped on him, cracked some ribs, kicked his balls in before they got me loose. Did time in Oklahoma for it. Pulled hard time, I mean hard." He flashed a smile. "How about that, huh? Blam, blam blam, just like nothing. *Me*. I didn't kill him, but I wanted to."

"Did you get over it, after that?"

"No. I'm still not over it. I never was man enough to forgive her." Joe patted his stomach and burped. "Guess I'm still not. You know, the one I got at home now, if she went chippying, I could take it. But that one—well, she was special, you know? Special. It still hurts."

Dan waited for Paula's mother to call her to the phone. It was nine-thirty in Anchorage, eleven-thirty in San Francisco. The Lower 48 comprised four time zones. So did Alaska.

Paula spoke softly. Her voice was tired, sad, although her words were cheerful at first. The children were well, everything was fine, they'd taken a weekend trip to Disneyland.

Dan apologized for calling so late. He had been caught up in an emergency meeting. The Teamsters were threatening to pull drivers off until something was done about road conditions between Fox and Livengood. They were calling the stretch, maintained by the state, "the Kamikaze Highway." APPLE disclaimed responsibility, but at the same time, offered to pay for state maintenance. Environmental statements might have to be filed.

There was silence from Paula.

"Are the kids asleep?"

"Yes," she said. "They wanted to wait for your call, but they were too tired. I put them to bed."

"I don't suppose you want to get them up, then."

"They have school, Dan. I can't."

"I see. They're in school down there, are they?"

She didn't answer.

"You are planning to come back next month, aren't you, Paula?"

"Dan . . ." Paula hesitated, then seemed to take heart. ". . . my dad told me today there's an opening in the California State Park System and he was saying it's just the kind of thing for a man with your experience. It pays well. Regular hours. You'd get out in the woods from time to time."

"You aren't coming back, are you?"

"I don't know."

"Paula, do you still love me? Enough to want to stay married to me?"

"If only I didn't," she said. Dan had to strain to hear it.

"Please come back next month." He closed his eyes, pressing his ear to the receiver so he wouldn't miss her words. "Don't make me choose like this."

"Don't make *me,*" Paula said.

"Boom," Tiny shouted over the bar at Maggie. Nasty coming in the door behind him called out, "Boom, here come the lonely, sex-hungry men from the big, bad construction camp across the bay."

"I liked you guys better when you looked at the pictures and didn't read the stories," Maggie called back.

"Something's got to go BOOM," Tiny hollered, and made his way to an empty table. "Jesus," he shouted, "look who crawled back into town."

Nasty caught Isaac Ahgutuk by the arm and dragged him over to the table. Clyde Baranov followed.

"So it ain't true about you," Nasty said.

"What about me?" Isaac sat down unsteadily, slopping his drink over the edge of the table.

"I heard you went to take a shit and died and the hogs ate ya."

Isaac considered the statement.

"How's that again?"

"Naw, hell, you gots to listen the first time, right, Clyde?"

"Native counselor got him back," Clyde told Tiny. "Isaac promised not to get drunk no more."

Tiny waved at Gloria. "C'mon honey, we got some wild pipeliners here tonight. Boomers loose in boomtown. We got promises to break over here."

The jukebox was blaring. It was too early for the band. Several copies of *Tomcat* were in evidence and Maggie laughed loudly at comments from those at the bar. Tiny took her in. Woman never looked better. And that Gloria. From what he remembered of the night he beat the checkpool, she'd been worth the money he'd stuffed down her panties.

A table of locals, two couples in their mid-forties, sat near Tiny, and he caught one of the men glancing over in disapproval at the noise he was making.

"Only thing true in that magazine was how these Montezers is all worked up 'cause they can't skin us out of our money quick enough."

The man looked away.

"I don't think it was raight of thet boy to be callin these folks jackals and vultures and that sort of thing," Nasty said. "Hell, I've known some raight pleasant vultures in my day. Least they waited till you was dead fore they tried to strip you clean."

"Like a raven?" Isaac asked.

Baranov told him he was stupid. Vultures were much bigger than ravens.

"Yeah, shit, these people here," Tiny said. The pipeliners turned to watch, sensing something in the air. "They're clannish all right. I been in Alaska for years, know Alaskan ways, but these people got no use for you unless you grew up here. I'm a good Alaskan. Lot of you boys are good Alaskans, right?"

Tiny pointedly ignored the two couples who were now threading their way to the door. Larry Ransom passed them on his way in and Tiny waved at him. Nasty stood up and grabbed a chair from the abandoned table and Larry sat. As he did, a shout went up near the door and two men were swearing.

Tiny got to his feet and Schultz, propelling himself through the crowd along the bar, gave him a warning look. Someone had landed a punch. A chair was knocked over and there was a heavy sound as a body fell against the wall and there was another smack of a fist against flesh.

"Shtop!" Schultz barked. "No more."

The cursing ended. So did the scuffling. The fringes of the crowd drifted away. Two men were dusting themselves off and one stuck out a hand. The other man refused to shake, turned on his heel, and walked out the door.

Gloria came to take the orders.

"Who were they?"

"Locals," she said, leaving no doubt on whose side she stood.

Larry studied her carefully, and when she asked him what he wanted said, "You."

"Busy night," Gloria said. She sounded sympathetic. "How about a drink instead and try again middle of the week?"

"Beer."

"See that?" Tiny said after she left. "That was townies in there fighting. Spoiling the peaceful atmosphere of this establishment. And here I thought *we* were supposed to be the animals."

"Those were the two at the next table, weren't they?" Nasty looked delighted.

"Goddamn animals," Tiny said.

"I like animals," Isaac said. "I like to eat animals. I ride animals. Make things out of animals."

"Have sex with animals," Tiny added.

Isaac nodded enthusiastically. "You know how everybody talk about fucking a bear?"

Nasty smiled. "Ain't all talk."

"Shut up," Tiny said. "You fuck a bear, Isaac?"

Isaac looked from man to man in the tight circle.

"When I was a boy in Barrow. The men in the village killed a polar bear and her cub and the other cub they tied to a stake on the beach."

"He's lyin," Baranov said. "Eskimo lies."

"Cub must'a been a month and a half. Size of a sled dog. Good, big sled dog. Four of us went down. I was first. I pulled mine out."

"His oosik."

"Shhh."

"Thought that cub was gonna tear it off. We couldn't hardly get near her." Isaac began to giggle. "Everyone wanted to fuck a polar bear. We tried all afternoon and all we got was torn clothes and scratches. But at least I actually tried to fuck a bear."

Gloria pushed her tray onto the table. "Honestly, the things you guys think to talk about."

Larry hung his head, laying the money on her tray, not even looking up.

After she left, Nasty motioned the table back into huddle.

"Time has come to tell you boys how it's done in the south."

Tiny began chuckling low in his throat.

"You through, dum-dum?" Nasty glared. "Now listen to this. I had a bear once, when I was twenty, just going into manhood."

"Hell you did," Isaac said. "Can't be done."

"I knew some soldiers fucked a moose," Clyde said. "They'd started calling it by a girl's name, then they hung a girl's hat on it, and then somebody snuck up and tied a bra around its neck. One thing led to another, you know, and these two guys fucked the moose."

"You gonna let me tell the story?"

Clyde shrugged. "I was just saying. They both got thrown out of the army. Don't want no moose-fuckers in the military. I can see it. Give the outfit a bad name."

"Will ya shut up?" Tiny said. "Let him talk."

Larry sipped at his beer. Rosemary had turned him down. Gloria was too busy. Tears started up in his eyes again and he faked a yawn, wiping them away.

"I ain't boring you, am I?" Nasty asked. "All right, it was that time of the year for the animals and it was that time of the year for me. I was out in the woods and I'd been walking around with a two-day hard-on. I was so horny I would've fucked the rotten end of a warm watermelon. Well, I'm going to say right now, a black bear sow in heat is the best piece of ass I ever had in my life, bar none!"

"You didn't," Isaac persisted. "She'd tear you to pieces. How you do it, huh?"

"Nothin to it," Nasty said. "I just shot her, ran over, stuck it in and had the dyin' quivers."

Larry took a cab out to the Crossroads Bar, four miles out along the highway. The bar sat well off the road at the junction to the old Copper Canyon Camp. Several tractor rigs were parked along one edge of the lot. The Crossroads was popular with both highway truckers and the teamsters from the project. Rosemary had recommended the place to Larry for its bluegrass music and good sandwiches. Dago John told Larry if he wanted to see the girls he was raffling off, he would find them at the Crossroads. So far, he still hadn't sold enough tickets.

Larry entered the low, red-painted building. It looked like a barn. There were tables around two sides, a dance floor and bandstand, and a bar on the far wall. The place was crowded. Up on the stage was the four-man band, a bass, banjo and two guitars. A few couples got up and attempted to dance, but only a character in a cowboy suit could match the rhythm. It sounded like he had taps on his boots. A few girls in long dresses were sitting at the bar, talking with the men, who stood two and three deep. Larry wondered if they were the ones Dago John had mentioned. He pushed past the tables and went into the bathroom. There were the usual "Keep on trucking, mother-trucker" scribblings on the wall, same as in the teamster shack across the bay. "Hydramatic illegitimatus = shiftless bastard."

Larry went to the mirror, met his frowning face, a beard almost thick enough to look good. He glanced up at the neat lettering patiently inscribed on the wall: THE TWO MOST OVER-RATED THINGS IN THE WORLD ARE MACK TRUCKS AND TEEN-AGE PUSSY!

Above, someone had scribbled: "I had a '64 Mack wasn't so bad."

For a good lay, he said silently to the glass, call Hope Ransom.

Larry pulled a five out of his wallet and held it in the air over the shoulders of two men standing at the bar. Here the crowd was only one layer deep. The bartender nodded at Larry to indicate he'd registered the fact he wanted something and would get around to it. Larry lowered his hand and turned to watch the dancers. After another ten minutes, he got his beer and moved down the bar toward the bandstand.

There was a short woman, dark hair, dark complexion, dark shirt and slacks leaning with one hand against the wall. Larry found a space alongside the woman, clear of traffic to and from the telephone, and stopped. He got the uncomfortable feeling the woman was watching him and he wondered if he should just lean over and ask her if she'd like to go somewhere. But where? How could you find a motel room in Montez without a reservation a week ahead? It had been so long, Larry had forgotten what to say, how to get started. Should he ask her to dance?

"You working on the pipeline?" he heard.

The woman had spoken to him but she looked straight ahead now, out at the bandstand.

"Yeah, been there since September."

The woman still watched the band, barely moved her lips when she talked.

"What do you do?"

"I'm a timekeeper."

"Doesn't pay so good, does it?"

Larry considered a moment. "Not like a teamster, no. But it's okay."

The woman smiled slightly.

"What do you do?" Larry asked, not knowing what else to say.

"I'm a madam."

Now the woman looked at him.

"Oh," Larry nodded, pulled at his nose, nodded some more.

"That blond girl with the cowboy, that's Angelique. Suzette's over at the corner table, the one with the pink dress. They're just two of my girls. The rest are working tonight."

"I'm interested."

"No kidding. I wonder how I knew that. You want to go tonight, just call a cab and tell him you want to visit Paree."

"Is that one of your girls?"

"That's me, but he'll know. Any cab in town will know. You don't happen to be a gambler, too?"

Larry shook his head.

"If you do go and want to come back later, you have to phone ahead to see a particular girl, got that?"

"Right." It was hard to hear over the noise and he moved closer to the woman. She smelled good. Larry wanted to go tonight.

"You ever come over without calling, you will not be welcome. I run a clean, safe house, everything very nice. But you have to call."

"Should I phone for a cab now?" Larry asked. "I'd like to go now if I could. That is, if it isn't too expensive."

"I don't talk business out of my home. Don't worry about it and don't call a cab. You'll find one out in front. Cab number five."

Larry finished his beer and reached over to set it on the bar.

"I'll do that. Thanks."

"My pleasure," she said.

Larry hesitated at the doorway of the tavern. Even if Hope hadn't gone to bed with Schall, it had been a long time for Larry. Six weeks now. And what if it did cost? Serve her right, both ways. He found himself trembling as if from the cold.

"I'm taken," the cabbie said, rolling down his window, but waiting to see if Larry had anything to say.

"I wanted to visit Paree."

"Hop in."

Larry got in.

"Two bucks," the driver said, not even putting the meter in gear. Larry produced the two dollars and the cab circled the bar, shot down a driveway, and stopped at the entrance to a trailer park within walking distance of the tavern.

"This is it."

"Here? I could have walked here."

The driver turned around. "And where would you go? There's twenty trailers in here. What, you gonna knock on doors? Can I get laid here? Oh, sorry, lady."

Larry nodded.

"All right," the man said. "You go down three trailers. It's the one with the grizzly bear decal on the door, little wooden porch. That's not necessarily the trailer you'll end up in, but that's where you'll start. Have fun."

Larry walked through the snow. A dog barked at him from inside a darkened trailer. The cab turned and circled back around the tavern. From the trailer park it was impossible to tell whether the cab would then have gone out on the highway. Snow had drifted around some of the trailers so that the owners had to shovel out not only paths, but windows as well. One drift completely covered a car set between the trailers.

Larry found the porch with the decal. The bear was on the attack, standing on its hind legs, paws out, mouth open, ferocious.

Larry knocked softly.

There was syrupy music coming from the trailer, a big 12-x-60-footer. He heard someone stirring and the door curtain flicked aside before the door was opened by a wide-eyed slender girl who looked no more than sixteen. Larry was sure he had made a mistake.

"C'mon in, honey," she said. "'Scold out there." Her name was Michelle.

They talked terms in the bathroom. Finally Larry counted out the hundred, wondering if the tingling he felt inside was from the promise of sex or the loss of so much money.

Hadn't Hope given away as much by having Kurt in their very own bed?

She checked him carefully for signs of venereal disease, even asking Larry to urinate, which he found difficult under the circumstances. Then she washed him.

"We run a clean house."

"So I've heard."

They went into the back bedroom.

Michelle assured him that there was no need to be alarmed if he heard any noise in the trailer. The other girl would direct any customers to one of the other trailers while Larry was there. It had been a busy night.

She slipped her wraparound off and threw it over the back of a chair. The room had a twin-sized bed, and over the blanket Michelle had spread a Snoopy beach towel. It showed the dog standing next to a bullet-ridden doghouse, saying, "Curse you, Red

Baron." Michelle lit an incense candle and an oil lamp and turned out the overhead light as Larry stepped out of his underwear and lay down, prone on the bed, as she directed.

As the girl rubbed oil into his back and began to massage him, Larry realized how much he had missed the simple fact of being touched by another person. At home he was always hugging Netty and Caitlin, giving Hope a friendly pat on the ass or getting one from her (had he really been so perfunctory, even there?). At camp no one touched him and he touched no one. Michelle had him roll over on his back and after she had massaged his chest he asked if he could just hold her for a while and touch her. The unfamiliar body in the candlelight, scent of jasmine in the air, soft music playing far off seemed like an impossible gift after the weeks of harsh, uncomfortable camp life.

The girl, though, grew restless and began to shinny herself down to the foot of the bed. She ran her hands over Larry's thighs and buried her head in his groin. Larry held back, resisted, and then urged her to straddle him, which she did. Then Larry began to wonder if he would come at all.

They changed positions and Larry looked at this strange girl beneath him, the small breasts, the slender hips, tiny, pointed chin, this girl writhing and groaning with his every movement as though this was too great a pleasure to withstand. The candle tickled at his nose. Snoopy shook his fist at her right breast. They were having sex; there was this strange woman, not Hope, under him and he was being unfaithful. The girl moaned, moved her unfamiliar hands along his back.

Hope had given herself freely to one who wanted her. For neither of them was there any pretended fulfillment. This was not the same. Still, Larry did not stop. He made himself groan and pretended, too, banging her down into the bed, trying hard not to hold back.

He had too much invested. Like Michelle, he was doing it for the money.

Larry loaded his breakfast tray with little regard for what he was going to eat. He had left the trailer last night in a worse mood than he'd been in when he rode the bus to town.

As he went to an empty table in a corner of the mess hall, he heard his name spoken sharply.

"Ransom! Get your ass over here."

It was Joe Akin, blond hair uncombed, sticking up crazily, eyes bloodshot, obviously at the end of a bender.

"Get your ass over here," Akin said again.

Reluctantly, Larry complied. He was too unhappy to talk to anybody, least of all someone who was drunk at five-thirty in the morning. Akin looked terrible and Larry told him so.

"I been up all night," Akin said, "drinkin' and thinkin' about you."

Larry bit into a piece of toast.

"You hear me, Ransom? It's going to be a long day today, because of you. I stayed up all night on your case."

"I didn't ask you to stay up for me." Larry crammed the rest of the toast in his mouth. "I don't feel like talking."

Joe reached over and caught Larry's wrist. He pinned the hand to the table. Larry started to protest, but something in Joe Akin's expression caught him up short.

"Listen to me, will ya? You been walking around here the last month like you got a patent on being miserable. Well you ain't."

"I know. You told me the same thing happened to you. But it isn't just what Hope did. It's everything since we came up here."

"Yeah, we heard it all, the whole sad story."

Larry started to pull away, but Akin had his wrist locked.

"I'm talking to you, Ransom. I stayed up on your account. I was drunk. I'm drunk now, but you're going to hear this, pal. You want to know something about yourself?"

Larry shook his head. "No. Let me be."

Akin smiled. "I'm not going to let you be. That's your problem. Everyone and everything has let you be. And that goes for your wife, too."

Larry looked up. Keep Hope out of this, he thought.

"Don't get me wrong. I like your wife. She's a nice woman, but like you, she's been living in a shell. You been too comfortable. Both of you. You could see it the way you acted when you went in the water. You were in shock. It's like you never expected anything bad to happen to you. And that shell . . ." Akin studied Larry's face. "it's hard to explain, but I got the feeling that you and Hope were just passengers on that boat. It was like you really didn't know each other. You had shells, but you weren't in a shell with her. Am I right? I can tell I'm right. You look mad."

Larry used his other hand to take a piece of bacon off the plate. He didn't reply.

"That's the trouble when people don't get exposed. They make comfortable shells and pretty soon they don't even get exposed to each other. But when you and your old lady hit that water, you got exposed good. When you were sick in the hospital, you got exposed. That airplane ride that scared you so bad, you got exposed. And you didn't like it. What happens out there on the East Coast? Don't people get exposed there? You call yourself a journalist? How can you write good stories if you haven't been exposed? Ernie Pyle got exposed. You ever read him? That's why he was good. But I'm not talking just writing. I'm talking about being a man and not a jerkoff. I like you, Ransom, and I'd like to think you're a man."

Akin's gaze wavered. Larry could sense the struggle he was having putting his thoughts together.

"So Alaska gave you some problems. So your old lady got screwed by some Kraut. What if you did nearly lose half your family in the water and went broke and had to live by yourself in a goddamn work camp? You're getting exposed. That's right. You ain't been exposed enough in your life and that's your whole trouble. I'd like to be proud of you as a friend. I don't want a jerkoff for a friend, huh? You want to be a jerkoff?"

Larry looked down at his plate of eggs and bacon.

"Hey," Akin said softly. "I don't tell you this to be mean to you. I only say this because I love you. You understand that, Ransom? I just don't want to see you be a jerkoff. You're in Alaska now and sure the country can kill you. But it's not what happens to you that counts. It's what you do, how you take it. The country can make a man out of you, too. You stay here in Alaska and you'll get exposed. And so what, huh? So what, you go in the water and lose your dough? So what? You're a man. You get out of the water and you get some more dough. That's all. You get up again and go in the fight. I wouldn't tell you this if I didn't love you. You listening to this?"

Larry nodded his head slightly.

"So don't be a jerkoff no more. Don't go around complaining you got exposed. You're not in the water now. You could be again. This ain't Walpole. You go around unhappy; shit, you ought to go around laughing. You're lucky but you don't know it. You got exposed. Some people go their whole life, don't get exposed. You want to sit on a fence all your life? You want to go around like a jerkoff, got to be comfortable all the time? Hey, you got it in you to be a man. Don't make me ashamed of you no more. Wouldn't hurt you to get exposed some more, either. Wouldn't hurt either of you. Am I making any sense? I know I'm drunk. I got to be. Up all goddamn night with the bottle, thinking about you. Long day ahead. Going to be a long one. But that's being exposed too, isn't it? I don't care it's a long one.

"Hey, am I drunk? Am I making any sense to you?"

That night Larry waited patiently at the phone to call Hope. As friends came out of the mess hall he smiled, spoke, exchanged gossip and crude observations. Akin hadn't been at dinner, probably had fallen into his bunk sound asleep when the shift ended. Larry stood in line, next up for the phone, and smiled at everyone who came through the open double doors. A stocky kid in his early twenties got up from a table just inside the doorway. From the way he was walking Larry guessed he'd been drinking most of the day. The kid had been terminated at ten in the morning for sleeping on the job and had caused a scene when the superintendent informed him of it.

"Who you looking at?" the kid asked Larry as he came through the door. "You looking at me?"

Larry was too happy to be either angry or intimidated.

"Not looking at anybody in particular. Just waiting to use the phone."

The kid, Del Hazen, hitched his pants up and looked at Larry with his head tilted to one side. They stood the same height and matched pound for pound, although Del's weight was all muscle.

"Using the telephone," Del said. "That's a good idea. I think I'll use the phone, too. Ahead of you."

He stood, waiting.

Larry smiled and gestured at the phone. "Sure, go ahead."

Del shifted his weight from one leg to the other and then cursed, turning on his heel and slouching back to the mess hall. He continued on up the aisle to the serving line and hovered over the dessert tray. Larry watched him while he waited for the operator to make the connection.

He explained to Hope in brief what Joe Akin had said over the breakfast table.

Del Hazen had picked up a piece of pie and then, halfway down the mess hall, began complaining that it was unfit to eat.

Someone hollered for him to shut up and Del stood by a full table, trying to get everyone to look at the pie. A man at a table by the door got up and walked toward the dessert tray. Del stopped him, showing him the piece of pie. He turned and Larry recognized him, the new sheet-metal worker up from Reno.

Sometimes drunks could be helpful and sometimes not.

He told Hope that basically Akin had made him mad. Whether it was intentional or not, Larry would get over the depression just to prove to Joe Akin he could do it.

Hope said she'd been worried sick about his letters, the constant ups and downs. She hoped this wasn't just some sort of manic stage that would be as far down the other way in a day or so. Larry said he didn't think so and then asked Hope to hang on for a second.

Del was shouting at the sheet-metal worker, Butch something. He was Italian. Small in the waist but big through the shoulders and arms. Butch backed away from Del, who was screaming about the lousy food. The two men, one advancing, the other giving way gradually, moved almost to the door. Finally Butch stopped and put both hands out.

Larry couldn't hear what he said but, the next thing, Del threw the pie on the floor and some of it got on Butch's shoe. Butch looked down. Del called him a Wop. All the way from the door, Larry could see Butch take a deep breath and let it out. As he seemed to relax, Butch suddenly lunged forward and brought his knee up into Del's groin. Del staggered backward and fell across a table. A carpenter at the table shoved him away and stood up.

"We got a fight here," Larry told Hope, and tried to describe what happened next. Someone at another table stepped between the carpenter and Butch, and then Del had jumped on Butch, swinging wildly. The other two men began to push and shove and one threw a punch. Del landed four or five solid punches. Tables began to clear.

"Give 'em room," voices called. "Let 'em fight."

Butch staggered backward and knocked a man into another man and they began to argue. Since one of the men was small, another, larger man got up from his bench and offered to take on the big guy.

"I can't believe it, honey, there's six people fighting, tables going everywhere, food on the floor. Jesus, they're knocking chairs down. Now four more guys are into it . . . they're under a table."

Larry stretched the phone cord as far as he could. It looked like a scene from a bad western. There was no logic to it. Larry saw two men fight who just happened to look at each other. The fighters were changing partners. The loose circle of workers that had formed around the fight had turned into a pushing, shouting crowd. The noise—dishes breaking, chairs and benches, even tables overturning, screams, curses, punches—was deafening.

Larry had to shout into the phone.

"What you doing?" a tough old bird just inside the mess hall asked Larry.

"Telling my wife about the fight."

"That so?" he said and swung wildly at Larry, just missing his nose.

"Hope," Larry shouted, "I got to go now." He handed the phone off and waded into the melee.

The next day he found Akin at the operator's dry shack.

"What in the hell happened to you?" Akin asked immediately.

Larry had a bandage across his nose and one eye was swollen shut. His right hand was wrapped in gauze.

"I got exposed."

Akin shood his head. "I guess you must have told Al Godwin what I said to you at breakfast."

"Do you mind?"

"I guess not. Of course, you shouldn't listen to a man who's drunk. I'm drunk I say a lot of things I don't mean."

Akin seemed uneasy, wouldn't look Larry in his eye, the good one or the bad one.

"You said good things."

"I wish you hadn't mentioned anything to Godwin about your wife."

"Why not?"

"Now I have to stay up all night with Al. You know, I saw him this morning and he's as depressed as you were. He figures if your wife could do it, anyone could."

"He's right."

In bed, full of aspirin to knock down some of the pain, Larry listened to country western songs being played in the next room. The partition was thin and he listened for a long time to the lyrics. In the Montez Club he'd listened to Leslie Collins, too. The songs were about men like him. He'd never liked the music before. It was the kind of thing truck drivers listened to.

Through the wall Larry heard about men who had gone away, missed their homes, lost their wives or wondered if they had, lonely men who laughed too hard at jokes and sometimes fought other men for the fun of it. Stories about men like him. Larry fell asleep to it.

Chapter Seven

MARCH DOES NOT BRING spring to Alaska. It brings the last solid month of winter, and with it suicides, cabin fever and a great restless urge for the snow to go away. Along the coast, the snow will begin to fade in April; inland, not until the middle of May. The department stores put out gardening tools, camping equipment, lawn furniture, bicycles, boats and outboard motors, and the families come in and touch these displays in wonder. Soon the gardening tools rest inside the doorway with the snow shovels, the canoe sits in the garage just above the summer tires, the bicycles are tested on a driveway or patch of bare pavement.

Hope Ransom, coming from New Hampshire, did not find the long winter as distressing as many newcomers. And, though Anchorage stayed at twenty or thirty below for a few weeks at a time, Hope had experienced such temperatures in New England winters, if only for a day or two at a stretch. The women she worked with expected Hope to stay home or come in late after snowstorms or the occasional thirty-five-below night. But Hope showed as often as they did and took the winter in stride. The two children grew restive in February, but Caitlin said she liked it when the wind blew and whitened the air with snow. It made her feel tough, special. Netty took up skating, which she hadn't done before, and excelled in cross-country skiing, which she'd learned in New Hampshire. The time passed quickly and Larry surprised them all with his full beard and black eye. The kids thought he looked like a pirate.

It was a good homecoming. The house was decorated with Eskimo and Indian paintings done by Hope's classes. Some of the parents had given her small ivory carvings and Hope had bought more. She was especially proud of the small ivory kittiwake and the snow owl from Gambell on St. Lawrence Island. A girl from Anaktuvuk Pass sold Hope a caribou mask of an Eskimo hunter for less than half of what stores charged, and a boy from a tribe in the southeastern region presented her girls with native "yo-yos" made of sealskin.

Some of the native villages, Hope discovered, were as deeply puritanical as towns in seventeenth-century New England. The village councils passed rules against drinking, gambling, visiting from house to house after 9 P.M., fighting. In one village, a woman pregnant out of wedlock would be confined to jail until the birth of the child. And so would the father be, if discovered. Violations could result in a public rebuke, causing unbearable shame for a member of the tribe. Repeated violations were met with fines and even, in extreme cases, expulsion from the village and "shunning."

Students brought in poems about alcohol and being terrified of their fathers, others about the joy of riding a Sno-Go, faster than a dog can run. Hope got recipes for cooking seal flippers, making jelly out of salmonberries and dozens of wild game dishes, including bear meat and sausage from caribou or reindeer.

After making love the first night home, Hope told Larry that she sensed a change in him. She felt for the first time that he was truly friendly toward her.

"I feel very friendly," he said, putting his hand in the small of her back and pressing suggestively.

"No, not that. Not just here in bed. I know you haven't forgiven me, but I think you want to. You're going to."

"Guess I'm jus' a one-woman man with a one-man woman in mah arms."

"You really shouldn't spend so much time in the Montez Club."

"Cain't live with or without her, no use to doubt her, she's a no count woman, hooooo . . ."

"Don't sing." She put her hand over his mouth.

"You got your poetry, I got mine. Stay away from Germans and we'll be fine."

She dropped her hand and snuggled up to him again.

"You know who you look like with that beard?"

"Who?"

"Especially since you took off some weight. Just like him."

"Who?"

"Ernest Hemingway."

Jim Miklov had finally brought Finch-Smith a 16 x 20 glossy photo of a pair of caribou, back-lit, one cropping the tundra and the other nobly standing watch, its velvety antlers catching the light. In the background stood an oil derrick.

Finch-Smith had the frame ready and he slipped the photo in and hung it on the wall.

"Rather striking, Jim, don't you think?"

Miklov looked up at his own photo. "Genius, Malcolm, sheer genius."

Finch-Smith smiled. "Well, it's certainly appropriate to my office. Seems that the first thing anyone can think to ask is if the caribou will be able to migrate when the pipeline is built. May as well get right into it."

Jim Miklov took a seat across the desk. "Only problem with the picture is how you take it. Does it mean, as I think it does, that the caribous are not disturbed by the presence of man, or does it suggest, as Emil Bacich insists, that these poor creatures are being threatened by the approaching march of technology?"

Finch-Smith studied the picture. "I'd side with the first reaction, of course, but then I've heard the stories about the caribou running up and down the workpad to get away from the mosquitos and take advantage of the summer breeze." There was more to that, in fact. The caribou were proving a positive nuisance on occasion, having to be shooed off runways so planes could land, wandering over to oil drills and buildings to scratch their sides in a landscape with no trees for over a hundred miles.

Apparently the first migration studies with a sample pipeline were inconclusive. Some crossed, some didn't. But the pipeline had been placed near Prudhoe, which was the end of their migration run. There was no great instinctual urge pushing the caribou on once they got to the test sections of pipe. Mountain passes didn't stop them. Traffic couldn't move on the haul road when a herd passed, so roads didn't stop them. Even when the herd settled at Prudhoe, the animals dodged back and forth across the road, climbing the embankments without difficulty.

It didn't seem to matter where in the world the reporter or visitor was from. What about the caribou, they asked, sidling up close, looking for an inside track on the big question, will the caribou be able to cross the pipeline?

Well, good, he'd have caribou right out in the open from the start now. Jim Miklov began laying out his latest run, slides of Copper Canyon for the next progress report, only a week ahead of the first pipe in the ground, glossy pictures of the Copper Canyon area and the Terminal. There were tank rings under construction. Most of the dormitories had been built. Fifteen in one section, two smaller sections of seven dorms each. There were twenty-nine in all, but one was a hospital dorm. The dorms ran up a hill, each set about a story higher than the one next to it. The two mess halls and the rec hall sat level just below a bluff on which stood the two sections of seven dorms.

"Looks like an army camp," Malcolm Finch-Smith said, separating the shots into those he would use for company information and those he might need extra prints of for the press. "I don't think I'd like to be billeted in one of those dorms at the top of the hill."

Larry Ransom came in the door and shook hands with Miklov.

"See you got whiskers," Jim Miklov said.

"Am I too early?"

"Not at all, in fact you're just on time. What's this big pool they're digging on the plateau just above the dormitories? It doesn't show on any of the plans."

"That," Larry told him, tracing the pool's eventual dimension, "is a temporary sewage holding area. Our treatment plant broke down, our water supply leaks, and in general, things are deteriorating quickly."

"That's a big pond," Jim Miklov said, measuring with his pencil against the size of a dorm.

"About half as long as a dorm by twenty feet. Ten feet deep." Larry looked at the pictures again. "They're further along now. It's almost dug out. They'll drain it with a line into the regular main that runs under the main dorm sections."

"That should make for an awkward ceremonial day. I had hoped to run a tour of the camp. How much sewage would you say they'll dump into this lovely cliffside lake?"

"They were talking two hundred thousand gallons by the time the sewer plant gets into operation. Not only that, they're running water in from Howland Creek by truck. Every day they have two or three guys filling and dumping. And a laborer to keep the water hole from freezing up."

"Sounds like a lot of crap to me," Jim Miklov said, leaning over the pictures. "Good thing the wind blows the other way most of the time."

"I just hope I don't get one of those dorms on the hill when I get back," Larry said. "Of course, they'll probably delay the opening now. The dorms are ready except for the sewer. At least the first fifteen are ready."

"How are you liking camp life?" Finch-Smith asked. Larry had written several humorous articles, but some of the most recent had taken a decidedly bitter tone.

"Hate it," Larry glanced up at the picture behind the desk. "Caribou, huh? You know I always wondered about that."

"Yes, Larry, there are caribou and we prefer to believe they will cross the pipeline, not that the line lies across the route for any great length. We generally parallel the caribou run."

"At orientation we were told the caribou barely survive the winter migration." Larry studied the picture. "I hope you're right."

"To change an overly familiar subject, Larry, had you considered finding work in Anchorage?"

"I'd like to if I could make a reasonable salary. You got something?"

Americans were so blunt. Finch-Smith liked the trait in Larry.

"I can't say for sure. But if you send me a résumé, there's a possibility something might come along, either here or elsewhere. If you're interested, that is."

"You'll have my résumé tomorrow. Six copies."

"Good. Mr. Miklov has recommended you highly and he thinks you shouldn't go on living away from your family."

Jim busied himself with his slides, holding them up to the light and squinting at them one by one.

"I wish I could hire you on as a temporary correspondent for the pipelaying in Copper Canyon. Do you think you might have the time to file some kind of local color story? Perhaps interview one or two of the main participants, the man who lowers the pipe in the ditch, the laborer who unhooks the cable. You wouldn't have to be present at the ceremony, although I might be able to pull some strings."

"Either way, I'll send you something."

"Course," Jim Miklov said, "that Tonsina crew is pushing hard to be ready. I think they want to be first."

"Yes. I wish we could instill that sort of spirit in all the camps. That was one of the points of starting the *Pipe 'n' Hot News,* you know. But there may be problems. Tonsina involves a river crossing and Dan Curry is very particular about timing. If we cross the river while it's frozen, it lessens siltation problems. There are several crossings where we simply can't work from April through November. Then again, we're having problems in the canyon with the rock structures. Curry has found fractures in the section just above the old railroad tunnel. I don't know what that will do. And then," he sighed, looking at the two men glumly, "there's the weather. Young is pressing me to nail down dates, times, details, and I can't begin to make arrangements until I find out what the weather will do."

"Expect the worst," Larry said. "Then you won't be disappointed."

Miklov put an arm over his shoulder. "See, the lad has learned something."

Dan Curry spent the first weekend in March in Montez, staying at Lavinia's and avoiding Gil Wolfe, who was also in town, poking into various aspects of the Curry family and their dealings over the years. Maggie called him to say that the reporter had been in the club and had talked with David, suggesting possible collusion between the police chief and the prostitutes. But a few nights in town convinced Gil that if David allowed prostitution at the Montez Club, he allowed it to flourish in the five other bars, particularly in the Crossroads and the White House. He seemed, Maggie insisted, overcurious as to the relationship between Ed Booth and Dan, and she wondered if the family could do anything about it.

Nothing, Dan said, but let him wander uselessly through the town, looking for connections that don't exist. The first pressure put on him by a Curry would certainly convince him of the case. Be nice, Dan advised, but don't buy him any on the house.

I wasn't about to, Maggie said, and invited Dan to dinner.

He declined. He needed some time to think and Lavinia's ark of a house was a good refuge. Dan and Lavinia sat together in the chart room watching the sunset tinge the mountains red, gazing at the unfamilir aspect of a bustling town clinging to the hillside across the bay.

"I think I'm going to lose Paula," Dan said after a long silence. "Ma, what can I do?"

Lavinia tapped her fingernails on the brass tube of an old telescope resting on an ivory table. Dan could hear her breathing in the darkness of the room, could see the glint of brass in the fading light.

"Danny, I always said you should marry an Alaskan girl, but you didn't. So, I guess you'll have to do what any Curry would do. Make mistakes. It's a family trait. Oh, don't look so disappointed, boy. I can see you, you know." She switched on the floor lamp. "What did you think? You could come here and I'd answer it for you? Danny. Just because I'm an old woman doesn't mean I'm wise. I may have a solemn speech or two in me, but they're going to have to wait for the proper time. You know, boy, you expect too much."

"Of you?"

"Me. Paula. Yourself. Everyone."

In mid-March Larry Ransom returned to Montez. His first evening back, with no work to do, he went into town early, joining the locals in the Montez Club. They kidded him about being a reporter, asking if he had seen the article in *Tomcat.* Larry agreed with them that it had been bad and allowed as to how people Outside had no grasp of the anger Alaskans felt at what they considered unjust interference.

"Just like this road they want to build to link Cordova up with the Richardson Highway," Bill Greenwood said. "The Sierra Club in California put the kebosh on it. Those people got no other way out except by air and water. You know what the average Sierra Club member earns a year?"

Larry shook his head. Greenwood was drunk and meant to be heard tonight.

"Forty, fifty thousand bucks a year. They want to keep Alaska wild so they can fly up, take a bush pilot out and hunt or whatever, have the state for a private game preserve. And there's plenty of hard-working Alaskans can't afford to hire a plane and do that."

"Amen," Farrell said. "Sierra Go Home. We don't care how they do it Outside."

"Bumper stickers," Maggie told Larry.

"Let the bastards freeze in the dark."

"Some clown in California doesn't want me to drive over to Cordova, doesn't want my uncle to be able to drive to Anchorage so he can buy something for the house. I can see the way it was, too. They called a Sierra Club meeting. Stop the Cordova road! So one evening all these rich Californians jump into their big, expensive cars and . . ."

"No, no, no," Farrell said loudly. "Little, expensive cars. They drive Saabs, BMWs, Porsches. Little, expensive cars."

Bill Greenwood shook a finger at Larry. "He's right. They jump into their Jaguars and tool on down the fine eight-lane highways and meet at somebody's two-hundred-thousand-dollar house and see if they can't do something about these selfish Alaskans who want to be able to travel around their state."

Tom Farrell applauded. Barney Hawkins, who ran the Montez Garage, bought Greenwood a drink. "Give 'em all drinks," he said, shoving money across the bar. "Bill's got it right. They screwed up the Lower 48 beyond repair and now they think we ought to pay for it. Alaska for the animals and the hell with the people."

"Barney," Maggie said, "I'm surprised to hear you say that. Aren't you always complaining that there isn't as much game here, that too many people are moving into the state?"

"I don't like people telling us what to do," Barney said at last. "If we're going to screw up, let us do it our way. Ah, hell, I don't know what I want. I like to hunt and I hate the hunting laws. You shoot a man here, you might get a few years; you kill a damn moose out of season and you'll be in real trouble. I can't figure it." He picked up his drink. "Anyway, the hell with Californians."

"I'll drink to that."

"Where you from?" Greenwood asked Larry. "Out east wasn't it?"

"New Hampshire."

"What do you think? You in to get the money and get out or do you want to stay?"

"I like it here. I could stay. You go for a drive and you see wild game. Go for a drive in New Hampshire and you see cows. I just like the way the land looks here. And the way Alaska is."

Everyone nodded at that.

"You know what makes the glaciers blue?" Greenwood asked. "You took my boat trip with your family, you saw the blue ice."

"Ice worms," Farrell said. "The dark blue streaks is where there's a whole nest of ice worms."

"Tell me about the fur fish." Larry sat back to get a better look at Farrell. "Are they found this far south?"

"I caught a fur fish near the glacier," Greenwood told him. "But he didn't have the pelt on him like you see in the Brooks Range."

Barney asked if Larry had ever heard the term "breakup."

"I'm confused on that," Larry said. "I thought it was in spring when the mud and slush got all mixed up, the thaw. We call it mud season in New Hampshire. But then I saw something in the paper about betting on the Tanana breakup."

"Not like a banana," Maggie laughed.

"What?"

"It isn't Tanana, like a banana. It's the Tan-a-naw River. Every spring there's a big pool and people buy chances to see if they can pick the exact second that the ice goes off the river. It's a big deal. You can win thousands on it. Judges go out, put up markers, line up sights, start watching the exact time on a chronometer. You can always tell a newcomer by how he says Tanana. Same as here in town, calling it Mon-tez instead of Mon-teez. Or not saying Val-deez."

"We have that back east, too," Larry told them. "Hav'rill for Haverhill."

"Now he knows how to say Tanana, he can get by anywhere in the state."

Barney waved a hand. "I got one for him. Kid, you ever hear of a Spenard divorce?"

Larry shook his head. Spenard was a section of Anchorage over toward the airport.

"Spenard divorce is when a woman gets tired of her husband and shoots him." He banged his glass down. "Guilty as charged. Six months, suspended. Next case."

Ed Booth came in, hung his parka behind the bar, and took a seat, rubbing his hands together. "Cold out there."

There was talk about the celebration Ed would be in charge of at Copper Canyon the following month.

"If we can get the snow cleared off and do some more blasting," Ed said, "I think we'll make it. God, I wish we could clear the snow around this tavern. Coming down the road it looks like we're about to be swallowed up by the drifts. You know, I don't see how these ravens and crows make it through the winter. I saw a couple of them huddled behind the sea wall. Miserable."

Larry had been surprised at the number of crows in Alaska. The first raven he'd run across, peering malignantly at him from a fence post in Fairbanks at thirty below, seemed an apparition. The bird was so big, so ugly, that Larry had almost lost his footing. In camp, the roof peak of the old metal dry shack was lined with crows every day. The men threw crusts of bread and the birds swirled down after them, cawing and squawking. Sometimes a single raven would land and a flock of crows would reluctantly give way as he strode among the pieces of bread, picking up the choice morsels. Over the water, sea gulls flew and called to one another. There were no songbirds. Only cawing, croaking, screeching birds. Once in a while a bald eagle would soar over the other birds, and if the eagle made a cry it was so high and distant Larry never heard it.

The men along the bar talked of birds and sea otters, fish they had caught, crabs, clams dug in Clam Gulch down on the Kenai Peninsula. There were bear stories, and Larry began to believe that if you spent any time at all in the Alaskan woods you would have either a funny or a horrible story to tell about a bear. A grizzly bear had eaten a photographer recently. A bear had come down off the mountain in Montez and chased some children until a motorist saved them.

Larry had heard some of these local bear stories and he added a few of his own, including the one where Joe Akin found a bear in the teamster shack. Larry hadn't been there for it, but his boss had.

The bar was a snug retreat for stories of cold walks down mountains, six-week camping treks through the Brooks Range living on Dall sheep and moving with the herd, tales of narrow escapes in the winter, bountiful harvests of salmon, and women, good and bad. Barney had taken a native girl to bed with only a blanket between them and the rest of the family. In the morning, the girl begged him to stay.

"You good man. You make my ass come glad four, five times,"

she told him in front of her mother, father, uncles, toothless ancestors in the smoky, smelly room.

Larry heard a familiar laugh. Little Nasty.

"Larry," Nasty said quickly, "you seen a woman in here, about five-foot-eight, square shoulders, one bad eye?"

"Jesus," Barney said.

Nasty glared at him. "That's my wife."

"That's Big Nasty," Larry heard over his shoulder. It was Tiny, looking more perturbed than usual.

"That right?"

"Why do you think they call me *Little* Nasty?" Little Nasty said. "She took a room over to the White House, but damned if I can find her there, here or anywheres."

He laid a hand up on the counter and Larry looked down at it.

"Nasty, I never noticed you had a finger missing," Larry blurted. "Did that just happen?"

"Ironworking's dangerous," Tiny said. "Specially if you don't know what you're doing."

Tiny held out his hands to show Larry how scarred and beaten up they were. Larry stuck out a finger.

"Timekeeping has its dangers, too. I once had a paper cut, right there on the end of the finger. And another time I nearly got scratched on a staple."

Tiny grabbed Larry's hand and turned it front and back, inspecting it. "Look at this," he held the hand up, disgusted. "He's got hands like a cunt."

Maggie turned away.

"Your face is funny, but you ain't," Nasty told him. "That there is the stupid, slab-sided son-of-a-bitch that took mah finger off. I seen dumber mules but I don't recollect when."

"Hey, get off my case, cracker. You been running your mouth at me all week."

Nasty held up his hand for everyone to see. "This clown's s'posed to be a big rigger. But he cut my damn finger off. Big nigger, more like. Some honcho we got pushing us out there. You know he paid the room clerk in camp a hundred bucks to get put in with the pretty boy that sings here nights?"

"You're tryin' hard. I told you to get off my case, pipsqueak."

Little Nasty hardly came up to Tiny's chest, but he faced the man like he was about to tear into him. "Ah could rig better'n you with mah eyes closed." He waved his hand, the stumpy finger at Tiny.

"That right? Well you know something. You can't weld worth a damn. No wonder the seven ninety-eight threw you out."

Everyone was laughing now as Nasty got up on his toes, trying to bully Tiny.

"Cain't rig 'cause you got your mind on that pretty boy, ain'cha?"

Tiny shook his head sadly. "Well, if I had to choose between him and your wife, from what I seen in the pictures, I got to say Big Nasty would run a close second." He turned suddenly and began to walk away.

Nasty moved after him, touched him on the shoulder. Heads turned at the bar.

"Feisty little bastard," Greenwood said.

Tiny shrugged Nasty off and took two more steps. "I ain't in no mood to play with you. And I don't want to meet your wife, please."

Little Nasty took a few scampering steps and kicked Tiny sharply just behind the knee. As Tiny turned, reaching down to touch his leg, Nasty drew back and threw a hard right to Tiny's jaw. It was early in the evening and the bar was only half full. Everyone in the club jumped at the sound of the fist against skin, the sharp crack of teeth, the unmistakable sound of another fight.

For Nasty, seeing Tiny stand there after taking a roundhouse was worse than wasting his last bullet on a rattler. There wasn't but one hope. He moved in and got the man, locked fingers, and went for the tit. And then the pounding. For a time the blows stopped hurting, but Tiny was getting to him. His ears were ringing. Purple lights went on and off behind his eyes.

Tiny hit, Nasty shifted and found a good bite down lower where the man's belly flab began. It was a lucky thing Tiny had his coat off and wore a light polyester shirt. Wouldn't want to be eatin' no flannel, startin' in through a down parka. Tiny slowed the rhythm of his punches as Nasty bit down. He could feel the man stiffen against him as he chewed. Ah'm a bulldog, Nasty repeated over and over, trying to stay conscious. The damn bear's gonna stove in mah head.

"This man's eatin' me up," Tiny screamed, his blows falling on Nasty's shoulders, the side of his head, his neck.

Nasty burrowed in all the more, ground his teeth into the fold of fat, chewing his way down until he could taste blood. He hoped it was Tiny's blood.

"Don't bite" Tiny shouted and beat on his head. Nasty chewed, got knocked away, dove in for a new bite higher on the chest and worked his teeth from side to side trying to bring the cutters into play. "You son-of-a-bitch. He's bitin' me to pieces."

Nasty heard a shrill woman's scream to one side but he didn't dare open his eyes. He ground his teeth into Tiny's flesh, getting more blood, tearing all the the harder when Tiny's punches jerked his head. Let the man's strength work against him. That scream again, high-pitched, awesome.

"She's got a barstool," someone shouted, and Nasty felt a surge of hope. It had to be Big Nasty.

He heard the blow of wood and immediately felt Tiny slump against him, the punches weaken. He grabbed a new hold and was clear under the shirt now, working on bare skin.

The wooden sound again and Tiny slumped further.

"Leave go!" the woman screamed, and there were confused shouts. "You bastard, let my husband alone."

Tiny put his hands down on Nasty's shoulders and pushed away. Nasty let go and fell back into the crowd. He felt other hands pushing him upright. His head ached so bad he couldn't see straight. Big Nasty was there suddenly, crying, a patch over her bad eye. And Schultz the bouncer was talking loudly in German. Nasty focused. Tiny stood in the center of the crowd, tears streaming down his face. He ripped the shirt off in one movement and the people in the bar murmured. Tiny's chest bled in five places. Nasty's teethmarks, angry circles, were everywhere.

"Look," Tiny sobbed. "Look what he done to me. The bastard ate me up." He turned to show others. Schultz stood there not certain of what to do next. "Get him," Tiny told Schultz. "He started it. He should go to jail." The blood streamed down his chest. "I'll get you for this, Nasty."

Nasty squeezed his eyes shut, managed to summon enough strength to stand alone. "You try it, you or the big Kraut. I'll eat you both up. Won't be nothing but bones left, either one of you."

And then someone was wiping Tiny's chest with a towel. Schultz was complaining that he couldn't get out of the corner because a man had pointed a gun at him. He'd find the man. Schultz was chewing on his fingernails, looking like *he* would cry at any minute. Nasty saw Larry looking at him and then felt himself start to black out.

The last he remembered, the drunk police chief had come stumbling into the club and said over and over, "Nobody leave. Nobody leave."

Dan used whatever spare moments he could steal to write to Paula or to phone her. April came and she was still hesitant about flying back up, yet unwilling to say that she might not change her mind. A week before the scheduled pipelaying, Dan Curry broke away from a meeting without explanation and drove home to call Paula.

"I can't take this," he said without preliminaries. "You write letters to me about what the kids do in school, about concerts you go to, the weather, anything but us. I know you asked me not to pressure you right now, but dammit, we're married, or supposed to be. Can't we talk about it?"

"Not with you up there."

"You know I can't just pick up and leave. I've got this pipelaying on April fifteenth at Copper Canyon. And problems with it." He pulled the desk calendar over and looked at it. "Look, honey, I could fly down the last weekend, Saturday, the twenty-sixth. Knock off for a week. I think I'm entitled to some emergency leave."

"Sure, Dan. If you think you can get away."

"Hey, what kind of talk is that? It's important. I'll be there."

She said she hoped so. They made a few attempts at further conversation. Then they hung up.

Dan wrote the date in on the calendar. Hell, if there was a delay, he'd find some pretext and shut down the whole project that week if he had to. He smiled at the enormity of that prospect and went to the kitchen to mix a drink. Didn't he have as much right to be jealous of San Francisco as she did of Alaska? Paula was always bringing it up. Alaskan girl. What the hell, Lavinia took her vacations in the British Isles, didn't she?

Dan poured himself a double scotch. For someone with a whole state as a mistress, he sure had one hell of a poor sex life.

In towns north of Thompson Pass, away from the temperate coastal climate, winter clung tightly to the interior of the state. In Copper Canyon and Montez, rain or sun brought thaws and mud. A reviewing stand was being built on the quarter-mile shelf above the old railroad tunnel. For a time, APPLE had considered using the temporary freight hoist built on the edge of the canyon to carry up the reporters and officials. The governor had been invited, a state senator, the mayor of Montez, and a handful of Alaskan celebrities. The shelf was inspected and found to have too much loose dirt packed near the cliff edge. Rocks might fall. The participants in the ceremony would have to be driven up the pioneer road, along the canyon wall, or flown in by helicopters. A landing pad was built near the stands. A rope fence would be erected between the stands and the pad and between the entire work area and the edge just to prevent accidents. It wouldn't do to lose a senator over the cliff with all the news media present. Ed Booth attended to everything, watched over the temporary lift that would now be used to transport the lumber to the clifftop and then dismantled until after the ceremony. APPLE would not want to be accused of creating an eyesore in such a scenic area. When the cameras and reporters went away, they could put the hoist back up. Booth reserved rooms in the motels, arranged for a luncheon at Sheep Creek Camp, which was actually closer to the canyon than Terminal Camp. The open sewage tank at the Terminal would be a problem, it had been discovered, wind or no wind. A sewer lake 20 by 150 feet just could not go unnoticed.

Rosemary Fay, the ex-schoolteacher, spent her days sitting in a school bus that had been assigned to the Copper Canyon crew for use as a warming shack. She pulled in alongside the rugged canyon wall and stopped just short of the old railroad tunnel. All day she opened and closed the doors of the bus for workers to come in from the cold. For a while she read books. Finally she left the door slightly ajar and began to explore the two-hundred-foot tunnel, hand dug and blasted just after the turn of the century. A local travel brochure said that rival companies, primarily from Cordova, Valdez and Montez, had sought to be the first to build a rail line from the sea to the rich copper deposits in Kennicott and McCarthy. The fifteen-foot-diameter tunnel was as far as they got when hired gunmen ambushed one of the crews. The next few days, gun battles raged throughout the canyon, and the companies withdrew one by one. At the end, nobody had the money or the will left to continue the job. The tunnel had been abandoned. A second attempt through Keystone Canyon led to troubles, and the new line was built from Cordova, a 194-mile railroad that brought ore out of the copper mines until they closed in 1938. Now that line, too, was abandoned.

Rosemary brought a flashlight and examined the rough, jagged walls and ceiling of the tunnel. It was so crude it looked like a natural formation. You might expect to find artifacts in it. Stone tools. Wall paintings. All she found was a mildly obscene notation in chalk. "D & L did it here, 6-18-67."

She got back on the bus, smiling to herself. One of the laborers, digging into a sack of cookies, clucked his tongue. "You must be ctazy, walking around in there. That place ain't safe."

His buddy reached out for a cookie, took it, reached out for another one.

"The lady's a historian, chump. That tunnel has a history."

"Even as late as 1967," Rosemary said.

The *Pipe 'n' Hot News* ran several articles on the big day when the pipe would go in the ground, a day that would write a new page in the history of the state. Both the Tonsina and the Copper Canyon crews were in a race for the honor of putting the first pipe down. It was, the paper said, in the great tradition of early Alaska, the race to the gold fields, the bush pilots' attempts to create one first after another, and even our own pipeline tradition, the race to complete the haul road. Finch-Smith found it all amusing, coming from a country where history tended to be measured in centuries. He took time from a busy schedule to place a special request with APPLE's employment representative. That same afternoon, the request was transferred to the personnel director at Bartel Construction: "Would you consider the release of a nonexempt employee from your payroll department to our public affairs division? The employee, a timekeeper for Bartel, Montez Terminal, is Larry Ransom. We would appreciate his release within two weeks of this date, if possible."

At Bartel, the request was passed from one hand to another. The director for the temporary facility called two meetings. Instructions would have to come from California. Two long-distance calls established clearly that the company did not have to release Larry Ransom but could after considering him for a similar position with Bartel. Did Bartel have public relations at Montez already? It did. The wife of one of the superintendents wrote up family news and amusing anecdotes for the company magazine. Larry's boss called him in and asked if he would submit a résumé. He couldn't tell him why. Something to do with a message from California. Larry left in confusion. He didn't know anyone in California.

The snow changed to rain and Larry took the work bus from site to site. He was wet, covered with mud, chilled from walking through slush. Still, there was a sense of exhilaration about being at the Terminal. The job covered acres of land that had been terraced into a steep hillside that rose high above the camp and diverged into a series of bare mountain peaks with steep valleys in between. The terminal had been hidden from the sun completely for seven weeks. On clear days, the sunlight poured down on Montez across the bay, but on the deep slope of the hill, Larry and the others never saw direct sunlight. Now the sun was high enough for it to shine through the valleys. There were four sunrises and sunsets a day for a while, as the sun left one peak, rose over the valley and disappeared for an hour or more behind the next peak. More often, as today, there was no sun at all in April. Even so, Larry stood in a drizzling rain at the junction of two work roads and looked down over the project. To his left, a high plateau held the tank farm, fourteen tanks, two-hundred-fifty feet in diameter. The rings of six tanks were now clearly visible, with the outlines of five more. Below the sharp cliff edge, out of Larry's sight, were the tanks for the ballast water treatment plant. Beyond that, at the edge of the water, materials were stored for pipeways, roads, control buildings. Out in the water a drilling barge took core samples for the offshore loading berths where the big tankers would dock one day. Larry looked back at the tank rings, half a million barrels of oil capacity each. Four of them would handle a day's oil coming down the line from Prudhoe.

Everywhere Larry looked, up on the high plateau, down on the sloping shelf that ran to the shoreline, he could see construction equipment in motion. The job seemed to have hit a good pace these last few weeks as the cold weather gave way. A line of Wabco Haulpaks, carrying thirty or more tons of dirt each, was moving from a material site somewhere below the tank farm. They were bringing the landfill to grade, while dozers pushed the earth into place. Other dozers worked the tank farm, clearing broken rock from the site of the last three tank rings. Graders worked up and down the utility roads, clearing the muck. Directly below, a team of ironworkers crawled over the steel skin of a new building going up alongside the company office building. The offices themselves stood on a hill overlooking the dock where another barge was being unloaded by two enormous American cranes, 225-tonners. To Larry's right, marching down the hillside, were the dorms and the temporary camp facilities.

The 75-ton P&H crane was working down in the midst of the camp buildings, erecting a new mess hall. On the hill above the camp, a generating station was being built next to the massive water tank. Between the tank and the edge of the hill where the barracks sloped on down to the shore, the honey wagon pumped sewage into the temporary pond. Larry could walk on down the hillside—if he could stand the smell. He stood a moment longer, no bus in sight among all that jumble of men and moving equipment (what great purpose it all suggested!), and decided to walk. He might find the Millwright foreman in the generator plant and he could count noses for the other timekeeper who'd be making the same circuit in an hour or so.

He followed the mucky access road, piled high with rotten snow on both sides, and came out at one edge of the clearing for the generator. He went to the building and looked inside. No one was there. He walked around the building. Usually there were four or five pipefitters and an electrician or two. Larry started on down the road when he heard a noise over the patter of rain, a deep groan from the water tank.

He hesitated a moment and then heard the groan again. The tank was a hundred feet away, a domed structure standing two stories high, the size of a house. It was surrounded by scaffolding, which had been put up the day before so the insulators would be able to work on it when they finished the new sewer pipe under the dorms. Such scheduling, Larry thought, hurrying now as he heard a scream and another moan. Had there been an accident inside? The sound was from the two-foot valve opening at the base of the tank.

It grew louder as Larry broke into a run and then skidded on ice, stumbling up against the side of the tank. He dropped his clipboard and quickly retrieved it, brushing the snow and water away. Then, cautiously, he knelt to peer inside.

"Ohhhhhhhmmmmmmm," he heard, and the dome repeated it. There was laughter. Larry's eyes began to adjust to the light. There were several men inside, gathered near the center of the tank. A white plastic coating, several inches thick, had been sprayed over the interior of the tank. It gave off a faint, eerie glow by the light coming in at the valve hole.

"Ahhhh," a voice went softly, and the voice was softly echoed. A cigarette glowed and Larry thought he recognized Gragen, the young pipefitter apprentice.

"What's going on in there?" Larry shouted, and he was answered by a jumbled voice that made no sense.

"What?"

There were other shouts, unintelligible. Larry gathered from the tone that he was, if not being invited, at least not unwelcome. He crawled into the room, pale at the floor, receding into darkness at the apex of the dome. He dropped his hard hat and the crack it made as it struck the floor startled him. He picked up the hat and tapped it lightly against the plastic floor. The sound was like a rifle shot. His footsteps were magnified many times as he walked to the gathering in the center of the room, where he caught a strong whiff of pot in the air.

"Hey, Ransom," Gragen said by way of greeting. "This is a real head trip." Gragen took a drag on his joint and passed it to Larry. Larry drew in and passed it on.

"Dig it," Coffee said. Coffee was a West Indian who wore a snakeskin necklace, flashed a gold tooth whenever he smiled, and spoke with little trace of an accent. If anything, he sounded English. Coffee tilted his head back and took a deep breath.

"OOOMMMMMMMMMM," he toned and it came back, "Mmmmmmmmmmm," the sound hanging in the dome for half a minute. He whistled two clear notes and the notes first repeated, then sounded faintly, then mingled and seemed to sound together, fainter, in and out of phase, until finally there was only a ringing in the air that fell to a tiny, insistent pressure against Larry's ear. At last it died away.

"You can't even understand somebody across the tank," Gragen whispered. "But isn't it a groove when Coffee whistles?"

Larry took the joint again, held his breath, passed it on.

Coffee whistled again. The men stood, listening.

"I have an idea," Larry whispered. "It might work if two men stood on opposite sides and faced the wall. Try it, Gragen. Face the wall and I'll whisper to you."

The two men went to opposite walls, their footsteps resounding in the dome.

Larry waited and then whispered Gragen's name.

"Yeah?"

"Can you hear me?"

"Yeah! Jesus, what a trip, huh? Wow. I hear you fine. Let's tell the others."

They returned to the center. A half hour later, when Larry left, the others were paired off around the tank, whispering, telling stories, giggling on a good high. At eleven dollars an hour each. Larry checked them off on the worksheet. Present. That was the important thing. Present and accounted for.

Someone had put a sign at the edge of the sewer pond, now three fourths full: POLISH SWIMMING POOL. Someone had written in smaller letters: No, It's a Conversation Pit for Texans.

A trail led down over the embankment where the pond stood. Below the embankment, dorm fifteen was getting its finishing touches—a snow porch at either end. Larry walked along the upper camp road to the second section. There was a crew working on the red-iron foundation for the last section. At the upper end of the pad a laborer cleared debris, following a rotary drill. Two rows farther down a backhoe squared off the holes. The other rows held upright iron I-beams either waiting for cement to anchor them or, if already set, for the 300-foot-long crossbeam that would support the modules. As the dorms were set on a steep slope, the lower leg of the steel beam foundation might stand as much as ten feet high while the uphill leg would be only a foot or two aboveground.

A labor crew sat idle, spaced out along a beam, waiting for a concrete truck to come up. They shared a long tarp, huddling out of the drizzle. Dago John was in charge and he waved Larry over.

"Got a smoke?"

Larry shook his head. John had borrowed so much off his own crew that nobody would give him a cigarette. He could always send John up to the water tank, turn him onto a new vice.

"Working hard?"

"Shit," John said, searching his pockets as if he expected for once to have cigarettes of his own. "What a waste of time. We've been here soaking for three hours, no truck. I don't know how this pipeline is supposed to get built."

"They say they're on schedule," Larry told him. "I think they must have figured in all the fuckups."

"We'll pay for it in gasoline someday," Dago John said. He looked as gloomy as the weather. "You'll see. They don't care what they spend. We're making it now, but we'll be paying for it when the oil starts to flow."

"On your salary you can afford it," Larry said, putting a foot up on the iron, resting one elbow across his leg.

"Yeah, you laugh. Wait until you pay a dime extra for a gallon of gas. They'll never get this thing built."

Larry shrugged. It wouldn't do any good to tell Dago John that the cost and scheduling people were pleased as hell. They'd anticipated delays, labor problems, disasters, you name it. By summer there would be fifteen or twenty thousand people working. With that many in the field, it didn't matter if a man worked three hours a day. Work would get done by sheer numbers. And some contractors, some crafts, were working hard. Damn hard.

"Ransom," John said, stroking his chin shrewdly. "What do you pay for a cord of wood, firewood, back east?"

"Depends. Anywhere from thirty to fifty bucks."

"You know how much APPLE is paying? Twelve hundred bucks."

Larry turned his head away in disbelief. Dago John caught at his sleeve.

"You see that pile of cut-up six-by-sixes, four-by-sixes down at the dock?"

"That's dunnage, isn't it? For loading at the dock." Larry had seen the pile and wondered at it. The forklifts needed lumber when they set crates and equipment down, needed it for clearance underneath. Larry guessed that the pile of wood, growing by the day, was for heavy summer shipments coming into Montez.

John filled him in. The laborers had been told to bring a four-man crew with chainsaws and a truck to cut up the wood. It was new wood, interior quality, shipped from Seattle. The men spent hours cutting down timbers, sawing away at everything down to two-by-fours, stacking it all in separate piles. So John asked why and found it was to be used as firewood in the modular housing being built for APPLE officials over in town. Last Sunday they had moved the first load, five men at the Sunday rate, twenty bucks an hour each. And that didn't touch the cost of the wood. He'd gone to see the labor supervisor and they sat down with cost accounting. It came to nearly twelve hundred a cord. By throwing in scrap lumber from other projects, the cost man announced that he hoped to bring it down to eight hundred.

"That's not even good fireplace wood," Dago John said. "Burns too fast. They could have gone to Copper Center, Glennallen, got wood delivered for seventy, eighty a cord. You wait. You go to buy gas someday, you remember that pile of wood down on the dock. You sure you don't have a smoke on you?"

Larry started on down and recognized Little Nasty under his welding hood. He walked over and spoke to him. Nasty was tacking a cross member in place.

"Don't be lookin' at the arc," Nasty shouted through his mask. "Don't even look sideways too long. You'll get a flash."

"What's a flash?"

"Burns your eye. Feels like someone put sandpaper under your eyelid. You'd be spending a few days hiding in the closet and wishin' to hell you had the nerve to poke 'em out and be done with it."

Larry turned around and waited for Nasty to finish. Nasty had transferred to the structural crew after the fight with Tiny. He'd stayed off work almost a week and when he came back he moved carefully, often sat down, and breathed hard, complaining that his head hurt.

"That'll hold it I reckon." Nasty pushed his helmet back and smiled at Larry. "How you doing, sonny?"

"I'm doing great." Larry tried to see past the welder's mask. "How's your head?"

Nasty eased the mask off carefully and bent forward. There were lumps still, one large one on the side that was a deep blue color. Odd patches of scalp showed through.

Nasty stood up. "Ah got bumps that ain't going away ever and some of mah hair's starting to fall out, but other'n that I'm fine. I hope that peckerwood dies of rabies."

"You haven't tried to get back together?"

Nasty shook his head. "Don't know that I ever will, now. Not until he apologizes."

"For hitting you so hard?"

"Naw. He insulted Big Nasty right out in public. He can damn well apologize in public . . . Say, I got Big Nasty a place to live in Anchorage and this summer we're going to bring a camper down here, maybe even get something permanent."

"That would be nice," Larry said. What else could he say about Nasty's wife?

"You know," Nasty said, "neither of us is much to look at, I guess, but we got us a good marriage, considering. We look out for each other."

Larry trudged on down the hill. He had a sandwich in his pocket and didn't feel like eating with the bosses in the camp office. On impulse he turned left at the bottom of the dorm road and went on past the office shack, past the fuel dump that stood between the shore and the dorms, and headed for the dock area where Tiny would be. It was raining harder.

The rigging crew was moving in for lunch; all over the camp the noise level slowly wound down. A siren on the office building announced lunch as if it were an air raid.

Larry had to turn away as the camp bus splashed by, spraying him with slush. Where were you when I needed you? he thought, and wished that whoever was interested in him from California would hire him down there. He could use some sunshine. Montez had gotten three hundred inches of snow and much of it still remained, in ugly, rotting heaps, eroded by the rain, becoming part of the ooze that daily swallowed tons of gravel put down to stabilize it. Even a Euclid truck had mired down in the landfill, its six-foot tires churning uselessly. The D-9 Cat that came to rescue it was forced to find dry ground and use the winch. Its treads, too, had threatened to bog down.

"Ya ever see this kind of rain?" Tiny said, stomping up the short set of steps into the dry shack. Larry followed. A yellow Master-heater sat beneath the overhang and blew hot air through a hole in the plywood. Inside, a row of pegs held coats, gloves, even a pair of boots. Tiny hung his coat and the rest of the crew followed. Larry put his jacket up with the others.

Sonny, the trainee, laughed as he sat down on the bench at the far end of the rough, wooden table. "Worse weather than Vietnam." He plunked down an orange and two fat sandwiches. "And I was there in the rainy season."

"Even mud season back in New Hampshire isn't as bad as this," Larry said.

"Shit." Tiny set a canvas bag on the table, sat down and began pulling out lunch. A thermos, sandwich, donuts, cookies, apples and cans of fruit juice. "I was in Korea, we had mud that'd swallow a tank right up to its turret while it was sitting out overnight."

The door banged open and Jack Price, the dock superintendent, began removing his raingear, cursing and fumbling.

"Watch your language, boys," Tiny said through a mouthful of food. "We've got a Californian in the room."

"This is the worst weather in the world," Price said. "And I mean the worst."

"Worse than Nam?" Sonny asked. Price had been superintendent on a job in Vietnam for thirteen years. Had married a Vietnamese girl. Larry had been cautioned not to use the word "gook" around him, even if Price, on occasion, did. Larry said he wouldn't.

"Christ, yes, it's worse." Price moved to the table and looked over the lunches. "Who's got something to eat?"

Sonny pushed a sandwich over and Price picked it up, cracked the bread like it was the cover of a book and peeked inside. "Screw bologna. Anybody got ham, roast beef?"

The old man, Dale, didn't say a word, but reached down in the bag and laid out three sandwiches.

"What are they?"

"All roast beef."

"What you got in there, a grocery store?"

The old man shrugged. "Once I got a sandwich with stale bread and now I grab four or five just to make sure."

"Here's another," Tiny said and threw a sandwich on the pile. "This mud ain't no worse than Korea, actually."

"Should have seen the mud in Anzio," the old man cut in, coughing heavily. "You couldn't dig a foxhole in that place. If you did and it rained, the whole thing'd close up on you like a grave. I never made a foxhole there."

Larry had nothing to say, not having been in a war.

"Yeah, it's bad here," Price said, taking the beef off four sandwiches and putting it all on one, throwing the extra bread in the garbage can by the door. "It's bad here because it rains all the time. At least in Nam when the monsoons came it rained a few hours and you got a break until the next day. In fact, you could just about count on it raining so many minutes each day. One rain and over for the day."

The door opened and the materials supervisor came in and moved gloomily to the table. His hair was dripping rainwater on the table. He didn't care.

"Bolls, you look like the cat drug you in here." Price offered him the bologna sandwich and Bolls took it and began eating without looking to see what it was. "We were talking about the weather, here, back in the Nam. How it used to rain hard there, but it would stop for a while."

Bolls frowned. "I was in Burma. Rained pretty good there. Not like Danang, but you know, for a couple of hours you couldn't see to drive through it. What the hell, even the tropics, Venezuela, it doesn't rain like here."

"Yeah, you put it that way," Tiny said, "we got worse weather in Montez than in Korea. I guess the mud there was bad because I was near a lot of rice paddies where the ground was soaked for a long time. Tanks were always getting stuck in somebody's irrigation ditch. Those farmers used to get pissed at us."

"Rain or not," Price said, "Vietnam was absolutely the best goddamn construction job there ever was. I mean the best job with not even a close second."

"No doubt about it," Bolls said.

"Why?" Larry asked. "What could have been so good about Vietnam?"

"You hear this asshole?" Price turned around to face Larry. "He wants to know what's so great about the Nam. Tell him, Bolls."

"The women."

A dawning hit Sonny. "I can see that," he said softly.

"The women?" Larry asked.

Price looked at him with pity. "Goddamn right, the women. You couldn't take a bath without three or four coming in to help you. And if you got tired of that bunch, you could snap your fingers and three or four new ones would come in. I don't think I ever had the same woman twice and I had me a passel of 'em, I mean I did some serious fucking."

"That was the place to do it," Bolls said. "They do things over there you wouldn't believe."

Silence.

At last Larry asked it. "Like what?"

"You don't need to know. With that beard and long hair you'd be beating yourself off every night and wondering why they wouldn't look at you. Guy like you, he'd be there all day with nothing while I was getting laid seven times. That long hair and beard shit don't go with them. You'd spend a year, never get a piece of ass, ain't that right?"

"That's right," Bolls agreed.

"Same thing in Korea," Tiny said.

Sonny looked at Larry and nodded apologetically.

"Maybe for a piece of ass I'd sacrifice it," Larry told Price.

Price went on. "Singapore's the same. Don't matter who you are, you get off the plane there, zip, they cut your hair and beard off or your ass is right back on the plane and out of there."

"Danang," Bolls said, "that was a good place. We had some times."

"All over now. VC got the whole damn country."

Everybody at the table seemed downcast at the thought.

"That's sad," Price continued. "But that ARVN was a lousy army. We called in an air strike on those bastards once. People were always stealing from us. Both sides. Not too bad most of the time, and some of our people were making a few bucks selling to the locals. But there was this bunch of South Vietnam colonels who were stealing us fucking blind. I mean they were cutting into the profit for all of us. You could get rich working there. But these guys were getting greedy. They were ruining it for everyone, and after all, we were trying to get a few airfields built.

"So we talked to the Air Force boys and told them our problem and let them know we would be very grateful for anything they could do." He rubbed his thumb and forefinger together for emphasis. "Very grateful. You men remember in the papers back then how we accidentally bombed a headquarters and killed seven

South Vietnamese colonels? Terrible thing." He made the sign of the cross. "Well, that put a stop to that kind of greediness for a long time. Those people knew who did it and why it wasn't no accident. Can you imagine? It was that good, back then. We could actually call in an air strike if we needed one. I was real sorry to leave that place."

"There's nothing like it," Bolls said. "Nothing."

"Bangkok, maybe. Singapore," Price said softly. "But it's not the same. It'll never be that good anywhere again." He paused. "There'll never be another Vietnam."

But it was actually another blues by Leslie Collins in the *Pipe 'n' Hot News* that made Larry realize he didn't belong in Montez anymore.

The song became the most requested number after "Yellow Ribbon" at the club. Copies were posted around the camp.

Even Tiny liked it.

TALKING TERMINAL CAMP BLUES

Well I got me a job on the old pipeline,
Working seven elevens and doing fine.
I was makin' money like a champ
And then they stuck me in Terminal Camp.
I wouldn't say my luck ran out,
But now and then I start to doubt.
It rains all day and snows all night—
That mucky slush is a terrible sight.

Makes me want to fight.
Jump up and shout
Go back inside
Hide
From Terminal Camp.

Seven and eleven in an old crap game
Is damn good luck by any name,
But seven elevens in Terminal Camp
Will bring you money and get you damp.
You'll cough and sniffle till your nose turns red

And every night when you lay in bed
You'll spread your fingers, crack your toes—
Just to see no webbing grows.
Terminal cramp.
Terminal damp.
Who turned off the sun?

Now I'm not sayin' I ain't happy here,
At least we got some broads and beer
Over in a town they call Montez.
Just the spot to find re-leeze.
Till you come down with the Mon-disease—
From Terminal Town.
Go on down.
They don't care how wet your money is.

L.C. from Montez

Part Four

Chapter One

WAVERLY, the office manager, called Larry Ransom in, hemmed and hawed and finally told him he'd been released.

"I'm fired?" Larry sat forward in the chair.

Waverly shook his head slowly, spoke slowly. "You've got the job you asked for with APPLE."

"Job?"

"The one I called you in about."

"But you wouldn't tell me what it was about."

"No, it was supposed to be confidential. I thought you knew about it."

"I didn't know anything. I gave in a résumé to APPLE on my R&R and never heard a word."

"Oh." Waverly considered this carefully. "Well, I should have told you. I assumed that you knew, even though you weren't supposed to know until the release was official, and that you only asked to make it look like you didn't know."

"I didn't know."

"You should have told me. Well, you did tell me, but not so I actually knew that you didn't know what we were up to. But you know now?"

"No." Larry got up. "But I'll make a call and see what I can find out. What does that mean, me being released?"

"Soon as we train a replacement you go. Should be a week. You know how it is."

Larry called Finch-Smith. "I've been released from Bartel. You know anything about that?"

"Good, good. Then I can offer you a job."

"Why couldn't you offer it before I got released? Suppose I don't want the job?"

"Not the way it's done, you see. I can't steal help from the subcontractors, but I can ask them if it's permissible to have a man. Once they release him, give up interest in the employee, then I'm free to make him an offer."

Larry pinched the bridge of his nose. "What is the offer, Mr. Finch-Smith?"

"Ah, yes. Where shall I begin? I suppose this all came about due to the Copper Canyon pipelaying. We've been writing speeches and press releases about what a historic occasion this is, what a history-making project the pipeline is, how each person who works on the line enters the pages of Alaskan history as surely as the gold rushers, that sort of muck. Of course, it's all quite true, isn't it?"

Larry agreed that it was quite true.

"Well, it seemed natural then that we should compile some sort of historical account of all this. Largest private construction job in modern history, all that gaff about the last frontier. As I say, all of it perfectly true. We've got the photo-historian. Miklov was there from the start, snapping pictures of the first surveyors, the first Cat train, everything. You can write, and as you're something of an old-timer on the project . . . you seemed the logical choice for the writer."

"Me? An old-timer?"

"Relatively. After all, you were here before construction began, toured the camps when they were hardly manned, crossed the ice bridge last year. If you can get to town right after the pipe goes in, you might even see this year's bridge. It should last into the first week of May. Jim Miklov was your strongest supporter, aside from myself. He says you've been here long enough and gone through enough to prove you're no tenderfoot any more. That wasn't the word he used. Something Indian."

"Cheechako?"

That was the word.

The job would pay between twenty-five and thirty thousand, as much as Larry was making away from home. More, considering the weeks lost to R&R.

"But what kind of history, Malcolm?"

Larry wasn't easy about working for a corporation. With the newspaper there had been a certain sense of freedom, particularly in covering feature stories. But a corporation? He told Finch-Smith he didn't mind selling his time to a company, as he had done in Montez, but when he wrote, he made his living by writing straight.

Finch-Smith told Larry that he'd said history and he meant just that. APPLE wasn't ashamed of its mistakes. After all, they were doing pioneering work, building in the Arctic. The company had attempted tremendous engineering feats in an area for which little practical experience existed. APPLE could be as proud of its failures as of its successes; they had added to the knowledge of the Arctic. Briefly, Finch-Smith listed the archeological work supported by APPLE, the cold weather studies, tundra reseeding, the revegetation programs, the geological sampling of an 800-mile section of the state, the fish and game studies, wildlife census, tagging, economic benefits.

"And," Finch-Smith said, "if you look at it honestly, the pipeline project got the Alaskan natives a better and quicker settlement from the state than they would have gotten in the ordinary course of events. Greed has its rewards. To get the oil leases and tax money, the state legislature would have signed anything. Native land claims looked like, as you say out here, small potatoes."

"No wonder you're head of public relations. I wonder what Emil Bacich would have to say to all that."

"Rubbish, of course. But, Larry, I very much want to see you put this book together for us. You'd travel the line, be on hand for the important events, the milestones, but you'd be home with your wife most of the time. Naturally, you'd have a great deal of research to do and you could spend days in the library, fly down to Juneau, visit with legislators. It wouldn't all be in an office."

"I think I'm being seduced."

Finch-Smith's voice rose noticably. "Don't know about that, old man, ha ha." He cleared his throat. "Do give us a call back on this, Larry. Be good to have you aboard."

Larry put the phone down.

"Good to have you aboard," he said to himself again and again.

Hope's response that night surprised him. To take the job would mean, of course, staying in Alaska until the project was finished, another three to five years, counting construction of the west tank farm. It might be 1978 before the line reached full production and that would be the earliest they could think of leaving.

"I was about to ask you if we should stay another year," she said. "I've been offered a contract next year for more money and I was hoping to tape-record some of the old people in the Pioneer's Home this summer. You know, in Walpole I was looking for diaries, digging in cellars. Here I can sit down with pioneers and ask them questions."

"What about the house?"

"Oh, the tenants want to stay on. And I'm sure if we sent Nancy a list, she'd go through the attic and box up the rest of our things."

"You know," Larry said, looking down the mess hall, nearly empty now, a few men hunched over coffee and desultory conversation, "when I first came up here I thought Alaska was it. I wanted to *be* Alaskan, the whole nine yards."

"The what?"

"The whole nine yards. Everybody says that here. But if I'd known last year what I do now, I'd never have left home."

"We could always go back to Walpole in the summer if you'd rather."

He told her he'd sleep on it.

As the fifteenth of April drew nearer, construction activity in Copper Canyon intensified. Dan Curry showed up on the weekend, four days early, to inspect the site. Dan rode a jeep to the top of the canyon and found Miklov taking pictures of the channel in the rock, the pipe strung along the ditch, most of it welded and taped, the row of side-boom Cats that had been moved into position and left along the pipeway. Ten of the Cats would pick up the pipe in heavy-duty nylon slings from their side booms and lower it, leapfrogging along the entire quarter-mile section, picking up at the head end, lowering at the back.

Problems had developed in a double-jointed section of pipe eighty feet long. It had been taped in advance by machine, like the rest of the pipe lengths along the ditch. When the last welds were put in, the plan was to hand wrap the joints, rather than drag a wrapping machine up on the already narrow and overcrowded ledge. Somewhere along the way, as the section had been brought up the canyonside, the machine bevel at one end of the half-inch thick steel pipe had been severely damaged. Further inspection showed a hairline crack, running four inches at an angle from the circumference. A replacement section was brought up and the eighty-foot length mounted on wooden skids near the reviewing stands. The visitors could then look at the pipe close at hand without getting in the way of heavy machinery during the ceremony.

By Monday, April 14, the workmen were beginning to dismantle the temporary hoist, and reporters, including Gil Wolfe, had drifted into Montez.

Planes were chartered from both Anchorage and Fairbanks to bring in the visitors. Two nine-passenger helicopters had already flown in to Sheep Creek Camp. The visitors would land at Montez Airport, tour the canyon, have lunch at Sheep Creek, be ferried directly to the grandstands atop the ledge, and then, after the ceremony, be flown to Montez airport for the trips home. That afternoon, the fourteenth, the weather began to close in, and an alternate plan, to fly the visitors into Tonsina Camp, bus them to Sheep Creek, and then continue as before, was readied.

By evening the weather had worsened. Weather reports, which did well to describe meteorological events in the area, much less predict them, indicated high winds through the pass and the canyon. It might not be possible for the choppers to maneuver. The canyon was narrow, with a river and highway sharing the floor. Two cliffs, one on the pipe side, breaking off at ninety feet, the opposite rising to some four hundred feet, created in Copper Canyon a sense of majestic and brooding stillness. On occasion, it also created a funnel for the winds. The temporary hoist was left intact, perched on the edge of the shelf, until the weather would clear.

During the morning of April fifteenth the ceiling dropped and winds in the canyon gusted to fifty miles an hour. In Thompson Pass winds hit eighty, held a steady sixty. It began to drizzle. Miklov, under orders to produce a good, dramatic shot of the pipe in the canyon, was disgusted. But there was a reprieve. Flights had been cancelled, the ceremony postponed.

Miklov and Gil Wolfe decided to spend the extra day exploring

Copper Canyon, Jim Miklov looking for good photo angles, Wolfe keeping his eyes open. At noon, Dan Curry came down the reactivated hoist to have lunch in the bus. Rosemary Fay seemed glad to have company.

"Understand you used to teach school down in Kenai," Dan said. As good a way to get a conversation going as any.

Rosemary set her coffee cup on the dashboard. "That was before I found out what bus drivers made." She watched the hoist come down again and four workmen step off. They walked over to the bus and she let them on. "You know, I like the way this place looks, even in the rain. The rock damn near glows if you catch it in the right light. Sometimes I . . ." She paused in midsentence. Had Curry heard what she was hearing?

Jim Miklov, standing at a bend in the canyon, shooting the lift area and tunnel with a wide-angle lens while Gil Wolfe held an umbrella, also paused, advancing the film lever out of pure instinct. And on the ledge, above, the men waiting to use the lift froze except for two laborers who ran to the canyon edge—a sprint that was to cost them their lives.

Ed Booth in town heard it in the same moment that a flock of crows rose as one from the tin shack on the terminal site and wheeled out over the slate gray waters of the bay.

Somewhere deep under the earth a massive door slammed shut. That was the sound. The multiplication of sounds. Hollow. Echoing. Profound.

As the first tremor reached the surface, Rosemary, still bent over the wheel, jammed her foot on the clutch and snatched the gear lever back. Already rock and dirt were falling in the canyon, on the bustop. The bus, in gear, gas pedal now flat on the floor, lurched as the ground itself lurched and bucked.

A broad cirque of rock fractured and refractured over an area nearly eighty feet across, twenty feet deep at the top, and Copper Canyon crumbled with a roar that drowned out the screams of those who rode it down.

The plunging bus smashed against a boulder just inside the tunnel entrance and then veered into the opposite wall.

Miklov, bracing himself the best he could (Gil Wolfe had been knocked flat by the first wave of the quake), snapped a picture of the yellow school bus in the tunnel entrance just before the rock slide hit. He grabbed his next shot from his knees—a montage of dirt and mud and a man and a bright, unpainted timber of still undamaged wood. The rumbling stopped. For a moment there was silence. Then a storm of dust. Up on a ledge, Miklov saw a movement, a leg. Someone was lying there.

Leopold LeClaire, a truck driver, had caused some head shaking when he went through the physical in Anchorage. Leo was forty-seven, seriously underweight, chronically short of breath. He'd had two heart attacks, one of them a close call, but still smoked heavily. "Are you dispatched as a bus driver?" the doctor asked him.

"Naw, heavy-duty trucker. I'll be pushing a rock buggy. It's easy, once I get in the cab. I rest halfway up the ladder when I'm climbing in."

"So you won't be driving other people?"

"Just rocks."

"Well, that's something," the doctor said and passed him, as he had passed the others. Considering the medical histories of some of the men who had passed through the clinic, it was, the doctor thought, a wonder that the company got any work done at all.

When the quake hit, Leo had been rounding the corner of Dorm Fifteen, just below the temporary sewage pond. He held his nose, eased the truck around the corner, and was about to gear down when he felt the spasm of pain in his chest. According to a carpenter, who was walking down the trail from the generator pad, Leopold LeClaire had braked the truck and turned sideways in the cab. The carpenter had dropped the small tool chest and started to run toward the truck when he heard the door slam (many workers and town residents were to compare the quake to a door slamming). He had dropped to the ground and the next thing he knew the truck was rolling downhill. He didn't know if LeClaire had died right then of a heart attack or died at the bottom of the hill. There wasn't enough of the man left, in any case, to make a determination as to the cause of death.

The truck, loaded with thirty-five tons of gravel and weighing just over thirty tons empty, came down the hill in either second or third (out of five forward gears) and picked up speed with every downhill foot. Each dorm was thirty feet wide. The space between the dorms was thirty feet. These dorms and spaces whipped by the right-hand side of the truck at accelerating intervals. As the truck drifted to the right, the dorms flashed by closer and closer to the runaway.

The snow-tunnel exit on the back end of Dorm Three was grazed. A moment later, the plywood enclosure at the end of Dorm Two was ripped open. Had the truck not caught the metal girder that supported the stairway at the west, or back, end of Dorm One, it is possible that Leopold LeClaire and his load of gravel would have continued on another 200 feet and plunged into Montez Bay.

Instead, the right front wheel tucked in and sent the vehicle directly into the larger of the two fuel dumps located between the dorms and the shore road. The east dump contained fuel oil and two four-by-six-foot propane tanks. The west dump held gasoline, diesel fuel and kerosine. Here, Leo's truck shattered the serviceman's shack, tore a hole in the protective dike, and wallowed in among the steel tanks.

The events of those first few seconds were hideously confused. Some said it looked like the gasoline tank in the fuel dump exploded and sent chunks of the larger diesel tank flying through the air: others said both tanks exploded simultaneously with the truck's own tank. The explosions that followed made a reconstruction difficult, but it was clear that the truck had plunged into the dump in a ball of flame and that the diesel tank had been shattered, one large, flaming section being hurled deep into the center section of Dorm One's roof. Dozens of small fires briefly flared on the ground and on buildings within a wide radius of the dump. Most of these went out.

But one small fire started deep in the rafters of the production kitchen, where a six-pound chunk of tank had torn through a corner of the ceiling. Because of the larger fire in Dorm One, no one noticed the kitchen blaze until much too late.

It had to be assumed that the serviceman, whose office was the four-by-eight wooden shack, had been killed in the first moment of the crash. No trace of him was ever found, and he did not turn up at home as so many others did in the general exodus that followed.

The wind, which had let up for the past half hour, started again in Copper Canyon as if on cue. The umbrella Gil Wolfe still clutched suddenly blew out. The dust began to clear and Miklov stood warily, hoping the quake was indeed over. A deep rumble, much like thunder, rolled down the narrow canyon walls. There were men lying in and around the slide, some partially buried. The fact that the hard rock fell first and the packed earth had only slumped and given away in sections had probably saved lives. It was a rough ride down, one of the survivors said later, but it had seemed almost a controlled descent.

As the sound, a deep-throated, hollow thunder, grew louder, countless heads turned upward. The noise came not from be-lowground this time, but from above. A family of tourists parked near Jim Miklov looked up. The workers who had been to the right of the fall, between Miklov and the canyon, steadied themselves and most of them were looking up. Isaac Ahgutuk, with one leg broken and the other buried in rock and gravel, opened his eyes, lying on his back, and looked up.

Everyone braced instinctively for the next wave of the quake. But no one was prepared for the sight of the eighty-foot section of four-foot-diameter pipe, wrapped in gleaming green tape, that tumbled out over the edge of the cliff. Turned in the air. Fell.

Doug Booth, lying on an outcrop of rock some thirty feet below the summit of the cliff, saw the sky fill with the green of the pipe, saw the overlapped half-inch of tape at each seam, heard the screams from below and shut his eyes. Jim Miklov, camera held to his chest, tilted his hands back, hoping he was on it, and pressed the shutter.

Finch-Smith had, after all, requested a dramatic shot of the pipe.

Larry Ransom had been on the shore road, coming back from the pool in Howland Creek where the water truck shuttle was operating. As the quake subsided he saw the ball of flame from the fuel dump, just hidden around a bend. He began to run.

Al Godwin had shut down his forklift for lunch and was on his way to the ironworkers' dry shack to eat with Tiny. He saw the toppling crates at one edge of the laydown area and Tiny and his crew running from the shack. They were well clear when the fuel tanks blew. Tiny even had time to take a few more bites from his roast beef sandwich.

The shore road diverged at the dock area. One branch continued straight on past the office building and ended in a junction with the road up to the tank farm. The other swung down along the dock. Godwin ran back to his forklift, yelled for Tiny, and powered on up the dock road. Tiny clung to the side of the twenty-eight-ton lift. Al prayed he had a firm handhold.

The firehouse stood on the main road opposite the office building. Superintendent Talford, in charge of the camp facility construction, was already climbing into the driver's seat of the one fire engine that had been put into service. The truck was a one-and-a-half ton flatbed with a six-foot tank, a hose reel and a rack of horizontal gas bottles—nitrogen propellant. In short, it was a giant, dry-powder fire extinguisher, primarily useful in small electrical and fuel fires, nearly worthless for large structural fires.

With Tiny now aboard the fire engine, Godwin followed in the forklift. The office building swarmed with secretaries and officials, running to get clear in case a second wave hit. The lights were still on, Al noticed, and he couldn't see much damage.

Talford braked the truck close to the fire, started to open the door, and suddenly backed up. Godwin put the forklift in neutral and waited at a distance.

"Goddamn roast you alive," Talford shouted. He and Tiny began pulling hose from the reel. The dorm roof was on fire and there was a truck buried in the fuel dump, a big rock buggy. Tiny moved toward the fire. What the hell had happened? Why the hell were he and Talford the only ones trying to fight the fire?

Talford climbed up on the truck, read the directions. Pull pin, push lever, squeeze nozzle. He looked at Tiny. Tiny would probably know to squeeze the nozzle. Talford yanked the ring free and slammed the lever down with the heel of his hand. The hose stiffened and a moment later a spray of powder, thick as water, poured from the nozzle, arched toward the flame, and fell to the ground some thirty feet short of doing any good.

A sudden mushroom of flame drove Tiny back farther. All the while, the ground between Tiny and the fuel dump turned a sickly white.

"You got to get closer," Talford shouted. "If that dump goes, we might lose the camp."

Tiny offered Talford the hose. "Get as close as you want, pal."

From his perch up on the forklift, Al Godwin had a better view of the dorm roof. The wind had come up again, whipping the flames, driving them toward the next and higher roof in line. They might lose the camp anyway.

Tiny ducked his head and turned his hard hat so the brim would shield his face. "Tell me if I'm hitting," he shouted and began to hit the revetment that encircled the fuel dump. It sizzled and bubbled up as it touched flame. Talford pulled more hose down. Tiny took a few more steps, arching the spray. Foam hit the side of the truck and turned brown, bubbled. Joe Akin and the camp manager were at the scene now, shouting encouragement. It was beginning to look hopeful. Then, abruptly, the foam ran out. Talford rapped on the tank. That was all there was. And no more fire extinguishers.

Joe Akin joined Godwin on the forklift.

"What a circus! They're calling the town fire department, but they can't be here for a half hour. You know what they need, don't you? A fire boat. Ease in along shore and pour Montez harbor up on that dorm."

"Yeah," Godwin said. "We need a fireboat. You got one handy?"

Larry Ransom and an assistant superintendent talked with the teamster foreman. Ransom hadn't been a fireman, but he'd done some news stories on the fire school in Walpole. The propane tanks might explode if they got too hot. A water shuttle could keep a constant stream of cold water on the tanks. A dozer could be run in to block the heat from the distant fuel dump and a man could crouch behind it with a hose from the trucks and spray water over the tanks.

"Goddamn risky," the foreman said.

"I'll do it," Larry told him. "What the hell. It's my idea."

"No argument." The dozer and truck moved into position.

Larry took the hose, which had no nozzle, and braced it against the treads on the Cat. The water arched up over the hood, but even when the pump hit full rpm, the stream barely reached the propane tank. When Larry shifted the water from one tank to the other, he noticed that the unprotected tank would begin to steam.

The assistant superintendent listened to the radio chatter. If the fire department from across the bay didn't get here soon, it was entirely possible that several dorms might be lost. There were fourteen buildings above the one on fire and one of the radio reports said the flames were now reaching out to the eaves of the next building. The fire could easily jump up the line, take out the adjoining rows as well. If the camp were destroyed, it would take a year to rebuild. That would mean a delay in construction on the tank farm and pipeline activity in Montez, a year's delay on the operation of the trans Alaska pipeline.

"I always did think those dorms were too close together," the assistant superintendent told Larry. "I said so in a meeting once."

The man hoped it would show in the official minutes. If the camp went, heads would roll. He put a hand on Larry's shoulder. "You know, Larry, I think I talked about this with you once, how the whole camp could go if there were a fire. And the lack of fire-fighting equipment. You remember that, don't you?"

Larry looked away from the hose. The pump was throbbing, the truck engine racing to power it, the fire roaring. If he'd heard the question, he made no sign.

When the pipe came over the edge, Miklov was sure it was going to crush the men lying in the rubble below. Fortunately it had fallen level. The narrow, circular slide had created an inset. The left end of the pipe lodged in a four-foot shelf, strongly supported by a rock column that jutted out just above the old tunnel. As the left end hit, the right end, with a shower of sparks and rock fragments, abraded the opposite wall and jammed itself into place some ten feet above the prominence on which Doug Booth lay.

Doug tried to think clearly. His leg was broken. His pant leg was soaked with blood. His back and right side hurt so bad that he could only breathe shallowly. There was just enough room for him on the outthrust of rock and no way down, no way back up. But the pipe had stopped. He studied it. What was holding it? The bare rock was already growing damp in the wind-blown mist.

There were shouts from above. Was Doug conscious? It hurt too much to reply. Doug waved an arm over the edge. There were groans coming from below. He'd seen others going over the edge, but couldn't remember landing here.

A pebble fell and pinked Doug's ear. He looked up angrily just in time to see the pipe drop an inch. They had heard the sound below, the tearing at the rock face. Someone had shouted "Look out!"

Doug regarded the pipe over his head. Look out. Sure.

The first report of fire in the production kitchen came in. The entire roof and one corner of the building were in flames, and workmen in the area were trying to remove vehicles, lumber, dry shacks, anything combustible.

Joe Akin asked Al Godwin to run him up to the production kitchen with the forklift. Some communications from the town came over the walkie-talkies. There had been little quake damage in Montez. Some broken picture windows, bottles on the floor at the liquor store, cracks in foundations. All fire engines could be spared and were on their way to the camp.

"Check with the state," someone said over the air. "There might be a tidal wave." It had happened before in Montez, but there had been an immediate drop in sea level followed by a series of waves, much like the back-and-forth slopping of water in a tub. As Al and Joe neared the production kitchen, a new voice cut in on the radio.

"This here's a trucker for Bayless and Roberts, and if you guys are looking for help on this shore road, you can forget it. I'm blocked by slides in front and back and I can see at least two places down the road that are covered with snow and rock. I think a whole bunch of mountain is down here on the road with me."

"Where are you, driver?" the camp manager asked.

"Mile three on the shore road. I hate to say it, but you people are cut off real good. Me, I'm gonna start climbing."

The teamster foreman, sent up the road in his pickup truck, reported that the driver had not underestimated the situation. In one spot, an avalanche of snow had buried the road thirty feet deep across a hundred-foot section. Beyond that, at a curve in the road, a rock slide had torn away nearly fifty feet of causeway built to preserve a tidal pool and marsh area.

Superintendent Talford watched the flames eat into the roof and upper story of Dorm One. The thin metal sheeting on Dorm Two began to peel away below the eaves. Water poured down the stairways of the dorm as the sprinkler system melted. Eventually the plastic water pipes would fail and the dorm would flood, too late to do any good. Talford sent a man to the main office to call the town fire department and cancel the alarm.

Water, washing down the hill from the dorms, poured into the blazing fuel dump and overflowed on the seaward side, carrying fuel out into the narrow cove below the dorms. Puddles of flame gathered in the road. Despite a heavy surf, the shoreline was soon afire.

Baranov was up to his waist in dirt, gravel and mud. "What you laughing at?" he said to Isaac Ahgutuk. "Don't you know I'm hurtin? Can't you see you got a busted leg?"

Isaac tried to talk, but only laughter came out.

People were slowly approaching the pile of boulders that blocked the old tunnel. No part of the bus was visible.

"You're crazy," Clyde told Isaac. He had feeling through his body. He hurt, but he thought that was a good sign. "What's so damn funny?"

Isaac bit down on his thumb. "You," he said. "No way I can help it. That look on your face when the pipe came over the edge."

"Hey," Baranov shouted. "Hey, someone get us out of here."

Near the edge of the slide, where the rubble thinned out, a man lay in a pool of yellow liquid that poured from a steel drum just visible above him in the rock. He bled from the side of his head and his shoulder was oddly canted to one side. The man looked dully at the gathering jelly. He moved his fingers in it as the mess rose to his chest and then began to seep over the edge of the depression in which he had fallen. "What is this stuff?" he asked a truck driver who had only just arrived on the scene.

"Looks like snot."

One of the drillers stood above the injured man. "That there is dynamite," he said. "Liquid dynamite."

The man looked down. "Dynamite?"

The driller told him the dynamite was not dangerous, unconfined and without a detonator. Then his eye caught a smooth, white surface, partly buried in mud. The driller carefully scraped the mud away and lifted the tiny, twin-wired cylinder, two and a half inches thick, three and a half long. It looked like a plastic container that you might buy yogurt in, but it was, in fact, a DuPont High Detonation Pressure Primer, the HDP-1.

"Barney. Cass," he called, and the two powder monkeys from his crew slogged over to see what he wanted.

The driller held up the detonator. "I found this. See if you can find any more."

There was a one-in-a-thousand chance, probably less, that a detonator and a pool of water gel dynamite might be locked up under a slab of rock and mud. But if another slide occurred, or someone carelessly threw a rock down. . . . The driller looked around at the jumble of rock, dirt, men and timber. Even a lone detonator going off beside a man could blind him or take off his hand.

He reached down to help the man in the pool of dynamite and tried to remember how much DuPont Pourvex Extra had been stored up on the canyon shelf. The hoisting foreman, who had been rockhounding downstream during the quake, came over to help. They laid the man beside the road and made him comfortable. The driller explained the situation.

As they talked, the hoist foreman, Mac, turned to face the stream. It was only a trickle. He pointed upstream to where the slide had dammed the river. "We're going to have to call for equipment from the camp."

"You can't do that," the trucker said, returning from his vehicle with a first-aid kit. "The shore road's out. Nobody's getting through. Not from the job site."

Dan Curry and Rosemary Fay, after stumbling out of the dust-filled tunnel, climbed over the pile of rock blocking the river. Behind them came the four laborers who had boarded the bus at lunch. Fortunately, none of them had chosen seats at the rear of the bus. Beyond the first five rows there wasn't much left.

Miklov snapped a picture of Dan and Rosemary looking down at the three desperate workmen clawing away rock from the tunnel, the trapped bus.

"Hey," Curry shouted from the rockpile. "What are you men doing?"

"Bus inside," one grunted. "You might help," he said and took another look. Dan came down off the rock and the whole crew walked over to where the driller, hoistman, Miklov and Wolfe were standing. The driller repeated the news about the detonators.

"Could be none. You can't tell."

Wolfe edged in toward Curry. "Was it you who told me blasting is a science?"

Dan looked up at the pipe, precariously bridging the cirque. "Who's on the ledge?"

"Doug Booth?" the hoistman suggested. He squinted up to the outthrust and then saw a tiny figure atop the canyon, the catskinner boss from Louisiana.

"Hey, JimBob, who's that on the ledge?"

JimBob crouched, peered over the edge, exchanged a few words, stood up. "Doug Booth. 'Fraid he might of broke his back. Leg hurt an' scared to move. Hey, I got six men up here but we ain't coming close to the edge 'less you need us. It ain't safe."

Gradually the picture was becoming clearer. The pile of rock sloped from the tunnel toward the downstream end of the canyon. In the center, dirt and mud had poured down along with part of the grandstand and the lifting hoist. Pieces of cable snaked here and there. Groans were coming from places where men weren't visible, possibly because they lay out of sight on the pile or were partially covered by rubble. Some of the men must have been completely buried. The driver was sent back to the truck to radio the town garage for help in the canyon.

Gill Wolfe faced Curry. "I know we're going to have to pull those men out somehow, but when this is over, I'm going to have some serious questions for you. This wasn't supposed to happen."

The driller put a hand on Gil's shoulder and drew him aside. Gil felt the pressure on his collarbone. "Dan," the driller said, "I can see we got to get them out, but what about the pipe?"

The men looked up again. There seemed to be nothing holding the eighty-foot length in place. If it fell, it would surely carry Doug away with it and then crush the people below. The pipe had already shifted position twice. Whether it was digging in deeper or working loose was anybody's guess.

And there was the problem of detonators that might or might not be scattered throughout the pile.

"You know," one of the men from Rosemary's bus said, "he's right; it could go at any time."

"Then again, it might not," Dan said. He walked up on the pile where Ahgutuk had started his crazy giggling again.

It was fortunate that the kitchen sat in a corner of the camp with a dug cliff on two sides. The dorms overlooking the mess hall and kitchen were high, out of reach of the flames. Akin saw that the danger to other structures here was less, albeit real enough. The wind, which was driving the dorm fire uphill, here drove the flames into bare soil. But if the wind stopped, or changed direction, swirling in from the west, the recreation hall would go, too.

Using hand signals, Joe swung Al Godwin around so that his forklift faced the wide end of the kitchen, which had been made of double trailer rows stacked on steel foundations. He brought Al in to the right-hand 12 x 60 mod and motioned him to run the forks under. The same forklift had set the mods on the iron last year. Now it could lift them off.

Joe gave the sign and Al brought the forks up. At first nothing happened. Al dropped the fork and revved the engine, lifted harder. The side of the unit buckled, panels cracked, part of the floor separated. All at once Al had the uppermost section of the unit in the air.

He tilted his lift and backed off. Running forward, he tilted again and threw the machine in reverse, coming away with a larger section of module. Most of the floor remained and the roof trusses slumped down where the room had been. Sparks flew. Pipes shot water. Joe Akin spun a finger and pointed. Al wheeled the lift and dropped the wreckage at the base of the cliff, coming back for another piece. After two more grabs, the dozer moved in, flattening the wreckage to make room. Operating engineers began to gather in the area, cheering the way Al Godwin forked chunks of building off the foundation and stacked them. Finally Joe called him down, sent another man into the cab, and left instructions.

"What's up?"

"The radio says we're gonna lose this camp if they don't put out the dorm fire. If we can do this here, maybe we can do something like it on the hill."

"Take out one of those monsters? They're three hundred feet long, man. Thirty feet high. I don't see no way."

Akin shouted at the APPLE rep, just climbing in his green pickup. "Hey, bossman, can you get us to the motor pool in a hurry?"

Ed Booth, in town to arrange with the motels for extra stayovers on the ceremonies, had recovered quickly from the fright of the earthquake. He and Maggie had looked their building over and switched on the emergency scanner to check other damage. Gradually he began to get the story, the fire across the bay, the trouble in the canyon. His phone rang. It was the APPLE auditor, who had just spoken to both B. R. Young and Roy Rogers on a conference hookup. Ed was to drive out to Copper Canyon and report back immediately on the situation there.

"Will do."

"Don't forget, they want the info like yesterday."

Ed said they'd have it, asked if he should call at the office or call Young directly.

"Call me," the auditor said. "I can patch you in by phone or radio. In fact, you better take your mobile unit and give us a report from the scene. But get on it."

Ed hung up. No doubt the man had done that with an open line to the head honchos. Get on it.

"Maggie, I'm going out to the canyon to look it over for the company. You want to come?"

Maggie had changed into jeans and sweatshirt. "I thought I'd go in any case. Do you suppose David will be out there?"

Ed shrugged. "I'm sure he knows about it."

David Curry, sitting in his office at the town hall, listening to the flood of emergency talk on the radio, answering a phone that rang as soon as he put it down, did know about the situation, but he found it difficult to concentrate.

His lieutenant, a real hustler who'd transferred in from the State Police, urged David to get on the scene and coordinate.

David thought about it between calls. He wished he had a drink, but he didn't dare take one with the lieutenant around.

"Well, chief," the lieutenant said again. "You going out there or you want me to go?"

David might have friends out at the canyon. He understood his brother Dan was somewhere around the cave-in. He owed it to the town and to himself. All these years in the department there had never been an opportunity to show what he could do. Certainly not since the last quake, and then it had been a family tragedy.

He picked up the phone, identified himself, and covered the mouthpiece.

"You go," David said. "I think we need the experience here in town to keep track of the total effort. And I know the people, I know what's available."

The lieutenant was already on his way.

Pinching the phone between his cheek and shoulder, David Curry talked to the school board director and used his free hands to open a bottle of bourbon that had been tucked in the back of his lower desk drawer.

Tiny stood with his hands in his back pockets, and Little Nasty moved in beside him to watch the fire take hold under the eaves of Dorm Two. Talford, the superintendent of camp construction, stood on the other side of Tiny.

"Would you look at that? Unbelievable. We could lose the whole thing."

"Dynamite could do it," Tiny said. "You know, take it down." Tiny pointed to the iron framework holding the dorms level. "If I had some plastic I could cut those legs right out from under, knock that damn building right down flat."

"We must have dynamite. They blast around here all the time. Get some."

"Wrong kind," Nasty said, addressing Talford as though Tiny weren't there. "They usin' that water gel. Anyhow, it would take too long. We had time, that building could be dropped as flat as a cowflop on a hot rock."

The superintendent was losing interest. "You guys figure out a way to knock it down or put water on it, let me know, huh?"

Tiny and Nasty stood side by side a while longer.

"Even sticks of dynamite, maybe TNT, we could do it," Tiny said.

The fire spread across the roof of Dorm Two. Dorm One showed flame at all the windows on the second floor and the building had begun to roar. It was a wind tunnel, sucking air. Each dorm consisted of two rows of trailers, stacked two high. There were five trailers on each row, twenty in all. They burned like matches, the fire sweeping from unit to unit.

"Five or six sticks on each post, wrap in some det cord," Nasty told Tiny, watching the fires. "We could make kindling out of it."

The ceiling on Dorm One fell in. Windows popped on the first floor.

"I didn't mean nothing about your old lady," Tiny said. A sheet of aluminum siding curled away from the building and drooped from the heat.

Nasty took a step back as flame billowed out to engulf the snow porch on Dorm One.

"You didn't get no infection, did you?"

The super walked past with two APPLE reps. "Water is what we need. Can't they bring the trucks in a barge or something? We need the water."

"What I don't understand," the one rep shouted over the roar of the blaze, "is why nobody ever thought of this before."

Ed Booth pulled into the canyon, stopping behind a row of cars from town. A number of local people were pitching in to help dig men out of the slide. Near the edge of the slide area, three bodies lay silent, arranged in the neat order of the dead.

One group was digging at the rock that had blocked off the river. According to one of the men there, the water had backed up the road to fill the highway tunnel, which was the only access into Copper Canyon from the north. With the high winds and bad weather, this meant that for the time being Montez was completely cut off from the world outside. Not that it hadn't happened before, particularly during the winter. Often Thompson Pass would shut down for a few days and air travel be suspended, stranding visitors in town.

Ed looked up the canyon face to the pipe wedged across the fall area. Miklov approached him, bringing a stricken Maggie by the elbow. Ed had been about to say what a terrible thing it would have been if the quake had come during the ceremony. Miklov looked grim.

"Was Doug in this?" The last Ed heard, Doug was working on the dorm construction across the bay.

Maggie pointed at the leg and arm dangling over the edge of rock some sixty or more feet up the canyon wall. "He's there. Under the pipe."

A voice squawked call numbers over Ed's radio and he realized dully that it was for him.

"Go ahead," he said.

"What's the report at the canyon?"

"I'm sorry," Ed said. "I've got something to do here. I don't have time for reports."

There was a pause. "Booth," the man said. "You know who wants this, don't you? This is a very serious matter. I don't care what you have to do. It can't be more important than getting the story into APPLE so we can deal with things."

"This is more important," Ed said. "APPLE can go piss up a rope." Ed let the radio drop to the ground and began to move back and forth, looking over the rock face on Doug's side and over the tunnel.

"Maggie, do you think you can drive back to town and bring Farrell out here with a backhoe, maybe a dozer? And have him bring some men. Tell him we have to move some rock out of the river and see if he can round up the Medevac team. He'll know what to do if you describe all this."

Maggie looked up at Doug, at the pipe, the harsh rock wall. She nodded. "Okay."

Joe Akin agreed that the dorms were too high to bulldoze, even using the Allis-Chalmers HD-41s, with their seven-foot blades. The HD-41s were the largest dozers in general construction use, although special needs, such as quarrying, might bring in articulated equipment modified from a pair of Caterpillar D-9s. The solution, Joe explained, might be down at the dock, where two two-hundred-foot lengths of steel cable had been bolted to barge moorings.

The HD-41s had been delivered only a week ago and were still having their blades "hard-faced," a process of welding nuggets of steel along the cutting edges of heavy equipment. The diamond pattern could take the daily abuse from tearing into rock; when it was worn away, new hard-facing was added, extending the life of the blade.

Akin told the master mechanic what he wanted and the dozers were turned over to him on the promise that he wouldn't tear into anything with the blades. Joe promised and grabbed a spud wrench and spanner, asking the three mechanics if they could come and help hang cable on the tow hooks.

At the dock it was a matter of some minutes to wrench the anchor bolts off. Then it took a concerted effort on the part of Joe, Al, and the mechanics to bring the wrist-thick cable eyes together and bolt them, making a single cable. The weight of the entire cable made it necessary to bring the dozers back to the end eyes rather than drag cable to the HD-41s. At last Al Godwin had one end of the cable on his dozer and Joe Akin had the other end on his. The master mechanic assured Joe that the bolt holding the cables together was the strongest part of the chain, not the weakest.

"You'll pull the tow hooks straight out before you tear the cable and bolts apart. But don't try."

Side by side, Al and Joe made their way up the hill, the 400-foot cable following reluctantly, flopping over, gradually straightening out.

The top floor of Dorm One was completely in flames and the fuel dump had exploded again, driving back the onlookers. Superintendent Talford came out of the crowd with Tiny and Nasty and stood, arms folded, watching the dozers crawl up the road toward the dorm. When they reached him, he jumped up on a tread.

"What the hell's going on?"

Joe motioned for Tiny, who came up and leaned into the cab.

"If Tiny and some of the welders could cut the front supports, we might be able to run a dozer down the firelane, wrap the cable around a dorm and tip it right on over. Pull one dorm right into the next one down and maybe rake it over with the cable to knock it down even more."

Tiny planted both hands on his waist and looked back at the dorm. "Ironworkers don't have that many welders. There's six supports we'd have to take out. Could be if we used the pipefitters, it'd work, but the men would be taking an awful chance."

The superintendent rubbed at his eyes. "Jesus, I wish I knew for sure I could do this. Nobody wants to take the responsibility. I mentioned knocking a dorm out to the APPLE reps and I thought they'd cry. They won't say yes or no, only how much one of these damn things costs."

Tiny reached down and hauled Little Nasty up on the tread. He explained the situation to him.

"Too dangerous," Nasty said. " 'Less we make an angle cut, enough to let the upper part of a leg slide on down along a joint." He indicated with his hands, a downward sheering motion. "That way it might tip some, but it wouldn't go all at once. More like a tree coming down. If it didn't go all the way off you might pull it down with that clothesline back there."

"I don't like it much," Tiny said, "to be honest. You might get away okay if two men started working back from the center so they'd have something solid behind them to duck under in case she slid down all of a sudden."

Al Godwin got off his dozer. "How's about letting me in on it?"

"All you have to do is turn around," Joe said, "let me pull the cable straight and follow me up the hill. We're going to give it a try."

Ed Booth got JimBob to come back to the edge of the canyon. They had a generator, JimBob said, and several operable Cats (but only two operators), two welding machines and several sets of slings and cables for moving pipe. It was enough for Ed to follow through on.

"I'm coming up," he shouted.

"Lift's gone," JimBob told him. "And the cable on the side booms don't reach that far."

"Climbing." Ed pointed at the rock wall. "Going to climb up."

JimBob put both hands on his head and walked back out of sight.

Miklov didn't like it. "You know, you touch that pipe, you might bring it down on your son. And the others."

"I know." Ed zipped his leather jacket.

"That's no easy climb," Miklov said.

"Well," Ed said at last, "I spent a lot of money to go through that guide survival school. I guess it's time to see if I learned anything."

Mac, the hoist foreman, and the driller came over from their digging.

"Booth," Mac said softly, "I know you're upset about your kid being up there, but you have to realize we have people working here. There's men stuck in that rock. You get up there and knock that pipe loose, you may kill a dozen people."

"That pipe's slipped three times since the quake," Ed told him. "If I don't find a way to grab hold of it, you still might lose lives down here. Don't tell me what the risks are."

"I don't see what you can do, Booth, but do us a favor, will you? Let *us* know about it before you try anything up there."

"You got it," Ed said and stretched his arms to loosen up. "See you boys in church."

He turned and walked toward the rubble blocking the old tunnel.

The driller made a move to stop him but Miklov caught him by the sleeve. "Let him try. He's a long-time Alaskan. He'll work it out or he won't go through with it."

"I think he's a long-time windbag," the driller said and went back to the rockpile.

Ed stopped to tuck in his pantcuffs, scuff the mud off his boots. He'd climbed the opposite side of the canyon five years ago, all the way to the so-called goat trail, the high path used by early prospectors trying to avoid the glacier route to the gold fields.

He buttoned flaps, tightened his belt, swung his arms, loosening up. Much of the tightness he felt in his muscles was from fear. The canyon face was wet, the winds were gusty, and Ed knew better than anyone how out of shape he'd gotten in the past few years. But he had done okay in guide school.

He took another look at the rock where Doug lay, moving his arm weakly from time to time, once raising his head, though not enough for Ed to get a look at his face.

You climbed by taking the first step, Ed told himself. The rock was damp, but it presented many ledges, cracks, disconformities, handholds, footholds, angles for the knee. He'd done it before. Ed placed a foot on an inch-wide ledge, stepped up, found a hold for his left toe, a handhold on the right. He raised himself and felt with his left hand, caught a deep crack, found another for his right foot, pulled himself up, moved the other foot. This was a higher climb than the side where Doug lay, but here the surface looked better. Ed didn't think he could climb anywhere else without equipment.

He was higher than the roof of the tunnel now and he paused for breath. The rescuers moved carefully among the rocks below, never knowing where another detonator might be hidden. The men who had been injured were remarkably stoic, Ed thought. They cried out only when moved. Otherwise they lay still and endured. Doug, afraid and alone, under the pipe, had made a sound only once: when the pipe showered a handful of rock fragments as it shifted. Ed was proud of the boy.

The hard part for a beginning climber is to keep his body away from the rock. Ed heard his teacher, the gravelly voice, the insistence, yet patience of the man. Get your belly off the rock, you don't climb with your belly, you climb with your hands and feet and, if it gets rough, with your chin and knees and shoulders and elbows. A belly is a bad climber.

Hitting a near-vertical stretch of rock with few holds, Ed did his best to push away from the cliff. Belly up to the mountain is where he wanted to be. Get the belly off the rock, four points, two hands, two feet, let's see four-point climbing.

Ed found himself breathing too hard and he pressed on until he found a setback in the rock where he could plant both toes and hold himself steady without straining. He turned his head. He was a third of the way up. He didn't bother looking down. He knew where he was. From thirty-five or forty feet it was all the same. Ed had passed the point of a broken leg or a few cracked ribs. From here he had to play climbing leader.

You men want to know how to be such a good climber that you can lead expeditions? I'll tell you how; it's simple. I learned this from an old man in Wyoming. All you have to do to be a lead climber is remember one simple rule.

What's that? Ed had asked, rising to the bait.

The instructor held up one finger. The leader . . . must . . . never . . . fall.

Ed felt his breath come back. He was sweating and the occasional gusts sweeping down the canyon plucked at his clothing, chilling him. He blew on his hands, surveyed the rock above, and began to climb again, climbing by the book, coaching himself every inch of the way. Several times he was forced to backtrack.

After a second rest, past the halfway point, he forced himself back into the climb too soon and his foot scuffed out of a tenuous hold. Three points will carry you. Lose a point and you have three good ones left. You can climb on three.

The instructor had climbed with one hand in his pocket, although he alternated the climbing hand from time to time.

Ed had three points but they were poor ones. His left toe ached from the strain of trying to wedge in a crack and remain rigid while he searched blindly with his other foot for a hold. He found the original ledge that had crumbled away and traced the line with his foot. It widened, but he would need to heave himself upward with his arms to get any leverage. If he failed he would lose the other toe hold and be left with two points. Tired as he was, he doubted he could hold on long with his hands. Ed drew in a breath and yanked himself up, kicking the foot down into the ledge as he came into position. Secure, he shut his eyes and pressed his forehead against the cool, damp rock.

The other cardinal rule of climbing is not to do it alone.

Ed was breathing quite hard now, but the rock face had begun to slope back and he was finding that he could make the occasional scurry up a gentle incline and that some sections had more holds than a ladder.

The face had taken Ed around the corner from the slide and he could no longer see the green pipe or the ledge on which Doug lay. The wind came and went and Ed found himself climbing the last ten feet in a trickle of water—the runoff from snow higher up the mountain.

He picked his way over the loose stones to the firmer surface of the shelf and jogged around the rim of the canyon to what was to have been the ceremony site. Half the grandstand had been carried away by the pipe, but there was little evidence of other damage. Probably everything damaged had gone over the edge. There was a heavy wooden platform left from the hoist and some timbers. The dirt slump had left a rounded, precarious edge to the canyon top. Ed could understand JimBob's reluctance to hang around the rim.

JimBob and a half-dozen men were sitting in a three-sided Kelly enclosure, out of the wind. They had built a fire with some of the wood from the grandstand. JimBob made room for Ed to sit on the wooden bench and handed him a thermos of coffee.

Ed outlined the plan. The seven men sat in silence when he finished. He could see from the looks on their faces that not one of them gave it a chance in hell of working.

The production kitchen was soon sorted into two piles, a heap of rubble and food against the cliff and the last few blazing units still on the foundation. Two dozers were pushing dirt over the mods below the cliff, and when they finished they began on the standing units, which were burning too ferociously for the front-end loader to risk moving in.

The fire could be buried if there was no other way of dealing with it.

At Dorm Three, Nasty and Tiny had cut the center supports and run out while Banjo-eye and the pipefitter foreman worked on the second set. Two more men, an ironworker and a pipefitter, waited with cutting torches to begin on the outside supports. The slant Tiny had cut was already shifting with a screeching sound of metal against metal. Banjo-eye and the foreman made the next cuts: the building groaned and panel rivets began to pop between units.

Already Tiny could see this wasn't going to work. The downhill wall had to slip off the footing and pull the uphill stack of mods along with it to topple the entire dormitory. All that had happened so far was a slumping near the center. The welder at the far end finished his cut and retreated as the steel began to rub and one end of the dorm dropped a foot, giving a definite overbend to the two-story stack of trailers. Then the last cut was made and there were protests of metal and wood throughout the unit. It seemed that the weight had shifted downward, that the downhill wall, toward the fire, had taken on a lean, but the foundation was simply too strong.

Eventually the steel would give, the pressures grow strong enough to snap the stress cables that ran between units, but by then the fire might have spread to Dorm Four and on up the hill.

Every dorm that burned meant one hundred less workers available to build the terminal.

Superintendent Talford paced back and forth, kicking at loose ground. The other supers and officials had gathered in the area, but everyone was perfectly willing to let him take the responsibility.

Two or three offered the opinion that a cable placed on the outside of the dorms from the uphill side might have a reverse effect. By crumpling in the outside wall, the upper story might eventually lean back into the cable and bring the dorm down against the next one up, spreading the fire even faster.

Dorm Two was fully ablaze along its roofline now, and it was only a matter of a few minutes before the flames plucking along the edge of Dorm Three's roof took hold.

Joe Akin began rounding up bystanders and pointing them to the loose cable that lay along the firepath between Dorms Three and Four. He had Godwin run his dozer back to loop the cable and then return to the far end. The men, some thirty or forty in number now, took the cable by one end and went up the steps, straining and heaving to bring the cable along. Other men joined in as soon as the problem became clear. Akin wanted the cable run down the center ground-floor hallway of the dorm from end to end. He showed Talford with one hand how the building could be pulled off the support so the downhill wall would hit the ground and yank the whole building after it. All they had to do was scrape the bottom floor, low side, off the foundation and the building had to fall.

"What have we got to lose?" he asked, climbing on his dozer.

Talford grimly explained the situation to the APPLE reps, one of whom took notes as he talked.

Godwin waved from the opposite end, letting Akin know his dozer was set and the cable hooked up. Joe sent Leslie Collins down to Godwin. He then borrowed a radio from Price, who seemed glad to give it up.

"You there, Collins?"

"Roger."

"Tell Godwin to start on down, easy, until we take up the slack."

He didn't wait for an answer, taking instead the roar of Godwin's powerful diesel. Joe cracked the throttle, edged down the road, veering to the far side away from the heat of the fire. The cable picked up tight, snapping through a few inches of the plywood snow porch before Joe could ease off.

"Collins, is Al set?"

"He is. Cable's snug."

"Okay. You make goddamn sure everybody stays clear. If this cable snaps it'll take off somebody's head sure as hell. Tell Al when he hears me open up he's to count to three and then run about ten feet. We'll see what happens."

There was another man now helping Larry Ransom on the water detail. Both propane tanks and the fuel oil tank could be cooled almost continuously. Water from the dorms flowed steadily from under the burning wreckage of Dorm One. The spillage was causing sudden runs of burning gas and oil from the west fuel dump. Once the flame had shot along the ground toward Larry. He was ready to drop his hose and run. The fire then changed direction, joined with a larger stream running down the shore road.

It seemed so unreasonable. A few men were working frantically to save as much of the camp as they could and the majority of project employees simply walked around and looked at it all, like tourists. Some were even taking snapshots. And a good many had gone into their dorms and begun removing the contents, stacking them at the far edge of the road leading down toward the shore.

The whole camp had taken on the air of some bizarre carnival. In the distance, as the fire claimed another section of the dorms, Larry could hear the shouts of the revelers.

A generator and welder were now in position on the rock shelf above Copper Canyon, and Ed Booth had borrowed two ironworkers' tool belts and fashioned a diaper sling for himself. The belts passed above and below his buttocks and were joined low in his crotch. Two half-inch-thick steel rings had been set in the belts for clipping on equipment or safety lines. Ed arranged the diaper sling so one ring stood out at the junction of the belts in front.

The sling caused Ed to walk with a swagger. He gathered up the coils of rope that had been intended for temporary fencing at the canyon edge, threw a loop around the crossbeam on one of the abandoned side-boom Cats, and pulled the rope taut. One of the men started the generator and plugged in the welder. The fifty-foot cables on the ground clamp and lead would be lowered to Ed when he got down even with the pipe.

Ed brought the rope as close to the edge as he dared and threaded the loose ends through the steel ring at his waist. The preferred method for attaching a rappel rope was through a carabiner or snap ring, but this would have to do. Ed stretched the rope out, trying to estimate the length. After he evened out the ends he guessed there was well over 150 feet, giving him rope to spare. Ed gathered the loose coils in his arms. "Down below," he shouted. "Rope coming down."

Dan Curry hollered for him to let it come. The work crew hauled the welder over and blocked the wheels.

Ed intended to rappel down about fifteen feet to the right of where Doug lay under the pipe and look the situation over. The welding tips would drop on command, as close to Doug and the pipe as possible. The men on top would be out of sight, but as Ed traversed the rock, pulling the cables with him, they could assist from above. The operation could be stopped at any point, the cables either left in place or hauled back up. Ed could continue on down to the ground if his presence constituted a danger to the stability of the pipe.

"You got the welding rod?"

JimBob nodded and handed a bundle of rods to Ed who tucked them firmly in his belt.

"We couldn't find a mask."

"No goggles? Nothing?" Ed hadn't considered that.

"Tried everywhere." JimBob eyed the sling Ed had improvised. "I'll tell ya—looks to me like you're settin out to kill yourself."

Ed pointed to the small dozer. "Has that thing got enough weight to hold the pipe?"

JimBob nodded. The pipe was the heavier of the two grades, weighing 285 pounds per linear foot. Twenty-two thousand, eight hundred pounds of steel hung over the canyon.

"You still ain't told me what kind of clamp you're going to weld onto the pipe so the dozer can drop a hook to it."

Ed pulled at the ring below his waist. "Couldn't find anything suitable. I'm going to weld the hook right to the pipe." A few of the men muttered and Ed didn't look at them.

"It's the only thing I can do."

"You know, Mr. Booth, that hook won't be good for anything after you do. It'll ruin the temper. Those things cost a few bucks."

"If anybody asks about the hook or any of this," Ed paused, "you tell them I authorized it. APPLE authorization."

JimBob took off his hard hat and handed it to Ed. "You better take this. The cables might knock a few pebbles loose when we drop them. Maybe knock some sense into you, too." He stuck out his hand. "Good luck."

Ed moved toward the rim and passed the rope up over his chest and left shoulder, down around his back, taking it off his right hip. He pulled in the slack, left hand extended in front of his body. The rope came tight and Ed leaned against it. Stepped back. Leaned again, letting the rope slide through the ring, up across his chest and down his back. Satisfied, he put on the pair of workgloves he'd found in the Kelly shack and leaned once more, clenching his right hand tightly as he fell backward. The moment he did, Ed stopped moving. He released the right hand and the rope let him move a few inches.

He nodded to the men. Rappelling worked the way he remembered it working.

"Coming down," Ed shouted over his shoulder. He took one last look at the ledge and the seven men watching him, and went over the rim.

The first time they had rappelled in class, Ed had been terrified. He'd gone slowly the first few steps, let himself drop a few yards, stopped himself cold. The mere fact of leaning back with only two feet on the rock face, allowing your body to grow almost perpendicular to the rock, was upsetting enough. But then you flexed your legs to kick away from the rock and let loose of the rope at the same time. It was a conscious cold-blooded suicide attempt, and everything to do with the instinct of self-preservation had told Ed to stay where he was. But he had overcome the fear and found in rappelling a feeling of childish delight, like being weightless or taking three giant steps. You kicked away and dropped fifteen or twenty feet, touched the rock lightly and kicked off again, dropping farther. In a few seconds you had descended a fifty- or sixty-foot cliff. There was nothing like it.

Out of sight of the men above, Ed took deep breaths, trying to remember the delight. He made a few tentative kicks. With no teacher, nobody to shout encouragement, he felt the old terror. The sling was a patch job; the rope was just something he'd found. He lay almost on his back, suspended only by a double length of rope that passed through the steel ring below his waist.

You have to learn to trust the rope. Lean into it, men, that's it, just let your weight go and loosen up. Bounce on the rock, let your feet come right up off the rock so the rope's the only thing, the rope, the ring, the piton, your partner, let the equipment hold you. Bounce on the rocks, side to side, hop back and forth.

Ed bounced, hopped, began to relax, danced back and forth in a small arc against the damp wall of stone. It was time. Ed glanced down, gathered himself and pushed off, releasing the tension on the rope. He dropped all the way to the pipe before he caught the movement. Now he could see the other end of the pipe, but not the end above Doug. Or Doug. Both were just around a corner and Ed realized he'd come down too far to the right.

He began his dance again, bouncing on the rock like a moonwalker, increasing the swing of his arc, a few steps toward Doug, then a reverse, then a longer arc toward Doug. Finally he swung out and looked around the corner right at the end of the pipe, only a foot away from his face. He saw Doug. The boy was conscious at least.

On the next swing Ed picked a small outcrop, ran past it and braced himself for the return arc. But one foot missed and Ed swung around wildly, banging his hard hat against the cliff, losing the hat, and wrenching his ankle. He banged a knee, reached out with one arm and steadied himself. He was back where he started.

Ed could hear a two-way radio crackle below. Dorm evacuation. Fire. They were having a bad time of it at the Terminal, he supposed.

Ed's ankle hurt but he could stand pressure. He resumed the side-to-side dance that would carry him to the pipe again. This time he braced well and came to a full stop, with his body halfway beyond the sharp corner. He was only fifteen feet above Doug. Below the boy it was sixty or more feet to the ground.

"Dad?"

"How you doing down there, son?"

Doug looked at him and then up at the pipe. "Well, I guess it's like you always say. I'm caught between a rock and a hard place."

"You got good company, boy—but don't let's quit yet." Ed called for the cables to come down about ten feet left from the rope, ten feet over from where he had gone down.

A shower of small stones poured down over the lip, followed by the lead and ground cables. Ed shouted a string of orders. More left, lower, little more, not so fast. At last the cables were level with him and he tied the rope off with both hands just above the steel ring on his belt. Ed took his hands away tentatively and threw all his weight against the knot. It held.

He caught the shorter cable, the ground clamp, and studied the pipe carefully. Ed was slightly above the center of the pipe and its circumference was jammed solidly against the rock face with only two small gaps. He had hoped to bring the hook down and get a bite inside the pipe as well. But at least there was enough of a gap to slip the grounding clamp over the half-inch-thick metal. He had been afraid that the pipe would be stuck flat so he could only lay the clamp against it. A magnet ground would have come in handy.

Ed squeezed the metal clamp open and reached across the top of the pipe. He edged the jaws over the circumference, letting them close a fraction at a time until he felt them take a grip.

The pipe hadn't moved.

"Hook," Ed said, and realized he was whispering. "Hook down," he shouted.

Another shower of dirt and pebbles. Then the massive steel hook appeared, moving slowly as the winch operator on the dozer fed him cable. It was perfect. The hook stopped six inches to the right and Ed grabbed it, two-handed. There was a screech of metal and rock. Ed let go of the hook, which swung back into the wall, and grabbed at the rope that held him. Down below, a woman screamed. Maggie. He wondered how long she'd been watching him. He hoped she didn't expect him to bring Doug down. It was a job for the local rescue unit. Ed closed his mouth, trying to work up some saliva.

The pipe had slipped, but only a few inches. The electrode was still in place, but it was now wedged tight against a ridge of rock. Again, Ed grasped the massive hook and called for a half-foot slack in the cable. He positioned the hook above the pipe, straining to get it dead center where it wouldn't slip off. The metal was damp. Ed called for more slack and countermanded the order as soon as the hook started to come down. Bracing his knee on the rock, Ed pushed forward and—almost ceremoniously—laid the steel hook atop the broad curve of the steel pipe. There was no movement, no sound. The pipe remained secure in the cliffside.

Ed reached into his belt and pulled out a welding rod. He fed it into the stinger. He was ready to weld and called out for the men on top to turn on the machine.

From below, Tom Farrell was asking whether Ed had his welding mask.

Ed waved an empty hand and studied the surfaces of metal that he would be joining together.

"You're going to get a flash like you've never imagined," Farrell hollered up. "You want to go blind?"

Not really, Ed mumbled to himself, and forced his knee into the rock again. So here goes nothing.

Maybe, he thought, as he brought the welding rod toward the cable and kissed a brilliant flash of light from the rod to the pipe, maybe I can squint, keep looking away. But he knew immediately that all he wanted was to shut his eyes tight. Ed felt the rod start to freeze and he snatched it away before it became irretrievably bonded to the pipe. He had to look.

"Ed," Farrell shouted, "you asshole, why don't you at least close one eye?"

Ed leaned down to look at Farrell. It was a good idea. Why hadn't he thought of it?

Ed turned back to the pipe and the steel hook that had to become one with it.

He shut one eye and squinted with the other, drew fire and began laying in the first bead. When the right eye couldn't see past the dazzle of purple, he shut it and used the left, going by feel where he could. After all, it didn't have to be beautiful, it only needed to hold.

Despite the possibility of a tidal wave (which was neither confirmed nor denied by the weather bureau), Bill Greenwood and the owners of two other big charter boats had decided to run to the other side of the bay and see if any injured needed evacuation. From the looks of the fire, it might not be long before the whole camp would need evacuation. Outside the boat harbor the thirty-five-knot winds had rolled up heavy seas, but nothing the men hadn't encountered before in Alaskan waters.

Up in her chart room, Lavinia watched the boats leave through her telescope and watched, too, the progress of the fire at the camp.

What Lavinia could not see she could piece together from the chatter on her CB scanner. Ed Booth was doing something in Copper Canyon. Eventually she would have to go out and see for herself. She always had believed in Ed. He came from good Alaskan people.

Al Godwin and Joe Akin made the first pull and succeeded only in ripping out the snow porch and entryways. The fire on the roof was going strong now. They decided to give it what they had before it was too late.

Akin spoke to Collins, asked him to hand the radio to Godwin.

"Yeah, this is Godwin."

"Listen, I want you to crack the throttle pretty good, but feather it. I'll give a sign to someone here and he'll pass it by radio to Collins. When he says go, just keep pulling until you hear from me."

Akin handed the radio back to Price and explained the setup.

He heard Godwin's diesel pick up speed and he eased the throttle out on his own dozer, keeping a foot on the pedal.

The cable jumped tight. The HD-41 began to claw downhill. The noise from the building was deafening, a sudden cracking that went on and on. At first it seemed as though the cable would cut through the modules without getting hold of anything substantial enough to pull the lower floor off the foundation, but as Joe looked back, he could see the outside walls start to come away. Water poured out of both ends now. Joe cracked the throttle, feathered lightly to give a series of jerks on the cable. And then it was happening: the whole bottom row of trailers began to slip out from under and the top units tried to follow. The end units came first and then the center, now canting out into space and then, under the weight of the upper stories, falling like a drunk to his knees. The roof came forward, the uphill wall tilted and for one moment it was a giant house of cards.

And then the motion stopped. The dozers shut down. The uphill wall, although tilted five feet or more out of plumb, simply would not let go. Somewhere in the depths of the structure, the steel stress cables were doing their job, while above, the cross girders, linking one side of the trailer stack to the other, refused to let the sections come apart.

The flames continued to threaten Dorm Four. Superintendent Talford climbed up on Joe's dozer and put a foot up on the engine hood. "Now what?"

Tom Farrell directed the rock removal in the river bed, bringing in a backhoe to scoop out a small channel at one edge, relieving some of the back pressure from the gelid lake that had formed north of the slide. The water, sluicing through the channel, helped the efforts of the dozen or so volunteers by constantly widening and deepening the gap. Moving on a broad front over the rock face, the men sought to even out the line of the slide so that if the water rose it would spill over a wide area and not suddenly pour down on the rescue team below. At high flood in spring, the stream often threatened the highway through the canyon, and the amount of water backed up now was as bad as some of the surges that came down out of Sheep Creek from time to time when a glacial lake poured out of a melt.

It was slow work. The location was bad for Farrell's heavy equipment, which would get stuck in the river and eventually sink itself. The job would have to be finished by hand. As the water came up even with the dam, it became impossible to stand in the icy flow and pick up stones. The men pulled back and waited for the channel to deepen. After the rescue work was done, they could dynamite.

Farrell left the stream and walked across the road. Maggie was on her knees in the gravel, pulling small rocks away from the end of a buried eight-by-eight timber.

"There's a hole here," she said, slipping her hand between the timber and rock to demonstrate it. As she did, Maggie stiffened and she yanked her hand free. "My God," she whispered. "I touched someone."

Farrell dropped to his knees and together they scrabbled at the rock, tossing stones aside, wrestling the larger rocks away until Farrell could look inside. He saw a black hand and heard breathing.

"A little help," he called, and three men from the river watch sprinted down. "We've got a live one in here."

The man lay under a long beam and a shorter crosspiece, and he was only lightly pinned at the waist by the shorter timber. He was unconscious, but Maggie recognized him from the club. He was a laborer. Nate something.

The three men lifted the beam and Tom and Maggie carefully pulled Nate free. They laid him on the rock, placing his head on a folded jacket.

The first of the ambulances had left with the man who had been stuck in a pool of liquid dynamite. He was convinced he would blow up at any second. The medics had loaded Isaac Ahgutuk on one stretcher and, as they went for Baranov, Farrell told them that Nate was in worse shape.

When Isaac saw who it was, he insisted they take Nate first. "Fix him before you fix me," he said. "That's Nate Jourdan. He owes me ten dollars."

The attendant pushed Isaac down on the stretcher and he was loaded into the ambulance. "Take Jourdan first, the hell with Baranov. Leave me, but take Nate."

The bearers brought Jourdan, still unconscious, to the ambulance and loaded him in. Then the doors were shut and the vehicle sped away.

The funeral home had sent a hearse and stretcher and Baranov muttered about it, all the way. Rosemary Fay shushed him and Clyde looked up at her sadly. "Did you know Eskimos are crazy?"

Ed Booth's eyes ached. The flash effect wouldn't hit until tomorrow sometime, but the intensity of the arc had given him a headache and his eyes felt swollen. At the center of his vision, in both eyes, he could see only a blaze of purple.

He touched the last welding rod to the hook and added a row entirely by feel, then let the tip fall back against the rock. Shutting his eyes was as bad as having them open. He could only dimly see the fillet he had laid in around the perimeter of the hook where it touched the broad curve of pipe. He had heard Doug groan once or twice and he tried to listen now, but the sigh of the wind through the rope and cable was too strong. Ed shut his eyes and pressed at them. Leaning back, unseeing, he called JimBob to pull up the welding cables and he heard them knock against the rock on the way up. Climbing down would be like rappelling in the dark.

"How's the weld?" JimBob asked, leaning over the edge.

"Good I think."

"Eyes?"

Well, he could see; he had enough peripheral vision to see where he was.

The pipe beside him dropped six inches. Ed could hear the warning shouts from below. He reached over and felt the cable. It was tight.

"Grab hold up there and see for yourself about the weld."

Ed waited. JimBob reported that there had to be several hundred pounds on the cable already. So it was holding.

"But I'll tell you, Ed," JimBob said. "We've been looking at the other end of the pipe and it don't look good."

Ed couldn't weld again. He knew he couldn't. He felt an ache come into his chest and for the first time in years he had an urge to break down and cry. "No," he whispered to the rock.

"It's sitting on a ledge, but the thing slants in. The last time the pipe fell, my man saw it roll a couple inches."

Ed clung to the rock, shaking his head.

"We figure if we can lower a sling on a cable from one of the side-boom Cats, we could grab the middle of that pipe and hold it for the next ten years if we had to. You think you could go out on the pipe and do that?"

"A sling?" Ed looked out at the pipe, trying to get a focus on it. The pipe bridged a gap and it was a wide bridge. On the ground Ed had walked the pipe easily. It was, in fact, almost too big in diameter to straddle at all. But this pipe was sixty or more feet up and wrapped with a rain-slick vinyl tape. The rappel rope wouldn't do him much good if he slipped. He'd only swing down in a long arc and hit the side of the cliff after a fall. But the pipe itself was too long for the hook he'd welded to help those below. Doug was safe now, probably, but if the far end came off, the pipe would reach all the way to the ground and dig a trench when it hit.

Avoiding the hot spot around the clamp, Ed pushed himself up to the pipe and tested the surface with one foot. It was slippery, but not as bad as he expected. Ed clung to the rappel line and took three steps out on the pipe. He sensed a shift in tension on the cable, but everything was holding fine.

Ed took another step and lowered himself to his knees, and then to a crawling position.

"JimBob."

"I hear you."

"I'll do it."

Ed slipped the rope out of his belt ring and tossed it back on the inside, between the pipe and the corner, so he would be able to retrieve it on his descent. Ed crawled low to the pipe, looking only at the wide green tape beneath him, sometimes going several feet with his eyes shut. He looked ahead and realized he was near the middle of the pipe. Then, caught by a gust of wind, Ed felt his point of balance shift. He threw himself flat, burying his cheek on the pipe. His left hand found the thin edge where one layer of tape covered another and he dug his fingernails in, scratching at the seam. He was slipping. Ed pushed at the slick surface with one hand while pulling frantically at the tape seam. He began to sprawl crossways on the pipe and then he stopped. His boot buckle had caught the tape. A two-point climb. Cautiously he pulled himself up to the center and lay still. Ed had a new rule for his climbing instructor. Just because a person *could* do these things didn't mean that he should.

"JimBob," he called. "JimBob."

"Yeah, boss."

"How am I going to wrap the sling around the pipe?"

"Cover your head and I'll show you."

Ed covered, and a wrench tied to the end of the rope sailed down just ahead of him and hung below the pipe. The rope touched the pipe on the outside and the slack reached up to the canyon wall. The wrench swayed.

Ed got the picture.

The only thing to do, Joe Akin reasoned, was to pull the cable back in the other direction, to cut the uphill stack of mods loose from the foundation. That way the whole building would be free to topple. Once down, they might be able to shove dirt over it, especially if they could come back with the cable and spread the wreckage thin, maybe drag everything down to Dorm One.

The two dozers reversed and pointed uphill. It took five minutes' work on the part of some fifty men to line the cable up properly. This time they would keep on moving, since the uphill slope was working against the big machines.

Joe gave the signal and the HD-41s began to chew their way up the hill. The cable, which had been caught under some of the wreckage at the center of the dorm, snapped free all at once, sending the two dozers racing and scattering the onlookers. The cable tightened again, tore out the uphill side of the entryways, and began to rip into the base of the mods. Again there were terrible sounds of wreckage inside before any effect was visible outside. But by the time the effect was made plain, it was too late to stop it.

The building settled out like a big letter A with its down legs pulled apart. The roof fell in on the center and the building spread over the whole distance from Dorm Four to Dorm Two. Opened up, as it was, the fire began to bloom over the entire surface. Joe and Al reversed direction again, but this time the cable was hung up on the steel foundations and buried under tons of wreckage. Now, instead of threatening the roof of Dorm Four, fire leaped at it from top to bottom.

Two city fire engines could have put the blaze out, but there was no pump on the Terminal that could send water 200 feet into the middle of the fire. The slumping pile stood about ten feet high at the ends, where it butted into the upper and lower dorms. At the center, where the roof had come down, it rose to about fifteen feet.

Akin unhooked and ran the dozer down the embankment to safety. On the other side Al Godwin did the same. The flames crackled, Dorm Two began to fall in on itself.

"Didn't really make it much worse," Al Godwin told Talford.

"Dynamite," Tiny said. "If only I had some plastic."

"Dynamite," Talford said. "I don't need dynamite, for Chrissakes, I need water. Water." He pointed to the shoreline, the waves, the boats warily approaching the dock. "That stuff. Only here."

Tiny looked up the hill, looked back down at the ocean.

"You want water bad? I mean real bad?"

Talford reached up and grabbed Tiny's shoulders. "Don't play with me, Tiny. If you can get water, get it, but don't play with me." Tears were in his eyes. "I don't care how you do it, who you have to convince, how much it costs. Water," he said, pulling Tiny closer. "Not dynamite." He looked at Tiny a moment longer and then let go. "Why am I talking to you? What do you care if the camp goes up in smoke? You get paid to rebuild it." He turned and stomped off toward the fuel dump fire.

On the roof of Dorm Six, twenty or more men had gathered. They were lowering ropes to pull up fire extinguishers that were being stripped out of the other dorms and the construction offices. Word was, they would make a stand as long as they could take the heat.

Tiny strode over to Nasty, put an arm over his shoulder and began walking him uphill.

"Nasty, you see that picture last month where there was a fire in a skyscraper and Steve McQueen blew up a big water tank to put it out?"

"I don't go to pitchers, less'n it's Clint Eastwood. And you know goddamn well that big water tank on the hill is empty. They ain't finished it yet."

"I don't mean the water tank." Tiny stepped up the pace, pointing to the short bluff above the last dorm. "The man said he wanted water. He said he didn't care where he got it."

Nasty stopped and screwed up his face. "The pond?"

"That's what I'm saying."

Nasty whistled. "Two hundred thousand gallons of shit? I don't know but what ah'd prefer to die by fire."

At the dock, the boats hung just offshore, while a crew member jumped onto the ramp and went in to inquire about injuries. There were only a few minor burn cases from the fire, but the medic was glad to be able to transfer the seven residents of his infirmary. And the secretaries, many of them town girls, wanted to get home to see if their families were all right after the quake. It had been hard for those who had lived in Montez in 1964 to sit by on the wrong side of the bay. The boats left full and promised to come back.

The blasting would be no problem. A drainage line had been started from the center of Dorm Fifteen to the sewer pond and that left only a plug of earth some 15 feet long, 10 wide and about 12 deep to knock out. A Mustang drill, the larger of the two models made by Joy Manufacturing in use for blasting on the project, stood only a hundred yards from where Nasty needed it. He started the compressor, hooked it to the drill and began walking the rig into place.

The Mustang—a 23-foot-high pneumatic hammer mounted on a narrow pair of caterpillar treads—crawled easily over the uneven ground into position. Nasty and Tiny decided to make do with four quick holes, canted in a slight diamond shape. The plug should come out with a narrowing gap that would restrain the flow of water and sludge the first few seconds. Gradually, of course, the pressure of the flow would widen the channel.

The drill could be canted at an angle, and Nasty, compensating for the uneven ground, made adjustments so the drill was plumb not to the dirt but to the surface of the pond. A Mustang punched holes, three to five inches in diameter, through hard rock at speeds of up to four feet a minute.

By the time Tiny could get back with the dynamite, Nasty would have four holes spotted and ready to load.

Nasty covered his ears as the drill pounded its first hole. Down below he could see the fire, the long row of dorms, the fools on the roof. Well, help was on the way.

Tiny had commandeered a pickup and driven up to the explosives bunker high on the west tank farm area. A powderman was at work outside the low building, set in a hollow against the side of the mountain.

Tiny walked into the building and the man chased after him.

"Hey, you can't come in here."

Tiny picked up a thick-walled tube of polyethylene, some eight inches thick, nearly three feet long. It said DuPont Water Gel on it. The tube weighed 60 pounds.

"What are you doing in here?" the powderman asked. "You don't even work for Hyatt & Rueter." He saw the hard hat, Bartel, altered to Fart.

"This stuff any good?" Tiny hefted it easily in his arms, picking up another tube and another.

"You can't take that," the man said, but his voice trailed off as Tiny easily carried five bags, 300 pounds, out to his truck and came back inside for more.

"Just in case," he explained, going back to the truck and moving to the smaller shed.

The powderman followed. "It's for the fire?" he asked, "right?"

"No, I'm constipated. Now tell me, buddy, what kind of detonator do I want?" Tiny tore the lid off a carton. "What the hell are these?"

He'd been expecting the small pencil-nub charges that he'd worked with in the past, those or det cord, which he used on big jobs.

"How big's your hole?"

"Four, five inches."

"You do know what you're doing?"

Tiny just looked at him.

"You'll want the HDP-1 then. Put in a couple of feet of the gel, then a primer, then gel and a primer every ten feet after that. Two per hole minimum." He fumbled through a drawer and pulled out a mimeoed sheet. "Here's some specs. Figure eight to ten pounds per foot, size hole you're talking."

Tiny took several feet of blasting wire and a hand-crank blasting machine.

The powderman watched him drive off.

Ed took the line and reached out to the left to get the line up off the pipe. But the diameter of the pipe was too great to get any rhythm going. Ed couldn't reach far enough to get a pendulum motion started across the pipe, could barely swing the rope parallel to the pipe.

He pulled the wrench up and tried throwing it up in a loop. The wrench merely jerked, swung in a tight little arc, banging the pipe. If only his eyes didn't ache so, he could think better. Ed sat upright. It was like straddling an enormously fat horse.

There was only one way left. Ed began to whirl the wrench over his head. When he judged the rope had gotten long enough, Ed changed the angle and threw the wrench down around the right-hand side of the pipe. It glanced off sharply, skittering across the top of the pipe and falling down to the left, the rope snuggling up against his thigh. He pulled the wrench up and tried again with the same result. Ed sat higher in the saddle and spun the wrench in a wider circle, snapping his right hand down sharply when the wrench was coming around behind him. A moment later his ear exploded with pain and Ed swayed out of position, slipping to the right under the impact of the wrench. He flattened himself, feeling the wrench under his chest. There was blood on his cheek. He touched his face with his fingertips. The wrench had caught him just over the ear, splitting some skin behind the lobe. No longer able to resist, Ed let tears come freely. Sobbed. It seemed a necessary thing.

"Ed," he heard. "You got 'er yet, Ed?"

"Yes. Yes, I got it. Now what?"

"You keep reeling in. We took a sling and some cable off one Cat and hooked it on another. Wrap it around and hang the free end on the hook."

Ed heard an engine whine and the rope began to slacken. Ed

threw the wrench down over the right side and took up rope, passing the free end down after the wrench.

A yellow nylon sling laced with steel cable appeared, dangling from one end, and Ed pulled the rope, wrapping the sling around the pipe. When he had the free end, he shouted for JimBob to hold up. The sling hooks hung two feet above the cable. Ed dragged the heavy nylon into place, dropping the double eyes onto the hooks, letting the wrench dangle below the pipe.

"It's on," he called. "Take it up a foot."

The sling rose. Another two feet of space remained between the bottom of the sling and the pipe. The wind blew the nylon against the side of the pipe. Ed looked at the canyon wall, where the rock had fallen. It was almost twenty feet away. If much tension was put on the cables here and at the other end, the whole pipe might come away and bounce against the rock wall.

Ed put one hand on the lift cable. He needed to snug it up against the pipe, but would be safer feeling for the change in tension.

Ed stood, moving his hands up the cable. The pipe seemed so much narrower. There was still that burst of flame at the center of his vision. Ed wiped at tears with his free hand.

"JimBob, take it up real easy."

The cable began to rise. Ed kept a hand against the foot-wide nylon sling. There was still slack. He reached inside as if tucking a sheet, punching out at the nylon. "Little more," he called.

Maggie saw it all, the pipe breaking free, Ed falling, the chunk of ledge that just missed Doug. Then she saw Ed below the pipe, his arm in the nylon sling, apparently caught between it and the steel.

The pipe continued its swing, boomed against the freshly torn rock side. Ed screamed. The rock hit ground, setting off two detonators that sprayed the area with fragments of stone and wire. Dan Curry took a fragment in his cheek. One of the laborers, lying injured on a stretcher, was injured anew as a half-inch sliver of rock tore into his thigh.

The rescuers turned from the cliff and tried to run from the new shower of stones. Rosemary Fay stumbled, reaching out to Dan, who raised a hand to his cheek. Maggie screamed, saw Ed's legs flop like a rag doll as the pipe bounced off the rock and struck again.

But he did not fall free.

"Take it up," Farrell shouted at JimBob. "Booth is under the pipe. Take it up, for God's sake, *up*!"

"Won't hold, going up," JimBob shouted back. "Pipe's gonna knock against them rocks. Break the weld. Knock him loose."

"You can't leave him there," Tom screamed as the north end of the pipe grated and rolled off the ledge on which it lay. It slammed against the mountain, and again Ed was tossed from side to side. He did not cry out. High on the side of the cliff, Doug Booth raised himself to a sitting position. "Pull him up." he called. "The pipe's crushing his arm." His voice broke off and he lay back.

The rescuers gathered at the road, looking up at the pipe, Ed hanging under it.

Two diesel engines roared atop the cliff and JimBob reappeared. He made a circular motion with his hands and slowly the pipe began to grate and bump up the cliffside.

Dan Curry put his arm around Maggie. "At least he's unconscious."

She stared up and said nothing.

On the way back with the dynamite, Tiny stopped off to tell Talford what he was doing. "Go ahead," Talford said. "I don't care. I'll tell the safety man to clear the area. Better than letting the whole thing burn down." Talford looked at the fire. One of the water trucks had been run up the hill and it was spraying the edges of the collapsed dorm, while men inside Dorm Four crouched below windows and ran a bucket brigade. It would work for a while, but in places the aluminum had started to buckle and peel off. It wouldn't be much longer before the wood burst into flame. "I don't know," Talford said, "it might even work."

Leslie Collins had cleared the last two sets of dorms and had gone up to check on the drilling. Tiny was standing over a small hole in the ground with a long sack of gel, which he slit open and let pour.

Nasty stood alongside with a detonator, already wired up, and he shoved it down with a long wooden pole while Tiny went on pouring gel. Tiny slit a second bag and poured about a third in, let Nasty drop another detonator and poured a few more pints in on top. They kicked mud and dirt down the hole and Nasty quickly tamped it in place.

"How's it coming?" Leslie asked.

The two men shrugged. Neither spoke.

"That's good dynamite for this kind of situation," Leslie said. He had been reading the blaster's handbook and the company safety manual. "If water seeps in, the Pourvex will displace it."

Tiny grunted. "Yeah, it's okay."

A pickup came down the rough trail from the generator pad. It was one of the APPLE reps, Preston Howard. He strode up to Leslie Collins, waving a hand at the two ironworkers.

"What the hell is this supposed to be?"

Tiny was stringing blasting wire toward a front-end loader that faced away from the blast area. He led the wires around the six-yard bucket and crouched out of sight.

Nasty ignored the man and tamped in the last of the dirt. He knelt to connect the loose wires to the longer cable.

Leslie Collins answered. "I believe they hope to drain this pond rather quickly so that it will extinguish the fire below."

"Wish ah could talk that good," Nasty said as he bent to connect the second pair of wires.

The APPLE rep put both hands out in supplication. "You can't be serious. It'll wash right into the bay. This is raw sewage. The EPA will kill us." He looked around wildly. "Who's the supervisor that gave the okay on this?"

"Talford," Leslie said, pointing on down the long row of dorms to the cluster of onlookers around Dorm Three.

"I don't believe it." Howard moved toward the blast area, turned, turned again. "And there's reporters in town, too. No way we're going to spill this pond, not unless we get something legal from the state. At least a decision from Anchorage."

He stopped walking and decisively reached to his hip, unsnapping the mobile radio.

From five feet away, Leslie executed a perfect racing dive, catching Howard just below the knees, taking him down and knocking the radio out of his hands. Nasty scrambled after it and knocked the rechargable battery out.

Howard twisted around, half covered with dirt and mud.

"You ever work construction before?" Tiny shouted.

Howard hung his head. "The radio?"

"Goddamn right, the radio. You could have blown up my buddy here." He helped Leslie up and dusted him off. "Both my buddies."

Leslie Collins looked at Tiny. Nasty came over and shook his hand.

"You done real good, Leslie. Real good. That jerkoff might have blown us all away." He held radio and battery in one hand and he handed only the radio to Howard.

The APPLE rep snatched the radio and dusted himself off. "All right. Okay, men."

Nasty raised a haunch, farted, and went back to the wiring job.

"I guess that's that," Tiny said. "It don't make sense to put the water on the dorms unless we catch it while the fire's low, like it is in Dorm Three."

Nasty finished and walked to the edge of the bluff. Howard had driven off in a shower of gravel.

"Busted my beans gettin it done in time."

Collins put his hand over his heart. "On my honor, those boys never did a thing. We were sitting by the hill and it went off. Must have been a CB radio. I don't suppose the man responsible would ever admit to being in the area, though." He smiled.

The three men snuggled in beneath the protective steel shell of the bucket and Tiny picked up the hand blaster, grasping the crank firmly.

"I've never been this close to a blast," Leslie said, glancing from side to side.

"Just keep your mouth open," Tiny said. He gave the crank a sharp turn.

As the pipe went up over the rim of the canyon, there were cheers from above and below. JimBob appeared at the boulder.

"He's got a crushed arm, looks like. We'll take him down the back way, run him to the hospital."

Another ambulance rolled in below. The attendants were not hospital men. They wore climbing gear, and they gathered at the base of the cliff. One of them dragged a steel basket stretcher. The men made the climb easily, drove pitons deep into the rock above the outcrop, slipped in rings, hauled the stretcher up.

One of the men had given Doug a shot and splinted the leg. He didn't cry out as the men, hanging from ropes, clustered around and eased him up, sliding the basket into place.

"Dad," he said in the ambulance. "Where's my dad? I want my dad."

"I know," Maggie hold him in a whisper. "I know." But the boy had fallen asleep.

Tiny knew the moment he heard it that he'd overdone it with the Pourvex. The ground shook, the noise was too sharp, the spray of rocks too great. In one millisecond, fifty windows shattered in Dorm Fifteen, and for several seconds after broken rock fell like hail.

The sound of the water rushing forward was a roar, and Tiny, risking more rock falling on him, stuck his head out in time to see a great wall of brown, murky water rush out of the gap, pour over the short embankment, and pound into the side of Dorm Fifteen. It sprayed up to the second floor, splashing sludge into every window. Then the water seemed to draw down and suddenly pour through the gap under the dorm. Tiny imagined the scene would be repeated on the next few dorms until the surge diminished. The explosion had pushed the water back from the gap, he realized, and it now came through in a second great wave, this time splashing clear to the roof and pounding in the side of the building some two or three feet at the center. The three men crawled out from under the loader.

The smell was overpowering.

At Dorm Three the sound of the water moving downhill held many of the men transfixed. But as the spray became evident around the edges of the dorms, the more prudent pulled back. Some of the water would be coming down the road. Dorm Six thudded with the impact: the men working on top dropped fire extinguishers and fell flat, clinging to ropes, rivets, each other. Dorm Five groaned and then the flood burst out under Dorm Four, scooping up loose panels, boards, sheets of metal, furiously tearing at the pile of wreckage, floating the rubble and flame toward Dorm Two.

A second surge poured under the dorm and suddenly Dorm Three, or what was left of it, was picked up, dropped against the burning hulk of Dorm Two, and submerged in a foul wash of foaming water.

Larry, alone now at the fuel dump, crouched behind the dozer and considered giving it up. The dozer itself was growing hot and the flames in the west dump were shooting higher. It was only a matter of time until his protective shield overheated. Or the propane might explode and set off the diesel tank on the Cat. Anything could happen. The last two loads of water had been brought and the drivers had waited for him some fifty yards downshore. Larry was beginning to feel like an idiot. Nobody was paying him to take chances like this.

He heard someone shout at him. Heard two people shout. And he understood their chant. It was "Run."

Larry dropped the hose in blind, sudden panic. Water, he thought, and ran toward the shoreline, realizing that he might not be safe there either, with the waves high and the water covered with burning patches of fuel. He heard a noise behind him, faltered a moment, and then turned to see the ground swell up with water, garbage, whole hunks of dorm siding. It was a wave, and behind it, another wave. He was lifted up, knocked down, tumbled under a wall of water, alternately dragged in the gravel and buoyed up to the surface, and then he was upside down, eyes open, deep under water. He heard a pounding in his ears, felt the stinging at his eyes, the shocking chill of the sea.

Then, as if waking from long sleep, he felt strong hands upon him, and the voice of Joe Akin. "Good God Almighty," Akin said, "it's you again."

Chapter Two

OVER IN TOWN, people began to gather at the hospital as families of miners will gather near the shafts, awaiting news. Some of the victims had been strangers, but many were Montezans who had taken jobs on the line.

The people had gathered in front of the emergency entrance, in the early afternoon drizzle. A taxi pulled up and one more got out to join them. Lavinia Curry had come down off her hill.

Lavinia wore a purple cape that she had brought back from one of her trips to Ireland. Under it she wore blue jeans and a sweater. Her hair was done up in a complicated bun at the back of her head, and if some thought she had come only because of concern for her son-in-law and grandson, there were others who saw in her a flash of the pride and courage she had shown in the old days, after the big quake.

The crowd grew to a hundred and fifty by midafternoon. The mayor was there, of course, along with the police lieutenant who had arrived at Copper Canyon in time to see Doug Booth come down off the cliff. Some of Farrell's men were still in the canyon, removing rock to let the river run free, but no more bodies or survivors had been turned up in the last hour. It was believed that no one was missing.

Lavinia stood at the edge of the crowd, holding Maggie, talking to her gently. Dan Curry was at her side, going into the hospital occasionally, bringing out reports. Doug's condition was serious, but stable. He had two broken ribs and a severely fractured thigh. A surgeon was still exploring the multiple fractures and extent of dislocation in Ed Booth's right arm and shoulder.

One of APPLE's green pickups rolled into the parking lot. Two men, an APPLE official and one of Bartel's project engineers, approached the crowd.

"Folks," the APPLE man called. "Can I have your attention a minute? My name's Klein and this is Mr. Pierce from Bartel, across the bay. As you know, we had a bad fire after the quake. We lost our production kitchen, our entire food supply. Everything. The fire knocked out three dorms, we had damage to the others, and it looks as though we'll be sending most of our help home for a week or so until a sanitation team can get in and clean up the area. We have had a major sewage spill and I have no doubt that we'll have a job getting the health officials to let us reopen."

Gil Wolfe moved out of the crowd, notepad in hand, waiting. He was covered with mud and grime from digging at the canyon and looked exhausted.

The mayor, a tall man with a bad cold, stepped forward, blowing his nose loudly.

"How can we help?" he asked.

"Well, as you know the canyon is closed and will be for a day or two; the weather has shut down the airports. We can't get our people out of here until the situation clears. I understand that the road leading up to the pass is also slow going because of small slides and rocks on the highway. Might be three days before we can start evacuation. That's a thousand, maybe fifteen hundred homeless men and women. They're being brought to town now by boat. Where can we house them? Where will they eat? If you can do something, naturally APPLE will more than cover your expenses."

"They might stay in the gym," the mayor said. "It'd hold two hundred. And there's a cafeteria."

"Eagles Hall could take fifty," a man shouted.

"How about the churches?" one of the women said.

Lavinia stepped forward. "I'll take twenty. I can't promise they'll eat like they're used to on the other side, but I've got staples. As to sleeping, I have rugs, a few sofas, bedrolls."

Klein, the APPLE man, thanked her and said the company had a full load of blankets and pillows in the warehouse, and that they would be shipped over after the people got across. "I realize," he said, "that there's one of us for every one of you in town, but if anyone else wants to take a few in their homes, APPLE will reimburse you fully, I guarantee it."

"I'll take eight," Maggie said loudly, "but you can forget about paying us. We've been through this before in Montez, after all."

"I'll take five."

"We can handle three."

"Put the Akulaws down for nine. Two-ten Nome Street."

The two officials took names, addresses.

A laborer with a bandage over the side of his face came out of the hospital and moved toward Maggie.

"Ma'm," he called. "I hope you don't mind me asking, seeing as you had all the problems in your own family . . . but could you open the Montez Club today?"

Dan started to protest, but Maggie would have none of it.

"If you can find a few bartenders," she said, "I'll open. Dan will take the first shift. All drinks two for one, half price the rest of the day."

Mr. Grant, part-owner of the White House, was standing nearby. Several people in the crowd had moved in to get a look at Lavinia, some for the first time in years.

"I'll do the same," Grant said. "Half price on dinner and drinks. Free soup kettle. And we can bed down twenty in the Club Room."

"Maybe we should go down to the dock," Lavinia said firmly. "Why don't we go to the dock and meet the people coming in."

The Montez Club filled quickly, and many of the townspeople

offering shelter found it convenient to come there and sign up guests.

Having been promised a mattress on a floor with Tiny at the home of the Greer family, Nasty whooped and slapped his buddy on the back. "I been adopted along with mah brother."

He took the written street address and slipped it in his pocket. Then he and Tiny ordered up another round of drinks. Service was slow and finally Dan Curry realized he was doing more to hinder than help. He came out to the floor, joining Larry Ransom and Gil Wolfe at a table. Schultzie had taken over the beer tap and seemed to be enjoying himself tremendously, occasionally asking the entire bar for *ein Prosit der Gemütlichkeit,* which he then led.

Gil had been talking excitedly before Dan came about the scoop he was getting on other reporters. Jim Miklov had arranged with Sheep Creek Camp for a bus to wait just north of the highway tunnel. Jim and a few others eager to get back to Anchorage would climb over the rockpile, wade the tunnel, which was now knee-deep in water, and catch the bus to town, arriving in the morning. Since none of the other reporters knew about it, Gil would provide the city papers with the first full story of the disaster. And wasn't this the way it should be? Otherwise, Gil said, the only version that would appear would be the official line by Finch-Smith.

Larry had suggested that Jim Miklov might turn in a story, but Gil felt he still had the edge. His would be written by the time he hit Anchorage. And he might phone if they stopped, to let the editors know it was coming.

More important, Emil Bacich was due to leave tomorrow evening for California for a conference on the environment. The Sierra Club would participate, along with Friends of the Earth and a dozen other environmental groups. Gil would either send his report down or go along with Emil.

He smiled. "You can imagine the results."

Dan Curry brought his drink from the bar. "Results of what?"

"What else?" Gil said. "The whole bloody mess."

Curry looked from Gil to Larry, sipped at the drink. "Yes, I suppose the quake will be nothing compared to the aftershocks. And you're right. They should be fined for what happened at the camp. That was inexcusable."

"Are you going to shut the project down?"

"Why should I?"

"Come on, Dan. If they could spill several thousand gallons of oil and sewage now, in a relatively small quake, what do you suppose will happen when they have eight or nine million barrels of oil and we get a really big one?"

"That's not a fair comparison." Dan explained the way the tanks on the hill were protected, told Wolfe there was a big difference between the permanent facility and a temporary camp. "You can't compare them at all. It's apples and oranges."

"I agree it's apples." Gil looked at his watch. "But there's no point in debating. Just let me wash up, and I'll be out of your hair for a while."

Gil paid for his drink and headed for the washroom.

"What's he got up his sleeve?"

Larry told Curry about Miklov, the bus, the story Gil would file in Anchorage, the California meeting.

"He won't be satisfied with a fine and our follow-up studies, will he?" Curry sighed. "You know, I'm going to be stuck here for a month now. I'll probably lose my wife over this thing, if I haven't already." Dan drained his glass. "Anyway, I'm glad you managed to find a job close to home, Larry. Finch-Smith told me about it. When do you start?"

Larry saw Gil leave the washroom. "Right now," Larry said. "Hey, Gil buddy, before you go there's one guy I want you to meet."

"Can't." Gil tapped his watch. "If I don't get that bus, I miss the ride, Emil, everything." He smiled. "You know, you've really done a lot for me, Larry. I wouldn't want you to think I haven't appreciated it."

"It'll take two seconds." Larry caught Gil's arm and dragged him to the table where Tiny and Nasty were drinking out of separate pitchers.

"Hiya, Larry," Tiny said. "Have a seat. Have a beer."

"Tiny, I want you to meet Gil Wolfe. He's a reporter and he writes for Alaska papers and freelances all over."

Tiny grabbed a chair away from the next table. "Any friend of Larry Ransom," he said.

"Bus," Gil said. "I . . . "

"Tiny and Nasty here are the two men who saved Terminal Camp and kept the pipeline on schedule."

Little Nasty clapped a hand on his chest. "That's me."

"Why don't you tell Gil all about it? I'm sure the folks back home would get a kick out of hearing about you."

"Bus," Gil said. "I . . . "

Tiny took Gil's elbow in one big hand. "I ain't busy, just busy drinking." He pulled Wolfe down beside him. "See Nasty and I, we've done dynamite work all over the country."

"We'll show you a pitcher book 'bout it, later," Nasty promised.

Gil suddenly caught on. "What the hell," he said to no one in particular. "Let's have another round, men. Ransom buying."

Chapter Three

IN ANCHORAGE and Fairbanks the initial pipelaying, accompanied by a barrage of press releases, was rescheduled for a river crossing in Tonsina. The events in Montez had caused some stir in the papers and on TV, but there had been six other deaths related to the quake, two in Cordova and the rest attributed to a one-car accident at Mile 82 on the Richardson Highway. Intensity of the quake was rated at between 6.9 and 7.2 on the Richter scale, with a duration of only five to seven seconds. The quake was centered eighteen miles northeast of Copper Canyon in an uninhabited area. The abandoned railway tunnel at Copper Canyon was held to be the main reason for the slide there.

The Tonsina crossing drew crowds from around the state to a 1,400-foot valley that comprised the entire flood plain of a branch of the Tonsina River. A ditch fifteen to twenty feet deep had been dug across the plain, including the eighty-foot active channel of the river, which was still frozen despite the warm sunshine of late April.

The press kits passed out by Malcolm Finch-Smith and his staff stressed that this initial pipelaying was taking place exactly one year after the right-of-way permit had been granted. A sign beside the river, where twelve side-boom Cats cradled a few hundred feet of the long string of pipe, said ONLY 799¾ MILES TO GO!

A bluff at the north end of the crossing served as a vantage point for visitors and observers, although many of the news teams and photographers had moved down onto the river, across the pipe ditch from the side-boom Cats clustered at the south end of the pipe.

Atop the bluff a reviewing stand had been built, and on this stand B. R. Young waited to address his audience. At the end of his speech Young would drop a red flag and the signal would be passed to the river-crossing superintendent, a thin, laconic Mississippian who couldn't understand what all the fuss was about. He'd done thousands of river crossings and so had the good ole boys he'd brought along from every corner of the world to be here today.

Larry Ransom and Jim Miklov moved in for some close-ups at the edge of the ditch, now filled with ice-clogged water. The pipe would be lifted at the south end and then the first two Cat drivers would lower their booms, unhook, and take up a position north, lifting a new section, helping to swing it out over the ditch, and so on. The pipe had been coated in concrete to overcome its buoyancy; both ends bent up sharply to follow the contour of the valley edge.

Larry, along with an IBM Selectric, which he'd always wanted, a secretary, which he'd never had, and a big office in the new APPLE building, in which he felt misplaced, had been handed a Hasselblad camera and accessories for photo trips with Miklov. He also had, in his pocket, a miniature tape recorder with which he could dictate notes that would be transcribed by the office pool.

He had copies of what would be said up on the hill, a quarter mile away. B. R. Young was supposed to finish his speech with the words, "But enough; we have come to bury the pipeline not to praise it," and then drop the flag.

Larry stood, back to the ditch, chatting with the movie crew from ABC television. Dan Rather was rumored to be on the scene somewhere, perhaps with the officials up above.

Larry, like so many others that historic afternoon, did not turn as the diesel engines revved up, but continued talking. And his camera, like hundreds of others, was not in use as the ceremonies on the hill began. Later someone said it was a handkerchief or piece of scrap paper that had blown past Young and been interpreted as the signal. Another claimed that the crossing superintendent had merely intended to demonstrate for a cameraman the gesture he would use, that an operator jumped the gun, and the others rushed to get in, thinking they had missed the signal.

Miklov clicked off two quick shots as the pipe suddenly swung up and out and plopped down into the water, sinking until only the top foot of concrete showed. A ripple of alarm went through the crowd, and most photographs taken of the historic moment showed the moment after, a sliver of concrete and a few hundred people peering down a water-filled ditch.

B. R. Young's comment, recorded for all time by Malcolm Finch-Smith, was "Jesus Christ, would you look at that?"

As soon as a third of the pipe was under, Miklov and Ransom dashed up the short ridge to their helicopter. Miklov, in front, directed the pilot. Larry took black and white photos with the Hasselblad while Miklov shot the color slides. They hovered, swooped down, pulled back, found the angles, and then, as an afterthought, flew up even with a rocky prominence onto which many of the visitors had climbed for a view not only of the pipe, but of the hills and snow-covered mountains beyond.

Three young boys on the hill waved wistfully at the sleek turbine chopper, the lucky men inside. Larry lowered his Hasselblad, waved back, and found himself looking at Gil Wolfe, breathing hard, some 40 feet off, wiping the sweat of the climb away with one sleeve. Larry continued to wave, but Gil Wolfe shook his head, stared, shook again, like a baseball pitcher throwing off a sign. And then he turned away.

A moment later, the engine whined and the chopper whisked Larry and Jim up and across the broad valley with its steep hills and sudden ribbons of icebound rivers, sped them toward the waiting plane that would carry them back to Anchorage in time for the late editions. Two narrow bands lay below, the pipe route and highway. Beyond, in all directions, Larry saw no sign of man and his making. He relaxed, touching his forehead to the cool plexiglas bubble, and watched Alaska unfold beneath him.